Runaway Alex

Alex & Alexander: Book One

Natalie Keller Reinert

Natalie Keller Reinert Books

Books By Natalie Keller Reinert

Learn more at nataliekreinert.com

Before

My feet hit the ground with a little puff of dirt. Grass won't grow in this spot anymore. My dad, the resident gardener, does everything he can to fix the bare patch outside my window. He doesn't understand why the thick runners of St. Augustine grass can't overcome the gray sand. Some day, I won't have to jump out the window anymore, and then the grass will grow back in a thick, lush, tropical carpet, and he'll never be able to explain it.

He'll never know it was because I was running away, every chance I got.

Although at some point, he'll probably wonder how I got so good at riding horses.

They said: "Maybe when you're older."

They said: "Get your grades up and we'll see."

They said: "Put riding lessons on your Christmas list."

I got tired of waiting.

Chapter One

I SQUIRMED IN MY hard chair and wished I was anywhere else. Well, not really. I wished I was at the barn, mucking stalls or grooming horses, or tacking up for a ride in the arena. College was like a cruel joke. You grew up, you got out of high school, and then *wham*, even more classes, even more work, even more putting up with being told where to go, when to be there, what to say.

I just wanted to be with horses. Was that so much to ask?

Across a desk scattered with papers and thick books, my English professor sat staring at me, her expression almost distraught. When she spoke, it was like listening to my mother the day she'd found out I was sneaking to the local stable and working off riding lessons. The same mixture of disappointment and disbelief. The same conviction that I was somehow throwing my life away just because I didn't want it to look like theirs.

"Just suppose for a minute that you *didn't* sneak out of class half an hour every single week, what would that be like for you? For your grade? For me, your poor beleaguered professor who only wants you to have a happy and productive life?"

Honestly, Professor Blake was so dramatic. She was always like this with me, every time I got caught leaving class early, every time I begged for an extension on a paper, every time I confessed I hadn't done last night's reading. When was she going to get it? When was she going to get *me*?

I had to tighten every muscle in my body just to avoid rolling my eyes at her. My biceps pressed insistently against the tight cuffs of my polo shirt, looking for more room. Her gaze fell on my bulging arms, and Professor Blake's eyebrows went up. They stayed close to her hairline for a moment longer than I thought was strictly necessary.

Yeah, you like these muscles? I thought, and then immediately felt bad about myself. There was nothing going on here. Professor Blake just had extremely expressive eyebrows, thick and skeptical, and I generally respected her for those eyebrows, because she had clearly never felt the need to sculpt her face into something it was not.

No, she just wasn't used to fit girls with hard muscles, and who could blame her? I wasn't like most girls at Calusa Community College. Here in the suburbs of Southwest Florida, being trim and tan and bikini-ready at all times was practically its own curriculum. Muscles might be *toned,* but never buff.

Me, I was something rougher than the norm.

I was a horse girl.

"Professor," I began, keeping my tone as contrite as I could manage, especially considering the fact that I was lying, "I am so sorry for missing so much class. But I *am* passing this class…"

"Barely, and that's not exactly why you're here, to just barely pass—"

"...And unfortunately my work schedule just doesn't let me stay for the entire class every day."

This was a half-truth. Diana didn't care what time I got to the barn, just as long as the barn was cleaned and the horses were ridden, fed, and turned out in their paddocks for the night. It used to be easier—Diana used to help out—but nowadays, she wasn't as a hands-on as she had been when I was a kid. Diana was doing other stuff.

Anyway, handling all the horses and barn chores wasn't too tough in summer, when the sun stayed up late to keep me company, but now the calendar had flipped to August. I was losing daylight in small, painful increments, a few minutes every day, like some sort of water torture.

I needed to start riding and chores by two o'clock to finish everything before the evening was officially turned over to the mosquitoes crowding out of the nearby swamps, and on Tuesdays and Thursdays, English Composition lasted until two thirty. *Something* had to give, and it wasn't going to be the horses.

I glanced at the clock above Professor Blake's left ear. Five after two. *Damn.* I'd been so close to getting out unnoticed. Everyone in the classroom had been bent over their notebooks while the professor wrote on the white-board. Taking their little notes, oh so studious, what a class of future winners! I didn't belong with them. I was good at running away to play with horses, not buckling down over books. *Play to your strengths,* my father used to say, not knowing he was giving me a mantra which worked against his own hopes for his only daughter.

I was good at undramatic exits. My notebook slipped soundlessly into my backpack; my chair slid silently back on the flat carpet. I was out of my seat; I was heading for the door; I was almost free and clear.

Then, Professor Blake turned around unexpectedly, saw me scraping out of the back aisle with my bag over my shoulder, and instantly announced everyone should pair up into critique partners. Distraction planted, she chased me down and pointed me into her office across the hall.

Now, she tapped her blunt fingernails against the battered desk. "Can you talk to your manager about your work schedule? I mean, this is important stuff. This is a required course if you want to transfer to a four-year university."

I didn't *want* to transfer to a four-year university. I knew better than to say this. I pressed my lips together, waiting for her to finish, wondering what actual repercussions there could be if I simply got up, walked out.

I mean, I was paying for this lecture, right? Couldn't I choose if and when to listen to it? It was so hard to know where the lines were drawn in the adult world. In high school, we were captives, but we were minors. It made sense. In college, for some reason, we still seemed to be locked into whatever whims our educators took. I was twenty-one years old—did I really have to take this?

It sure seemed like I did.

Anyway, my parents were the ones paying for it, and they wouldn't back me up if I left. I needed their goodwill right now.

The clock ticked out another minute.

My afternoon was slipping away.

Her fingernails drummed away, her voice carried on. "Plus, you're a very strong writer. You have a lot of raw talent which could really lead to an interesting career down the road. Even if you don't know what you want to do with your life yet—"

I knew what I wanted to do with my life. I wanted to train racehorses. No writing required. Why wasn't there a career course for horse girls? Everyone wanted to tell me how to be a lawyer or a doctor or an accountant. No one was giving me a single hint on how to follow my *actual* dreams.

"...And that's fine, you don't have to choose a career right now, but you don't want to shoot yourself in the foot with poor grades now, when it would be so easy for you to get through here with honors, get a scholarship to a four-year college..."

I shifted in the hard chair, waiting for her to finish.

"Alex, I just don't feel like I'm getting through to you." Professor Blake leaned back in her chair and sighed.

I couldn't blame her for being frustrated.

We had been here before, Professor Blake and I, closeted away in her tiny windowless office, just enough room for a cluttered desk, a dangerously-tilted bookshelf and an overhead light which never stopped humming. If my earnest English professor thought I would find anything alluring about the scholarly life in this little white-plastered cell, she was deluding herself. My whole world was outside, in the bright shining sunlight, surrounded by horses.

"Professor," I began, ready to say my piece, "I'm going to be a horse trainer. That's my dream. That's my *only* dream. There's not going to be much call for English composition in that field. I'm just here because my parents told me I have to get my associate's degree if I want to keep living at home." *And I can't afford to live anywhere else.*

My parents thought enough enforced higher education would eventually rub off on me and give me a desire to finish a bachelor's degree.

They were wrong. I just wanted to live rent-free in my childhood bedroom because being an unpaid trainer/barn manager at Calusa Lakes Equestrian Center wasn't the slam-dunk career move one might think. That was okay. I wasn't going to be there forever. Someday, I'd find a way out. I'd dug myself into a little bit of a hole in life, but it wasn't too deep to escape.

I hoped.

Professor Blake blinked at me and shook her head. "But Alex, you've been here three years and you're just now getting through a basic, required course. You're so smart. How is this possible?"

"I only take two or three classes at a time," I explained. "And none in spring, because we have so many horse shows between January and April." The spring show season was when Diana sold horses like crazy, to middle-income, middle-class parents who got caught up in the excitement of ribbons and championships. Or, rather, she used to. That market had dried up and this year we hadn't done our usual spring business...mainly, because Diana wasn't sober enough to keep students in the sales cycle from First Riding Lesson to First Show Horse.

Or even to keep students and boarders at the barn. The fact was, I was the last woman standing at Calusa Lakes.

"And how old are you?"

"Twenty-one," I answered. "Just." Although most days I felt forty-one. Trailing around after Diana for eight years could do that to a person. Last night I'd had to pick her up at the Land Ho Pub—*after* I'd ridden six horses, finished the evening barn chores, turned out the lights, and gone home for the night. Driving her home from the bar wasn't a new chore, but it was happening more frequently. The Land Ho's weeknight bartender had put me down as Di's emergency contact not long after I'd finally gotten my driver's license and an old Honda Civic to drive around town. She'd said she was just hedging her bets against Diana being able to pay for rides home, and she'd been right.

"Twenty-one is too young to just give up an your education," Professor Blake informed me mournfully. "You don't know what you're going to need later in life."

From my pocket, my phone beeped urgently with the alarm I'd set to help me stay on top of my constant commitments at Calusa Lakes. This was my fifteen-minute warning of a scheduled farrier visit. If I missed Randy one more time, he wouldn't come back, and I didn't know who else would come out when Diana was so slow about paying her bills. "I'm really sorry," I said, standing up. "But I have to go meet the blacksmith now."

"The *black*smith—"

"Farrier," I amended. "We just say blacksmith so non-horse people will know what we're talking about."

Professor Blake blinked at me, her expression helpless.

I winked and ducked out of her office.

I felt bad for people like Professor Blake, I really did. She wasn't the first one to corner me for a come-to-Jesus about my grades, or try to take a special interest in me. Professors came after me from time to time, usually about midway through a course when they realized I was phoning in my essays and exam answers, and told me how talented and special and intelligent I was. How full of potential, how utterly limitless, how worthy of accolades and high salaries—if I would just show up regularly, and study once in a while.

I didn't doubt they believed these things, but that kind of conviction in education was why they had become teachers. I told my Thoroughbreds similar things all of the time, and that was why I was a horse trainer. I believed in my retired racehorses and their potential to learn new careers; I wanted them to show up and think about the things I was trying to teach them instead of just figuring out how to fake it around the arena.

The professors were just trying to train me. That was fine, that was understandable.

But I wasn't going to be trained.

The Florida sun was blazing overhead as I escaped the chilly school hallways, and when I got into my car I had to roll down the windows to let the air conditioning blow the hot air out. I took in my current situation: I had the farrier, six horses to ride, and a hay delivery to put away before nightfall. I still had almost five hours to sunset. I could do this.

Piece of cake.

My phone rang just as I started to reverse. I sighed, put the car back in park, and answered unwillingly. "Hello, Mom," I said in a monotone.

"You're supposed to be in class," my mother said.

"Then you shouldn't be calling me."

"Your ringer would have been off."

"What is this, a sting?"

"Just a check-in," she replied crisply. "To confirm my suspicions. I thought I saw you driving up Dixon Avenue last Tuesday at two o'clock."

Damn. I'd gone up Dixon to grab some Wendy's. I was starving and that was the only reason I'd strayed so close to my mother's office. The *one time* I had enough money in my pocket to eat something I hadn't pocketed from the pantry on my way out the door...

"This is your last shot to get your A.A.," my mother reminded me, her tone ominous. "If this semester ends and you're still not on track to graduate next June, the rent is coming due."

Rent in Calusa wasn't cheap. My parents had been threatening to charge me market rate on my bedroom for a while, which would require one of two things to happen: either Diana would find some money and start paying me again, or I'd have to quit, give up my job at Calusa Lakes Equestrian Center, and find a job with a paycheck. Novel idea, right? It wouldn't be as simple as just finding a barn manager with a solvent checking account, though. I'd have to find a place where they actually wanted to hire me. Sad but true: I knew enough to run any stable in town, but I didn't have the right kind of resume.

Most of the other equestrian centers in the area were posh show barns. They made their money as Diana used to, on bringing up new students into show-ring riders. That had been Diana's job—mine had been schooling young project horses, which were sold on before we had a chance to move up the levels.

So, I could ride the toughest off-track Thoroughbred in town, retired racehorses barely two steps off their last start, but I couldn't put an upper-level horse through its paces in either the dressage ring or the jumping arena. I didn't have any teaching experience, either. All I was really good at was getting on racehorses, figuring out how their brains worked, and reverse-engineering them to the basics so I could teach them to jump.

After eight years of sneaking around, begging forgiveness, and outright defying my parents for the right to work for Diana, I had no marketable abilities to show for it.

Someone *might* take me on as a junior riding instructor, or to muck stalls and scrub buckets, and actually write me a check or give me an envelope of cash every week. If they did, though, I'd be running around after girls five or ten years my junior, holding their horses at shows and sweeping up after them at night.

It was incredible to me how much work I'd put in and how little in actual, cash-earning skills I'd gotten out of it. Frankly, the only proposition with a more wasteful ROI was college.

I could do it, though. If I had to, if there was no other way to keep a roof over my head and horses in my life, I would bite my tongue and swallow my pride and head to a show barn to start over. There was a very clear roadmap in this industry, which led directly from my childhood as hardworking student in a local lesson barn to an adulthood as a tanned and wisecracking trainer with dozens of adolescent girls and average horses surrounding me.

The problem was, I didn't want that future at all.

What I wanted to do wasn't show horses. I wanted to work with *race*horses.

I couldn't explain why. But just like the love of horses is a deep, primal, inexplicable thing which some people simply arrive on this planet with, I was deeply in love with racehorses for no easily definable reason. I could line up reasons, of course: I adored Thoroughbreds, so sleek and so noble and so flighty and so bold, a contradicting lineage of inbreeding and outcrosses, a breed developed by kings and queens. I loved that racing was competing in the most pure form of sports: *my horse is faster than your horse!*

That was my true dream. I just wanted to be surrounded by fast horses. Riding them. Caring for them. Cheering for them. Leading them into the winner's circle, my name next to theirs, the headlining stars of the day.

Unfortunately, Calusa was a little short on racehorses. Down here in our soupy corner of the peninsula, the most desirable horses came with auto-changes on the hunter course and a five-figure price-tag, or a good head for cows and a trail-riding resume that included every swamp in a twenty-mile radius. The Thoroughbreds I rode here weren't the cream of the track; that's how they'd ended up in a lesson barn that wasn't even the cream of the county. I didn't know how to go from retired racehorses to current racehorses. I didn't even know where to start.

I blinked. The world through my windshield had gotten a little blurry. I'd spaced out for a minute there after my mom had said the rent was coming due.

My mom, still on the line, huffed an impatient sigh. "Alex? You understand me? *School,* Alex. School or rent."

"I understand," I replied woodenly, looking at the car's digital clock. Two-twenty. Where did the time *go?* My head-start was long gone. My misspent youth was coming for me. I was on my way to another unpaid afternoon at a failing lesson barn, and the only way out was to go work at a different lesson barn where they'd pay me. Sounded so simple, right?

So simple, but it meant my dream felt farther away than ever.

Chapter Two

I WAS ALREADY LATE and I was risking Randy's wrath, but I was suddenly starving. Depressing news will do that to a person. So, I scrounged some spare change from the car's cupholders and stopped at Wendy's anyway, hoping I'd annoy my mother in case she happened to be looking out of her office window. Then I put the pedal down, one hand on the wheel and the other on my extra-large Diet Coke, and managed to get to the barn just as the farrier's truck backed up to the barn aisle.

After the rough start, my afternoon began to unwind smoothly. The horses stood nicely for the farrier. The usual afternoon rain held off, but a nice sea breeze blew through the barn. The hay guys actually brought enough help to put away the delivery for me, a minor miracle.

Diana didn't show up. Her absence counted in the positive column. There'd been a time when I'd missed Diana, but these days, I looked forward to the uncomplicated silence of the empty barn. I could just get through the horses and chores without her interference and mood swings.

Smooth starts should be a warning for anyone in the horse business.

I should have known.

I had been at this long enough to have known. Instead I smiled at fate, waved goodbye to Randy, and started pulling saddles and bridles out of the tack room. "We're gonna get out of here by sunset," I told my first horse as I led him up the aisle to the cross-ties. "You and me, buddy, we're crushing this day."

Thunder rumbled around the distant pine forests to my east. I hustled through quick flatwork rides on the sales horses as lightning flicked in the distance—so far away, its electric stabs at the flat horizon were tinted pink and yellow by dust in the air. The clouds kept their distance, though, and I was able to get through my rides without being in any real danger.

Really, everything was going *so* well that by the time I hopped on my last ride, a little Thoroughbred mare with a nice face and a nicer disposition, I had stopped looking anxiously for Diana's truck. I allowed myself to believe she wasn't going to show up at all today—after all, she'd been taking unannounced absences more and more often, lately.

Without Diana around, I could get through my rides without drama, and that was the main thing. Every ride brought each horse a little closer to a sale. Every sale brought the possibility of a commission for me. Sure, that was a very faint, very dim possibility, since after the last two horses sold, Diana hadn't actually had any money left after covering the hay and feed bills. Still, selling her horses was the only chance at cash I had right now.

If I did a great job training, and a horse sold for a decent amount, I stood a chance of making some money. Maybe I could save some up, move out of town, make a change.

Maybe I could pay my parents their rent money, and drop out of college.

At this point, any change to my current dead-end trajectory, no matter how small, felt like a pipe dream. Still, I had to have faith in myself. I had no one else to turn to.

If people just stay off my back, I can make this work.

"You're a good girl, Misty," I told the little mare. She was just learning to jump cross-rails after I'd put a couple months of groundwork and flatwork into her. She'd come from Diana's usual racetrack source, a tight-lipped trainer named Lucille. I thought with a few more months of training, she'd make some little girl a nice hunter for schooling shows.

I was taking Misty around an easy little course, trotting around the turns and giving her plenty of room to balance before each fence, when it finally happened: Diana's truck appeared in the distance, a billow of white dust rising from the sandy farm road. My stomach turned over.

I glanced at my watch, which only made things worse. The time was twenty after six, which meant she had hit Happy Hour at Land Ho and decided after a few doubles that it was time to give Alex another riding lesson. Since it had been three weeks since my last lesson, and I was technically still her working student, she wasn't wrong about the overdue account—but I wasn't sure how much I wanted to learn from a buzzed Diana. I was doing just fine on my own these days, anyway.

I tried not to be nostalgic, but I couldn't help missing the old Diana: the tough-luck trainer who had taken me in as a skinny little middle-schooler and taught me to muscle my way through barn chores, auction horses, and recently retired racehorses. This farm was close enough to bike to from my house, and that's just what I'd done, hiding my bike behind the backyard shed so I could sneak out of the house every chance I got. After they'd finally caught me sneaking out of the house to work off riding lessons, my parents had okayed one *paid* riding lesson per week, on condition that I pay more attention to my homework. They had no idea how many hours I worked for all of the unpaid rides I was still getting, or they would have nailed my window shut.

I would have found another way out. There was no keeping me away from horses.

Diana, no businesswoman and chronically curious, had never run a top show barn. Instead, we'd danced around all sorts of disciplines: one summer was all dressage, and one winter we devoted ourselves to eventing. I love it, because I learned a little about a lot, and because my goal was always to end up in racing, anyway. I didn't have to be competitive at horse shows. I just needed to know how to stay on a horse in every situation.

Unfortunately, her dabbling became her undoing. Dedicated Calusa equestrians with cash to spend preferred to specialize in one sport. Students came, students went. We sold them every horse we could while they stuck around. Most of the stock came from Lucille, Diana's racetrack pipeline. By age fifteen, I graduated from riding the advanced horses, the ones ready to sell, to becoming the test-pilot who got on anything new to see what they could do.

In the years since I'd graduated high school, things had gone from bad to worse for Diana; a housing crash hit Calusa hard and the spare money for horses dried up amongst the suburban families who had once paid for lessons, show fees, leases, and board. She'd had to sell the farm's huge front pasture to keep the hay bill paid, and the new neighborhood which sprang up there seemed to send her around the bend.

Where horses had once grazed, pink and yellow houses had sprouted like oversized Easter candies, gleaming obscenely on lawns tinted the chemical-green of plastic grass. The children in those new houses were transplants from up north; they seemed to be allergic to sweating in the sun, and went to air-conditioned gyms to learn gymnastics and karate. As business grew worse, Diana's drinking had gone from an evening treat to a nightly bender, and with her decline in sober hours, the few boarders and show students she'd had left finally drifted away in search of riding instructors who were more...well...*stable*.

I was the only one left, the only one who had stayed with Diana, and if I was starting to see I'd backed the wrong horse, it's not like I'd had a lot of choices. When I'd first showed up here, thirteen and red-faced from a steamy bike ride through the deep sand of the driveway, Diana was my only option if I wanted to be around horses. Other girls, blessed with parents who had the time to drive them to the fancy boarding stables on the other side of town—not to mention the willingness to let their daughters devote themselves to horses—had more choices.

I took what I could get, and even now, in these desperate times, I was grateful for what she'd given me.

Now, though, I just wanted to get out of the arena before she did something to spook Misty.

"Let's go, girl," I told Misty. "We can finish before she gets out here. One more time around the fences, and we can call it a day."

As I eased Misty into a working trot and gently guided her toward the first jump, Diana's truck door slammed. I flinched without meaning to, and the mare shied sideways. I dropped my hands low, and spread them to form a V with the reins, giving Misty a clear path forward to follow. It was a good trick for novice horses which Diana had taught me years ago.

"Your arms are the train track rails," she'd said, positioning my elbows a few inches from my hips as I sat on an anxious young horse, "and your horse's nose is the point where they disappear in the distance." It was a pretty mental picture which made a strange amount of sense, and it always worked a treat.

Trying this trick now gave me a twinge of sadness; it reminded me Diana had been amazing, once. She had changed my life, introduced me to horses in every way, and then gone off the rails. I'd watched the same scenario play out before with other trainers. I'd heard the stories, listened in on the gossip.

"That's just what happens," Diana had growled in her rusty voice to Sandy Martin down at Southern Horse Tack and Feed. I'd been fifteen, and they'd been talking about another trainer's sudden disappearance from the horse show circuit. "Woman wakes up one day and she's got thirty horses to feed, half her clients haven't paid her in months, and all the bills are due at once. She just goes. I've seen it a dozen times in the past ten years alone."

Sandy Martin had agreed, nodding along sadly, and then written up Diana's feed bill. It had been over four hundred dollars. I remembered the sense of shock when I'd seen it, the first moment I understood my mother's oft-repeated: *Horses are for the wealthy, Alex.*

Was that really just what happened to women in the horse business: they cracked up, went bankrupt, turned to alcohol or disappeared? If I'd felt like I'd had a choice, maybe I would have explored something else which didn't have such a specifically tragic ending. I *could* concentrate on school. Get good grades, become a journalist or something; I'd always liked writing. On a school trip to New York one summer, I'd vaguely imagined myself living a cosmopolitan life as a writer, slinking through city streets in a chic black coat, but it had been a short-term fantasy, nothing more, because horses were all that really mattered.

Misty steadied and pricked her ears at the little jump ahead, trotting forward with an added spring in her step as she anticipated the moment she'd have to lift herself over the cross-rails. She liked jumping, she just had a little bit of a spook in her, but as long as I kept her focused—

"*ALEX! Wait up a minute, will ya?*"

Misty's head shot up and she hit the brakes; her fuzzy ears were nearly at my chin by the time I got her moving forward again. I coolly gathered my reins and steered her around the jump. The little mare huffed and pranced, staring across the arena with pricked ears. I followed her gaze with my own, and sighed. Diana had opened the arena gate and was crossing the sand between us with unsteady strides.

"Hi, Diana. Don't worry, there's no need for a lesson," I called, trying to steady Misty with my hands and seat. "We were just wrapping up."

"No, no, no, no," Diana slurred, shaking her head vigorously. "I *owe* you a lesson. That's part of our *deal*. So listen up, I want you to get a nice left-lead canter and take her over that line going away from the gate. Six strides exactly in the middle. You'll have to sit up and balance her between the fences." By the last word, her voice was perfectly crisp and clear.

It was truly amazing the way Diana's drunkenness fell out of her speech when she started teaching. She had an on/off switch for riding lessons. She'd still be good if she had any idea what was going on around her...but since she'd essentially abandoned the farm to me, she didn't. And so she didn't know Misty wasn't ready to canter a jump course.

Thunder growled, slightly nearer now, and a cool wind licked at the sweat on my face. I tried to dissuade her gently. "Misty's not quite up to cantering lines yet, Di. She's still trotting in and cantering out over cross-rails. Maybe next week? I'll just take her in now...she's pretty sweaty, don't you think?"

"She's fine," Diana said dismissively. "And no time like the present to start her cantering lines. Why wait? I'm sure you're just being a little too cautious, Alex. I know you're new to training horses, I understand that, that's why I give you the easy ones. So let's move her up a stage. Let's go!" She clapped her hands at the end of her little speech.

Misty jumped at the sound. I could feel how unnerved the mare was by our raised voices, and the newly rising wind, which was beginning to whistle around the barn eaves and rattle the lighter jumps, wasn't going to help. The storms were closing in at last.

That was a good excuse to go in, right?

"Whoops, it's going to rain!" I announced brightly, ignoring the line about being given the easy horses. I was riding *all* of the horses these days, but you can't win an argument with a drunk person. "Could be lightning! We'd better go in."

"Grandma Alex!" Diana crowed. "Spooked by a little storm! That's not how I brought you up. Let's get out there and jump."

Her words struck a weird chord in my mind. *That's not how I brought you up.* As if Diana had been my mother—and there was no doubt I'd seen more of Diana over the past few years than I had of my own mother. I'd spent every moment I could with this woman, and for what? I was twenty-one years old and I was still riding half-broke horses for a trainer who was in an accelerated state of self-destruction. Sure, my mother never could have taught me to ride horses, but I still felt a stab of guilt to think I had given her up, so young and so thoughtlessly, for Diana.

"I'm taking her in," I insisted. I tried to ride Misty past Diana, but the drunk woman reached out and grabbed the mare's bridle. Misty flung her head up, foam from her mouth spattering across Diana's cheeks, and started hopping in an anxious circle, with me clinging like a burr to her mane, my heels jammed down against the stirrup irons for security. "Let go, Di, you're freaking her out."

"Messy brat," Diana growled, swiping at the foam on her face with her free hand. "Hold still, mare! My God, what an idiot! *Stupid* mare!" Her words were slipping back into a slur.

Misty was heading for a panic attack, and the tighter Diana's hand grew on her bridle, the harder the mare yanked backward, threatening to rear. I could feel her balance shifting, until she was so light on her forehand, there was almost nothing connecting the mare's front hooves to the ground.

I grasped at Diana's arm with my free left hand, trying to shake her loose. "Knock it off, Di," I snarled, my patience gone. "You're drunk and you're going to get me hurt."

Diana's arm was tight and ropy beneath my fingers, the sinews in her wrist like thick, taut wires. She was still strong as hell, and she knew it. "Oh, call me *drunk,* will ya?" she spat, glaring at me as she shoved her arm back and forth, trying to shake me free. With my other hand, I was clinging desperately to Misty's reins as she tugged at the bit. Part of me wondered how long it would take to get the mare over this little debacle. "Nice to know what you *really* think of me after everything I've done for you!"

She let go of the bridle without warning, and Misty darted backwards, her hooves scuttling beneath her, leaving me behind. I went face-first into the hot white sand at Diana's feet, just as thunder shook the air around us and the first cold drops of rain began to fall. I pushed myself upright while fat, round raindrops plopped against my cheeks. The water's coolness slid down into the corner of my mouth before I could wipe it away, and I tasted the metallic tang of clouds and lightning.

It was quickly replaced by a blast of vodka fumes. Diana was leaning over me, laughing mirthlessly. "Whatcha doin' on the *ground?*"

I grabbed her arm to pull myself upright and then turned away, looking for my horse. Misty was cantering around the far end of the arena, head up and reins dragging. Even as I started trudging toward her, arms up in hopes of slowing her down, she put a leg through the reins, stumbled a little as the leather pulled taut, then bolted forward again as the reins snapped with a whip-like *crack.*

Her eyes were round and panicked, and she raced past me with her tail flagged as the rain began to fall in earnest.

"Super," I muttered. "Absolutely fantastic."

So much for keeping things going. As long as Diana was around, I'd always be teetering on the edge of disaster.

Chapter Three

To say I got home late that night was an understatement. The clock had ticked well past eight thirty and I was still fairly wet by the time I had parked my car on the brick pavers my dad had sunk into the lawn alongside the driveway—a present for me when I'd finally done the Adult Thing and scraped together enough in saved commissions to buy a car which could get me to school and, less importantly to him, the barn. Riding a bike in the Florida suburbs was a seriously sweaty and dangerous business, but my parents had been so eager to see me give up Diana's farm, they'd refused to help me buy a car.

Right about now, I couldn't entirely blame them for their motives.

All I wanted was a hot shower and to sneak some dinner from the fridge. My parents would be furious that I'd been at Diana's so late—being twenty-one but living at home without a paying job meant I was an adult in numbers only. I was still subject to their rules, their lectures, and their unmistakable disappointment.

Well, maybe they'd be watching TV in their bedroom, and I could skip the scene tonight.

I opened the front door slowly, and sighed. *Nope.*

My parents were sitting in the living room, watching TV. There was no way to creep past unseen, as our house didn't really have a foyer. There was the front door, a patch of tile to capture the pounds and pounds of sand that every Floridian dragged inside each year, and then the living room. Florida houses were very open-plan. It helped the air conditioning circulate. It was not conducive to skulking or sneaking.

Their heads swiveled when I came in, looking like a pair of owls spotting a moth. My father muted the television while I staggered around on the tile, struggling to pull off my wet boots. Nice of him, I thought, to provide good acoustics for the upcoming interrogation.

"We expected you home *early* with all that rain," my mother began. "Not an hour and a half later than usual."

"There were complications," I grunted, tugging off one drenched boot sock.

"Complications?" Her voice took on that heavy, sarcastic tone which signaled a fight was coming.

"Yeah," I replied shortly. "Complications. As in, work got complicated and the rain didn't help and everything took longer than it should have."

Obviously, I couldn't tell them the truth. What, I was going to tell my parents how I had chased my last ride around in the rain, then dragged the mare past a screaming Diana, who proceeded to barricade herself in the feed room so I couldn't feed the horses their dinners, meaning I had to wait until she finally fell asleep before I popped the door off the hinges to get past her and scoop the night's feed, and then while the rain was still drizzling down I had to turn everyone out for the night, splashing through ankle-deep mud in the dark?

I'd left Diana in the feed room, the door leaning against the wall, and could only hope that raccoons didn't creep in and eat her.

I wasn't telling my parents any of that. Sure, this job wasn't *ideal*, but it was the one I had. I'd figure out a way to fix all this, make it work out.

"Did these complications have to do with the drunken messages Diana's been leaving on our house phone?" My father's voice was dry, which was *his* dangerous sign.

"There were messages?" I was trying to keep my own tone level, but my heart suddenly began to pound in my ears. "What messages?"

"Between six-thirty and seven-thirty, I'd say we got about a half-dozen messages. We weren't picking up, but we did listen in. Would you like to?"

That was when she had been in the feed room. She must have been calling the house in between yelling at me. Which...could not be a good thing.

"No," I decided. "I would not. I'm just going to take a shower. Tonight was crazy, yeah, but it was a blip. And the weather didn't help."

My mother stood up and took a half-step toward me, then stopped and crossed her arms over her chest, as if she'd meant to bridge the distance between us but found she couldn't. We'd let it grow too wide. "Alex, you won't be going back there. That woman is dangerous. Unhinged."

"Someone has to take care of the horses," I pointed out, stripping off my other wet sock. "She isn't going to do it."

"Even if you wanted to be noble," my mother said, "she isn't going to let you."

I had no idea what she could mean.

"Plus, they're not your horses," my father said, as if this mattered in the least. "It's time you stopped going there either way. She will be forced to deal with them herself. You can't go out there safely anymore, and they're not going to starve without you. She won't let them starve once she knows she doesn't have you to do her work anymore."

"I think that's a *very* optimistic viewpoint," I objected. "How can I risk it? And what do you mean, I can't go out there for my own safety? Look, I know Diana's gone downhill over the past few years, but that's hardly—"

"*Downhill?*" My mother snorted ungracefully. "She's in a total state of collapse. I doubt she's even paying her bills. Those horses aren't going to be there much longer, whether you're around or not. And you're *not* going to be there. It's over. We're calling it on this whole mess."

The tile floor was cold beneath my bare feet, and I wanted a hot shower and dry clothes and something to eat, in that order. But there was something in my mother's voice that made me pause. Something in the way she said *you're not going back there* which made me think: *Oh, no.*

Something which triggered a defiance, deep down inside, which would never quite disappear from my personality. I knew what I wanted, I knew who I was supposed to be, and I would never stop fighting for my right to be that person. I couldn't.

"Listen, I have to go out there," I said resolutely. "I'll look for a better solution, but until I find it, I have to be sure those horses are cared for. Horses come first."

"Absolutely not," my father retorted. He stood up and took his place alongside my mother. They stood side by side in the living room, the blue glow of the television flickering over them, and gazed at me sternly, their faces unyielding. This was a united front.

But, I was twenty-one years old. Had they forgotten this? They couldn't just boss me around like a child.

I tightened my toes atop the cold tiles. "Guys," I said, enunciating carefully, "abandoning those horses is not an option. I am sorry. I will be careful around Diana."

"Go listen to the last message," my mother said, and something in her tone—something almost regretful—made me do it.

I went into the kitchen, where the house phone sat on its charger atop the counter, alongside the spill of daily mail and magazines. The voicemail light gleamed bright red. It would play the last message first; I didn't have to hunt for it.

I hit play.

Diana's words were slurred; her message was anything but.

"Your daughter is a spiteful bitch and if I see her on this place again I will meet her with a shotgun. You hear that Alex? I swear to God. Calling me a drunk! You must think you're something pretty special! But you're a nobody, riding my cheap horses because you're not good enough to ride anything else. Good luck out there, Alex. You better not show up here again."

I sat down on a kitchen chair and stared at the patterns in the plaster on the wall.

My parents came in and observed me impassively, like zookeepers watching a sick animal.

"She didn't mean that," I said eventually. "She was drunk."

But being drunk was nothing new for Diana, and she'd never said anything like that before. Also, I'd never fought her off before. Or called her drunk to her face.

This was a night of firsts, I guessed.

"Do you have any tack out there?" my father asked.

"No," I answered numbly. I didn't *have* any tack. I'd never made enough money to buy my own saddle. My helmet always stayed in my car after there'd been an unfortunate incident with a large spider. My paddock boots were sitting by the front door, drooping with dampness.

"Saves us *that* trouble," he grumbled, and left the kitchen.

My mother sat down at the chair across from me, resting her elbows on the kitchen table. "I'm sorry it ended this way, Alex," she said, and her voice was more gentle than I'd heard it in years. "But look at this as a sign. Now you can focus on college. In a few months you'll be back on track to graduate in June. Then you can get your bachelor's. I know you were fighting it, but, honey," her voice softened still more, "this is all for the best."

I put my head down on the table and tried not to cry.

Could it be, after all of this fighting, that she was *right?*

Chapter Four

I DIDN'T GO BACK to Calusa Lakes Equestrian Center.

Well, that's a lie. Of course I went back. Just...not all the way. I knew I couldn't go back to the barn, but I couldn't let the horses go so easily. Not without knowing what would happen to them. I had to be sure Diana would show up and feed.

The next morning, I waited until my parents had gone to work. Then I went out to the garage, wheeled my bike into the driveway, and hopped on. It felt strange to cycle away from my car, parked in its spot by the house, but I had my reasons. Cars were harder to hide than bikes.

The front pasture where I'd once fed horses carrots and tried to work up the courage to go ask for riding lessons was long gone, but the deep, white sand driveway still ran between two of the pink houses, and a big field still stretched between the driveway and the barn. I pedaled along the grassy center of the driveway, sweating in the late-summer heat, until I reached a thicket of sabal palms and palmettos that grew along the pasture fence. I pushed the sharp-edged fronds aside, hoping there weren't any snakes keeping the place warm for me, until both my bicycle and I were hidden from the driveway. Then, I sat down on a palm frond, thinking it might keep ants from biting me in the ass, and looked through the wire fence towards the barn.

The horses were standing near the gates, geldings in the closest pasture and mares in the next one, swishing their tails and nipping irritably at one another. It was late and they should have been brought in already, should have eaten their grain and be working their way through their hay by now. I saw a chestnut gelding we called Neville nip at a small bay named Marty; this led to some squeals and kicks that spread like wildfire through both little herds. They were anxious about their upended routine, and their anxiety spread to me.

What if she didn't come?

The morning humidity was no joke, and I was already sweating in the shade, so as the sun crawled upwards, the heat really began to sizzle. I knew the horses were hot and upset, and I wanted so much to go bring them in. It went against everything in me to let horses get distressed like this.

Still, the messages she'd left had been so vicious, and the threats had sounded so real. I had to accept the truth: I was afraid of Diana—and maybe I had been for a long time. I just needed to know the horses would be okay, and then I could move on, find a new plan.

If they weren't?

I didn't know yet.

So I hid out there behind the palm trees, swatting at clouds of gnats and whining mosquitoes, waiting. Finally, well past nine o'clock, I saw Diana's truck appear at the end of the driveway. I pushed myself back into the palmettos, feeling sick to my stomach. If she saw me...I had nowhere to run, trapped between the wire fence and the dense palmettos. What if she was starting the day well-sauced? What might she do to me? I had awful visions of getting run down by her truck.

The truck passed harmlessly behind me, bad shocks squeaking over the rutted driveway. Then there was nothing left but a lingering odor of diesel and hot engine.

I drew in a deep breath.

I could have left then, but I waited. I had to be sure.

I watched her bring in the horses. I watched the pasture gates swing wide in the gentle sea breeze. I watched her take the hose off its reel and drag it into the barn to start filling water buckets.

That was it, then.

I got on my bike, and I pedaled home, my head swimming with confusion. Diana really was taking responsibility for the horses, which meant last night hadn't been a drunken fluke. She'd known what she was doing when she'd left those messages. She'd known I wouldn't be there this morning to feed breakfast. She'd meant it.

Except...what if she hadn't?

Maybe, I thought with a burst of unwarranted hope, maybe she'd just woken up at a decent hour and chosen to go to the barn in the morning, the way she used to, when things were better. Maybe she was wondering where on earth I was, why I hadn't shown up to bring the horses in and feed. Maybe she'd call and check on me.

So I decided to wait. I'd stay close to the phone. I went home, sat in the kitchen, worked on an English assignment, and waited. I made myself a ham sandwich and waited. I carried the phone with me to the couch and waited. I fell asleep. I woke up in the gray light of an afternoon rain shower and checked the answering machine. There was nothing.

Around seven, as the storm clouds scattered and the evening light began to slant into golden rays, I biked back. One more time.

This time, I didn't make it to the clump of palms before I turned around and headed home again. There was no reason to hide, no reason to hang out. I could already see the horses, turned out in their pastures and grazing contentedly. A pink and purple sunset began to bloom lushly over the stable as I absorbed this knowledge: she'd done the entire day without me. She hadn't called me. She hadn't wondered where I was. She'd told me to stay away, and she'd meant it.

Just like that, my time with Diana was over. My time with horses was suspended.

I had no idea what to do next.

Even with the knowledge that I was unwanted around the barn, I developed an unhealthy, obsessive habit of checking on the horses each morning. I sat in the lee of the palm trees and waited for Diana's truck. I took a book with me some mornings, to catch up with homework and stave off boredom. I watched for the horses to be led into the barn, and when I was satisfied she'd shown up and fed them their breakfast, I got on with my day.

I didn't have any classes until ten, and there was no rush to get anywhere else, so I biked home slowly, meandering without purpose, turning down streets lined with identical pink houses, delaying the boredom waiting for me at home by boring myself with my surroundings. There was just so much *day* when you didn't have horses to fill the hours. The space between breakfast and dinner had become a yawning, empty space for the first time in my memory.

So, sheerly out of boredom, I went to all of my classes. I listened to the lectures. I turned in my homework and did my reading. My grades started to skyrocket.

I was completely miserable.

My professors noticed the uptick in my work, even if they didn't catch on to my mood. Professor Blake in particular was delighted at first, and then confused. She was maybe more perceptive than most. Or maybe she looked at me and saw a person, when others saw one more student in an endless procession of students. She was different, somehow.

"Alex, something has changed."

How astute of you, Professor Blake, I thought, grinding my back teeth like a frustrated Thoroughbred. "How so?" I asked, keeping my voice neutral.

"Your grades, to be frank." The older woman hovered above my desk, an armful of papers clutched against her side. She plucked a packet from the top and slapped it down in front of me. "You *worked* at this, and it's very good. I've never seen you write more than the minimum requirement before."

Her voice had brightened, and I felt myself bristle. Oh, so now Professor Blake was delighted with me! How could a person be so obtuse? Here I was sitting right in front of her, truly dying of unhappiness, separated from the only things that mattered to me in life, and she was *congratulating* me. I wanted to scream and scream and scream, and I would have, too, if I had thought it would do any good. I settled for bitter anger instead.

"Yeah, well, I guess I had nothing better to do than write this paper," I snapped, hurling the pages into my open bag without glancing at the notes she'd scrawled across the title page. "It was this or take another nap, and I'd already slept a few hours that day."

Professor Blake's expression was instantly hurt, her thick eyebrows coming together in a frown. "Listen, come see me after class," she commanded, her voice tight.

"I'd rather not," I mumbled, already embarrassed at the way I'd spoken to her. Challenging authority was not my usual approach to life's difficulties. I was much happier just running away from them.

"It's not a request." Professor Blake turned on her heel and walked up to the front of the room, ready to start the class. A few heads turned and watched me. I was the quiet one who never spoke to anyone. Maybe I was getting interesting at last. But I kept my eyes down, fastened on my book, and their attention eventually wandered. Professor Blake began talking about James Joyce. I *hated* James Joyce: all his wandering thoughts, his made-up words, his refusal to say what he really meant. So instead of listening or reading along with her, I drew pictures of horses in the margins of my book, swirling forelocks and pricked ears and elegant legs hovering in suspended motion, until she finally dismissed the class.

Then I dragged myself to her office across the hall, feeling like I saw far too much of this place.

The humming light bulb had finally died, and both the new quiet and the reduced lighting were improvements, but Professor Blake's office was otherwise unchanged from my last visit. Really, though, how much could a tiny box just large enough for a desk, two chairs, and an overloaded bookshelf ever change? I slid sulkily into the creaking extra chair, my knees pressing against the desk when the professor leaned behind me to close the door.

"Okay, Alex, what's going on? I thought you'd just decided to take things seriously, and I was happy." Professor Blake sat down behind the desk and rested her elbows on the little stack of books covering the surface. She clasped her hands and gazed at me, those amazing eyebrows coming together in the middle. "But now I'm wondering if you're okay."

"I'm *not* okay." The words came words bounding out of my mouth before I could stop them. Three simple words, but I hadn't said them before. Who would I tell? It wasn't the kind of thing I could tell my parents, and I didn't have any real friends anymore. When you're the last one to stick by a collapsing person, everyone else you thought you knew tends to vanish.

"Well, what's going on?" Professor Blake asked gently. "Let me help."

I lost everything I cared about and I don't know what to do about it, I thought. Aloud, I said: "I was working at a horse farm for a really long time, and I lost the job, and it's been really hard not being around horses."

She sighed, as if she should have known my issues were all equine in nature. "Horses really are everything to you, aren't they." It was a statement, not a question. She'd finally figured it out.

"They're everything. Yes."

"Well, Alex, in that case, you have just got to find a way to have them in your life. Just a little bit. Maybe you get a different job at a different farm. Or you get a job that lets you afford to pay to ride a horse from time to time, just to scratch that itch."

I sensed the beginning of a familiar lecture, the one with the line about getting a great job so someday, I could afford to own as many horses as I wanted, and board them at the nicest stable, and show them at the best shows every weekend, as long as I put in the years of study and earnest, urgent paper-pushing required to earn an upper-middle-class salary. I tipped my head back against the back of the chair and closed my eyes, prepared to let it happen, like a dental procedure or a vaccination.

"Or is that not good enough?"

My eyes flew open. Professor Blake was gazing at me sadly, and I realized, with a shock, she was the first adult I'd ever spoken with who hadn't taken the first opportunity to tell me horses were not the answer. I picked my head back up and met her gaze. "It's *not* good enough, no matter how hard people keep trying to sell me on it. I don't *want* a normal life."

Professor Blake shrugged. "Well then, Alex, you have got to think bigger than Calusa."

Chapter Five

W**HAT DO YOU WANT** to do? Besides train horses, I mean. Drill it down for me."

We were sitting over coffees in the campus cafeteria. I took mine black, the way Diana had shown me coffee was supposed to be enjoyed—or tolerated. I was never really sure if she'd *liked* what she'd thrown into her Thermos every morning. The faces she'd made were inconclusive.

Professor Blake, to my surprise, did the same. Took her coffee black, that is, not made scowling faces every time she sipped it.

"What do you mean, *drill it down?*" I asked. I was a little suspicious of this entire conversation. Would this ultimately be a ploy to make me settle for college, after all? I *wasn't* doing one of those equine management degrees, if that's what she was going to suggest. The class descriptions were like, "Accounting, but make it horses!" No, thank you.

"I mean, get really, *really* specific. Maybe I won't understand it, but you will. Don't be broad and say you'll take anything. That's how you get by, but that's not how you build a life you love. Broad strokes show you the road...but they're not the destination."

I'd never heard anything like that before. "Huh," I murmured, stalling while I thought. I sipped at my coffee in hopes of finding more brainpower via caffeine. *Better living through chemistry.* "So, like…I need to come up with the job I wish I had right now, training and skill notwithstanding?"

"Exactly."

"Oh! Well, in that case, it's racehorse trainer," I announced, without having to think another second. "I want to be a racehorse trainer. That was easy, actually."

Professor Blake's eyebrows drew together in the middle, a dark beetle of dismay. "Oh God, you really do, too. I can tell by how quickly you said it."

I nodded, wondering why everyone always reacted like that. I'd wanted to be a racehorse trainer for as long as I could remember—well, that wasn't true, when I was *very* young I'd wanted to be a jockey, but it was pretty clear by age twelve I was outgrowing that dream—and the general consensus by family and friends was that my life goal was Not Good.

Horse racing was dangerous, run by criminals, and possibly unethical. These were the *very nicest* reasons given to me by naysayers. Horse racing was not for nice girls like me. Horse shows were our domain. Memorize your course, jump your jumps, and don't worry about horse racing.

I wasn't giving in that easily, though. Maybe the sport *was* run by criminals. I didn't know. How was I going to know for sure until I'd been to a racetrack, worked with a trainer, learned the ins and outs of the business? Plus, even if that was the case, there had to be some good people in racing. You couldn't get thousands of horses to the peak of physical perfection without some seriously good horsemanship in the mix. Anyway, racing was so objective. The fastest horse won. It made a lot more sense to me than all the little rules and personal prejudices judges had when they placed horses at a show.

So yeah, I could admit it: I didn't know what went on in a racing stable. I couldn't afford to subscribe to magazines, but whenever I went to a tack shop I flipped through the racing journals, absorbing the trainer interviews, trying to find out what they *really* did with their horses. Somehow, these trainers, mostly men, managed to say a lot without saying anything at all. No matter how much I read, I didn't know how they trained. I didn't know what they fed. I didn't even understand how their tack worked—they used English saddles, but smaller, right? Surely there was more to it than that.

Maybe everyone in the Calusa riding community was right, and I'd hate working in racing. There was no real way to find out without actually trying it. I couldn't see any way to get past my racing obsession until I'd been a part of it for at least a little taste.

I didn't say any of this out loud. The question hadn't been about *why*, it was about *what*. I just waited for Professor Blake to process this information and, hopefully, tell me what to do next.

I sure didn't know.

"Fine," she sighed, recovering herself at last. Her eyebrows returned to a neutral position, and she sipped at her coffee, looking thoughtful. "Where around here can you learn to do that? There must be a career progression. You start out entry-level, you learn, you make your way up. Is there anyone in the racing business down here?"

"It's all up in Ocala," I replied. "There's no racing here. Nothing but show horses and pleasure horses."

"You make them sound so undesirable."

"They're fine, but if you want me to be absolutely certain of what I want to do, they're not it. I've been working in that business for almost ten years. You know what? I just realized this, but I have to leave." I said the words with conviction. *I have to leave.* Things were clicking in my brain, the steps were starting to slip into place. I needed money, a destination, a plan. Suddenly it was all so obvious.

Professor Blake nodded. "So, how do you get to Ocala? Do you start applying to jobs? That's what, three or four hours away? You'd have to get up there for interviews, find a place to live..."

Therein lies the problem, Professor. I chewed at my lip as the old frustrations rose up. If it had been easy to leave, I would have done it already. "Here's the thing. I don't have any money. Or experience with racehorses. I've seen a few ads for jobs up there, but they're not for beginners." I'd seen online listings calling for grooms, exercise riders, even farm managers, but they'd all required experience with *current* racehorses—not ex-racehorses learning to be show horses.

"That's tough." She considered her coffee for a few moments. Then she looked back at me, her brown eyes brightening. "I know. You need a contact, a place to start. Let me ask you this: if you could work for anyone in Ocala, who would it be? Do you have a name? A company?"

"Alexander Whitehall," I said, without hesitation.

I absolutely idolized Alexander Whitehall, a long-jawed English horseman with sun-bleached blonde hair and a humorous expression. He always looked as if he'd just heard something ridiculous, but he'd get in trouble if he passed it on, like an overgrown schoolboy who just learned a new dirty joke. I wanted in on the joke, but of course I didn't really know him. Alexander Whitehall was from the pages of those racing magazines.

For a few years he'd been all over the racing news. He was newly-arrived from the U.K. and making a splash on the American east coast tracks. I loved that he came from England; I loved that he came from a racing dynasty; I loved that he was here on his own, trying something new, making his own name in a country with different rules. That took courage, and conviction: two traits I admired in anyone, possibly because I hadn't yet been brave enough or sure enough of myself to leave my own poisoned employment.

I hungrily read every interview he gave, hoping I'd learn something, *anything,* about how to make it as a trainer like him someday. His horses were known for being sound and happy, and his beautiful Ocala farm was always described as if it was an equine Shangri-La, all green pastures and breezy barns.

Then, a year or two ago, he'd vanished from the headlines. New hotshot trainers arrived on the scene and took his place in the pages. Racing loved freshman sires, debut seasons, horses who won the first time out. This affection extended to apprentice jockeys on hot streaks and trainers so new, the plastic on their licenses was still warm. Freshmen and seniors got all the coverage; you seemed to need a huge season for mid-career stardom, and Alexander Whitehall just hadn't had one lately.

I figured he was in a slump. Apparently in racing, fortunes rose and fell in cycles. You got slumps, and you had to wait them out. I knew he'd be back someday. In the meantime, I missed seeing him in the magazines. Alexander Whitehall was easy on the eyes.

Professor Blake was nodding. "And he's in Ocala?"

"As far as I know. He used to be."

"Maybe you know someone who knows him. Have you ever thought about that?"

"I'm in the wrong side of things. I'm not a racehorse person."

"But it's all horses," Professor Blake said. "You have to know someone who can tell you something about it, maybe call up a connection for you. Right? Even if it's six degrees of separation, if you keep calling the next person on the list, you'll get to Alexander Whitehall eventually."

I looked back down at my coffee. I'd hoped this wouldn't be her suggestion. Because there *was* one person who might give me a clue how to break into racing. The problem was, if she was still Diana's friend, I didn't like my chances.

"Right?" Professor Blake persisted.

"Maybe," I admitted, grudgingly.

"Then you have to make that call," she said, shrugging. "If a little phone anxiety is the only thing standing between you and your dream, count yourself lucky."

❧❧❧ ❧❧❧

The woman on the other end of the call didn't want to give me Lucille's information, and I was getting annoyed. I'd been trying to get a phone number out of her for a solid five minutes with no results. It was time to resort to the only thing that talked in the horse business: money.

"Come on, this is a *business* transaction. I need to talk to Lucille Cornett or she's going to lose money on a sale. Do you want her to find out you cost her money?"

In my experience, everyone hated thinking they could lose a single cent, and for broke-ass horse-people, this went double. For me, having rarely brought home more than a few dollars that wasn't already earmarked for gas so I could drive straight back to the stables to do it all over again, losing money was still a foreign concept. I hadn't actually found any money to lose yet. Still, I figured, I could work this phobia to my advantage.

If this racetrack secretary would just fall for it.

"Miss, we can't just give out personal contact information," the woman insisted. She had a sharp Southern twang which was growing more backwoods by the minute. "You have got to understand my position here."

"*Ask* her, then!" I burst out, wrung dry of all patience. "Take my number, call her up and ask her, tell her to give me a call. Tell her it's the girl who trained Swan. I got her a lot of money for that horse."

Would Lucille Cornett remember a retired race-mare named Swan, who left her care four years ago and counting? *I'd* never forget her; she was the first horse Diana had handed over to me on day one with the instructions: "Calm her down and make her into a kid-friendly show horse."

Swan had been one of the many horses Lucille had hauled down to Diana's barn. How many dozens of her retirees had I ridden over the years? I couldn't even remember them all to make a list—but I remembered Swan.

I'd taken Swan the Racehorse apart and put her back together as Swan the Children's Jumper. Diana let her stick around longer than most, because she was so talented, and consequently I'd fallen for the mare in the process. I fell hard. I loved her, from nose to tail. I rode her every day, in every weather, including during a squall from an approaching hurricane which nearly blew me out of the saddle. There was no storm strong enough to keep me from Swan. When other horses in the barn developed a bacterial skin infection common in Florida, I hid a set of brushes just for Swan so she couldn't catch it from them. I did my homework in her stall, listening to her chew her hay.

Six months later, Swan sold to a middle-school kid from a fancy neighborhood for a decent five-figure price. I saved my sobs for my bedroom at night. Diana had already made it clear that there was no crying allowed in the barn. "There are always more horses," she would say, and she was right about that. Even as a teenager, I had learned it was foolish to fall in love.

Swan was just the beginning for me, the year my role shifted from student to trainer. I became an off-track Thoroughbred specialist thanks to Lucille's unending supply line of retired racehorses, but to this day, Swan remained my biggest triumph by far. I'd never managed to get Diana that much money for a horse again.

She'd just been *such* a nice mare, and the extra time had let me really get her going.

I was banking on Lucille remembering that one and only really good check Diana had sent her for a consignment horse, but maybe it wasn't that much money to her. How much money did it take to make a racehorse trainer look up and smile?

"Fine," the racetrack secretary was sighing. "I'll tell her. I'll give her the message."

She took down my number, then the call cut off abruptly. I put the phone back on its charger, leaned back in the kitchen chair, and waited for her to call me. I had nothing else to do, and if Lucille was as broke as she'd always *looked*, she'd call me.

The phone rang nearly an hour later, and I was jerked out of the uncomfortable sleep I'd fallen into, my neck cricked against the wall behind my chair, my left foot mysteriously asleep where it rested on the footer of the kitchen table. I shook my foot to try and wake it up while I answered the phone.

"I don't know who this is." Lucille's voice was more gravelly than ever. "But I'm calling you back anyway."

"It's Alex O'Connor," I replied. "From Calusa Lakes? The working student?"

"Oh boy. Did Diana finally crack her skull open?"

"No. I mean, maybe. I haven't been there in a while. She kicked me out."

"Was she drunk?"

"Very."

"That seems to be her state these days," Lucille said knowingly. "You're better off. I was thinking it was time to cut her off, find a new trainer. So you're the white-haired girl that rides all the horses. Rode, I mean. And you're looking for something new, I guess."

"Yeah." I crossed my fingers and looked at them as I searched for words. "This isn't really about making money. I'm sorry. I...I'm looking for work. I want to work in racing. I thought you might—" I trailed off. Should I really just ask her? Should I really just say his name?

He was a world-famous trainer.

I felt like I was shooting a little high for my first time out. I pinned my lips together, holding in the syllables.

"Oh, this again?" There was a pause, and a whooshing sound which puzzled me until I realized she was taking a drag off her Marlboro. "Nuh-uh. You asked me before, and I told you then. My answer's the same. Stay away from the racetrack, Alex. Keep training those show horses. You find another place to ride, I'll send you one to sell for me."

"I want to learn about *racing,* though. That's what I want to do." I tightened my fingers around the phone, trying to keep the hurt out of my voice. "Racing is all I've ever wanted to do. And I've been stuck doing show horses all of this time but now I have a chance to get away and—"

"I can't help you," she interrupted. "I can't hire you. I couldn't afford to keep a girl like you on my staff."

I was too confused to reply.

"But if you really want to work with racehorses, go to Ocala. Stay away from the racetrack—I mean that, now." Another pause, another drag. "But the breeding farms, Ocala...that's a pretty good place to be, even for girls. You can learn there. Everything you need to know is on the farm. And it's the right time of year. Yearlings are coming in. The September sales are on right now, tons of babies on their way to Florida for baby racehorse school. Yeah. You could probably manage in Ocala for a season."

My mouth was dry. Alexander Whitehall was somewhere in Ocala. Lucille was pointing me in his direction—maybe not by name, maybe not specifically, but...

"Can you...do you know anyone...do you know..." The words *Alexander Whitehall* wavered at the back of my throat, but I couldn't get them out. It was too absurd, like asking for the moon. I'd settle for whoever I could get.

"You don't need my help with anyone," she said. "Just go up there, drive from farm to farm. Look for help wanted signs. Drive in and ask if they're hiring. That's how we do things. It's not too formal. It might take you a few weeks, but you'll land something."

Okay, I thought. Then something else occurred to me. "What if they want references? Diana—"

Lucille had a sigh like a hoof-rasp. "Everyone knows Lucille Cornett. You can use my name. But that's it. And don't call me if it all goes south. Racetrackers eat nice girls like you for breakfast. Don't expect this to last. Don't burn any bridges at home."

Lucille hung up.

Ocala, I thought. The dial tone buzzed in my ear. It wasn't the plan I'd hoped for, but it was still a plan.

Now, how was I supposed to actually make it happen?

Chapter Six

IT WOULD BE NICE if you were supportive," I told my mother. Sarcasm, of course. I knew my parents weren't going to be supportive of this move. It was everything they'd never wanted for me.

"It would be nice if you weren't ruining your life," my mother snapped back. Her fingers tapped the doorframe; I knew she wanted to turn away and slam my bedroom door, but at the same time, she couldn't just walk away from a perfectly good fight. Giving in wasn't in her. "Alex, we have given you every opportunity to make the right decisions, and we have given you every allowance when you made it clear you weren't ready to take adulthood seriously, but this is going too far. You absolutely cannot move out right now."

I paused in my packing, a scrap of cotton tank top that I liked to ride in dangling from my fingers. "Or what, Mother? I'm twenty-one, and I'm pretty sure you told me I had to pay rent or leave."

She rolled her eyes. "Don't call me Mother, we aren't in a Victorian melodrama. And *or what?* You're right, I can't ground you. And I did tell you to pay rent or leave, if you couldn't get school under control. But you did that." She paused, momentarily stymied. "And anyway, you have a couple of months left. It's not even October yet. You had until the end of the year."

"I leave now or I leave in January, the end result is the same but I waste more of my own time," I said airily. I was cool and confident because I could be. I had sold my textbooks back to the school bookstore and sold my good show boots, the ones I wouldn't need in the racing business. So now I had a few hundred dollars, enough to get to Ocala and stay in a cheap motel while I found a job and a place to stay. My mother had no more hold on me. The car was mine; she couldn't threaten to keep that. Really, all she *could* do was tell me that if I went, I couldn't come back, and what exactly would that accomplish? Why would I want to come back?

Lucille had warned me not to burn bridges, but Lucille didn't know everything.

"Alex, listen to me a minute. Stay, and we'll help you find a job with horses around here."

I dropped another tank top into my suitcase. "You don't mean that," I scoffed.

"I do. We could—we could even find you a little piece of property to rent. You could start your own barn. Get a few horses to train, get some boarders." My mom's face was dead serious. "We could help you get set up with your own business. Since this is what you really want. I can tell you mean it. Let's just...let's just take a minute and think how we can make this work."

I looked at her in disbelief. "You'd really do that for me?"

She glanced at my suitcase. "If you stay, sure. But running away to Ocala is the wrong move. I hope this shows you how serious I am."

For a last-ditch effort, she hadn't done too badly. I was actually taking her offer seriously, which was pretty impressive considering I'd already committed myself to heading to Ocala—and I was the kind of person who made up my mind and kept it that way, even when situations began to make it perfectly clear I'd made the wrong decision. Diana was a perfect example of this trait.

I thought about the potential in her offer: I could have my own little barn, an arena with homemade jumps, some boarders and some students, some horses in training. Lucille had said she'd send me a horse to sell. I'd have a project horse to start my sales business. Instead of running away with my entire life savings—it was four hundred and fifty dollars, thanks for asking—I'd be getting my own training career rolling from the comfort of my childhood home.

Plus everything that came with the lifestyle, a warning voice reminded me. I'd have horse shows on the calendar every weekend from October to April, and the day-in, day-out grind of teaching horses to canter quietly around a hunter course, of telling children to put their heels down and to stop yanking back on the reins and to put their tack away instead of leaving it in the barn aisle to get tripped over while I was trying to feed.

Starting this year, and lasting for the rest of my life.

I couldn't do it. Not now, not while I had momentum.

Professor Blake had been right; I had to make my dream come true or abandon it altogether. I was living half a life right now—maybe less, since I wasn't riding at all. This was the moment, and if I didn't take it now, at twenty-one with nothing tying me down, when the hell was I going to take it?

Sure, going to Ocala was insane...but it was probably insane to stay here and trust my mother to follow through on this little plan. Sure, sticking to show horses gave me a slightly higher chance of success and a lower chance of traumatic injury, but in this case, success might be the one reason why I never lived the life of my dreams.

The promise of success might be the one thing holding me back.

"I don't want to train horses here," I told her. "I'm sorry. I don't want to be a hunter trainer or a riding instructor."

"But Alex, you're good at being a hunter trainer."

"I'm good at English, too, but I don't want to be an English teacher. Just because I'm good at something doesn't mean I want to do it forever."

I didn't want to horse show, didn't want to canter around a hunter course as slow and steady as could be, didn't even want to tear around a jumper course. I wanted to ride *Thoroughbreds*, as fast as they could go.

And fast Thoroughbreds were in Ocala.

Alexander Whitehall was in Ocala, too, and I couldn't stop thinking about him now that Professor Blake had put this idea into my head, this crazy idea that I should go straight to the top and knock on his door. I was going to give it a try, anyway. I had this crazy idea that if I moved fast enough, I could catch this dream before it escaped me entirely.

"I'm sorry, Mom," I said, going back to packing. "I really am. But this is what I need to do right now. I have to at least give it a try. I have to *know.*"

"Fine," she replied sharply. "But that's the only time you'll get this offer. If you leave now, don't come back here unless you're ready to commit yourself to full-time college and get yourself a real job. This is your last chance to make something happen with horses. Prove us wrong, Alex. I really want to be wrong. If you come back broke, that's it. School. Degree. Job. There is absolutely no discussion on this. Do you understand?"

It would never come to that.

But...could it?

I nodded slowly, realizing this really, truly was my last chance. I either made it happen, or I came back and gave it up. She'd made the offer. She'd extended the olive branch. I felt terrible knowing I'd turned her down flat. She was my *mother*. I would have loved it if I could have made her happy for once.

I had to swallow the lump in my throat before I could speak. "I understand."

My mother left my doorway. A few moments later, I heard dishes crashing in the dishwasher. She was going to take it out on the crockery and cutlery, then. Well, I appreciated the passion. It meant she cared. I sniffled, and wiped a stray tear from my cheek.

This was harder than I'd expected.

My father was next in line, but he didn't have much to say. He just stood mournfully in my room while I threw the balled-up contents of my sock drawer into the front section of my suitcase.

"You're really doing this?" he asked after a little while. "You're *sure*."

"It's important to me, Dad. And I'll never have another moment as good as this one. Yeah, I'm taking a couple Incompletes on classes. But they're really not important."

"You're really privileged, Alex, to be able to do this," he said grimly. "So don't forget that you have a safety net to let you run away and chase a dream. Your mother and I want to see you be happy."

Professor Blake had told me the same thing when I'd told her I was going. She reminded me not to forget that I was privileged, that I had a safety net if I failed, that I was lucky I couldn't fall through the cracks. I thought she made light of the underlying truth, though...if I came back, it was to live by someone else's terms, rather than my own. Could a safety net also be the trap?

I hadn't asked her that. I made a joke instead. "Yeah, I have a safety net...unless I get dumped on the track by a racehorse galloping at forty miles an hour," I'd reminded her cheerfully, skipping my dramatic internal reaction. "No safety net there! Then I just have a helmet and a prayer."

Professor Blake had raised her eyebrows. "Don't tell your parents that. And please, never mention it to me again, either. The last thing I want to do is think about that time I sent one of my students off to be trampled to pieces by a horse."

"My chances are good," I'd assured her. "I'm used to galloping tough horses."

Of course, I wasn't, not really. I was used to riding difficult young horses in an arena, with fences to contain any stupidity. I had never galloped around the alluring curves of a training track. I had never even seen an exercise saddle or a training track or a racing stable in real life. I had no idea what was waiting for me, besides early mornings and strong horses.

My father wasn't finished. "I just don't like to see you running away from your problems."

I zipped up my bag. "The answer to my problems isn't here."

"Finishing school and having a place to stay without having to worry about rent isn't the answer to your problems?"

I smiled at my dad with real fondness. There are some people who are never, ever going to get it, and all you can do is sympathize. "I know it sounds like it should be, Dad, but it isn't."

I considered all of the things I was running away from: the lectures on growing up and giving up horses, the yawning void in my life with no horses in it, the hurt I had felt when I checked on the farm all those mornings and saw that without me, Diana had resumed working each morning, as if *I* had been the problem all along, as if I had enabled her drinking and the absconding of her duties and the downfall of her business simply by being the Reliable One, and most of all, the stinging realization that everything here was wrong for me, just *wrong,* and I needed to start over somewhere new.

It all bubbled over and I turned to him, my empty hands spread, tears pricking at my eyes.

"I can't stay here, Dad. I have to do this. And if not now, what will I do with these *feelings?*"

The whole thing was becoming way more emotional than I had expected. I turned away quickly, hoping he'd leave before I started to cry in earnest.

My dad seemed to know this without my telling him, because before he wandered out of my room, he put a green fold of paper on my dresser. When I picked it up a few minutes later, I saw it was a hundred-dollar bill.

My cheeks were still wet when I tucked it into my wallet.

Chapter Seven

THE FIRST HORSE FARM to appear along I-75 was still more than half an hour south of the exit I'd planned on taking, but I took the sight of it as a sign I was doing things right, that I was nearly there, that all of my dreams were within reach. Maybe that was too much credit to give one little farm, but hey, this place looked *ritzy*.

Despite being pressed against the six-lane interstate, everything about it pointed to a working racehorse training center. There was a long barn topped with a fancy cupola, a round pen, and the swooping curves of a training track—the first one I'd ever seen in real life. The white PVC rails gave me a rush of adrenaline. A real-life *racetrack!* Okay, fine, a training track, but *still!* This was a place where racehorses worked!

I wanted to pull off the interstate and just admire those rails for a while, but I-75 traffic is essentially just a lot of semi-trailers jockeying for position and I probably would have died, so I settled for gazing at it longingly as I passed.

As my car whizzed past at seventy miles an hour, the last thing I noticed was a paddock just outside the barn, where a herd of young horses with shortish tails were milling around. They were displaying the various stages of horses waiting impatiently for their dinners: chewing on each other, kicking each other, and running up and down the fence.

I drove on, wondering how old the horses were. Yearlings? Two-year-olds? The youngest horses Diana would take on were three-year-olds. Lucille had said this was yearling season, but I had never dealt with yearlings.

Well, it was just one more unknown I was driving towards.

All of these unknowns weren't deterrents, though. They were just adding fuel to my fire. I should have done this *years* ago, I thought, flooring the gas pedal to overtake a slow truck ahead of me. I should know these things! I shouldn't just know about adult horses who have already been tacked and backed and are ready to start over fences...I needed to know *everything*. Training, racing, breeding, breaking: I wanted it all. I would be Alex O'Connor, the well-rounded racehorse trainer.

By the time the Ocala exits began to crop up, I was shaking with excitement—and yeah, some nerves, too. Now there were horse farms on both sides of the interstate. Some were sprawling and grand, all hilltop mansions and white-railed training tracks. Some were just little fenced-in squares with a mobile home squatting in the middle, a couple of horses grazing on sandy ground next to discarded tractor pieces. I could already see Ocala was a mixture of rich and poor, elegant and rusty, newcomers and old Floridians.

I supposed wherever I was heading, it would fall on the shiny interloper side of the divide. The racehorse people hadn't sprung up from the native culture. They'd come here in search of sunshine and green winter grass, and built an empire of money in the center of a rural backwoods.

Then there was no time to wonder any more, with the exit I'd marked as mine rapidly approaching. I'd picked it out of a book of I-75 exits: cluttered pages of maps which marked the amenities at every junction from South Florida to Michigan. The book promised a cluster of cheap motels and fast food joints which would be well-lit all night long. They were the kind of places which advertised rooms for truckers from thirty dollars a night. I figured if I ran out of motel money too quickly, I could find some safe-ish places nearby to park my car. I didn't *want* to live out of my old Civic (and my parents would have an absolute fit if they found out) but I wanted to be prepared for any situation.

Because I couldn't go home now.

I'd never get this chance again.

I pulled off the interstate and drove a little way past the normal cluster of exit commerce, looking for a quiet parking lot to just sit still for a bit, take some deep breaths settle my nerves. I'd never checked into a motel alone before, and just the thought of going up to that Econo Lodge front desk and asking for a room was putting me on edge. The reality of what I'd done was setting in for real now. I had to be a grown-up like *actual* grown-ups were. Not just working hard with horses all day long, but interacting with strangers like hotel clerks and farm secretaries.

For some reason, this part felt even scarier than the rest.

As I looked for a place to sit and breathe, I made a mental list of everything I had to worry about. (I like to be productive this way.)

One: I didn't have a plan.

Two: I was afraid of an unseen front desk clerk.

Three: I was planning on driving around Thoroughbred farms asking for work from people I didn't know, and on top of my list was the farm of a famous trainer. A famous trainer in a slump, but even so.

Four: When put like that, I guess I *did* have a plan, but it was still a terrible one.

I pulled behind a barbecue restaurant which had a big, shady back parking lot, and found a quiet spot beneath an oak tree. I rolled down the car window and took a few deep breaths of humid September air. Ocala was still hot, but it seemed cooler than Calusa, and the breeze was laden with woodsmoke from the restaurant's barbecue pit. My stomach rumbled encouragingly. "I wish I had enough money to buy you barbecue," I told it. "Maybe after I get a job."

Crap. Was I really going to find a job?

"This is fine," I said aloud. "This is fine, this is fine, *this is fine.* You're going be okay. You'll get a hotel room, you'll map out some farms, tomorrow you'll get a job. Easy. You're fine."

I closed my eyes. Maybe if I envisioned my dreams, they'd come true. There was a book about that. I'd flipped through it in lines at the grocery store, waiting to pay for another twenty-pound bag of carrots to keep my horses sweet.

Oh, my babies. An image of Misty, lipping at my fingers as she took a carrot after a ride, flooded into my brain. *No,* I scolded myself. *Only look forward.*

A new farm, that's what I would picture: black-board fences, rolling hills, green pastures, horses grazing under the sun. A training track. Riders galloping. A trainer on a bay stable pony, who turned to look at me. His lazy smile lit up his tanned face.

A truck door slammed nearby.

I sighed with irritation. Was it *really* necessary for someone to park next to me when the entire freaking lot was wide open? I'd gone into the back corner for a reason. You'd think that way out here in the country, people would have some appreciation of privacy.

I opened my eyes and looked over at the interloping truck, parked a few spaces away. A tall man was leaning over the tailgate, moving around some cargo, which must have shifted while he was driving. I waited for him to go away. I *willed* him to go away.

He stayed, stubbornly rooted to the ground, immune to my psychic commands. He went on fiddling with something in the truck-bed for what felt like hours. I watched him long after I should have lost interest and looked away. I watched him until it felt like my eyes were glued to his every movement.

I watched him until I felt like I knew him.

Finally, he lifted a tiny exercise saddle from the truck's bed and deposited it into the truck's cab. For safekeeping, I guessed. It was the first time I'd seen an exercise saddle in real life, and I wished he'd kept it out a few minutes longer. I wanted to get closer, run my fingers across the leather, study all the differences between its tiny shape and a more familiar jumping saddle.

He turned his head casually as he put it away, looking around the parking lot with no real purpose. Then our eyes met, and my heart seemed to lurch to a complete stop.

I *knew* him.

My heart took off again, galloping like a runaway racehorse. I could feel a pricking in my thumbs, a trembling in my limbs.

Our gazes held. I could see a startled expression sweep across his features—those familiar features, that face I'd known forever.

For the longest, most confusing moment of my life, I thought: *it's you.*

And I'd swear he thought the same thing.

Then, he looked away, distracted by a voice, someone else calling for his attention. It was a woman. I felt my stomach lurch. *What about me?*

And then I thought: *Just what is* that *supposed to mean?*

"Just a minute," he called across the parking lot. When I heard his voice, that clipped accent, I knew it was true.

This man, who had set my pulse to dangerous levels and made me feel like I was reliving some past life, was Alexander Whitehall.

And I'd clearly lost my damn mind.

❧❧❧❧❧ ❧❧❧❧❧

Here's the awful truth: I had a picture of Alexander Whitehall pinned to the bulletin board over my desk, back in my old bedroom, back in my parents' house.

I know, I know.

I didn't have the picture up because of *him,* though. (At least, I hadn't thought he was the reason.) It was really because of the horse he was leading, a dashing beauty named Beginner's Goodbye, who had been a pretty big deal four years ago. That had been during Alexander's rookie hot streak. In admiring Beginner's Goodbye, of course, I'd absorbed a fair amount of Alexander. He'd been holding the reins with a masterful air, his right hand raised to pat the sweaty neck of the dark bay horse, his eyes focused not on the cameras aimed in his direction or the entourage following him to the winner's circle, but on the horse he had trained.

Yes, *fine*, I will admit that while I'd been daydreaming about training a horse like Beginner's Goodbye, I hadn't been immune to Alexander Whitehall's many charms. Like the way his deep blue eyes were surrounded by friendly crinkles when he smiled, or the country squire style in which he dressed, those flat tweed caps and those long, tawny overcoats. It was a fashion sense which seemed firmly rooted in the past. Or perhaps this was just how British horse-racing glitterati still dressed. Either way, I loved it.

He wasn't wearing a coat now; September was too sultry for long-sleeved anything. Dark blue shorts, a short-sleeved white shirt, nothing fancy—just a regular guy out for an early supper at a barbecue joint. His skin was more tan than I remembered from the picture in my room, his hair an even paler tint of gold. He was taller in person, too.

So there was a perfectly rational reason for recognizing him, I told myself, even though I knew there was no rational reason for the unmistakeable heart-lift of seeing him, of feeling I had known him my entire life, of feeling I'd been *waiting* for him my entire life, just waiting to get our work together started.

Nothing could explain anything crazy like that...but, thankfully, the feeling was already starting to fade. My heart was returning to its normal rhythm, and all I had to do now was turn this chance encounter into the single greatest networking move of my life. Alexander Whitehall was a few dozen feet away. He could give me a job. If I convinced him to do it.

If I could get out of the car. That part was important, but I was struggling with it.

My hand was on the door handle, but I couldn't make myself pop it open. What would I say? *Hi Alexander, I'm such a big fan! I just moved here with no experience, can you give me a job?*

That was crazy. He'd laugh at me, it would be horrible, I'd die, the end.

Or...maybe he wouldn't.

Alexander Whitehall was a nice guy; everyone in the magazines said so. He'd put me down easy, if he didn't have any use for me. He'd be polite; he'd probably offer to connect me with someone who *could* help me.

So that was that. I had literally nothing to lose. I'd gotten this far, why not embarrass myself a little bit in front of my idol?

Plus, if the fates had arranged for me to meet Alexander *freaking* Whitehall in the parking lot of a barbecue joint, who was I to question them? The fates would definitely be pissed off with me if I didn't at least *try* to follow their lead.

What, I was going to mess with the *fates?*

I took a breath, summoned everything I had, and opened my car door.

Alexander was jingling his truck keys from palm to palm, looking almost nervous. His eyebrows were clinging together in a frown; his lips were turned down. I remembered his bright smile from the magazine picture, from my daydream of just moments before, and wondered how I could get a first-hand look at it.

"Nice weather," I said, and then I wished I'd just kept my mouth shut.

The pale eyebrows lifted, and I saw the faintest hint of a smile. "Do you like roasting in autumn, then?"

"I'm used to it," I replied. I started to cross the pavement between us. Brown lizards ran across the cracked asphalt, scattering into the lazy runners of grass at the parking lot's edge. "Actually, it's cooler here than back home. I'm from Calusa, near Naples?"

He shook his head. "I've heard of Naples, but I've never been to that end of Florida. Is it nice there?"

Why were we having this conversation? It felt like we were speaking our first words on a blind date. "I've been driving all day to get away from there," I answered.

He leaned back against the truck. "Where's your final destination?"

I took a breath. "Here," I replied. "I mean—not this restaurant. Ocala."

"You might change your mind if you try it. The restaurant's very good."

"I will, sometime. Since I'm staying here."

His gaze flicked over me. I was wearing shorts and sandals, not jeans and boots, but something must have given me away as a horse girl. "Working at a farm here?"

"I hope so." I had stopped about six feet away from him. I couldn't remember what to do with my hands, so I shoved them into my back pockets to get them out of the way. "I have to ask, aren't you—"

"*Alexander!*" a woman shouted. "Really, why are you keeping me waiting again?"

He glanced towards the restaurant, his slight smile disappearing. "I'll be there in a *minute,*" he retorted. His blue eyes focused on me again, flicking up and down as if he was trying to figure out who I really was. "Sorry about that. She gets shirty when she has to wait. You should see her at airports."

I grinned. "I think I'll pass."

"Heh. Wise. Well, I'd better go and shut her up. Good luck to you." He straightened up. "Where did you say you were working?"

"No, I'm not—" I summoned everything had. "You're Alexander Whitehall, aren't you?"

"You've found me out. Oh, no. Is this a summons? Have I been served?"

His smile was infectious. I found myself taking a step closer. "Can I admit something? It's really crazy but...you're kind of just the person I wanted to see. I'd really like to work for you. I'll do anything. I can groom, I can clean stalls—" Forget being a rider, I just wanted to follow this man back to his farm and never let him out of my sight again.

"Whoa, wait a minute!" he laughed, holding up his hands. "You came here to see *me?* So you could muck out my stables? That's a long drive to shovel some manure."

"I didn't really come for that," I explained, feeling like an idiot. "I want to learn about horse racing. Everything about it."

"Oh, I see." His expression grew more serious. "Well, what can you do?"

"I can ride retired racehorses. Lucille Cornett will give me a reference. I talked to her and *she* said to come up here now, that it was yearling season and everyone would need riders, that I had enough experience to do it—"

"Lucille Cornett!" Alexander sounded surprised. "You know her?"

"Really well," I lied. "I've known her since I was thirteen." This part was true. "How do you know her?"

"Everyone knows Lucille." Alexander looked at me thoughtfully. "So you rode Thoroughbreds for Lucille?"

"I've been retraining Thoroughbreds since I was a kid," I said. "Lucille would bring her retired horses to our farm, and I'd train them and sell them for her." I cut out Diana. She wasn't part of my life anymore. She wasn't part of my story anymore. From here on out, she no longer existed.

"Horse shows, is it?"

His voice wasn't dismissive; I had to take that as a good sign. "That's all there is in that part of Florida, yeah. Horse shows and trails and rodeo. I had to come here if I wanted to work in racing. And that's why I'm here. Lucille told me to just come to Ocala and ask for work. She said everyone would be hiring now. Because of yearlings." I realized I was repeating myself. "But I'll do anything, really. I can work my way up to riding. I'm very good with horses, I can manage a barn, handle basic veterinary stuff, wrap legs..."

He nodded, his eyes still scrutinizing me. He seemed on the verge of speaking when the woman started shouting again. Our heads turned in unison, but I couldn't see her from where I was standing. She was hidden by the restaurant wall. Her voice had no trouble carrying.

"Who is *that*? You're keeping me waiting while you talk to some *girl*?"

I bit my lip, but Alexander just rolled his eyes. "For God's sake, would you go inside and calm yourself? I'm talking business with this young woman and you're being terribly rude."

"Business? I'll bet it's *business*. You know what, Alexander? I don't want to eat lunch with you. I don't want to work things out. I'm off."

Now he looked interested. "You're off?"

"I'm leaving. That's what you wanted, isn't it? You wanted me *gone*, didn't you?" Her voice was getting hysterical. I saw another couple heading for the restaurant change their path so they could take a wide trajectory around her. I wondered what she looked like. I started to edge forward. If I was just a little closer to Alexander...

He walked to the end of the truck and slapped his hand against the tailgate. "Yes, damn you, I wanted you gone! Why do you always make things so hard?"

Her reply was unintelligible, but there was definitely a shriek and a curse mixed in. I heard heels slapping on pavement, and then Alexander leaned back against the truck, looking as if he'd just run a very hard race.

I bit my lip and then, figuring I had nothing to lose, I asked, "Who was that?"

He shook his head. "She'd call herself my *assistant* trainer, I suppose." He glanced my way, then pushed off from the truck. "Sorry you had to see that."

"It's fine," I said, and then I pushed it one step further. "Looks like you have a job opening."

Alexander burst into laughter. "I knew I liked you," he chortled. "There's something about you that...well, anyway. Cotswold Farm. Five-thirty a.m. Come up to the training barn and we'll put you on a horse, see what you can handle. Does that sound okay?"

I bit back a scream of my own. "That sounds good," I managed to choke out. "Thank you. You won't regret this."

"No," he said thoughtfully. "I don't think I will. I'm looking forward to it." A thought struck him. "Wait a minute—I don't even know your name."

"Alex," I replied with a weak smile. "Alex O'Connor."

"Is that so?" Alexander fixed me with beaming blue eyes. "Alex. I'll see you tomorrow."

Chapter Eight

I SPENT THE NIGHT at the roadside Econo Lodge in a state of nervous rapture. I had a job interview the next morning! With Alexander Whitehall! This couldn't be happening! What if I messed up? I might as well die!

"What could you mess up?" my mother asked. Her no-nonsense demeanor, usually so distressing—couldn't she just *feel* something instead of being *logical*?—was suddenly comforting.

I'd called her after my lonely dinner, a hasty and greasy take-out bag from McDonald's which left me feeling even more anxious than the prospect of driving out to Alexander Whitehall's farm in the morning. "I don't know," I sighed. "I'm just scared I'll mess up. Not in any specific way, just the grand, universal usage of *messing up.*"

"Listen. You know what you know. You were straight with him. You already told him you haven't worked with racehorses before, so it's not like you have to display any knowledge besides how to handle horses in general. You'll be fine."

"It just feels too good to be true," I admitted. "This guy is like...an icon."

"It does feel too good to be true," she agreed. "But it *is* true, so there you have it."

This was the sort of unassailable logic which made my mother fantastic in crisis situations but tiresome in everyday use. She was right after all: there was no denying the things happening were, in fact, happening.

"That's a good point," I told her, somehow managing to keep my tone sarcasm-free.

"So, get some sleep and go for it. How early do you have to be there?"

"Five-thirty," I sighed.

"In the *morning?*"

"Unfortunately, yes."

Setting an alarm for four o'clock in the morning felt absolutely awful, but it turned out to be a non-issue, because I woke up at three forty-five in a cold sweat, having dreamed I'd been put on a vicious, monstrous version of the Black Stallion and been informed my entire interview was to get the horse around a racetrack absolutely packed with other horses, and things were Not Going Well when I jerked out of sleep, approximately two seconds before my nightmare-self hit the nightmare-ground, where I supposed I would have been trampled to death.

There would have been no going back to sleep after that kind of wake-up call even if I didn't need to be up in fifteen minutes, so I was comparatively cheerful when I flicked off the alarm function and took myself into the damp little motel bathroom, where I took a twenty-minute shower and drew in deep breaths of foggy air, trying to stave off a panic attack.

Dressed in jeans and paddock boots, with a polo shirt I hoped made me look professional, I walked past the sleeping semi-trailers, wet pony-tail dripping down my back, and bought myself a coffee and hash browns for breakfast. The grease and caffeine sat curdling in the pit of my stomach as I climbed into my car, twin bad decisions accompanying me as I drove off to face the beginning of the rest of my life.

Ocala was a dark place at night. As I drove west from the interstate, the stars grew more fiery, and the velvet-blue sky turned inky-black. There were no street-lights out here, the moon was nowhere to be found, and where oak trees overlapped the road, their shadows felt like something absolute, the darkness bottomless and yawning. The headlights of my poor little Civic were almost too powerless to pierce the country night. The winding roads and rolling hills added to the alien feeling. With the landscape so different from the flat plains and endless straight roads back in my corner of the peninsula, I really felt like I'd left Florida behind.

I'd certainly left the version of Florida I had known my entire life.

Occasionally the car's headlights picked out an ornate wooden sign and I'd give a little gasp, realizing I was passing a farm I'd read about in a magazine or heard of because some great horse from history had been bred there. I was in the land of champions now. I longed for the sun to hurry up and rise so I could see the farms properly, but Florida has a lazy, late sunrise even in the longest days of summer. Now, as the calendar was winding down through autumn, I was still an hour away from even a hint of morning.

Occasionally another car went by, or was waiting at a stop sign for me to pass; sometimes I could see lights in a distant stable, squares of yellow marking stall windows where horses were eating their breakfasts, but for the most part, I was totally alone in the dark world.

For a child of subdivisions, this was mostly scary, but a little bit wonderful. Let's say a seventy/thirty split.

Cotswold Farm had a big wooden sign at its driveway, marking it as one of the fancier farms in the neighborhood even if I couldn't see what was hiding behind the border hedges and thick trees clustered around the front gate. The driveway took me through a gate that was wide open, although I could see a call-box for less hospitable times of day. Far ahead of me there was a set of tail-lights showing the way, and as I wound through what seemed like a huge complex of pastures, the lights of barns showing up on hillsides to either side, I watched that car ahead of me winking in and out of sight like it was a mobile lighthouse. At least there was someone else out here, and I wasn't the only one wandering this big, dark, pre-dawn wilderness.

When I finally rounded a corner and came upon the lane to the training barn, where Alexander had said to report at five-thirty, I felt a rush of relief. There was so much light! A long stable stretched out ahead of me, two open-sided shed-rows, flanking a square little central aisle where a huddle of people were standing around, drinking coffee and chatting. At least half the stalls that I could see were housing horses, their noses buried in feed bins clipped to their metal stall grills.

I'd only seen barns like this in magazines. It was different from the center-aisle stables, pole barns, and glorified sheds I was used to. This was efficient, streamlined, and beautiful.

This is what I want, I thought hungrily. *This is a racing stable.*

This barn told me I'd made it. Everything happening now was part of the dream. I wasn't just chasing my dream anymore. I had caught it; or I had at least grasped one of its elusive, rainbow feathers.

I had a sudden urge to call Professor Blake and tell her, but there was no chance she was awake yet.

I parked my car a little distance from the small collection of pick-ups and aging SUVs pulled up in front of the barn, and immediately felt a wave of shyness too strong to ignore. The barn, sprawled in front of me, suddenly felt unattainable, as if I'd come as close as I was going to get. They'd find me out the moment I walked in, and send me packing back to the show-ring where girls like me belonged.

Look at this place! an inner voice cackled. *You, working here? You don't belong here!*

A moment ago I'd been flying high; now I was ready to dive into a ditch. My stomach fluttered, my hands shook, my heart pounded. If I tried to stand up, I knew my knees wouldn't carry me.

I'd gotten all this way; now I couldn't get out of the car.

Panic attack, panic attack, you're having a panic attack. Probably too much grease and caffeine, not enough protein or water. I took a few deep breaths. *In, out.*

You were invited here. Alexander told you to come.

Slowly, I felt myself regaining control of my breathing, felt my stomach ease its churning. I still wasn't ready to get out of the car, though. I had a handy inner voice, logical and cool, pointing out the clear advantages to simply running away.

You don't have to do this. There are easier ways. You don't even know what they're like. They're probably awful people. Everyone says to stay out of racing. Why are you even here? This place is too big for you. Too grand, too rich, too special. You're not any of those things.

Ah! My inner voice was making a great point. Maybe this *was* too big a place to start. So, okay. New plan. I could just sit here for a little while, wait for the crowd in the aisle to disperse, and then drive away and never speak to anyone! I could go back to the motel, regroup, and then possibly look for work at another, smaller barn. One that wasn't run by a world-class trainer. One with slightly lower expectations. Wouldn't that be nice? So much easier.

Oh, that sounded tempting.

I was still deliberating when there was a sharp rap on the driver's side window. I jumped, I shrieked.

Someone nearby laughed, a short, sharp bark. I looked through the window and saw a grinning face looking in at me, nearly at my level. There was a very short man outside my car, and now I was caught. No driving out without being seen, now.

I unbuckled my seat-belt and slowly opened the car door.

"Hello there!" the short man greeted me. "Are you new talent? We're 'bout to get started riding."

He had a lot of enthusiasm for five-thirty in the morning, I thought darkly. And a Southern twang which made his words ring just a little too loudly for anything before, let's say, noon. Still, he had a very friendly smile plastered on his face. At least there was that.

"I'm here to see Mr. Whitehall," I managed to choke out. My throat was suddenly very dry. "He said to meet him here at five-thirty."

"Well, that's right now! Come on out and I'll introduce you."

I thought about brushing him off, maybe saying I knew Alexander already, but the little man was bouncing around with so much energy, I just let him own the moment. Anyway, I was back to shaking and I thought I might not be able to get any more words out. So I climbed out of the car and followed his bow-legged progression into the training barn, past the fascinated eyes of the riders standing in the aisle, and through a blue metal door into a rather barren barn office.

Seated behind an old laminate desk, his hands folded behind a little wall of fat paperback books and a big open journal, was Alexander. He looked up at me and a smile stretched across his face which lit my entire body on fire. I had to restrain myself from leaning over the desk and placing a good-morning kiss on those upturned lips.

My God, I thought. *What was in those hashbrowns, LSD?* I managed to settle on a returned smile.

"Alex O'Connor," he pronounced warmly, as if he had been practicing my name for this very occasion. "So good of you to come."

"Alex!" my escort exclaimed. "Well that's funny. Is it short for somethin'?"

"Alexis," I managed to say, working the breathy syllables around my pesky, pounding heart, which had somehow gotten into my throat.

"Alexis is a beautiful name," Alexander remarked. "I'm surprised you don't keep it."

"I—um—it felt—" I didn't have an answer. My stock reply was that it was too romantic for a tough girl like me, but that wasn't the impression I wanted to give this man.

"I apologize, I didn't mean to pick on you," he said quickly. "What a way to start, right? Walt, for God's sake, make me stop. Say anything."

Walt bounced on his toes. "We've got horses to ride. You want Alex here on anyone in the first set? Alex? What kind of ridin' have you done?"

I could still leave. I could go right back to my car and drive back to my parents' house and we could start over again. I didn't have to get on a racehorse and follow this tiny, energetic, kind man into the darkness and try to stay alive while my heart surged into a wild, out-of-control gallop every time Alexander Whitehall spoke to me, or looked at me, or existed in the same space as me.

I realized Walt was looking at me, head cocked. He'd asked me a question. His wizened face looked a little concerned by my silence. I desperately tried to recall what he'd asked.

"I'm sorry?" I tried to pull myself together. "Sorry, I missed that."

"I said what's your experience like? Track, yearlings, what have you done?"

"Oh." I swallowed. *You know what you know.* "Ex-racehorses. Retraining."

"Hmm." Walt regarded me. In the background, I saw Alexander tilt his head, waiting for Walt's pronouncement. "We got some easy ones," he said finally. "I'll put you on them. We got three for ya this morning. Then we can decide."

Alexander nodded. "Three rides. That's a good assessment."

"I'll get her kitted out," Walt said. "Meet me in the tack room in five." He bounced out of the office.

Alexander came around the side of his desk and perched on the edge, hands crossed over one leg. He was wearing neat brown trousers and a chambray shirt; he had scarred Blundstone boots on his feet. I glanced back up at his face and absorbed the full force of him, taking in those dark blue eyes with deep laugh lines etched on either side of them, the eyes of a man who stared into the rising sun, unblinking, as his gaze followed his horses.

"They don't know what happened yesterday," he said quietly. "She hasn't been around in a while. She said she was going home to visit her parents."

"The assistant, you mean?"

"That's right. So don't mention her to anyone, please."

"Of course not," I said quickly.

Alexander smiled, a conspiratorial look in his eyes. "I have a good feeling about you," he said. "Are you ready to start?"

"Yes," I replied, finally in control of my voice again, finally certain this was real, this was happening, this was right. "I'm ready."

❧❧❧❧ ❧❧❧❧

Walt was waiting for me in the tack room next to the office, a brightly-lit space filled with saddles and bridles and a wall of industrial washing machines. He fitted me with a safety vest. It was old, the green cover sweat-stained and the zipper a little tricky, but he said everyone had to wear them. "You *can* buy your own," he allowed, "but they're a couple hundred bucks. Might as well let Cotswold Farm foot the bill. That way if it gets trampled on, you don't have to go buy another one. You got a helmet of your own?"

Trampled on? I seriously hoped not. "I have my own helmet," I offered. "And—chaps? Should I wear half-chaps?" I was wearing the snug jeans I liked to ride in, but my gear was still in the car.

"Yeah, go and get what you need. Leggin's are a good idea." Walt drank some more coffee and bounced on his toes as I raced out of the tack room. Some riders were standing outside the door—*my coworkers*—with curious expressions on their faces. My brain took a quick snapshot as I ran past them: two men and a woman, all wearing deeply-lined faces and tired expressions.

Racetrackers eat nice girls like you for breakfast, Lucille had said, right before she hung up on me. I wondered if they were really that bad.

Walt seemed fine, anyway. High-energy, but fine.

I zipped on my half-chaps and plunked my helmet onto my head before I went back into the barn, leaving the chin-strap dangling as if I was still a hunter rider between classes. The trio of riders had disappeared. Walt was alone in the aisle, writing on a big white-board hung on the wall between the office and tack room doors.

I peered over his shoulder. There was a grid of boxes running across the board, with the numbers one through ten written across the top. He'd added *Alex* to the list down the side, and he'd just finished writing in the first three boxes next to my name. They were clearly horse names.

1: Chessiecat

2: Miss Vampire

3: Nordic Empress

I looked at Walt. "These are the horses I'm riding?"

He grinned, showing off an erratic collection of teeth. "You got it. I do horse assignments every morning. These are the sets—" he pointed to the numbers running across the top of the grid— "So you just look and see who you're riding in the first set, take your tack down to that stall, and saddle the horse. After you're done with your ride, you untack the horse and set the tack at the next stall. Help the groom hose the horse, get your next horse tacked, shout for a leg-up. It goes like clockwork. You'll learn it so quickly, it'll be second nature in no time."

Most of the words he'd said to me were familiar, but the procedure was totally alien to me. I gave Walt a sheepish smile. "Do racehorses come with an instruction manual?"

"Don't worry," he chuckled. "I'll set you with Ricky. He's the nicest groom in the barn, trust me. Ricky'll help you learn it all." He turned around and bellowed: *"Ricky!"*

There was a bang as a nearby horse objected to his shout and kicked a wall. "Knock it *off,*" a cross voice told the horse.

A small, beachball-shaped man appeared in the aisle. He had shaggy black hair, a thick mustache, and a tie-dye shirt over baggy cargo shorts. Definitely not a rider, then. "Whatchu want, Walt?" he asked, his accent somewhere between Latin and Southern.

Walt clapped me on the shoulder with so much power, I had to bend my knees to absorb the pressure. "We got a new girl. She can do Wallace's fillies that are back from the track; they know what they're doin'. She just needs to learn the ropes. Can you help her with them? And when she's done with them, you can keep her as an apprentice for the rest of the morning. She knows horses, just not racehorses. Wants to learn how we do things." He glanced at me for confirmation, and I nodded. "If you want to work through noon, like the riders do, you'll have to do it on the ground."

"That's fine," I said quickly.

Ricky shrugged. "Sure, why not." He waved a hand at me. "Lessgo, new girl."

This is it. "Well, thanks," I said, sliding out from under Walt's grip. "I guess I'd better—"

"Don't forget your tack!" Walt went into the tack room and emerged with an armful of equipment. "This is your saddle, pad, bridle and girth. They go from horse to horse. Adjust the bridle to fit each one. Every horse gets a new saddle towel and a new girth cover from the stack in the tack room, the dirty ones go in the laundry baskets. Absolutely no sharing! Prevents fungus." He deposited the tack into my possession. *"Now* you're ready!"

As I went past the barn office with my tack-laden arms, I glanced inside. Alexander was back behind his desk, writing away in that big journal. A training diary? He looked up at me and my steps momentarily arrested, my entire attention resting on whatever he would say. My lips parted in expectation. For what, I couldn't have said. But I knew it would be something big. Something game-changing. Something which acknowledged this crazy, inexplicable pull between us.

Alexander smiled benignly at me. "Have a good ride," he said.

Chapter Nine

WELL, I RODE A racehorse for the first time and I didn't die.

I'm not sure how, though.

Nothing about that first ride was like any "normal" ride I'd had up until that point. Eight years spent riding horses of all ages, shapes, sizes, mental situations, and physical conditions did not prepare me for the strange sensations and huge demands of balancing atop a racehorse, of galloping headlong down a dark pre-dawn track, of the strange and simple challenges posed by the minuscule exercise saddle.

I had imagined my first ride on a track for years, but it had always been a blissful thing, a lot of *chase the wind*-style poetry curling around my daydreams while I took that first step towards a life of speed and grace.

The *actual* first ride, though it took place on a sweet bay filly named Chessiecat, was a chaos of darkness, whipping manes, and thudding hooves through a space which seemed to funnel a horse towards speeds I'd never experienced. The unrelenting depth of the Ocala night made sound and touch impossibly important when we were in the wells of darkness between orange street-lights. My ears and my skin were assaulted with new, beautiful, terrifying sensations—sometimes all three at once.

The jingle-bell song of a buckle rattling against some metal ring with every stride.

Riding so close to a fellow rider that our stirrups clinked together.

The feel of muscles and bones pressing against my legs through the thin leather of the exercise saddle.

The unrelenting pull of the filly's mouth against my grip, the burn in my shoulder muscles growing more fiery with every ride.

The tremble in my thighs before we had even rounded the last turn.

Everything hurt, everything was frightening, everything was new.

But I didn't die, and that in itself was amazing. When I'd first been hoisted into the tiny saddle by a stone-faced Ricky, I'd thought the end was nigh. Sitting on Chessiecat, tying up my fat racing reins in a knot, feeling her shift beneath me in a saddle which was more bareback pad than anything, I couldn't feel much relationship at all between the skills I had spent my short life mastering, and what I'd need to stay in the saddle out on that track.

We rode in, I dutifully stripped my filly of her tack, I followed Ricky's orders, and we did it again. A second horse, a second terror. Again. A third horse, and the fear began to abate, although my muscles were screaming.

The sun slowly came up over Ocala as we worked through those first three sets, and by seven o'clock the morning had arrived and I was done riding for the day.

I had galloped three racehorses, on a training track, and I was a new person.

Okay, they weren't tough horses. They were three-year-old fillies, nearly four if you counted their upcoming official birthday of January first, just a few months away, and they'd had the latter half of the summer off after racing the previous spring. Alexander liked to give horses a few months off, especially in summer, to just be horses. These three were all just starting to gallop again. They were sluggish, lazy, more than ready to pull up when I stood in the stirrups. They knew their jobs and were happy to teach it to me, especially if they could throw in a few little tips of their own on how quickly to head back to the barn.

"You came at just the right time," Walt told me. "In two weeks they'll be too strong for a newbie. Of course, we'll be doing the yearlings by then. Not too many this year, it's a slow one for us. You should have been here three years ago. This place was booming! Seven or eight riders in every set, every day! We had horses coming out of our eyeballs."

We were riding the third set back to the barn, the horses walking contentedly along a mulch path leading between the track and the training barn. Straight, lined with palm trees, it also led almost directly into the sunrise and I had my eyes cast down to my filly's neck, watching her black mane rise and fall with every step. She had been a nice ride. *Nordic Empress,* I thought. *Pretty name.*

Aloud I asked: "Why are there fewer horses now?"

Maybe there was an easy answer to why Alexander had fallen out of the public eye over the past few years.

Walt shrugged. "He was relyin' hard on a partner and they've had...difficulties. He doesn't do all this himself, y'know. Used to be she'd send us ten, twelve yearlings from the Keeneland September sale, plus everything we bred here, plus all the horses of racing age coming in and out of the barn. There just used to be more."

Walt said *she,* and I wondered if it was the same woman from yesterday, or if Alexander just had a tendency to fight with women he was doing business with. I glanced his way, ready to ask more questions, but he was already looking ahead to the barn, where the grooms were coming out to meet us. Conversation over, work to be done.

Ricky came out of the training barn, hands on hips. "Lessgo, lessgo, off that horse so I can give her a bath, please!"

Walt tossed me a toothy grin. "Ricky'll get you right. He's a taskmaster, that one." Then he reined his own horse away, leaving me to ride Nordic Empress into her stall, Ricky hot on my heels. I watched him go, wondering what else Walt knew about Alexander's business, and how tough it would be to get it out of him.

I wanted to know everything. I *needed* to know everything.

I held my filly for Ricky as he hosed her down and sluiced the excess water from her coat with a sweatscraper, then scooped up my tack and went back to the tack room while he handed her off to a hot-walker. Walt had said everything got cleaned or put in the wash daily, and I figured that went for leather, too, so I tossed the saddle pad and towel into the big laundry basket and got busy with a bar of glycerine soap and a sponge. Alexander came in as I was attacking the bridle with vigor.

"So, done riding for the day?"

"I guess so." It was weird to be finished with work before seven-thirty. This was when I had usually fed breakfast at Diana's. *Don't think about Diana.* "I liked the fillies, and the rides went pretty well. It's not as different from riding in a jumping saddle as I expected. I mean, it's different but...there's instinct there, too. Am I making sense?"

Alexander grinned knowingly, his eyes sparkling with amusement. I refused to acknowledge the little flip-flop my heart gave, not that my heart cared if I gave it any credit or not. "Perfect sense," he assured me, "for people like you and me."

He reached his hand out—I thought for a wild moment he was going to touch my cheek—my heart stopped flipping over and start racing wildly—what should I *do?*—and then his fingers closed around the bridle's cheek-piece.

"Bit of loose stitching there," he observed, rubbing his thumb on an errant thread. "I'd better get that down to the saddler's shop in the next few days. You can't be too careful with racing tack. When you're done with it, set it in my truck cab, will you? It's the big green one, with the farm name on the side."

I nodded. "No problem," I managed to say.

His hand retreated back to its rightful place at his side, and I was left with the upsetting realization that I was projecting all kinds of romantic tomfoolery on my boss. This was *not* the way to get started in the horse racing business.

Well, someone like Lucille might shake her head and say it was the *only* way for a girl to get ahead in racing, but I wasn't that cynical...not yet.

I pushed my lips together, trying to tamp down the nervous flutter of the butterflies in my stomach, and launched a new assault on the bridle, pulling the straps loose from their buckles to get at the neglected leather underneath. I decided I'd keep scrubbing it until Alexander went away, and then I'd take a few deep breaths and try to get my pulse back to normal.

It felt like a good plan, except that Alexander wasn't in on it, so he went on standing a few feet away from me, watching me work, and I began to suspect he wasn't going to go anywhere until I was done.

We were at a stalemate.

Why? Was he waiting for me to say something? Was this some sort of polite Britishism he'd learned as a child, being brought up all lord-of-the-manor and a-gentleman-always-stands and that sort of thing? If so, *crap*, that was all, because I couldn't think of a thing to say. Nothing conversational, anyway. There was plenty I wanted to know about him, so all of my questions were nice, normal pleasantries like, *Why are there fewer yearlings now?* and, *Don't you want to be a leading trainer again?* And maybe I'd throw in, *What's the deal with the partner, is it the assistant who left yesterday or some other woman you can't get along with?*

I was pretty sure, even with my own limited social skills, these were not great topics to further our limited acquaintanceship or help any sort of relationship bloom between us.

"That bridle is looking pretty clean," he said.

I made the mistake of glancing at him and his grin made my fingers fumble on the bridle, I dropped my wet sponge on the floor, and it bounced across the room.

Alexander! I thought, chasing it. *Stop looking like that!*

His smile was mischievous, his eyes were crinkled up in that way I'd loved before I'd even met him. It was as if the picture of Beginner's Goodbye had come to life.

Well, minus the horse.

He picked up the sponge right before I snagged it, and our foreheads nearly thumped as we both straightened at the same time. Our eyes met, and it was like a magnet held our gazes locked tightly together. He had a tiny brown dot in his left iris. My breath came ragged; there was a humming in my ears. His lips were parted slightly, but as seconds ticked back and neither of us moved, I realized each of us must be waiting to see what the other person would do.

It had to be him. I didn't have the faintest idea how to make the first move. I touched my tongue to my dry lips. "Alexander," I started to whisper, but no sound came out.

Hooves on concrete broke the spell. Alexander whipped around, and my gaze flicked past him to the open door. In the aisle, a horse was trotting through, one of the male riders urging him on. He glanced into the tack room and I saw him make an *oops* face with his mouth and eyes.

Alexander's jaw tensed and he went to the doorway. "Juan!" he shouted, "I have *asked* you not to jog through the middle!"

"Everyone's ahead of me!" Juan hollered back, his voice already coming from a distance. "Sorry boss, I need to catch up!"

Alexander sighed with exasperation. "I ask them not to ride through the center. I don't like their hooves hammering on the concrete if it's not necessary. It's such a minor thing...I don't see why they can't listen."

"I don't know," I echoed. "I won't do it." Was that it? The moment was over?

I watched his gaze flick around the room, darting from my face to little objects around the tack room: the stacks of thick foam pads, the bridles hanging on the walls, the tiny saddles on their racks. After being so close, the space between us was frustrating. I wanted to chase down Juan and yell at him myself.

"So, listen, Alex...you're staying on, right?"

His words surprised me. "Yes. If you'll have me."

"Please stay," he said, finally letting his gaze settle on my face. "You'll be a good rider, once you've got your legs. You said yesterday that you wanted to learn it all, and we can arrange that. Since you're only riding part-time, you can work with the grooms, learn the rest of the trade, does that sound all right?"

"That sounds perfect. I really do want to learn all of it."

"More people should be like you. You can do better than just getting on horses and learning to get them around the track. There's far more to racing than that." He picked up the bridle I'd been cleaning and ran his thumb over the loose stitching again. "You need an understanding of the whole horse. Not everyone realizes that."

I wondered if he was talking about the vanished assistant. "Of course. I ran the barn at my last farm. I definitely want to be more than a person who just gets on horses."

His smile flashed at me again. "We'll get you where you want. I see good things for you, Alex."

I was so focused on his smile, I barely heard his next words. Something about housing. "What's that, now?"

"Housing," he repeated, tilting his head. "You'll need a place to stay, won't you?"

The training barn had open rafters, so there was no barn apartment hiding above the stalls. I wished I'd seen the rest of the farm. There must be dorms squirreled away somewhere. "I will, yeah. Are you offering?"

"Well, there's the mobile homes. They're not grand. But they're mouse-free and non-smoking. I think we can make you comfortable here. The riders are paid per horse and have the option for renting a room, but you'll be working all day, so I can give you housing plus salary in exchange for a full-time schedule, six days a week."

"That's awesome. I hadn't even expected housing."

He grinned at me. "Were you planning on living in a motel?"

"No, of course not." I'd been planning on finding the cheapest possible accommodation in Ocala, but I didn't even know how to start looking, so this was incredible news.

"Of course, you'll probably have a roommate. I don't think more than one. I'm not sure who is actually living here right now. Emily handles housing. The farm secretary."

I bit the inside of my cheek. I'd never had a roommate. I'd barely been around other people for the past few years. Only child, solitary horse trainer...I was only used to my own company. What was it like, living with someone else? Did I even want to know?

The amusement in Alexander's eyes told me my conflicting emotions were obvious. "Whatever you're thinking, I promise you it's not that bad. I don't run a labor camp here. It's just a few mobile homes for employees. They're fine. Really."

"Sorry, I'm sure they are." I busied my hands again, putting away the saddle soap and sponge. "Honestly, thank you. For the job and...everything. Taking a chance on me—" I stopped myself before I disqualified myself even more. "I promise to be a good investment," I finished.

"Just settle in and ask lots of questions," Alexander advised me. "Head up to the office when the grooms break for lunch. It's the little building by the house."

He left the tack room at last, leaving me alone with my *very* clean bridle. I looked at it for a moment, tempted to wrap the throat-latch around the cheek-pieces in a figure-eight, the way I would have done with a hunter bridle. It was so similar to the bridles I'd worked with all my life, just a plain bridle of brown leather with small steel buckles, but the leather was doubled, the stitching was more robust, and there was no noseband—just a little loop of nylon attached to each bit ring, where a curb chain would hang on a double bridle.

It was built for tougher labor than a hunter bridle.

I left the bridle out, so I would remember to put it into his truck, and put away the cleaning supplies.

"Time to go learn how a training barn works," I said to myself, trying to ignore the new ache just making itself known around my shoulders. Racetrack Alex would have to learn to cope with tougher labor than Horse Show Alex ever had. Considering my upbringing, that was really saying something.

I went off down the shed-row, looking for Ricky, and wondering which one of the people I'd met this morning was my future roommate.

Chapter Ten

Emily, the farm secretary, held up a single brass key after I'd gone through all of my new hire paperwork. A plastic, diamond-shaped keychain dangled from it, like something from an old roadside motel. There was a big number 3 on the keychain.

"Pretty easy to remember," Emily announced. She had a soft Southern accent and a kind smile. "House number three, room three. Same key for both doors. Sorry, housekeeping's not included."

I grinned back at her. Emily had made me feel comfortable up here in the barn office, offering me coffee while I was bent over the release forms and tax paperwork. I guessed without Professor Blake to talk to, I'd been missing the presence of a supportive female to get me through all of this sudden change. "I can handle the housekeeping, but...any chance of room service? I've never been much of a cook."

"Nothin' doin' sweetie, but hey, there's a microwave and a freezer. You'll be fine. My teenage son lives on microwaved pot pies and I can't see any ill effects yet."

I turned the key over in my hand, lingering in her presence. "Are, um, are there other people in the house?" I ventured. Maybe Alexander had been wrong about that.

"Just one," Emily said, going back to her files. "Jacinta Bell. She's a rider, too. You probably met her this morning."

She's a rider, too. I savored those words. The last one, specially. *Too.*

I'm a rider.

A rider.

The rest of what she'd said came into focus. Jacinta had been the lone female in the barn this morning. She hadn't said much to me.

"Jacinta? Yeah, I met her." Sort of.

"Good. I'm sure you two will get along fine."

I wasn't so sure about that, based on our lack of interaction this morning. Then again, I didn't know anything about her. She was a sturdy-looking woman who had seemed pretty wrapped up in her horses during the sets I'd joined, but she'd been loud and talkative during our mid-morning break, which began when a woman everyone called the Taco Lady arrived in a battered minivan and started doling out homemade tacos and tortas. Then she'd gone back into riding mode, and I'd gone back to work with Ricky and the other grooms.

"No chance of my own place, right?" I tilted my head and smiled.

Emily gave me a doubtful look. "It's pretty dark back there. And quiet. I think you'd be better off with some company."

"Oh, that's all right," I began, thinking that if there *was* a way to score my own trailer, I'd better jump on it. "I really don't mind being alone. I'm used to it."

Emily gave me a level look, the kind of stare only a practiced mother could summon, and I felt like all my secrets had been bared. Emily could clearly tell, just by looking at me, that I'd never lived alone, never even left my childhood bedroom before. "Trust me on this one, kid," she said flatly, and I had no choice but to agree.

"Got it," I replied weakly.

"Good." Emily nodded briskly, happy the chain of command had been re-established with her on top. "So, the housing court is behind the back pastures. Just drive all the way back and follow the driveway where it jogs a little to go through the back fence-line. They're right there. The trailers are numbered. Your room was cleaned last on...hmm...in June, actually. So it might be a little dusty."

"Well, the Econo Lodge at 75 is pretty dusty, too, and I'm sure I'm not the first guest in that room since June."

Emily allowed me a sideways grin. "One thing I love about riders," she chuckled. "You're sure not hard to please."

Great.

I took a last look around the office before I walked out. I liked the space very much. It was a comfortable little rectangle filled with Thoroughbred imagery, with a sitting area just inside the door, bookcases against the wall filled with sales catalogs, and cardboard organizers stuffed with magazines. My eyes hungrily took in the titles on their covers: *The Blood-Horse, Florida Horse, The Thoroughbred Times*—there must have been years of them stacked up in those shelves.

Emily noticed my interest. "You can come up and read those anytime you want," she told me. "If there are clients in here, just nod hello, take a few, and bring them back later. If there's no one around, well, just make yourself comfy. There's always coffee."

I wanted to hug her. *"Thank* you," I told her, giving the view one last admiring glance. "I'll do that soon."

I'd come back, and dig into those magazines, and catch up on everything I didn't know about racing.

Maybe I'd even figure out what was going on with Alexander and his nameless partner.

I sat in the car and looked at the housing court, thinking: *I don't know what I expected.*

Dimly, I suppose I'd pictured a little collection of cabins, like we were all living on a dude ranch. That would have been cute. Sure, Alexander and Emily had clearly said *mobile homes* and *trailers,* but these things also came in log-cabin designs, and everything else about Cotswold Farm was so perfect, I could easily see Alexander extending the farm's good looks back to the help's living quarters.

One thing Emily hadn't been wrong about? This place would be very dark at night. The rear of the farm was divided into two or three big pastures, with enormous granddaddy oaks forming a shadowy border with whatever farm lay beyond, but I had to drive through a gateway in the back fence to enter the housing court. By now, the lights of the barns were very far away.

Arranged around a shady circle of white sand, and overhung with old oak trees, the three single-wide mobile homes sat sinking onto old axles. Drooping wooden stairs led from the sand up to their rusting screen doors. Green streaks of mildew and mold marred their aging white finish, and Spanish moss fallen from the oak branches overhead dangled from their flat eaves. The trailers didn't quite look like they were ready to rust away to nothing, and the entire scene was fairly tidy, despite their need for a good pressure-washing. But the housing court was still older and more tired-looking than what I'd hoped for.

A cat made of black-and-white fluff sat washing itself on the mossy hitch of the first trailer; it paused mid-lick to consider me and my car, then went back to grooming. Apparently I was not interesting enough to interrupt its bath.

Each mobile home had an old brass number screwed into its front door. Both numbers One and Two appeared empty. Number Three had three window air conditioners humming away. That must be the spot.

I parked as decorously as I could in front of the trailer, pretending there were stripes painted on the ground to avoid looking like a chaotic hillbilly who just left my car any which way, and went slowly up the stairs. My bags were still back at the Econo Lodge, which I had booked for a few more nights, so this was really just a reconnaissance mission. If things were really bad, I told myself, I didn't have to stay. I had options.

I wasn't sure what they were, but I had to have them.

I peeled back the screen door and fit the key into the front door, one of those cheap metal jobs with the wavy white surface that seemed to come standard with old mobile homes, and knocked gently as I pushed it open.

"Hello?" I called, my voice echoing into the cool air within. "Anyone home?"

Silence. Well, silence and the reassuring roar of the air conditioners. Jacinta must really like it cold. The atmosphere inside was absolutely arctic. I kind of liked it.

I was standing on a patch of linoleum just inside the door, but I was already in the small living room. I looked around, sizing the place up. The trailer's interior didn't seem *too* bleak, especially if you liked brown. Everything in the room was a slight variation on a shade of milk chocolate: brown carpet, brown couch, brown faux-wood paneling on the walls. To my right was a short hall, with three doors, all closed. To my far left was a little bar, with the kitchen lurking behind in darkness. It also seemed to be predominately brown, although a lighter shade. Was there such a thing as a more cheerful shade of brown? If so, I thought the kitchen might be it. A chipper, welcoming brown space to cook food.

I took a suspicious sniff. Old places in Florida usually smelled of mold, mildew, rot—normal Florida scents, but not what you want in your home. Instead, the fiercely cold air smelled like a lot like my motel room: cheap, fruity cleaning products and the metallic tang of filtered air.

"Not bad," I decided, relieved.

I ventured into the little hallway and saw more numbers tacked onto the doors: a brass two and a porcelain three. The bathroom didn't get a number, apparently. I put the key into door number three, at the end of the hall.

"Big money, big money," I prayed, pushing it open to see where I'd be living for the foreseeable future.

Well, it was clean. Tiny, and brown, but clean. The wide front window looked out on the bare circle of sand in front of the houses; a side window was plugged with a growling air conditioner. The bed was a single, and sagged in the middle. It was pushed against the wall beneath the window; an old dresser leaned on the wall next to the door. A set of sheets had been left folded on top of the striped mattress for goodness knew how long; there was dust on top of the pillowcase, just as Emily had warned.

I was considering the state of the dresser—were those mouse droppings on top? So much for Alexander's mouse-free guarantee—when I heard the humming of an engine outside, and then a car door slamming. The front door opened and closed. I stood very still, like a deer listening to the crashing footsteps of a nearby panther. Maybe if I didn't move, it would go away.

"Hello?" A woman called. "That you, new girl?"

I came into the hallway and found Jacinta waiting. She'd worn a stoic expression in the saddle, but now she was smiling. "So, you're moving in with me?"

"Yeah," I said, feeling about as awkward as I'd ever felt in my life, which was pretty serious. "I hope that's okay."

"Aw, it's no problem. Remind me your name? It was so busy this morning, I didn't catch it."

"I'm Alex."

"Another Alex! Heh." Her accent was…Southern? Or just country? There was a definite twang there. "Emily called my cell and said to expect you. I'm glad you're here, actually. I could use a roomie. It's been quiet since everyone in House Two left."

"Why did they leave?"

"Oh, old Pablo bought a house out in Dunnellon. It's a long-ass drive but they make it every morning." She stood upright and saw my confused expression. "Sorry, forgot you didn't know everyone yet. Pablo's in the yearling barn, and three of his sons are in the training barn. They're all grooms, except Juan. He just started riding, like you, but you learn fast by getting right into the saddle. No better way to do it. But you rode horses before, right? You know how to sit."

"I'm new to racehorses, but not Thoroughbreds."

"That so?" Jacinta looked interested. "Oh, I know. You're one of those horse show girls. Velvet-hat girls."

"I mean, that's all I've done but...I've been riding Thoroughbreds off the track for a long time."

"It's no problem," she assured me. "We fix up horse show girls *all* the time. Now, you ready for a margarita with your new roomie or what? And then I need me a nap."

⚬⚬⚬

Jacinta went to bed early, despite her post-margarita nap which lasted until three o'clock. By the time I came back from town with my things from the motel and some basic groceries, the darkness outside was absolute and the trailer was quiet. I glanced at her bedroom door, next to the kitchen, but there was no light peeking around it.

Fearful of waking her, I moved quietly through the kitchen, putting away my peanut butter and granola bars and bread. Shopping had been a weird experience. I'd never had to shop for myself; my mother had kept the kitchen stocked. I'd been helping myself to whatever she put into the cabinets for my entire life. Outside of the occasional stop at Wendy's or Subway when I was running short on time between school and barn, I'd never really had to feed myself. The grocery store run had been a cross between terrifying and exhilarating. What did I need? What could I afford? What could I even cook for myself?

I put four frozen pizzas into the freezer and nodded grimly at them, an affirmation to myself that I wasn't going to starve to death, anyway.

I might perish of loneliness, though. The night outside was utterly silent. I could hear Jacinta's air conditioner gurgling away, but the living room unit seemed happy with the trailer's ambient temperature and, as I walked to my end of the trailer, the buzz from behind her closed door faded away. My unit was quiet, too, waiting for the warmth outside to slowly nudge the bedroom's temperature back up.

With no air conditioning rumbling, no neighbors chatting, no traffic: the country silence seemed to press against my ears. I waited for a sound: a croaking tree-frog, a distant dog barking, a whip-poor-will clucking, *anything*, but minutes passed by and the quiet only grew more formidable.

Maybe Emily had been on to something when she said I was better off sharing a trailer. If sharing a house was this lonely, hard to imagine what having an entire place to myself might feel like.

I thought of Alexander's big house near the front of the property, a weird box of concrete and glass leftover from the eighties, and wondered if he grew lonesome on these dark nights, too. What was he doing right now?

"Probably sleeping," I muttered. "Get over it. You need some background noise and something else to think about."

I dug around in my suitcase until I found my clock radio, and plugged it in for a little company. Static immediately crackled from the speaker. I sighed and started rolling the knob around, searching for a signal. The radio stations I found were...well, let's call them eclectic. First a mariachi band, then country, then...more mariachi?

"Damn, Ocala," I muttered, impressed with the sheer quantity of mariachi music. I was pretty sure back home there wasn't even *one* mariachi station. Two on the FM dial was an interesting achievement.

I kept scanning: classic rock, no thanks; more country, no thanks; a Christian minister mid-exhort, no thanks; a quiet-spoken moderator talking about politics, no thanks; an earnest speaker orating in recognizably National Public Radio tones, no thanks; another classic rock station playing the same song as the first one—well, what were the chances of that?

I came to the end of the dial. *Crap,* I thought. No pop music? No top forty? No alt rock? My choices were ministers, mariachi, middle-aged rock classics, or mumbling about state politics?

I rolled back down to the NPR station, reasoning that at least it would sound like I had a friend, albeit a very boring friend, in the room with me.

An hour later I was fully unpacked and sprawled across my newly-made bed, listening to a nasal-voiced man named Ira Glass talking with a woman who had gone back to Poland to find the family who had saved her mother from a concentration camp. It was the most enthralling thing I'd ever heard on the radio. And it definitely felt like I had friends in the room.

I climbed under the bed's top sheet after the show ended and lay awake for a while. The air conditioner in the window occasionally cleared its throat and woke up for a few minutes, but otherwise the quiet was absolute. The room was utterly dark. I could have been in a mineshaft. I could have been in a box at the bottom of the sea.

Suddenly, I felt a surge of homesickness I never could have predicted, a pain in my stomach and chest which left me breathless. Uncertainty plunged through my heart, followed immediately by regret. Why had I left my *home?* My parents, my bedroom, the pattern of light on the wall where the street-light bled through the window blinds? I didn't even have Ira Glass to keep me company now, and my unhappiness was overwhelming.

Then I heard it, filtering through the vents of the still air conditioner, soft and distant but unmistakeable.

The high-pitched whinny of a horse.

I got up almost without thinking, slipped on my paddock boots, and went out into the night, closing the door very gently behind me so as not to wake Jacinta. Outside, the silence pressed down on me. I stood on the sagging steps, uncertain.

The horse whinnied again.

I followed the sound.

My eyes adjusted slowly—even in total darkness, the earth is somehow lit—and I walked up the sandy driveway, beneath the line of oak trees marking the farm border, until I reached the pasture fence. Out here under the open sky, the full strength of the Ocala night hit so hard I had to grab onto the fence, just to feel grounded to something. The stars overhead were so hot and close, I might as well have been out there beyond the atmosphere, spinning into space.

"So that's the Milky Way," I said aloud, but my voice vanished into the warm, muggy night.

There was another whinny, and the rustling of hooves in grass. A dark head, with two pricked ears, blocked out some of the stars. Then I felt a warm muzzle pressing into my arm, the prickles of whiskers, soft breath.

"Well, hello there," I told the horse, reaching up to rub its neck. The horse's mane was shaggy, but not too long; someone had trimmed it a few months ago. Who lived in this pasture, I wondered. Retired racehorses, maybe, or broodmares getting a year off from making babies? More horses were coming now, their hooves sliding through the long grass with a sound like a stage whisper.

I drew my hand back as the horse I was patting turned to look at the newcomers, and waited while the usual herd dynamics played out. A few other horses managed to sidle up along the fence and nibble at my shoulder or pluck at my fingers, each one chased off in turn and replaced by a new horse higher on the totem pole, until at last I was left rubbing the neck of a blaze-faced bay with a long, womanly forelock.

"You *must* be mares in this field," I told the horse, "because I just can't see a gelding or a stallion having a forelock like that. You're like a Horse Barbie."

The horse turned its face into my hand, rubbing against my fingers until I gave in and scratched the itchy spot between the eyes. White hair rained down on my pajama shirt like prickly snow.

For the first time in a little while, I felt like I was going to be okay.

Chapter Eleven

T HE NEXT MORNING CAME too quickly. My alarm clock played to an unappreciative audience for a solid ten minutes; then a knock on the door woke me up. "Hey, new girl," Jacinta called. "I think you're sleeping through your alarm."

I sat up and fumbled with the switch. A late moon had risen and there was a surreal bluish light flooding the bedroom, which somehow made the early hour even more disorienting. "Thank you," I croaked. I always sounded like a frog in the mornings. "Sorry."

"You're fine," she breezed. "I'll fix you some toast. Just this once."

I didn't want Jacinta to make me breakfast, as if I was still living at home, enjoying a pity party from my mother because of my early work start, but at the same time, I very much wanted toast. "Thank you," I called, struggling out of bed. "I'll be right out."

We drove up to the training barn in our separate vehicles. Jacinta said she liked to ride at another place after we finished with horses here. "Until we start the babies, we only take out five or six sets in the morning," she explained over peanut butter toast, eaten leaning over the kitchen counter. "In about two weeks, we'll have yearlings coming out of our ears and have more like eight or nine sets. We'll be riding until noon or later some days. You ever ride that many horses?"

I nodded. "I usually rode five or six a day, but for about forty-five minutes each." I didn't mention that the new riding position in the exercise saddle had me breathless and sore within about ten minutes of mounting.

Jacinta looked impressed. "Well, thank goodness for that," she said. "You need stamina for this job."

When we arrived, the other riders were already in the barn aisle. I knew their names now: Walt, Pablo's youngish son Juan, and a morose-looking young cowboy named Billy. They were drinking coffee from travel mugs and looking at the white-board. As I walked up, Walt leaned in and erased a horse's name from my fourth set.

"Good morning, newbie," he said. "Just the same three for you today."

Billy sighed heavily. "You'll be done before eight o'clock," he told me sadly, as if this somehow ruined his plans for the day.

"Oh, don't worry," Walt said. "We got plans for her." He winked at me.

I felt distinctly nervous. "Plans?"

Jacinta chuckled. "You gonna send her to the stallion barn to pull manes?"

"I oughta have *you* do it," Walt shot back. "They all look shaggy as hell and Maureen's been complaining about her arthritis in her fingers."

"Boy, I ain't pulled manes in ten years. You send me up there, I'm taking scissors and I'm giving all those men bowl-cuts."

"I bet you would, you crazy mess," Walt told her affectionately. "Nah, Alexander said this kid's staying in the training barn to learn the ropes. She's Ricky's assistant now, once we're through with her."

"Wait, what you say?" Ricky came around the corner with a full hay-net and a scowl. "Was that my name?"

"New girl's gonna help you with your horses again today. After she rides her three."

Ricky looked at me and shrugged. "Okay, no problem I guess." He stomped off down the shed-row with his hay.

"You did all right yesterday. You'll have him eating out of your hand in no time," Walt assured me.

"Ricky's a softy," Jacinta added. "Buy him an orange soda at break time. He loves those."

"Always offer to hold the horse before he asks you," Billy suggested. "He don't like to ask girls to do things."

"That's true," Jacinta said seriously. "Lotta guys like that here. Everyone thinks racetrackers are a buncha creeps. And don't get me wrong, we got our share. But we got a lotta old-fashioned gentlemen runnin' around, too."

I glanced into the office, hoping to see Alexander, but he wasn't there.

"Oh, not *him,*" Jacinta snorted. "I mean nice fellas like Ricky. Not stuck-up folks like Alexander."

"Jacinta!" Walt scolded. "That's your boss."

"He ain't here, is he?" Jacinta laughed, a sound like rocks rattling in a bucket. "Aww, I'm just jokin'. He's fine. But he's not like us. He's somethin' different from us."

"That's enough," Walt said, shaking his head. "Let's mount up and get goin'. He'll get here when he gets here."

I chewed at my lip, watching the other riders march into the tack room to gather the morning's equipment. I couldn't help but feel disappointed by Jacinta's words. If riders were beneath Alexander's notice, what did that mean for me? For us?

Assuming, of course, I hadn't just made it all up.

Chessiecat was a nice mare to ride, even if she was a redhead with a dished profile. It was the kind of face Diana would call ditzy. "Too much Arab in them," Diana liked to say about dish-faced horses, but I remembered Lucille defending one of her drop-offs once: "We call that kinda head *feminine*, Diana, not that you'd know anything about it."

I rode Chessiecat alongside Walt's filly, feeling an unfamiliar ache in my hips and shoulders which had everything to do with this new style of riding, long stirrups and no padding in the saddle, and a horse who pulled against me in order to get her most efficient galloping stride. A morning breeze rattled the palm trees lining the horse-path, and she tossed her head and threatened to spook, but she didn't really mean it. She just felt good.

"You like her?" Walt asked as I used my hands and heels to get her hooves back on a straight line.

"She's not bad," I said. "She has a feminine head," I added, trying out the phrase.

"That she does," Walt agreed, surveying my mare. "Really pretty. Jimmy Wallace never sells a pretty filly. He keeps all the lookers for himself."

"That's her owner?"

"Yeah. Old friend of Alexander's. Goes way back, to England even. He's a New Yorker." Walt sighed. "Don't know that I always trust those New Yorkers. Fast talkers. They'll get ya into anything, and they'll keep their name outta everything. But Alexander, he's always known Jimmy. I guess the guy's okay. There's worse folks in this game."

I had an instant impression of Jimmy Wallace: tough cartoonish guy, slicked-back hair, pinstriped suits, said *fugeddaboutit* a lot. "Is he ever around?" I asked, hoping not.

"Not often. Maybe in winter. He spends more time in south Florida. All the rich bigwigs like Gulfstream in the winter. They can keep it, far as I'm concerned. South Florida is one big pile a'concrete. I like this better." Walt gestured wildly at the shadows of trees and the dark blue dome of sky overhead, complete with pale laughing moon, and his filly swerved hard. He didn't react, just laughed and let her find her way back onto the path. I watched him, studying his riding style: not picture-perfect, but quiet and unconcerned. The young horses seemed to like it.

"Gulfstream's open now, isn't it? Do we have any horses there?"

"None," Walt said. "They're all here."

"But...why?" How could a racing operation of this size not have any horses running? There were at least seventeen horses of racing age, between two and six, in the training barn right now. I was on one of them. I got that Chessiecat was coming back from a lay-off, but seriously, no one else was ready to run a race?

He laughed. I could see the white rail of the training track approaching; our chat was almost over. "The whole point is to run 'em, right? I hear ya, Alex. But Alexander's been real cautious this whole year. I can't decide if he's watchin' his step or just tryin' to make her mad."

"Her?"

Walt glanced sidelong at me. "His partner."

"What's up with her?" I asked, going for it. "You mentioned her yesterday. No one else has said anything about her."

"Better off that way," Walt said with a shrug. "Maybe she's not around anymore. I think she's out of the picture except for the money. I sure *hope* so. She ain't no fun when she's around."

I kept my mouth shut. She'd been around, all right. It was strange to start a job with a secret this big.

We reached the training track, the groomed surface seeming to wake up the horses. Chessiecat hopped and snorted, ducking her head while I sat back, hoping she'd settle.

"Okay, crew, let's jog!" Walt called, nudging his filly into a trot. Chessiecat immediately tossed her head and started cavorting sideways, and for the rest of the set, I was too busy trying to stay in the saddle to think about Walt's tone when he'd said I was better off not knowing about Alexander's business partner.

❦❦❦❦❦

By the second set, Alexander had shown up and mounted his pony, a solidly-built mare named Betsy, so that he could accompany us to the track. From horseback, he could better see what we were up to out there; he could jog or gallop alongside our horses, or even catch a loose horse if necessary. There were a lot of good reasons to have the trainer on horseback, Walt told me as I rode beside him, but all I could think of was Alexander's presence, and wonder if he was watching me more closely than the others.

I kind of hoped not. As much as I wanted his attention, I wasn't having the prettiest ride. After we'd trotted a lap, we turned around to gallop, and I quickly started to feel the burn in my arms and thighs, with an ache in my knees for good measure. Naturally, Miss Vampire decided that this morning was a good time to be a tough ride. The dark bay filly jigged sideways and pulled hard in the jog; then, when we turned around and galloped around the track together, she alternated between shoving her head down in the bridle and throwing her head straight up.

I was actually afraid she might hit me in the face with her rock-hard skull, so I stood up in the stirrups, placing my weight well behind her withers. Miss Vampire tugged on me even harder.

"No, you gotta bend at the waist, Alex," Walt yelled. "Plant your hands at the yoke's neck-strap and straighten your arms! You're just making her mad sitting so far back."

I tried to listen, but it was so different from the English half-seat I'd been cantering in for my entire life, and when you added in the stress of those ears snapping right back in my face...the entire situation had my nerves jangling. My arms were exhausted from trying to hold her back, my legs were exhausted from trying to hold myself up off the saddle, and now this crazy mare wanted to knock out my front teeth with the top of her stupid head. I was starting to feel desperate. I was starting to feel like I wanted off this ride.

Walt pushed his filly closer. "Listen up. You put your weight down on her neck, take hold of both reins in your left hand, and straighten your knees—trust me, it all works together."

Shaking, scared, I followed his advice. I hooked both reins into my left hand, took a stronger hold with my right, pushed my knuckles down, straightened my knees a little, and—*magic.*

Everything stopped hurting. The mare stopped rooting against the bit and straightened out her gallop. If she was still being bullish, at least I stopped feeling every tug deep in my shoulders.

"She's pulling against herself now," Walt explained. "Every time she digs down on the reins, that cross you have pressed against her neck takes the pressure. The reins are doing all the work for you. Ever wonder why racing reins are so damn wide? They gotta take a lot of strain."

"This is genius," I gasped, looking down at the hard-working mare. Her neck arched and her black mane fluttered along the crest, a scalloped accent to her bulging muscles. "This is *witchcraft.*"

"Race-riding," Walt said with a grin. "You're a gallop girl now."

The words sung in my ears the rest of the way around the track. *I'm a gallop girl now.*

Alexander neck-reined his mare onto the track after we finished our gallop, the horses blowing and hot in the steamy morning air. He waited as we walked the horses up to the inner rail, stood them for a moment with their noses looking at the grassy infield, then turned them back to leave the track.

"It's called 'backing them off,'" Walt explained. It was how we kept horses from learning to take off and gallop right through the track's on-off gap after a workout. I thought it was a useful little trick we could have used in the regular horse world.

I noticed Miss Vampire was still a little anxious, so I made her back up a step as well before letting her turn after the others. We were a few steps behind when we went through the gap to the horse-path, meaning that when Alexander turned Betsy to head back to the barn, he brought the mare right alongside us.

I wished he hadn't. This wasn't when I wanted Alexander to see me. I was red-faced and dripping with sweat, and I thought I was sitting badly in the exercise saddle, as well. My sore hips weren't exactly good for my equitation.

Still, I gave him a lopsided smile. "Morning," I said. "Think I'm getting the hang of it?"

"You're a natural," Alexander replied smoothly, returning the smile with a little twinkle in his eyes. "It's tough learning to switch between a classic seat and a galloping position. I saw you figure it out about halfway through. Things went a lot more smoothly then, didn't they?"

"Oh, much more. I guess I thought galloping was like riding in an exaggerated two-point position."

He laughed at that. "Most people here wouldn't even know what you meant by that term."

"Well, you know, just leaning forward..." I trailed off, feeling embarrassed. My mare snorted and sidestepped, bumping shoulders with Alexander's horse.

"I know. I was a Pony Club brat, too."

"Oh, I wasn't in Pony Club," I explained, trying to straighten Miss Vampire, who suddenly seemed attached to Betsy with glue. "I was just a working student my whole life. I've mostly been riding green horses since I was thirteen. I'd get them jumping courses and then they'd sell."

"Hard knocks teach more than books," Alexander observed. "I think it's worked well for you."

Startled by the compliment, I turned my head to meet his gaze—and Miss Vampire lurched left into Betsy again, shoving my knee into Alexander's. I jerked the reins to haul the filly back to her own path, but not before I felt blood rush to my face, adding a fresh tomato hue to cheeks which were definitely already pink from heat.

"Sorry," I muttered, squeezing the reins in hopes of settling Miss Vampire, who had decided prancing was the next best decision. "She's still a headstrong girl."

"We all like a headstrong girl," Alexander murmured.

I felt an electric shiver run through my skin. Had he—was he—

I hazarded a sideways glance and saw Alexander looking blandly ahead, watching the other horses. Of course he hadn't been flirting with me, and I was crazy to think so, and—

His eyes flicked back to meet mine, and I felt as if I'd been caught with my hand in the cookie jar. His smile was slow and knowing. "Keep it up, Alex. I'll see you back in the barn."

He put his heels to Betsy and sent her jogging ahead to the head of the line.

I let Miss Vampire jog the couple of strides to catch up with Juan's filly, but I was barely paying attention as we walked in, and if Juan said anything friendly, I didn't notice. I was too busy internally screaming.

Chapter Twelve

I HELD MISS VAMPIRE for her bath outside the barn, and failed hard at trying not to watch Alexander moving down the shed-row, looking over each horse who had gone out in the second set.

"What's the matter with you?" Ricky grumbled as the filly swung her hindquarters around when he tried to sponge under her tail. "Pay attention to this horse, okay? It's worse when you half-help."

"I'm sorry," I gasped, trying to get her to stand still. I could feel Alexander approaching, standing just a few feet away, watching me. *He's watching the horse,* I told myself. I kept my back to him and took Miss Vampire's halter in both hands, shaking the noseband to distract her from the activities going on around her backside. To distract myself from thinking about Alexander.

I told myself it had to stop. That this was a crush to get over *immediately.* I was not in Alexander Whitehall's league. He consorted with celebrities and royalty in owner's boxes. I remembered seeing a photo of him at Royal Ascot, wearing the required top hat and cravat, and looking fantastic in both. That was the sort of person Alexander Whitehall was: an old-money, old-school horseman who rubbed shoulders with princes and queens. Jacinta was right; he wasn't like us.

But there's something there, a determined voice reminded me. *You know there's something there.*

Our easy conversation in the restaurant parking lot, that moment in the tack room yesterday, those lingering glances from the saddle: all of it added up to something I shouldn't give up on yet. And weren't horses the greatest equalizer of all? A shared love of horses brought together people of all ages, all backgrounds. A walk through any boarding stable on a summer evening could prove that point. Our age difference didn't matter, and neither did our very different backgrounds. We were the same. We should be having long conversations, talking horses and whatever else we wanted to talk about. We should be friends.

And yeah...we should be more than that.

❧❧❧❧ ❦❦❦❦

"I have one more horse for you today," Alexander called.

I turned around, my hands still on Miss Vampire's halter. My drifting attention was the only invitation she needed to nip at me, and I narrowly missed getting chomped by her razor-sharp young teeth. I swatted her on the neck and took a step back from those choppers.

"I have Nordic Empress in the next set," I told him.

"In the fourth set, you're taking out a new one. I already told Walt." He looked pleased with himself. "You'll suit him really well,

I think. He wasn't sure, but I said you two would go together beautifully."

My first colt. Would he ride differently from the fillies? "Who is he?"

"A three-year-old colt I have a partnership in. He raced in the spring, but he's been off most of the summer—he was growing like a weed and all out of proportion. But he's been jogging for the past two weeks and I think he's ready to do a turn at a gallop with the group today. Are you up for it?"

Did I have a choice? I was tired and sore, and Nordic Empress was going to task me in about fifteen minutes. Another horse on the tab sounded like a nightmare, but riding horses was my job.

"Of course," I chirped. "What's his name?"

"Wings and Prayers," Alexander said. "But call him whatever you want. I believe my partner calls him Weeds and Prickers." He gave me an apologetic shrug, then went off down the shed-row to look at the next horse.

Ricky peered at me from under Miss Vampire's arching neck. "Wait for me before you tack that colt, Alex," he said, his voice low. "He's not the easiest horse in the barn."

The words did nothing to add to my confidence, but I just nodded and went along with it. This was my life now. Getting on new horses every day, hoping for the best, sticking to whatever I could.

I'd wanted to learn about horse racing—well, now I was in the thick of it.

Wings and Prayers might have grown out of the worst of his three-year-old imbalance, but he was still a gangly horse: big bones, big head, big shoulders, big hind end, all connected by long skinny neck and long skinny body. He didn't look put together quite right. Add in his plain chestnut coloring, with just a small white star between his eyes to break up all of that muddy brown color, and a short tail which barely reached his hocks, and he made a particularly unimpressive specimen. Except for his height.

"Is he like, seventeen hands high?" I asked, standing in the horse's doorway with my saddle over one arm.

Ricky, who had been hooking the colt to his tie on the back wall, shook his head. "Close enough, though."

"Damn," I muttered. I pushed back the stall grill and went inside. The colt eyed me closely, but he didn't pin his ears or swish his tail. He just looked interested. I could handle tall and interested. It was tall and murderous where I drew the line. Luckily, horses like that were pretty rare.

I glanced at his pathetic tail. "What happened there?"

"Probably got chewed on while he was turned out with some buddies. He was out all summer. You know colts, they're so dumb." Ricky produced a hoof pick and started cleaning out the colt's hooves, rapid-fire, while I put down my tack in a corner and grabbed a curry comb. I had to dodge some teeth to get the job done, and I quickly saw why Ricky had said he wasn't easy: Wing, as I immediately abbreviated his name, didn't like to be pushed around. When I asked him to move off the wall so that I could reach his other side, he acted like I was trying to shove an aircraft carrier out of port, and there was a lot of tail-swishing and teeth-clicking every time I accidentally touched a ticklish spot—which seemed to be most of the horse.

Still, by working together it took us about three minutes to produce a clean colt who was ready to be saddled; in three more, we had a tacked-up horse who was ready to go. The racing life was speedy both in and out of the saddle.

"You're quick at this," Ricky grunted, tightening the girth another hole. "You groom before?"

I thought of the many years' worth of students I'd taken care of, back before Diana's self-destruction had chased them all away. Prepping horses for riding lessons, often six or seven in a single lesson, then stripping and bathing them all while the next lesson went out. Horse show days that lasted fourteen, fifteen hours, dragging horses back and forth from stalls to warm-up ring to show-ring. And then there had been the last few years, working alone with six or seven horses in the barn. Yeah, I'd groomed before.

"You could say that."

"That's good. We need people who know their way around a horse."

From the way he said it, I guessed some people were truly just riders and nothing else. "I want to be able to do everything," I said.

"Well, if you want, after the riders done today, we practice doing up legs," Ricky told me. "Wrapping Thoroughbred legs is different than wrapping show horse legs. Okay...you ready to get on this thing?" He held out a cupped hand.

By now, I knew how to manage a leg-up, though I wasn't very good at it. I put my hands on the saddle, bounced, and straightened my arms, pushing up at the top of my jump. Ricky caught my bent left knee with his hand and pushed me the rest of the way into the saddle. We'd only done it a half-dozen times, so sometimes I made it, mostly I didn't.

This time, I got most of the way into the saddle—but the colt's added height made things more challenging. I had to scramble into the tack while the colt turned anxiously, wheeling around Ricky, and then shove my weight deep into my right stirrup to straighten the saddle, which had slipped to the left. I glanced ruefully down at Ricky as I took the reins in hand and got them knotted up securely.

"I swear I'll get better."

He winked at me. "I know you'll get better." He pushed open the stall grill to let me out. "Get better on top first, we can manage on the ground."

"Okay, Wing," I told the colt as we headed down the shed-row, "I need you to be cool out there for me. Think you can manage that? Be cool?"

Wing shook his head, and his straggly brown mane bounced on his thin neck. He felt strange between my legs. I had just begun to acclimate to the ultra-close feel of the exercise saddle, but the fillies had been full-bodied, almost chubby. This lanky three-year-old was like a pile of bones between my legs. I felt as if his vertebrae were scraping my seat bones.

"You're a scarecrow, aren't you, Wing?" His ears flicked back to listen to me. They were as long and skinny as the rest of him.

I knew Wing wasn't a malnourished horse—his sheer size gave away the quality of food this horse was eating—he was just a teenager who hadn't yet recovered from a rapid growth spurt. I could tell by his uneven, fast-slow-fast walk that he was still getting used to the new length of his legs. I just hoped he wouldn't stumble and toss me over his head once we were galloping.

One by one the other riders joined me, and after we'd carousselled around the shed-row for a few turns, Alexander rode out, mounted up on Betsy, to lead our little parade out to the training track. I braced myself for another close encounter, but he stayed alongside Billy the whole time, speaking in low tones to the quiet cowboy. I didn't know whether I felt relieved or disappointed, but as Wing began to stretch his neck and look around, I decided I'd better focus on the horse and not worry too much about Alexander.

I walked Wing onto the track just behind Walt's colt. Passing Alexander, I glanced his way—I couldn't help myself—and he gave me a wink. "Just give him a loose rein, let him find the bit, and try not to worry."

Try not to worry. I nearly burst out laughing. "Sure," I said, flashing him a sarcastic grin. "No worries here."

I'd just let a three-year-old racehorse coming off his summer vacation go for a gallop on a loose rein and not worry about what might happen.

"Tuck him in tight behind my colt," Walt called over his shoulder. "You can run right up this boy's butt and he won't mind."

Squeezing Wing up behind Walt's colt, I let him break into a trot, keeping my seat close to the saddle in case he stumbled over those big front hooves of his. The colt had a choppy, bouncy stride at first, the kind that was sure to give a rider a backache, but by the time we'd rounded a few turns, he managed to smooth out. More comfortable now, he pushed his nose out, asking for rein, and I gave it to him. Soon he was jogging along the outer rail like an old hunter in a flat class, and if I felt like I was balancing on a two-by-four, at least it wasn't a runaway bronco two-by-four. I didn't have to gather him up again until it was time to whoa, turn, and stand up for a few moments in preparation for our gallop.

Walt looked over at us. "You okay there?" he asked.

"All good," I said, trying to keep the surprise out of my voice. My body was sore and I was drenched with sweat from a morning of riding, but at least Wing seemed like a good boy. Better than I'd expected, anyway. "Ready when you are."

"Okay then, crew. Let's take a nice easy gallop."

I tucked Wing along the inside rail again, just behind Walt's pretty chestnut colt. Jacinta came in alongside me on a mahogany bay colt with three white socks. "Flashy Boy here wanted to join ya," she laughed, dragging the colt's head away from Wing with one forceful arm. "I think he discovered his balls but he doesn't know what to do with 'em."

"Yikes," I offered, watching her manhandle the colt, who was grunting suggestively at Wing. The bay colt was a beast, as well-developed and muscular as a grown horse, with a huge ridge of muscle along the crest of his neck. "He can't just be two, can he?"

"He shore is," Jacinta drawled, leaning back against the reins. "*Way* too much testosterone in this ol' boy. He'll have to get cut before he's any good at the races, watch and see."

Despite Jacinta's mobile sex machine, we had a nice gallop. It was a nice morning. The sun was halfway up the sky; a flock of ibis flew over and landed in the infield to scout for bugs and tadpoles in the grassy pond, and in a nearby tree, a red-shouldered hawk was yelling his head off about something.

I let my joints move loosely, flowing with Wing's surprisingly fluid canter, and felt a little disappointed when we'd made our second circuit and the workout was over. Wing ducked his head, nostrils flaring, and I knew he was thoroughly worn out.

"Oh, that's probably why you're being so good," I told him. "I know how you boys are. Big babies when you're tired."

Alexander nodded as I took the puffing colt over to the gap, still keeping close to Walt's steady ride. For a moment I thought he was going to tell me I'd done a nice job, and a smile began to crease at the corner of my lips as I anticipated a compliment. Then Jacinta's colt whinnied, another one of those studdish neighs, and Alexander's gaze swept past us. "Jacinta," he snapped, "give that colt a boot in his ribs and get him past Betsy without incident, please."

"Yessir," Jacinta panted, and I heard the thumps as she planted her heels in her big colt's ribcage. Startled, he darted past us, his head high and his eyes wide. Jacinta just whooped and kicked him again. The other horses shied and jinked away, and I shortened my reins as Wing ducked sideways, tossing his head like he wanted in on the trouble. Somehow, I kept him going, and we made it back to the barn without any issues.

But when I slid to the ground, my body ached like I'd been hit by a truck.

Between the aching muscles and the upheaval in my heart, everything about this job was hurting more than I'd expected.

Chapter Thirteen

AFTER WE'D HOSED OFF Wing and handed him over to a hot walker, I started mucking stalls alongside Ricky. My thighs might be absolutely shattered from the galloping position, but cleaning stalls was, at least, familiar ground for my upper body. I'd been a little afraid the farm would use straw for bedding, something which had to be cleaned with heavy pitchforks, but Ricky said straw was just for broodmares and the racetrack. "Too expensive for every day down in Florida," he explained. "Shavings is cheaper."

And lighter, I thought cheerfully.

I quickly learned that when the riders and Alexander were out of the barn, the grooms felt free to gossip about everyone on horseback. This made the busy time during rider's sets, while we cleaned stalls, scrubbed water buckets, and filled hay-nets, extremely interesting. The stall walls were made of cinder-block, but the center of each wall was filled with the hollow blocks that let light and air through, along with plenty of conversation about the goings-on around Cotswold Farm and Ocala at large.

"You hear what happen at Tony Donovan's place?"

"I hear his wife caught him with that assistant trainer he brought up from Miami."

"You hear right. You know what she did?"

"What's that? She cut off his balls?"

"Nah, man, she paint his stallion barn *pink.*"

Guffaws all around.

"That right?"

"The whole barn is pink as a baboon's butt."

"Ain't a monkey butt blue?"

Laughter. "Man, I don't know. But that barn is pink."

"Imagine if that happen here. Boss-man would die if someone ruined his perfect little stud barn."

"Maureen would murder anyone who tried. When's the last time you saw her anywhere but that barn?"

"She does the broodmares on Sunday when Kimberly's off."

"That's not all she does on Sunday."

Snorts.

"You don't mean that."

"He doesn't know what he's talking about. Boss isn't messing around with grooms. He's got fancier pieces than that."

Whoops, not the gossip I was hoping to hear. I finished my stall and pushed the wheelbarrow out of the stall door, thinking it was time to escape this conversation. If I walked down to the manure spreader right now, I wouldn't hear whatever came next—

"Oh, I heard that's all over."

I stopped walking.

"Heard *what's* all over?"

"Adriene. I heard she went back to England."

Someone whistled.

"Tough loss."

"If you like ballbusters."

"She had legs up to *here.*"

"She was a nasty thing though. Working for her? I ain't miss it."

"Nasty in the barn, nasty in bed!"

"Yeah, let's send him flowers—"

With a grunt, I dug in my heels and pushed the wheelbarrow down the shed-row. *Adriene.* That was her name.

And she'd been more than just his assistant. The knowledge curdled in my stomach.

Ricky was waiting for me when I came back, a hay-net in his hands. "How are you at making balls?"

"Excuse me?"

"Making a hay-ball." He held up the empty net. "You can't just drop a few flakes in the hay-net. This is science. Come on, watch me."

Ten minutes later, I was trying and failing to make my hay-net look like a soccer ball, as instructed. Ricky was trying and failing not to laugh at me. "That's a football," he chortled, as I held up my cylinder-shaped creation, "but the wrong kind."

"I've never heard of making it a ball!" I wailed, finally feeling frustration well over. "What is wrong with filling it with the flakes of hay and leaving them square? That's how we do it at home and it's never caused any trouble."

Ricky just shook his head. "Too much space in the net that way. Racehorses can't get a single loose inch of rope or they'll hang themselves. Think about it. We get them fit, then we stick them in a stall all day and night. They got too much energy. They get hurt way more easily. Most of these horses get some turn-out but when they go to the racetrack that ends. Someday you be at the racetrack, too. So learn your lesson now, no bad habits later."

Duly chastised, I went back to adjusting the prickly hay, trying to fluff it into a ball-shape. "You think I'm going to the racetrack?" I asked after a moment of struggle.

Ricky shrugged. "I think Alexander grooming you for a big job."

I smiled to myself. *That* made up for everything: the exhaustion, the aches, the gossip, this damned hay-net. If Alexander really thought I had potential, if he'd believed me that first day when I'd intimated I could take over his assistant vacancy, then I was going to do everything in my power to prove him right. I rocked back on my heels and pushed the hay-net back to Ricky. "Please show me one more time," I said meekly. "I think I can get it if I just watch you."

Ricky grinned. "Okay, horse show girl. It's like *this...*"

That first week was long, but I gave everything I had to learning the ropes of the training barn. Long past eleven, when the other riders headed out for lunch or second jobs, I was still in the stalls with Ricky, "doing up" legs of horses who needed a little support from standing bandages, poultice, or sweats. After that, I took on housekeeping. I cleaned tack, folded saddle towels, rolled up wraps while they were still warm and fresh from the dryer. In the afternoons, I dragged horses around (or tried not get dragged by horses) as I put walking horses on the hot-walker, and turned out others in paddocks. Some days I stayed late enough to help feed the horses dinner and turn out the younger ones, who spent the night in paddocks in front of the training barn.

I didn't hear Adriene's name again, although I learned the grooms liked to pair Alexander with a cavalcade of female names, so it was possible hers had meant nothing. Still, that first conversation had given me a bad feeling I couldn't shake, a premonition which made about as much sense as the heart-lift I felt when Alexander walked into the barn each morning. They said she was gone, so I shouldn't have had anything to worry about, but even then, I knew no woman would give up on Alexander that easily.

If Adriene wasn't a common topic, complaints about Alexander were, which surprised me. Sure, everyone liked to complain about the boss, but there seemed to be a pervasive belief amongst the grooms that the farm was going downhill, the horses weren't running their best, and Alexander just didn't care.

I had never thought of Alexander as anything but the very best, a top trainer who was enduring a regular slump, but as I listened to these mutterings, I realized there might be a bigger reason why he'd disappeared from the magazine covers lately. Every trainer had hot streaks and cold streaks, but was it possible Alexander was simply not the devoted trainer he used to be? After all, he had *no* horses at the track right now, no one running in the lucrative fall meet down at Gulfstream, and it didn't seem to be the fault of the horses, who were all quality.

"He just don't care no more."

"I bet he sell up in a year's time. I've been through this before at other places."

"None of these big fancy places last that long. They always get bored and want to move on."

"Rich people, man."

I absorbed their chatter while I shook shavings through my manure fork, knelt in deep bedding to wrap legs, and scrubbed water buckets out with a handful of twisted hay. It gave me plenty to think about, but my wonderings went nowhere.

I simply couldn't imagine how anyone could accumulate success and develop a beautiful property like this, only to lose interest in keeping it going.

No, there had to be a good reason. I kept my ears open, waiting for the clue which would tip me off, give me an insight into Alexander's apparent inaction.

The work-days grew longer as my body took more and more of a beating and kept on ticking, and Saturday morning lasted so long it felt like a punishment. Even so, I hesitated when Walt told me to take an early weekend at noon.

"I can stay and work," I assured him, afraid to give up any ground I'd gained during my first week. The other riders were talking to me now, giving me space and even a coveted folding chair in the center aisle when the mid-morning break rolled around. The grooms seemed more amiable, too. I didn't want to get some extra time off and look like I was skipping out on the barn crew.

Walt just grinned at me. "You look wiped out," he drawled. "And no one is killing themselves on a Saturday afternoon around here. Everyone will clear out early. Go home. Get some rest. You have a day and a half to recover for a new week."

I didn't chance asking twice. I went home.

Home to my bed, the saggy little mattress smelling a lot sweeter now that I'd called my mom, found out what brand of detergent she bought, and replaced the dusty smell of the sheets with something familiar and floral.

When I woke up at four o'clock that afternoon, to the music of distant thunder and a shaft of golden sunlight sifting through my blinds, I felt refreshed for the first time since I'd come to Ocala. *Now for a quiet evening and then back to bed early,* I thought contentedly. I'd just get a snack to start, maybe watch some TV.

I walked into the living room, and froze.

Jacinta grinned at me from the sofa. She was holding a two-liter of Pepsi in one hand and a bottle of Jack Daniels in the other. I guess I'd startled her just before a dollop of each went into the plastic tumbler on the coffee table.

"Oh...hi, Jace," I said weakly, trying to cover my surprise.

I'd spent so much time working, I'd barely spoken more than a few bleary-eyed "good morning" and "goodnight" wishes to Jacinta here in the house. She generally went to work at other farms in the afternoons, and came home in the evening to shower, eat something frozen or some fast food she'd brought home in a greasy, delicious-smelling bag, then topple into bed.

I'd see her in passing, and we'd nod, and she'd say something like: "Long day today, mmhmm," and that was the last I'd see of her until the next morning.

I'd almost convinced myself I didn't *have* a roommate, just someone who used the back bedroom to sleep. To be confronted with evidence of one, and one who was planning on getting her drink on while I'd been dreaming of sprawling on the couch to watch a movie, was pretty disconcerting and plenty disappointing.

"Hellooooo, Alex!" Jacinta crowed. "Girl, it is the *weekend!*"

"Yes," I agreed cautiously. "Happy Friday, I guess. Haha."

"Get you a cup down and I'll mix you up a drink." Jacinta waved the bottle of Pepsi expansively.

I did not drink Pepsi. I came from a Coca-Cola home.

"That's okay," I demurred, backing up into the hall. The bathroom beckoned; I could hide out in there for a while, then go back to my bedroom. "I was just about to take a shower. Thanks, though."

"Well, you need one for the road!" Jacinta pointed to her own wet hair, pulled back so tightly her reddish forehead looked stretched and painful. "Shower drinks are the best drinks!"

I had worked for a drunk for a long time, but I had never heard *that.* Jacinta was clearly on another sort of planet altogether. She seemed like a cheerful drunk, though. Diana had been sad and angry. With a pang of sadness, I wondered how the Calusa Lakes horses were doing. Then I pushed the thought of them away. I couldn't do anything about that now. They had to stay in my past.

"Really, it's fine," I insisted. "Thanks, though."

"Fine, suit yourself." Jacinta shrugged and commenced her own pour. "But you *are* coming out with me tonight."

"Excuse me?" I was doing no such thing.

"Take your shower, take your shower," Jacinta said, waving me away. "Get cleaned up. And then, *dinner,* Alex. I'm taking you to dinner tonight. New roomie stuff. We're overdue for some getting-to-know-you fun."

Chapter Fourteen

DINNER TURNED OUT TO be an overstatement. We stopped for burgers and fries from a no-name place on Highway 441, then kept driving deeper into farm country. Thoroughbred farms unrolled along each side of the road, and late-September yellows and browns peeked from the full, northern-looking trees that grew so happily in north Florida. A yellow and pink sunset prepared to unfold across the western sky, bright pastels burnishing the distant heights of thunderstorms over the Gulf of Mexico, less than a hundred miles west.

I watched the clouds spread their feathery tops with a nostalgic feeling. We were almost to October. Florida's rainy season would be over in a week or two, and the summer storms had already been few and far between in the week I'd been up here. I loved the crash and bang of an afternoon storm.

Jacinta didn't notice the weather or the sunset. She was fully focused on the road, which was good, considering she'd been drinking Pepsi and Jack an hour before. Something told me her tolerance was pretty strong, anyway.

"This is going to be great," she announced every few miles, but she didn't give any details. After what felt like an hour but was actually half that, she finally put on the truck's loud blinker and pulled off into a gravel parking lot across the road from a training track. I stared through the dirty windshield at a little wooden storefront with a crooked front porch and a line of detached semi-trailers behind it.

A big plywood sign by the road read: THE HAY PLACE.

"Jacinta, this is literally where people buy hay," I said.

"So?"

The semi-trailers even had signs posted on their doors: Alfalfa, Peanut, T&A, Timothy, O&A. All different types of hay. It was clearly an actual hay store. "Do we need hay?" I looked back at the storefront. "This place is closed. Where can we get hay on a Saturday night?"

Jacinta snorted.

Then a couple walked past me, decked head to toe in glittering Western outfits, and I realized that in Ocala, things weren't always what they seemed. I looked back at Jacinta. "What's going on?"

She grinned devilishly at me. "It's the weekend, baby! Let's go!"

I followed Jacinta around the back of the store, and sure enough, that's where things were just getting rolling. A long, low addition had been built onto the store, and I'm not saying it started life as a makeshift stable but...it *definitely* started life as a makeshift stable. The beams were set at precise twelve-foot intervals, for one thing. There were still some screw-eyes at water-bucket height scattered around, for another. And if you still weren't convinced you were standing in former horse stalls, the hay-rack bolted to the wall behind the DJ's folding table was a definite giveaway.

But despite this place's equine origins it was now a full-fledged, if low-ceilinged, country disco. The ceiling was studded with flashing lights in every color of the rainbow. Men wearing cowboy boots clutched bottles of Bud Lite. Women dolled up in everything from tube tops and jeans to rhinestone-studded dresses drank from red plastic cups, dancing with each other and casting appraising glances over the unattached guys. A DJ in a backwards cap and a NASCAR t-shirt was rocking out to a house version of a country song I'd heard at the grocery store.

I felt like I was in some sort of reality television experiment. Everyone around me looked really happy to be there, though.

Jacinta had started gyrating to the music, but the song ended and she stood still for a minute, looking around with what could only be described as starry eyes. I was happy for her, but also confused for myself.

"What is this place?" I asked her.

"The Hay Place," Jacinta said simply. "Everyone knows The Hay Place. It's the best!"

"But this is insane," I protested. "We're in a barn behind a hay store!"

A new song burst out of the speakers and threatened to overload the local power grid.

"WHAT?" Jacinta shouted.

"THIS IS INSANE!"

"YEAH!" Jacinta grinned at me, then bounced over to a card table covered with coolers of ice. She gave the guy behind them a ten and plucked two bottles of Bud Lite out of the ice. "HERE WE GO!"

I took the bottle she waved in my face and we toasted with an exuberant *clink,* and Jacinta started wiggling around to the music, getting funky white-girl style. I joined in with a *when in Rome* sense of duty.

Dancing was hard work! By the time the song ended I was panting, thirsty, and happy to swallow most of my beer in a few gulps. It tasted weak and sort of yellow, but it was very cold and that seemed to be the most important part.

A lanky man slapped Jacinta on the butt as he passed by on the way to the beer table. I looked at her, alarmed, but she just shook her head.

"That's Rinker. We used to race-ride in Oklahoma together. I beat him most of the time."

"You did not," Rinker said from behind her.

"Did too. Got the meet records to prove it."

"Dang old peacock," Rinker muttered, and stumped off.

"You were a jockey?" I asked, a little astonished. Jacinta was taller than me, and didn't exactly have a stick figure.

"Sure enough," she said. "Then I got too heavy even for little bull-ring tracks." She took my empty bottle, turned back to the beer table, and procured two more bottles. The music came roaring up again, a heavy raggaeton beat.

I watched Jacinta, former Oklahoma jockey, give herself over to dancing. She shook out her thick, ash-colored hair, she waggled her hips, she closed her eyes and waved her arms in the air. She was having some sort of religious experience under that low ceiling, those flashing colored lights, and let me tell you, The Hay Place crowd was *loving* it. Suddenly we were in the center of a chanting crowd.

"JACINTA!"

"YES, GO JACINTA GO!"

"JACINTAAAAA!"

Everyone knew her and, it soon became clear, everyone knew just how crazy she got. I let Jacinta take center stage and backed off a little, looking for a nice quiet corner where I could watch without being watched. The room was getting crowded and hot, as more and more people arrived for their Saturday night action.

I'd finally settled into a dark corner, leaning my cheek against the wall in hopes of finding some residual coolness from a time before the air conditioning was overwhelmed, when a young guy caught my eye and came dancing in my direction. I bit back a groan. This was not my hope for the night. I was not looking for some gallant cowboy at The Hay Place.

Still, I had to admit he was nice-looking, and as he emerged from the crowd I saw he wasn't dressed like he'd just dismounted after a Western Pleasure class, unlike most of the other guys here. In fact, we were dressed pretty similarly, in dark denim and a basic top. I was wearing a navy-blue blouse; he was wearing a cornflower-blue shirt. The resemblance was actually kind of hilarious, and I managed to smile as he bopped over to me, pushing back smooth dark hair, and flashed a pearly smile.

"Well, hello there! Are you having a good night?" he asked in something approaching a normal volume.

I realized it was a little quieter in the corner and we could talk like humans. "I am," I lied. "It's a nice change after working all week."

"Oh, I know! Where do you work?"

"I work for Alexander Whitehall at Cotswold Farm in Reddick," I replied.

His eyebrows went up, as if he hadn't expected such a blueblood address. "Nice," he said appreciatively.

I was pleased to note my employer's name lent me a certain something.

"You?" I assumed he was a rider for another training center. Were there rivalries here? What if he was from an arch-enemy barn? That could be a thing here. It was definitely a thing in Calusa. Barn politics were part of horse show life.

"Oh, I'm not in racing," he said, shaking his head. "Sorry. I ride jumpers."

A real, live horse show boy, right in front of me! I couldn't contain my surprise. "*What?* Really?"

"Is that so crazy?"

"I just...I always wondered where all the guy jumpers come from. You know how every Grand Prix competition is just guy, guy, guy? Well, at regular horse shows, it's all girls. So I wondered where all these hotshot guy riders were coming from. Now, I guess I know. It's Ocala."

He was laughing at me, but I didn't mind. "Come outside," he said, touching my elbow gently. "It's hot in here."

I hadn't been to a party in years, and I'd never been to a club. Too busy with horses, not particularly interested in the noise. But there was something about this exact moment which made me understand why people did this. Why they put on skimpy outfits and drank terrible beer and danced under colored lights while a bunch of strangers watched. Because you might have a half-second like this one, when the music suddenly dimmed in your ears and you were keenly aware that someone was looking at you like you were the most interesting person in the room.

Tonight it happened to me for the very first time, and the feeling was more intoxicating than the cheap beer could ever be.

So I went out into the humid Ocala night behind a guy who rode jumpers, even though we hadn't even shared our names yet, feeling like I was in a movie.

A weird movie, with a nightclub built into a feed store, but we can't all be Oscar nominees.

The sun had set while we'd been in the windowless club, and beyond the thumping, pulsing walls there was a restful darkness, and the peeping of tree-frogs, and the prospect of spiderwebs if we walked too far. Maybe the collective outdoors knowledge of all these horse-people was what kept everyone outside fairly close to the building, but the jumper guy still managed to find a quiet place near one of the hay trailers where we could feel at least a semblance of privacy without stumbling into a jumbo arachnid.

"Three-string alfalfa," I remarked, reading the sign on the front of the trailer, dimly lit by a street-light over the parking lot. "I've lifted a few of those this past week."

"Are you a *groom?*" the guy asked, sounding maybe more shocked than necessary.

"I'm doing a little bit of everything," I said. "Learning how to run a training barn. I'm Alex, by the way." I kept my last name to myself, in case he turned out to be crazy.

"Miles."

"Really?" I'd never met anyone named Miles. He didn't look old enough for such a title. He looked...young, actually. Ought to be in college young. Like me.

"Wait a minute! What's wrong with Miles?"

"It sounds like an English professor, that's all. It surprised me."

"What would you have named me?"

I considered what I could see of his face: his boyish good looks, his dark hair falling over his forehead, his smiling lips. A door opened and closed, allowing a brief wash of red and yellow spotlights to stream across his features. The party lights gave me a flash of inspiration. "I know...Elliot."

"*Elliot?*"

"You have a little bit of a teen dream movie thing going on. Like, if you were thirty but you played a sixteen-year-old on TV. Look, if it wasn't Elliot it would have to be Phoenix."

"Jesus." Miles ran a hand through his hair. "I don't know how to take this."

"That was a *very* Teen Beat hand gesture."

He smiled at me wolfishly. "So you think I'm a teen dream, huh?"

"I guess I do," I said coquettishly, aided by the Bud Lite in my system.

Miles pressed a hand against the hay trailer and leaned over me. "What happens next in the dream?"

"I'm not sure," I demurred. "I'm not a teenager."

He burst out laughing and pushed back from the trailer. "You're a tough sell, Alex."

I let him think that, happy to know even if I was going to be totally inept at talking to a guy, it could at least come off as cool skepticism.

"So are you going to let me take you out?"

"Hmm?" Still cool. *Good job, Alex.*

"Come on. Let me take you to dinner. Something a little nicer than a hay place."

"This *is* weird, right? It's not just me?" I gestured to everything.

"Oh, it's weird all right. But that's just part of Slowcala's charm."

I considered Miles's smile. He seemed nice enough. I was interested in how he'd ended up riding jumpers, where the mythical Boy in Horses actually came from. Should I be into this guy, or holding out with Alexander? Where were things going with Alexander, anyway? *Nowhere,* the beer told me confidently. *You're holding out for the wrong guy. Hang out with this guy, he's nice and he likes you.*

Thanks, Inner Beer Voice. I made up my mind. "Okay. You can take me out."

"Good." His smile grew lazy and he tipped his head forward. I had a moment that was half-excitement, half-panic, and then I heard Jacinta.

"Alex? You out here?"

"I have to go," I said, ducking out from under his arm. "That's my ride."

"Oh, you're not really pulling a Cinderella act on me, are you?" Miles shook his head with mock woe. "Wait a minute—are you from Orlando?"

"I'M COMING, JACINTA!" I bellowed. "Look, I don't know her that well and I don't want to get left here by accident." I dug my phone out of my pocket. "Put your number in."

He punched in his number and handed it back. "Call me, though. Really."

"ALEX?" Jacinta roared again.

"Tomorrow," I promised. "So we can make plans." I took off running before he could say anything else.

Jacinta was remarkably sober. I'd sort of expected a walking disaster to be waiting for me, but she was standing comfortably outside the front door of the club, chatting with a few other leather-faced horsewomen. "Did you have a nice time?" she asked.

"I did. This was fun."

"Good. Well, ladies." Jacinta turned and waved to her friends. "It's past my bedtime. Have a safe night." She started through the gravel towards her pick-up.

"Do you...do you need me to drive?" I asked hesitantly.

"And get us lost?" Jacinta glanced at me and realized what was concerning me. "Oh, bless you! I only had the two beers. That's why we're leaving now. You don't want to drive drunk on Saturday night around here. Cops know what's up. Get home early and get tucked into bed, that's the safe way to do it."

"Sorry." I slid into the passenger seat of the pick-up. "I didn't mean anything by it."

"No, no, that's fine. I'm glad you had a good night out. Ocala can get boring real fast. A little bit of dancing, a little bit of necking, well that always cheers me up." Jacinta chuckled and turned on the truck.

I gazed out into the dark night as she drove the winding roads back to the farm, thinking over my accomplishments. I had been here just about a week and I had a job, a place to live, and the prospect of a date. Well, look at me! Look at everything coming up Alex!

And the good feelings stayed with me until we drove past Alexander's house and I looked up at a yellow square of window, only to see his silhouette inside. Was he gazing out at the starlit farm, or was he looking back at his own reflection?

I wished I knew.

Chapter Fifteen

I WENT FOR A walk on Sunday afternoon. There wasn't much else to do. I'd slept past sunrise, a novelty in itself, then had a nice breakfast at a Waffle House with Jacinta. Afterwards, I let her drive me around Ocala, showing me the tack shops and horsemen hangouts she thought I should know about. By lunchtime, she had dropped me back at home and went out to ride a horse for a friend. I thought about taking a nap, but decided against it. I felt restless, not sleepy at all. I found myself putting on my shoes again.

The horses who lived in the back pasture were grazing in a shady corner near the driveway, so I took them some carrots from the crisper drawer. That first night I'd been here, I'd thought they were mares, but subsequent pauses to chat with the little herd during daylight hours had shown me they were a trio of geldings. Each of them bore battle scars from tough lives. One had a big knee, another had a scar running up his hind leg which looked like a gray rope pressing through his fawn-colored hair. I decided they must be retired racehorses who hadn't been sound enough to move on to new careers. This was the old-timer's field.

"I appreciated you guys so much my first night here," I told the horses as they crunched on the carrots. They blew curious breath on my empty hands, and the chestnut with the big scar gave me a few solemn licks on my palm, then they wandered a few feet away to get back to the serious business of grazing. I settled on a knot of tree root to watch them for a little while, enjoying the shade and the soft breeze, letting my mind wander and trying not to think *too* hard about the heart of a man who gave his retirees a big pasture and a peaceful life in the midst of a bustling farm.

Then, footsteps crunched on gravel and I looked up quickly, surprised anyone would be out this way. The afternoon was beginning to cloud over, thunder rumbling promises of rain off to my unseen east, where the sky was hidden by towering oaks. Anyone out this far from the main buildings now was risking a soaking. But here was Alexander, walking up the driveway, his brown leather shoes coated with a fine layer of white dust. When I saw him, my heart did that funny/stupid lift which was becoming my standard response to his presence, and my stomach felt as though it was filled with bees, humming and swarming.

I lifted a hand and waved, as if everything inside was totally fine.

Alexander sighed as he reached the shade and reached up to doff his hat, a trim straw affair I thought I'd seen him wear to the races in years past. "My God," he said, "September gets more like August every year."

"I was thinking it's not as stuffy here as it is in South Florida," I said teasingly, although I was half-lying. The humidity *was* lower here, but not the temperatures. "Up here in the great white north, seasons are different."

"You just wait a month, Alex," he laughed, coming to stand beside me and gaze out over the pasture. The geldings had moved away, but they flicked their ears in our direction, just in case Alexander should crinkle a plastic wrapper or snap a carrot. "By late October we'll get a night so cold you'll be scratching at my door, asking to come sit by the fire."

I tightened my lips, imagining snuggling up with Alexander by a crackling fireplace. "Maybe I'll just get an electric blanket," I said lightly. "Unless you'd prefer I wake you up on this supposed cold night we have coming."

I sensed his head turning, felt his gaze on me, considering me as if I wasn't quite what he'd expected. For my part, I just stared straight ahead, keeping my gaze on the grazing horses. I wasn't a flirt, I wasn't experienced at those practiced turns of phrase which seemed to fascinate men. If I said anything to keep his attention now, it was all coming straight from my gut—my brain had nothing to do with it. The less thinking, the better, quite honestly.

The silence stretched between us, a humming live wire, until I couldn't take it anymore.

"Who are these guys?" I asked suddenly, nodding at the geldings. "They all look pretty fat and happy."

"Ah, the old men." Alexander studied the geldings. "They're just retirees I couldn't easily find new homes for. It happens. The bay there—he had knee chips that just kept coming back, and I said one surgery was enough for any horse. The chestnut with the scar was in a traffic accident while shipping from Gulfstream and the muddy-colored one is just..." Alexander shook his head, chuckling. "He's just *bad*. I sent him out to three different trainers after he was done racing, and he came back from every single one within a month. He raced for five years and he won all over the place, but sometimes they can't settle down into normal life after that. He wasn't even any good as a track pony."

I'd seen that before, with some of the older horses Lucille had brought Diana. The longer a horse spent at the racetrack, the more foreign a life of squealing children and hours trotting around an arena became. "Looks like *this* is normal life, though, if you think about it. Grass, sunshine, sky."

He looked back at me, and just for a moment I thought: *This is the moment, I could take one step closer to him and—*

"Alex, you know—" Thunder interrupted his words, the sound still distant, but deep enough to make the ground seem to rumble. This was a nice, polite storm which wasn't trying to sneak up on us. "I suppose we're in for a storm," he carried on, though in a flatter tone than before. "I was just going to walk up to the stallion barn. You're welcome to join me, if you don't mind waiting out the rain there."

It was silly—I was just a few hundred feet from the safety of my trailer. But I could hardly let him go now. "I'd love to," I said.

❧❧❧❧❧ ❦❦❦❦❦

We swapped horse stories as we walked along the driveway and turned up the hilly lane to the stallion barn. I could hardly believe it was happening, when I gave myself time to think about it—which wasn't very often, because I would stop myself as soon I'd begin. A second or two of wild roaming in my thoughts and I'd miss the point of whatever racetrack parable Alexander was telling me, and wouldn't be able to comment with more than an insipid "Wow!"

So I focused on his tales and volleyed back with stories of my own. For every tale of an impossible two-year-old who became a stakes winner, I had one about a forgettable off-track Thoroughbred who possessed a secret talent to jump like a gazelle, perform a dressage test with aplomb, or carry a child with the softest of strides. I really had gone through an amazing number of horses for my age, I thought at one point, pulling out yet another wonderful story from my memories. Dozens and dozens, most of them Thoroughbreds, all of them in and out of my life in less than six months.

Soon it became pretty clear we were competing for Most Amazing Horse Story, and by the time we'd gotten to the stallion barn I had already fired off my favorite: Swan, the little bay mare Lucille had delivered to Diana and whom I had turned into a twenty-thousand-dollar windfall. (Not to mention my ticket to Ocala.)

"Lucille Cornett's mare, you don't say," Alexander mused, walking into the dark barn. I liked the stallion barn. It was small, just a few stalls on either side of a short center aisle, but the little space felt cozy. The four horses who lived up here peered at us through the stall bars and there were a few deep, rather suggestive neighs.

"What do you think of her?"

"Lucille is a real old-school horsewoman. She's had a tough go of it. Some people work in this business their whole lives and they never cash in with a really good horse. She's one of them."

"So, not like you," I suggested. "What's the difference between the two of you?"

Alexander looked around his little barn, then gazed past me. I turned and realized the view out of the doorway was sensational: this barn aisle commanded the whole farm, from the broodmare pastures in the front, all of the way back to the oak trees lining the back fence. I saw the three geldings in their field, the glint of metal that was a last shifting ray of sunlight hitting my car through the trees, and the dark line of cloud approaching from the east over their wind-tossed branches.

"Money," Alexander said.

"What?" I'd already forgotten what we were talking about, utterly distracted by this breathtaking view. I was looking at the training track in the distance, imagining myself galloping around it each morning. *Me.* I was a *rider* on this spectacular spread. Two weeks ago, I'd been a miserable college student. That life felt like a million years ago.

"You asked the difference between me and someone like Lucille? I said money. Whether it's yours or someone else's, you have to be able to spend, and spend, and spend if you want to get to the winner's circle. You can't do it on guts and passion. That's a fairy tale."

The clouds swept over the farm, a rush of white rain roaring with them. I took a few steps back as lightning flickered over the training track, thunder crashing around us. "You're saying only the rich make it in racing?" I had to speak up as the raindrops pelted on the metal roof.

"I'm saying you *need* money. It doesn't have to be yours, you know. But you have to know where to find it, and you have to know how to use it. That's not an easy skill for a lot of people. Lucille? She's never been close to being in the black. If you made her twenty thou on a horse, that was probably one of her bigger paydays. There's nothing wrong with that in the grand scheme of things—she's still a good trainer, and there's a place for her, but...knowing there's room for a certain type of person doesn't mean you want to *be* that person, either. I'm sure she'd rather be in my position."

"What if you hired her?" It made sense to me. He respected her, he had money, he had good horses. She could do well here.

"Lucille isn't for hire," Alexander said. "That's part of what makes her great, and part of what keeps her poor."

"Have you ever been for hire?" I wasn't sure what made me ask it. Maybe it was the chatter of the grooms, the way Ricky had said Alexander's heart wasn't in it anymore. Maybe it was just a lucky guess, or maybe it was simply that I knew Alexander with a deep familiarity which made absolutely no sense, and I knew how he'd answer before the words left his mouth.

"I've always been for hire," he said stiffly. "That's where all of this comes from."

He sounded disappointed in himself, and my heart went out to him. I felt a trembling, dangerous desire to reach my fingers out, bridge the bare inches between us, and take Alexander's hand in mine.

All at once, I did it.

He glanced at me once, quickly, and then his fingers laced tightly through mine.

So we stood side by side, hand in hand, and watched the rain push through, taking the bright flashes of lightning with it. After maybe a quarter of an hour, the storm was spent, raindrops slowing to a musical drizzle overhead. A cool breeze played up the hillside and swept around my cheeks, still flushed from the walk and the white-hot strain of being so close to Alexander.

Buried in my back pocket, I felt my phone begin to vibrate. *Not now,* I thought desperately as it hummed away.

Alexander glanced down at me. "Don't ignore that on my account. I just need to leave a note for Maureen. Excuse me a moment." His fingers slipped from mine as he turned away, but I felt the warmth his grip had left behind. I closed my fist tightly to hold it in, and sighed as I pulled out my phone with my other hand.

"Hello?" I said, putting the phone to my ear. "This is Alex?"

"*Alex,*" a male voice said, sounding immensely satisfied. "This is Teen Dream calling."

Oh God. The guy I'd met last night. What was his name? Miles. I glanced over my shoulder to check for Alexander, but the barn aisle was empty. The feed room door was open, though, just a dozen feet away. He was going to hear me.

How could that possibly matter? There wasn't going to be anything between us. He was my boss. A man who had glittering women with legs up to there, as the grooms said. I was a sunburned college dropout in cut-offs, and Miles wanted to talk to me because he liked me. Alexander just wanted a little company on a slow afternoon. I should take this call, I told myself. I should be realistic.

"Alex, are you there?"

"Hi, I'm here. Sorry, funny connection out here, you know how it is."

"The rural life! I know. So listen, dinner this week? Do you get any time off?"

"Not really. Just Sundays. But my evenings are free."

"I almost always have a show on Sundays, but what about Wednesday night? Do you like pizza?"

"Any kind but frozen. I've had enough of those this past week to last a lifetime."

He laughed. "Weird, but okay. Tell me about it on Wednesday. I'll pick you up around, say, seven?"

I almost agreed, then remembered the front gate. Emily had told me it was open all day, but a timer closed it after working hours, and I wasn't supposed to give out the code. "I better meet you there. Can you text me directions?"

"You got it. Okay, Alex. Until Wednesday."

I put the phone back into my pocket and busied myself peering in at the stallions until Alexander emerged again. They were older horses, two with gray around their muzzles, sunken hollows above their eyes.

"Sounds like you have a date," Alexander observed cheerfully, and I wished I'd let the call go to voicemail.

"Just dinner with a new friend," I said evasively. "Have to meet some people now that I live up here!"

But Alexander paid me no mind. "Ah, the rain is stopping," he announced. "May as well head home. I have some paperwork to get through this evening." He set off down the hillside without giving me so much as a farewell glance.

I stood in the stallion barn for a few minutes longer, watching him put distance between the two of us. My disappointment was thick in my throat. Had I ruined something just now? Or had it been nothing to him to begin with? How was a girl supposed to know these things?

When he'd turned up the barn lane and disappeared from view, I turned back to the stallions. I knew better than to mess with them; Maureen, their groom, was fiercely protective and didn't like anyone in the barn without her around to chaperone. She arrived early each morning and turned them out in their individual paddocks until she judged the sun too hot for their precious backs, then she brought them all in and gave them soapy baths like they'd gone out for morning gallops. I suspected she came back late every evening and tucked in each one of the imposing horses, with a kiss on the nose and a little lullaby.

"I'd like someone to kiss *me* goodnight," I told the closest horse. He lifted his head briefly at the sound of my voice, then went back to his hay.

"Fine," I said. "I'll leave."

I started to walk out of the stallion barn and head out into the watery afternoon sunlight, but habit made me pause and glance over the aisle before I left, just checking for anything which might go wrong while no one was around. I noticed the feed room door was still open.

"I'll just shut that," I said to myself, and went back inside. I already felt like I shouldn't be up here alone, like Maureen would swoop in and chase me out with a broom.

I really meant to just push the door closed, but curiosity got the better of me and I glanced inside. The feed room was more than just a box stall-sized space given over to trash cans of grain and a few shelves of supplements; it was a lovely, wood-paneled little room, complete with a desk and chair, a bookshelf filled with binders, and one wall devoted to a neat rack of the usual plastic tubs, feed scoops, spare buckets, and various supplies. Two metal trash cans and a stack of feed bags sat underneath. Everything was so glaringly clean, it was obvious the entire room had been dusted this morning.

"Maureen runs a tight ship," I muttered, and went inside for a closer look. I glanced over the supplements and medicines, but finding nothing more outlandish than a tub of bee pollen, which could be fed to horses with allergies or as an all-around health tonic, I turned to leave. I felt nervous being here alone. No one came up here without permission. But then again, Alexander hadn't told me to leave...he hadn't even waited to see if I was going to follow him.

Maybe this barn wasn't such a taboo, after all.

Emboldened, I went behind the desk and sat down in the old rolling chair, giving it a proprietary swivel. No squeal or whine—it was perfectly greased. Even Alexander's chair down in the training barn had a resigned sigh in its spin. The desk was of aging laminate, but it was dust-free, and topped with a spotless desk calendar. A big black diary like the one Alexander used as a training record sat in the center, and I pulled it towards me, expecting to find records of vitals and vet visits.

I wasn't prepared for the bristling black figures which filled the pages.

About half the book was filled, without seeming regard for the dates stamped at the tops of the pages, with names, numbers, arrows, and question marks. At first it all just looked like gibberish, but as I turned the pages, names and numbers began to jump out at me. There were horse names, stallions in this very barn and horses who were winning at the races, and others which bore enough resemblance to prominent stallions to tell me they were progeny. There were years, there were the grades of stakes races, there were numbers which might have been purse takings or stud fees or both.

I drew my finger under one line and stared at it hard, trying to decipher it.

Country Lad 92—Vice Versatile 99 G2 250000 ? Brightliner 13000. A-

The numbers after the names had to be years, so Country Lad was born in 1992 and Vice Versatile in 1999. The G2 would be Grade Two Stakes, the second-highest tier of race, and the 250000 must be earnings of a quarter million dollars. That made sense, although whether it could be earnings for a race, a year, or a career were up in the air. All the rest: the question mark, the name Brightliner, the 13000, the A-, those still had me stumped.

And then there was a note on the next page: *A wants top nicks by Oct—full bookings by Nov—commits to full year??*

"Who is A?" I asked the book. An owner, I guessed...or the partner?

Was it the woman? Adriene?

I turned the page, but there was nothing else. The rest of the book was blank. When had he last written in this book? The cover was clean, the ink was sharply black. On the first few pages, though, it had started to yellow a little. The most recent notes were dark. If they were from the past few days, it meant he'd been talking to whoever A was.

And if it was Adriene, Walt was wrong when he'd said she wasn't in the picture anymore.

The sound of tires on gravel came through the open doorway. My heart leapt into my throat and I slammed the book shut, anxiously shoving it back to the center of the desk where I'd found it. I nearly fell over the swivel chair as I pushed past it, and my hand rapped the corner of the desk as I jumped out from behind it. I was only at the door of the feed room when the truck door slammed and I knew I'd been caught.

So I did the only thing I could think of: I looked around for something to do. *Look busy, the boss is coming* had been my life's motto since I was thirteen. Diana didn't like a working student who sat around.

Finding a job in Maureen's perfect barn was my greatest challenge yet, but luckily my eyes happened upon a basket of clean leg wraps that was just barely overflowing. I gave the basket a little shake with my knee and the top wrap tipped out, its tight coil coming undone and flowing across the concrete floor in a waterfall of hunter green. I snatched the wrap and started rolling it back up.

And that's what I was doing when Maureen came in.

We'd met briefly in the training barn, but now she didn't seem to recognize me right away. She stood in the doorway, a small woman with tight brown curls and a turned-up nose, and fastened suspicious hazel eyes on me. "Who're you?" she demanded.

I finished rolling up the standing wrap. My speech was memorized already. "I'm Alex, from the training barn. I was up here with Alexander waiting out the rain and some of the wraps had fallen out of their basket, so I was putting them away before I left."

Her eyes narrowed, taking in the wrap in my hands. "You were up here with Alexander?"

"Yes...you didn't see him walking back up the lane?" Maybe I'd been up here longer than I'd realized. I didn't dare look at my watch to find out.

"I didn't," she groused. "But okay. You can go back to the training barn now. I'm here to feed dinner."

One of the stallions nickered, as if he recognized the word *dinner*, and the others all chimed in as well.

I hesitated. It felt weird to walk away while there was work to be done, even if today was Sunday and I was technically off. "I can help you if you want?"

"No, no, it's only four horses," Maureen said gruffly, but I thought her face softened a little, as if she liked to be asked. "I'm used to working on my own."

"Well, bye then," I said, putting the wrap back in its basket. "Have a good night."

I felt her gaze on my back as I walked down the driveway. Like Alexander, I didn't turn around.

But that was a mistake, I realized later, sitting on my couch and puzzling over the notes in the book. Quiet, efficient, loyal Maureen probably knew exactly what was going on with the business, Alexander, and Adriene. I should have stayed and charmed her into telling me.

Now the whole puzzle was going to drive me crazy.

Chapter Sixteen

B Y THE MIDMORNING BREAK on Monday, the training barn was abuzz with some exciting new gossip: Alexander was sending two horses to the races.

I had come down to the center aisle after handing off a freshly-bathed Wing to a hot walker, following my nose as the spicy scents of our breakfast floated down the shed-row. The Taco Lady had arrived, her minivan's trunk popped up so she could hand out that day's selections. There were always tacos, flimsy corn tortillas bursting with their payload of spiced meat, cilantro, and chopped onion, but some days she made other treats: tortas, flautas, and sometimes even delicious tamales, wrapped in palm leaves and tied with string.

"I saved you a chair, Alex," Jacinta crowed as I handed over a few dollars to the smiling Taco Lady and took my foil-wrapped tacos from her. "Had to fend off Juan to do it. Sit on a bucket when there's a lady present, Juan!" she added, cackling at his sour expression. There weren't enough chairs for everyone, but flipped-over buckets which had previously held industrial quantities of WindFresh detergent were plentiful. Juan balanced himself carefully on top of one.

I gave Juan a meek smile of thanks and settled into the chair. "So, who is going to the races?" I asked. "Ricky said two horses were going to Gulfstream on Wednesday and staying there to run over the weekend."

"None of yours," she said, biting into a taco. "Envision Light, Walt rides him in the last set most days, and Appleton Nelly, that goofball filly that Juan rides most mornings." She waved at Juan, who was still glaring in our direction. "Juan, what odds will you give me on Nelly?"

He snorted. "Don't waste your money. She no ready for that company. She gonna run like a rat."

"Same with Envision," Jacinta snorted.

I was flummoxed. "Why would he send a horse who isn't ready?"

Jacinta shrugged. "It happens."

But it *didn't* happen. Not with Alexander Whitehall, anyway. He was well-known for his above-average success winning with first-time starters, and conditioning horses to the exact moment of peak performance. "A great conditioner," the journalists had called him.

Until he stopped winning. Now, they didn't call him anything at all.

The entire situation just didn't make sense. I shook my head and unwrapped my own tacos. The morning break was always short; the grooms would finish first and slip away to get the next set ready, giving the riders a few extra minutes, but I had already ridden my four. It was time for me to turn back into Ricky's apprentice.

Better eat and forget Alexander, I told myself. *He's really not your problem.*

I couldn't let it go, though. I watched every horse as they rounded the shed-row that morning, and spent a little too much time peering across the paddocks to the training track, trying to get an idea of how the horses in each set were working, and consequently falling behind in my chores. Ricky had to catch a horse for me in the shed-row when I wasn't finished cleaning out the stall in time, and the look he gave me was withering. *Weak,* his glare said. *Not good enough.*

I was so embarrassed, I rushed to empty my wheelbarrow and overturned the whole damn thing on the ramp to the manure spreader. This did not improve matters.

Alexander was missing half the morning, but he came back for the last set and walked out behind them, not bothering to tack up Betsy. I hustled through my last stall, leaning the stuffed hay-net against the wall to be tied up once the horse was walked dry, and managed to fill up the water buckets just before the riders came back. Juan wheeled his horse into the stall as I pulled the hose back into the shed-row, tucking it up along the wall for safety.

The horse Walt had just brought back was one of the rumored shippers: Envision Light, a chestnut gelding who had been back at the farm for several months after a spring in Tampa, according to Ricky. He was four, a veteran of ten starts, and had won just one race.

Walt stripped his tack and stepped back, looking over the horse. "He look okay to you?"

I glanced at the steaming colt. He was breathing hard, but he didn't look too blown by the workout. "Hot, but he just needs a bath."

Walt nodded. "Good enough. That was an okay gallop. He could be more fit, but he's sound. I'll work him tomorrow—we'll do breezes tomorrow, so he'll get a good work in before he ships to the track. Breezes are fast works, timed," he added, in case I didn't know already.

"Will a breeze tell you if he's ready to run a race?" I asked, trying to buckle the halter. Envision leaned against me, trying to rub his sweaty head on my shoulder. I had to shove him off to get the halter fastened.

Walt shrugged and looked back over the horse, his expression skeptical. "It'll probably tell us he's not ready for Gulfstream company," he admitted. "But that's where the racing is right now, so that's where he's going. If he loses, it won't be by twenty or thirty lengths, anyway. I don't *think.*"

"Still, isn't it hard on horses to lose races?" I asked, knowing I probably sounded like a naïve child, asking about a horse's feelings. "They're competitive, it must be tough on them...mentally, I mean."

"It's tough on them all around to lose a race. Every race is tough. Puttin' them in the gate when you know they don't stand a chance...yeah, that feels kinda wrong. But it's not our call, kid. And sometimes you get results. Sometimes you take a chance and you get your picture taken."

"It doesn't sound like Alexander," I persisted. "I've read all the old interviews. That was never how he did things. He wasn't a guy who won races by taking chances. He won them by being ready. He knew where to put horses."

"You're right," Walt said, ducking under the stall chain with the saddle over his arm, the girth trailing through the shavings. "But things haven't been the same for Alexander these past few years. And maybe we shouldn't be judgin' him without knowin' what he's dealin' with."

I'd started to lead Envision to the doorway, but the warning tone in Walt's voice made me pause. The horse tugged at me and I gave a little jiggle to the chain over his nose, reminding him not to get too pushy just because he was a big strong racehorse. *Walt knows something,* I thought. *Walt knows what's going on.*

My mind went back to the diary in the stallion barn, the cryptic horse names and numbers, the dashed lines and question marks. *A signing on for another full year.*

Whatever had brought Alexander down over the past three years, the scribbles in that book were tied up in it somehow. I wasn't looking for a mystery. I wasn't the kind of person who watched crime shows and tried to guess the ending. But there was something unexplained about Alexander's fall from the top of racing, and his lackadaisical attitude towards it all.

I just knew that somewhere in those notes was the key to Alexander's decline.

And if I could figure it all out, maybe I could help turn things around.

Alexander was working in the barn office when the workers started to scatter, some for a lunch break and some for the day. I lingered in the tack room, rolling up some bandages still warm from the dryer, until the last car door had slammed and the last rumbling, rattling old pickup had disappeared from the barn's parking area. Then I swallowed and squared my shoulders. If he wanted me to watch and learn, he had to be ready for me to ask questions...right?

I paused in the office doorway for a good minute or two, unnoticed by Alexander. He was bent over his work, writing steadily into a fat notebook. Every now and then he glanced over at a little open booklet, or thumbed through the pages of a glossy magazine. Every page seemed to be a photo of another horse. Most were conformation shots, the horse standing up straight and tall, gazing into the distance, but a few were racing images. After a moment's puzzling, I realized it was a stallion catalog, showcasing Thoroughbreds available for breeding.

Breeding season began in February. I supposed late September wasn't too soon to start thinking about stallions...but what of the four horses up in the stallion barn? How many more bloodlines could Alexander possibly want for his two dozen broodmares?

Or were they A's horses?

I cleared my throat at last, ready to be noticed. I was tired of mysteries. It was time to ask questions.

He looked up, his eyebrows coming together, then sliding apart as he realized it was me. An expression of pleasure flitted across his features, and I felt my heart lift in response. He *wanted* to see me. I mattered to him. For a moment, the purpose of my visit vanished and we were just two people in a room. Two people who liked each other.

"Alexander," I said gently, "you're working through lunch?"

"Only a little late. Adri—someone wanted these matches sent over as soon as possible, and I thought I'd just knock them out here rather than facing Emily down in the office. She always has an almighty pile of messages for me to work through."

I leaned on the cold metal doorframe, trying to look casual, although I'd heard the way he'd skipped around the name of whoever wanted his files. He'd been saying Adriene. She was A, then. "What sort of matches are they? Is this for breeding? Can I see?"

"Certainly. Come and have a look."

Well, it wasn't a secret, whatever he was doing. I stepped up to the chair facing his desk and paused. He hadn't turned the catalog or his papers around for me to see. Very well, then. I went around the desk and stood next to him, leaned over his elbow, breathed in his scent of leather and cotton and clean soap, and felt just a little dizzy at his nearness.

Normal boss-employee relations.

Alexander seemed unaffected by my presence, but I probably smelled more like hay and horse sweat and, *hopefully*, Degree Extra-Strong, so I decided not to be offended when he didn't turn to me with stars in his eyes and declare his undying love. Maybe after a shower. We had time. "So, this is a stallion catalog, right?"

"A register, or a catalog, that's right." He tapped the photo of the horse he was looking at. A big, strong-looking bay gazed into the distance. Green pastures and black-board fences stretched across the background. "My client wants to breed to one of four stallions, and she needs recommendations for each of her mares. There are programs which crunch all the numbers, but I'm a bit old-fashioned...I'd rather make notes on each one to accompany all of that high-tech reporting. I've done most of the work, but she had a few more names for me to look at today." He slid his notebook over for me to look at.

I ran my eyes over the strong black handwriting. I recognized some of the names. "This," I said, placing my finger on a line. "Where it says *Not for Love x 2.* That means the stallion has Not for Love in his bloodline twice?"

"Close," he said, smiling up at me like I was a favorite pupil. "The prospective foal would have Not for Love twice, on the stallion's side *and* the dam's side."

"And that's a good thing because..."

"Not for Love is a successful sire from a very influential family, but *not* from the stallion Mr. Prospector, which can be a bit hard to find in the particular cross we're looking for. We're trying to outcross away from Mr. P. for this mare. And he's everywhere, Alex...that stallion's progeny are absolutely everywhere." Alexander shook his head, clearly overcome at the thought of all those Mr. Prospector grandbabies flooding Thoroughbred farms across the nation. "Which is fine, but we can't have every horse bred three by three to Mr. P., now can we?"

"No," I agreed, because it sounded bad, not because I totally understood. Breeding was definitely its own animal. I'd have to focus on it seriously once I'd learned more about riding. And conditioning. And racing stable management. "But a *little* inbreeding is good, right?"

"It can be, certainly. Or you can try for an outcross, too. You try one, then you try the other." He tapped his pen on the book, looking thoughtful. For a moment I thought he'd say something else, but then I realized he'd drifted away, lost on the currents of his own musings.

I shifted on my feet, desperate to get him back. When his attention was focused on me, I felt wrapped in a warm glow. When his thoughts wandered, the air around me turned cold. "What about Envision Light?" I blurted. "What's his cross?"

He turned his gaze back to me. "Funny you should ask," he said. "A grandson of Mr. Prospector, who is by Raise a Native, on his sire's side. And Envision has Raise a Native *twice* on his dam's side, but *not* through Mr. Prospector. It's through a broodmare named Suspicious Native, and also through Alydar."

My eyebrows went up. *"Alydar,* the one who came in second in all three Triple Crown races? He lost them all to Affirmed, who won the Triple Crown, right?"

"But he won almost everything else there was to win, yes..."

"And then he died under mysterious circumstances?"

Alexander nodded. "Although that particular outcome didn't result from his breeding, so I leave it out of my notes."

"Can you believe that's one of the first racing stories I can remember reading? It was a feature in *Horse Illustrated.* I think it was like, the second issue I ever got. And it had a big article on Alydar and whether he *really* kicked his stall door and broke his leg, or someone arranged the break for the insurance money. My mom thought it was inappropriate reading for a child."

"An unfortunate introduction to the sport," Alexander said. Already, I could hear the distance coming back into his voice.

I was losing him. "Does Envision Light have anything else cool in his pedigree?"

"I can't recall anything. He's an average sort of horse."

"But, he's ready to win a race next week, so that's exciting for him."

There was a pause while Alexander considered his answer. It was long enough to make me realize Walt was right. The horse wasn't ready to win at Gulfstream, and Alexander knew it.

"He's had a long lay-off," Alexander conceded eventually. "He's not training very brightly. He needs a race to wake him up."

"But he has a shot," I persisted. "Surely you wouldn't ship him all the way to south Florida if he didn't have a shot."

Suddenly Alexander closed his book, and I stepped back, feeling a change in his posture. He was angry with me. Or—maybe it wasn't me.

He didn't look at me as he began gathering his stallion register and files together, putting them into a neat stack. "You're new to this game," he said gruffly. "Not every decision is the trainer's to make. Sometimes an owner says to go run the horse, and you go find the best race you possibly can. If he runs badly—well—then that's another conversation to have. The only real question is how long the owner will put up with it, before making a change."

He stood up from the table and I felt myself being dismissed, but I hung on for another moment, pressed by some demon to continue digging until he gave me the truth—or just enough information to confirm my suspicions.

"Does Envision have the same owner as the mares you're working on?"

"Would you like to go through my records? They're in the office. Tell Emily you're feeling nosy and would like a rummage through the business files." He was properly upset with me now.

"I'm just trying to understand how it all works." I set my jaw and forced myself to meet his eyes. His blue irises were stormy and dark, narrowed down at me beneath fiercely-drawn brows. My pulse leapt, but I kept my tone steady. "I'm here to learn about the whole business, remember? Not just to get on horses and get them around the track. That was what you said."

Throwing his words back at him seemed to do the trick. His eyebrows unknotted ever so slightly, and he studied me for a moment, as if trying to decide what to do with me.

I had a few ideas, but none of them were really appropriate to the moment. Still, he was damned sexy when he was looking riled up.

"The answer's yes," he said finally. "I have one major owner who is my biggest partner right now. She owns most of the horses in this barn. She owns half the broodmares. And she co-owns my two younger stallions."

I've always been for hire, Alexander had said in the stallion barn. *That's where all of this comes from.*

None of this was really his. The truth, after watching him from afar for so many years, was staggering. Alexander Whitehall had been presented to the public as a gentleman of old family, a Mr. Darcy of horse racing, with ten thousand per year and an estate in his own name.

In reality, we'd all just been fawning over his accent and making some big assumptions about his income.

Alexander was pushing past me, his hand on my arm, gently steering me out of his way. "Go and get yourself some lunch," he said as he passed. "You're needed up here this afternoon."

I stood in the empty office for a few moments after he left—so long that Walt nearly closed the door on me. He saw me at the last moment and opened it again, looking startled. "And what are you doing in there, Miss Alex? Alexander went back to the house. He won't be back this afternoon. If you're waitin' for him, go ask Emily to call him up for you."

"Oh, no. I was just thinking, I guess. We were talking and then he left—I wasn't snooping through the desk or anything!" I laughed, and Walt grinned.

"Naw, I wouldn't suspect you of anything too crazy. Maureen, now, she told me she nearly fell over some blonde girl in the stallion barn and she was all sorts of put out over it...but that's just how she is. Likes her privacy up there."

I scooted through the doorway and let him close the door. "Walt, do you know the name of the lady who owns Envision?" I asked, trying to sound casual. "Just wondering if I've ever heard of her from my racetrack friends." As if I had ever known more than one person involved in racing. As if Lucille Cornett could really be called my friend. But knowing her had had gotten me this far...

"Oh now, you want to know about the owners." Walt slammed the bolt home on the office door and we started walking towards our cars. "I'd stay out of that."

"Messy?"

"Extremely. But I've told you that. It's always messy with partners."

"So Envision is the *partner's* horse, too?" I knew he was. "What's her name?"

Walt hesitated. "You don't want to get mixed up—"

"Adriene?" I asked. "Is her name Adriene?"

Walt shrugged. He looked out over the paddocks, where a few older horses were grazing, swishing their tails and stomping away the midday flies. "Well, do you know Adriene Hartwell?" he asked suddenly.

Hartwell. "Do I know her?" I repeated.

"You said you might have heard of her from your racetrack friends." Walt peered at me. "So do you?"

"Oh." I was flustered. Say yes, and he'd want to know how. Say no, and he'd want to know why her name came to my mind so quickly. "I think I've heard her mentioned," I lied hurriedly. "But I can't remember when it was. Just a striking sort of name, you know? It sounds..." What had the grooms said about her? *Alexander has fancier pieces than that.* "Fancy."

Walt chuckled, seeming satisfied with my answer. "It sure does," he agreed. "Real fancy. Well, go to lunch. See you in an hour."

I got into my car and sat for a moment, hands on the wheel, waiting while Walt got into his pick-up and drove off down the lane. I had food back at the trailer; there was no need to go pick something up. I could enjoy my air conditioning for a while, put on some clean clothes, rest up for the afternoon's barn chores.

Or I could go up to the office, start opening magazines from that treasure trove on the bookshelves, and see if I could learn anything about Adriene Hartwell.

Chapter Seventeen

EMILY WAS HUMMING AS she typed, a tuneless little song which was starting to make me a little crazy. I wished she'd turn on the radio or something; then I remembered that every white person in Ocala listened to the same classic rock station, playing the same ten songs over and over, and I decided I'd better be careful what I wished for.

What I was *really* wishing for, of course, was some mention of Adriene Hartwell in the past year's issues of *The Blood-Horse*. I'd been flipping pages and skimming text for almost my entire lunch hour, paying close attention to any story about Florida-breds or Florida racing, but so far, nothing was coming up. I was beginning to see that it was very easy for owners and breeders to vanish in this game; the trainers picked up most of the press, followed very distantly by the jockeys—which was amazing, since they were the actual pilots during the races—and only the very top-tier breeders got any mention at all.

By the end of my lunch hour, the only thing I'd learned for certain was Adriene Hartwell wasn't an owner at any big farms like

Claiborne or Spendthrift or Three Chimneys and, well, I'd known *that* already.

The alarm beeped on my phone and I looked at the scattered magazines I'd spread across the coffee table. Emily's humming stopped. "Was that you?" she asked.

"Yeah, it means my lunch is over," I sighed. "Let me clean this up and I'll get out of your hair."

"Oh, you're fine," Emily trilled. "You're quiet as a mouse, didn't even remember you were here." I heard her desk chair creak, and her clicky little heels crossing the tiles, and then she was standing over me, looking at my magazines. "Did you find what you wanted?"

"Just learning," I lied. "Just trying to absorb everything as quickly as possible."

"Oh, you don't have to know all of this." Emily stooped and started gathering magazines into the crook of one arm. "I barely know the front end of a horse from the back end, and I've been working in this business since I got out of college. You know how to ride, so what else do you need?"

I guessed Emily wasn't used to ambitious riders, but I was definitely surprised she didn't know anything about horses. "You're not a horse person? How would you end up working in the racing business?"

She laughed. "Around here it's just the local business. I guess I'd be working in timber if I lived up in Georgia, or, I don't know, oysters or something if I lived up around the Big Bend." She started dropping the magazines back into their slipcase. "But don't let me stop you if this is how you want to spend your lunch hour. Maybe you'll get a promotion! I guess Alexander could use an assistant with some smarts. His partner was his last assistant, but she seems to break the place every time she comes through the front gate." She glanced at me through her eyelashes and pursed her lips mischievously. "Oops. Don't repeat that."

Nice try, Emily. Now I was on to the story, and I wasn't about to let her quit on me. "Why did she leave? What happened?"

Emily gave the front door a dramatic look before she responded, as if she expected Alexander to materialize. "She went back to England. They had a huge fight. It wasn't the first time, either."

Jackpot! "When was this?"

"A few months ago? Maybe more. It was during breeding season so...yeah, I'd say six months ago. Alexander was doing okay through the fall last year. Then she came back in January and started working up in the barn and calling herself a trainer, and it just went to hell. He brought all the horses back from the tracks and they had a blowout. *Everyone* was talking—" Emily stopped short and cocked her head. "He's coming."

"Alexander?" My heart did its thing.

"I heard the house's side door slam. It sticks, you have to really bang it." Emily smiled that mischievous grin again. "I'd ask the maintenance guys to fix it, but then I'd lose my Alexander alarm."

I heard footsteps on gravel. I started scrambling to pick up the rest of the magazines and drop them back into their cases, as if I could possibly get them all put away and sneak out before Alexander came inside. What if he guessed what I was up to? After all the questions I'd asked in the training barn, it was at least *possible* he'd realize I was doing some heavy research on his past.

Alexander came into the office, bringing a gust of humid air in with him, and stopped short when he saw me.

Our eyes met, and I felt a ripple of electricity charge between us.

Emily just went on putting magazines away, oblivious.

His gaze tugged away from mine and he glanced over the magazines. I watched his eyebrows go up.

I dropped my last few issues into their case and slid them hastily into the bookcase, eager to get out before I had to explain myself. "I better get back to work," I mumbled, slipping past him. I skipped into the parking lot and started speed-walking to my car before he could say anything.

∽∽∽∽ ∾∾∾∾

I was dead tired and absolutely starving when I got back to the trailer that night. Maybe skipping lunch to study magazines hadn't been my best idea. I might have managed better if we hadn't gotten an hour's extra work tacked onto the day.

Maureen had come back from her lunch break with the dire news of a strangles outbreak at a show barn south of Ocala, and Walt announced we'd have to take every horse's temperature twice a day, starting immediately.

"It's a nasty disease, and people can carry it around with them," he explained. "And it stays in the soil for years. If any of the big farms catch it, there'll be quarantines and it might bounce around some, so...we're just going to make sure we stay ahead of it."

Taking temps was a very time-consuming, very dirty, and, occasionally, very dangerous undertaking. After some quick negotiations between Walt and the other barn managers, I found myself carted off to the broodmare barn with Kimberly, the broodmare manager, to help her with the two dozen mares in her care. Since most of the mares lived outside, we fed them an early dinner in their little outdoor stalls, called catch-pens, which allowed us to get in and take their temps while they were eating.

"Okay," I said, once all of the mares were in their catch-pens. "How are we going to do this?"

Kimberly extracted a clipboard from her golf cart. "One of us will take temps and the other one will write them down. We'll go halfway down and switch. Which end do you want first?"

I considered the job ahead. If the mares were still eating, they'd be more likely to ignore the person fiddling with their tail. Once they were done, they'd be pushy and ready to leave. "I'll do temps first," I offered, and Kimberly agreed.

She handed me a glass thermometer. "Harder to read than digital," she said, "but more accurate."

Catch-pens weren't big enough for the mares to turn around—they had to back out when they were done eating—but they were still plenty wide enough if an athletic Thoroughbred horse wanted to wiggle around and cause trouble for a groom who just needed to slip a thermometer under her tail for a quick minute and then get the heck out of Dodge. The older mares were cooperative and ignored me, but the younger mares tended to take things like this personally. When tails were wrung and ears were pinned, Kimberly leaned over the fence and took hold of the mare's halter, speaking to her in low, threatening tones, which mostly did the trick...but still, by the time I reached the halfway point, I was nursing several bruised toes, a sore elbow which had been slammed into a fence-post, and considered one of my fingers to be permanently crooked.

"That was painful," I croaked, sliding between two fence boards.

Kimberly handed me the clipboard and took the thermometer. "That's horse life for ya," she said with a wry grin, and ducked through the fence herself. "Just be glad you're not doing the two-year-olds or the yearlings."

I was very glad I had been sent down from the training barn; when I got back up there to help with evening feeding, I saw Walt walking with a decided limp and Ricky pressing two fingers against a cold soda can. "You miss all the fun," Ricky told me, wincing as he adjusted his grip. "Tomorrow, I'm telling Walt you stay up here and help us."

Ugh, tomorrow we had to do all of this again! How long was this going to last? I shook my head. "I'm good, thanks. Kimberly and I make a great team. Wouldn't want to split us up now."

"This better not last long," Ricky muttered, throwing Walt a spiteful glance. "I don't get paid enough to shove tubes up horses' butts all day long."

It was true, I thought, walking back down the lane towards home. None of us got paid very much, certainly not for the danger we placed ourselves in every day. Riding paid more than grooming, and grooming paid more than hot-walking, and everything paid more than maintenance, the domain of two guys who drove around the property with paint brushes and toolkits, constantly nailing up fence boards or touching up door-frames scarred by long yellow teeth.

But I knew all of this low-wage, high-risk work was going to be worth it in the end. *Racehorses,* I thought happily, looking around at the pastures and paddocks. The retired geldings in the back pasture saw me coming; one whickered, hoping I had some treats in my pockets.

Damn. I'd skipped lunch and now I didn't have anything leftover for the retirees. I rummaged in my jeans pocket and came up with a folded-over wrapper; inside there was half a granola bar, gooey with melted chocolate chips. My stomach rumbled immediately; I'd eaten half of it this morning and run out of time to finish when a set came back from the track, then forgotten all about it. I could have devoured it in a single bite now, but the geldings heard the wrapper crinkling and they were coming in a hurry. The chubby bay actually broke into a trot.

"Fine," I told them, and, leaning over the fence, I gave all three horses a bite of granola bar. They pushed and strained to get at my hands, long tongues lapping, hoping for more. Then the bay bit the chestnut and they both squealed. "Get out of here!" I scolded them, waving my hands. "Shoo! Git!"

The geldings spun and took off running, snorting and bucking.

I watched them for a moment, thinking about Alexander—the sort of person who kept a couple of retired geldings safe and happy at pasture even though their earning potential was nil. Horses weren't free just because they were on grass; they still needed hoof care, vet check-ups and treatment, grooming and feeding, all sorts of hands-on stuff. Most people wouldn't keep them.

Alexander wasn't most people, and that was why I kept coming back to the puzzle of Envision Light, the horse who wasn't ready to run. Why was he sending the horse too Gulfstream? Was someone else really calling the shots?

The questions troubled me all the way back to the house.

Jacinta made us dinner while I was in the shower. Mac and cheese, from the store-brand box, not the blue one. But hey, free food that I didn't have to cook? Score.

"Thanks for cooking. What's the occasion?" I asked, pulling my wet hair into a bun.

"You had to do all those temps today. I don't want you getting scared off and quitting." Jacinta grinned at me, spooning up a heaping bowl of mac and cheese. "I know we're losing a couple horses, but the yearlings are coming up to the training barn next week. It's gonna get busy and we'll need everyone. Plus, yearlings are fun. You don't want to miss this."

"The yearlings, huh." I'd been waiting for this. I was nervous about the prospect. Riding the older horses was one thing; teaching youngsters to gallop around the track? I was pretty sure this was going to hurt. "Everyone keeps talking about them and I have no idea what's coming."

Jacinta laughed. "It's gonna feel like all babies, all the time. First week, we're just bouncin' around the shed-row and that don't take much time, but soon we'll start takin' them out in the fields, workin' them in drills, and then once they know all their manners, they'll be goin' out for morning gallops just like the big horses. We'll be ridin' past noon for a *while.*" Jacinta opened a can of seltzer and took a deep gulp. She sighed with satisfaction. "And I'll take a little break from ridin' extra horses all around town, which will be awfully nice."

"Right." I took a bite of mac and cheese. Hey, store-brand was just like the blue box. Who knew? The flavor and texture reminded me of dinners at home, and by extension my mom, and I made a mental note to call and check-in with her before too many more days passed.

She'd like to know I was going to be riding full-time soon, instead of just a few horses early in the morning. It felt like a step in the right direction.

"You wanna watch some TV? I got some old Breeders' Cups on tape, they're in the VCR."

"That would be great," I agreed happily. Mac and cheese, horse racing on the TV, and an ex-jockey sitting next to me ready to explain everything I'd ever wanted to know. This was the life for me.

"Let's go way back," she suggested, picking up the remote. "Wanna see when Alexander won the Turf a few years back?"

"Yes! That was what, four years ago?"

"Yup. A big deal. He was young to win such a big race." Jacinta glanced at me sideways. "Still young, to have so much."

I filled my mouth with pasta to avoid answering. What was that coy look of hers? What was she implying?

What had I let slip in her company?

Jacinta fast-forwarded through the usual Breeders' Cup commercials: stallions standing at stud, expensive brandy, watches for millionaires. It was funny to live amongst racing people, the actual folks on the ground who ate, breathed, and slept horse racing, and contrast these commercials against our actual lives. Everything geared towards the rich owners and players had nothing to do with the real business of raising and racing horses.

"Here we go." Jacinta let the tape play. That year, the Breeders' Cup races had been held at Santa Anita, in southern California. The sky above the track was a stoney gray, and the turf course looked a little drought-stricken, but the palm trees lining the homestretch were all Hollywood-glam, and the stony mountains just beyond the track were an incredibly striking backdrop. "He's got the three horse in this race."

"It's Virtuous, right? One of the stallions up in the barn. The young one." I leaned forward, excited to think a horse just a short distance away was on screen right now. He pranced through the post parade and then was sent away to warm up alone, his white socks skimming over the track in a ground-covering gallop. "It's so British to start without a pony, isn't it?"

"Yup," Jacinta agreed. "But you see it more and more, I think. Especially in turf, because European horses *win*. Alexander showed up and everyone said, 'Oh no, a Brit's coming to take our turf money,' and they were right for a long time."

Until they weren't. I took another bite and watched Virtuous gallop up the track.

The race itself was a typical turf battle, with one horse leading the way until the homestretch, and then a sudden surge of competition as the other horses were put into an all-out drive. When Virtuous finally stuck his nose in front, he was just three strides from the wire and had emerged from a pack of six; there was a photo for the second and third place finishes.

I loved watching the dark horse run, but it was the winner's circle I was really waiting for. If Adriene owned half the stallions today, did that mean she'd owned half of Virtuous four years ago? Would she be there? I put down my bowl and leaned forward, elbows perched on my knees.

The camera found Alexander. He was wearing the same outfit he'd worn in the picture I'd cut out of the magazine, when he'd posed with Beginner's Goodbye—the photo was probably from the same day, now that I thought about it. The long tan jacket, the smart dark trousers and shirt, the flat cap: he was the very image of a British horse trainer, and with those laughing blue eyes and those pale eyebrows and that long jaw...I drank in four-years-ago Alexander hungrily. What had changed about him in the past few years? Not much, although I'd have to say he didn't look nearly as happy today as he had that day.

Well, he'd just won the biggest turf race of the year.

But still.

He was talking into the fat felt head of a microphone, but I wasn't listening, I was peering into the faces behind him, willing the camera to pan out just a little, give me an idea of who was in his entourage.

"Adriene, say a few words," Alexander said, turning his head.

I froze.

A lovely woman appeared beside Alexander. She could have been a movie star: white skin, coils of raven hair, diamonds shimmering in her ears and at her throat. She was wearing an elaborate blue hat and a pearly smile as big as the Ritz.

"He's a wonderful colt," she said, her crisp British accent a perfectly feminine version of Alexander's. "We think the world of him, and I know this isn't his highest achievement. There's more to come."

It was the voice from the barbecue restaurant.

Jacinta nudged me. "Look at Alexander's face."

I tore my eyes from Adriene and peered at Alexander. His smile had slipped, and he was looking sideways at Adriene with a pensive expression. "What is it? Was this the colt's last race? I can't remember."

"Yup. And he knew it the whole time. But she thought she was takin' him to Europe to run. And Alexander turned her down flat."

"How do you know that? Were you here then?"

"I heard it from Maureen," Jacinta said contentedly. "She was in the room. She said the fight nearly brought down the pictures on the wall, and when it was over Miss Adriene went pouting back to England, and she didn't come back for a whole year. As soon as Alexander started to win a few, she was back, and the whole thing started again. Maureen says she can't stay away from him when he's winnin' races. She has to have her hand in the pie. But when she's here, it all goes to hell."

I sat back, feeling slightly winded. "So she just keeps coming back and wrecking things?"

"From the sound of it. I've only been here since last fall, but when she came back in winter, Walt just shook his head and said *here we go again.*"

Adriene was the slump. I blinked at the television, not seeing the horses on the screen, just the diamonds flashing on the woman who wouldn't leave Alexander alone.

Jacinta put the tape on pause and got up. "I'm getting more, you want some?"

I realized my bowl was empty. "Definitely. I'll get it, though." I followed her into the kitchen, wondering what else I could reasonably ask her about Alexander and Adriene. Was it just simple curiosity to wonder if a man was seeing a woman? Or would that immediately come off as being too interested? I wished I'd had more girlfriends over the past few years. I'd have a better idea of what was normal and what was a dead giveaway. The last thing I needed was Jacinta getting the idea that I *liked* Alexander or something crazy like that.

Something crazy...like that. I heaped my bowl with reckless abandon, suddenly feeling like I had a big sad hole in my belly to fill up. Because it *was* crazy. No matter what I learned about Adriene, or whether Alexander was really single, or whether there was some hole in his life or *whatever,* it was crazy to think we could ever be together.

I was trying to shoot way out of my league just by thinking about it. And that was what all of this was, in the end. It wasn't idle curiosity. It wasn't even as if I could step in and save things, push Adriene out and give Alexander the distance he couldn't seem to buy for himself. It was just a burning need to understand what Alexander's past was, so I could try and fit myself into his future.

It's not going to happen, I told myself, following Jacinta back into the living room.

Time to move on.

I had a date with Miles in a few days, I reminded myself. It would be good for me to meet someone else. Who knew what might happen? Maybe Miles and I were an awesome match.

Chapter Eighteen

T**HE PIZZA PLACE WAS** on the other side of Ocala, but I didn't mind the drive. I was still taking in the novelty of living in a new place for the first time in my life.

I took a few wrong turns, but I also passed some magnificent horse farms, the sorts of places you only saw in magazines...places like Cotswold Farm, honestly. The realization made me shake my head in wonder. It was still so hard to believe I was really here, living this life—but being out amidst all these other showplace farms helped me distinguish the reality from the dream. This *was* my reality. I was a rider, I was learning the sport of horse racing, I was living at one of the most beautiful Thoroughbred farms in Ocala. It was all real.

The only dream was my crush on Alexander, and hey, I'd get over that eventually, right? I was driving to a date. That was a good first step. Maybe Miles wasn't the man I dreamed of, but at least he had come across as really nice and uncomplicated. As far as I could tell, he wasn't harboring a dark secret, and he didn't have a long history of dating extremely beautiful, extremely rich women.

These factors could only be considered positives when comparing him against my boss.

The restaurant he'd chosen for our date was a tiny storefront in a strip mall, wedged between an old Winn-Dixie and a dusty-looking fabric store, and looked like it hadn't been redecorated since the sixties. I liked the whole dripping-candles-in-wine-bottles vibe. It was like we were in *Lady and the Tramp* or something.

Still, I made a mental note not to order any spaghetti and meatballs. I was not about to recreate any adorably romantic movie scenes. I was just here to get to know Miles a little better. Maybe Miles would be perfect. Maybe we'd fall in love and we'd support each other—I'd go see him at horse shows, he could come cheer for my horses at the track. There could be a happy, idyllic horsey future waiting for us. You never knew, right? Hope for the best.

Prepare for the worst, my helpful brain reminded me.

I went into the restaurant, muffled bells chiming.

"Alex," Miles called, standing up from his chair. He had a little round table in the front corner, and the evening sunlight cast a golden light on his features. He was more than good-looking, I realized with a pleasant jolt of surprise. He was really, *really* good-looking. The flashing lights inside The Hay Place hadn't let me get a good look at him, and most of our conversation that night had taken place outside, in the dark. He was even more of a teen dream than I'd originally given him credit for.

I suddenly hoped I didn't look *worse* than I had originally appeared that night.

"You look wonderful," Miles said, smiling. "Come and sit down."

He held out his hand and as I came closer, he leaned forward and gave me a light kiss on the cheek.

I was blushing as I sat down. *Less of that, please,* I urged my face. I didn't need Miles to know what a novice at dating I was. If I could count the number of post-high-school dates I'd had on one hand, that was definitely none of his business.

"So," Miles began, holding out a floppy menu of plastic-covered pages, "like I said, not fancy. But if you follow my lead, I think you will be very happy. Any allergies?"

"None," I said thankfully.

"Anything you absolutely will not eat?"

"Nothing comes to mind."

He exhaled. "Oh Alex, thank God. I was so afraid you'd be a vegetarian."

I burst out laughing, and he smiled even wider, looking as if everything was going to plan.

"Perfect. So let's start with garlic knots, then work our way through the house special pizza, and finish with tiramisu."

I felt my mouth watering, but I had to shake my head at the excess. "I can't eat all of that! I won't even be able to get on a horse in the morning!"

Miles tilted his head at me, suddenly concerned. "Oh, no. Please tell me you aren't trying to make jockey weight. I like to eat too much for that kind of restraint in my life."

"Nope." I laughed at the very idea. "You see how tall I am! That's just a *lot* of food. But honestly, no one has ever mentioned weight to me. And some of the other riders are pretty solid. I'd say jockey rules don't apply at the training centers, or at least not with the horses I'm riding."

"I can't wait to hear all about them." Miles leaned forward. "Tell me about racehorse life, Alex."

He placed just enough emphasis on my name to make my heart jump.

I'd never heard anyone say my name quite like that.

The garlic knots were soft and savory, and I somehow managed to limit myself to just two slices of the perfect pizza so I would be able to pay proper attention to the tiramisu, but all through the fantastic meal, Miles commanded the lion's share of my attention. And he, in turn, seemed captivated by everything I had to say. He asked a hundred questions about my life, where I'd come from and where I wanted to go, the horses I'd ridden and the horses I wanted to ride, my reasons for coming to Ocala and my reasons for choosing racehorses over show horses.

He asked, and I replied, at first speaking politely over cooling portions and then more openly, around bites, laughing and covering my mouth as our words spilled over one another. I was delighted to have an audience who actually cared about my equestrian life, who didn't think my hopes and dreams were foolish, but fascinating.

He was pretty intriguing, too. I was still charmed to have located that rarest of finds, a horse *boy*, and I plagued him with constant questions. He admitted his parents owned a few foxhunters in his home state of Virginia, and had been all too happy to encourage their son in his passion for horse showing. He'd come to Ocala when he was nineteen to work with a prominent jumper trainer, and he had been here for the past five years, leasing stalls and training alone when it suited him, and working for other trainers when he felt like learning something new.

"I worked for Daisy Brenner during HITS Ocala back in spring," he said, tossing the Olympian's name out like it was nothing, and spooning up some fragments of the remaining tiramisu. "Over the summer, I went up to Lake Placid to get on some horses for her, but this winter I'm mainly working alone. I have stalls at a big equestrian center out on the west side of town, close to HITS, so I'll stay there through at least next spring."

"Your life sounds glamorous," I admitted. "I bet you even live in a real house, don't you?"

"Close," he said with a wink. "I live in an apartment over the barn owner's garage. All by myself."

"Oh, that sounds nice! All by yourself! I have to admit, I wasn't really prepared for having a roommate. She's turned out to be pretty cool, but it was still a shock. And I'm not sure the trailer we're living in is exactly up to code."

"That happens a lot here." Miles gave me a sympathetic look. "Farm owners and trainers seem to think grooms will live anywhere. Or riders," he added quickly. "I know you're not just a groom."

"I wouldn't ever say *just* a groom," I began, but he cut me off with a little bark of laughter.

"It's okay, Alex. There are levels in this game. You've leveled up to rider on your first run—don't think that doesn't mean something."

"Well," I sighed, leaning back to take the pressure off my full belly. "I don't know the rules here. What's the next level, then?

Because that's what I want to focus on. I don't want to just be a rider, either."

"For racehorse people? I think it's head rider, or foreman...what they call you depends on where you're at."

"And what's my prize for getting there? More money? My own trailer?"

"I don't know, I'm not a racehorse person!" Miles laughed. "But I imagine you work with the trainer. Maybe you become an assistant trainer. You're going to have to ask your roommate. She's showing you the ropes, right? She brought you to The Hay Place, so she must know her way around."

"Well, like I said, she was a jockey." I guessed I should ask Jacinta more about the business, but I didn't like to feel like a novice nuisance, always pestering her for more information. I usually waited for her to volunteer her knowledge.

"It sounds like you're in good hands. But if you get tired of being a jockey, you can always come get on a jumper. I have a few greenies who could use a nice light hand."

"Thank you! That's...that's very nice of you." I was startled by his easy offering of horses to ride. But he looked a bit smug at my thanks, so I decided to put a stop to that. "How much do you pay?" I asked with a wicked grin. "I have to be sure it would be worth my time."

"Oh, I pay," Miles said without missing a beat. "I'm *very* generous." He winked and favored me with an over-the-top old man's leer. I had to wipe away tears of laughter.

By the time the check was paid and the coffee cups were sipped dry, I felt like I'd truly had the ideal first date. It was one for the books: good food, good-looking guy, good conversation. We'd laughed so much my cheeks hurt, and when Miles walked me to the car, I stood stalling, with my fingers on the door handle, sorry to go home when there was so much more to talk about with him.

Then, suddenly, I realized I didn't know what to say. Darkness had fallen while we'd lingered over dinner, and the nearest street-light was burned out. In the soft orange glow from the next light down, I could see Miles's face shaping into lines of intention.

He was going to kiss me.

I wanted him to, I really did, but I was twenty-one years old and I'd never been *properly* kissed and I felt like an absolute idiot. Suddenly I wanted to throw up from sheer nerves. And if I did, that would be the end of it. You didn't come back from vomit at the first kiss. Even I knew that.

"Hey, Alex," he said softly, "what's wrong?"

I leaned back against my car door, hoping to put a little space between us. Just in case something bad happened, digestively speaking. "Nothing's wrong," I lied. My hands were behind my back, pressed against the window. He took a step closer, eyes searching, and I tilted my head back to watch him, not realizing that doing so was the exact gesture of consent he was waiting for.

As his face came closer, I closed my eyes in sudden panic.

But the kiss was soft, and undemanding, just a light press of his lips against mine, and I felt my taut muscles loosen as I realized things weren't so bad. I wouldn't say I kissed him back, but I didn't want to push him away, either. It was nice. It was a nice first kiss, to go along with my nice first date. As Miles leaned back, he brushed his knuckles against my cheek, and I smiled at him.

"Goodnight," I whispered, anxious to get into my car before he saw that I was shaking.

"Goodnight, Alex," Miles whispered back. "Be safe. I want to do this again."

I drove home into the dark Ocala night, thinking about his kiss, and feeling terribly guilty that I wished it had been Alexander's lips on mine.

Chapter Nineteen

ON THURSDAY MORNING, WALT announced that the yearlings would come up to the training barn on Sunday, and we'd start riding them on Monday. "Cut out any other jobs that begins before noon," he announced. "You'll be here until one o'clock most days, until they're doing regular track work."

"I coulda used some warning," Juan grumbled. "I was going to start a friend's horses out in Williston next week."

"You still can," Walt told him. "In the *afternoon*. But you're needed here while we get them started, and this job is your first priority."

"Well, I'm glad," Jacinta declared, putting on her helmet. "I'm sick of drivin' all over the county tryin' to get in enough horses to pay my car loan."

"Now you can stick to good old Cotswold horses," Walt agreed. "It's easier ridin' in one place, that's for sure."

"And they're better horses." Jacinta stuck out her arm so we could all admire a lurid, swollen bruise just above her wrist. "This is what that goddamn colt of Willy Perez's did to me yesterday. Turned around and bit me just as I was tightenin' the girth."

"Where was your groom?" Juan asked.

"No grooms at Willy's," Jacinta scoffed. "Just some old man muckin' stalls. He laughed at me when I yelled. So then I chased him with my whip until he stopped laughin'."

Walt followed me down to Chessiecat's stall. "You hear what Jacinta said about Willy's?" he asked as I set my tack up against the stall wall.

"Yeah. She came home groaning about it last night, too."

"I just want you to know how good you got it here."

I looked back at him. His face was serious, his eyebrows drawn together. "Something wrong, Walt?"

"I just want to be sure you stick around. When the yearlings start coming in, people start moving around. A lot of barns put out their Riders Wanted signs. You might hear someone's paying more money, maybe got better dorms, and the truth is, what really matters is the horses you're on. You want to ride quality. Well, these are the best horses in Ocala."

It had never occurred to me to look for work elsewhere; I was touched Walt thought I had that kind of confidence. "There's no chance I leave, Walt, unless..." I stopped myself. I hadn't meant to say *unless* at all. Because of course the condition for my leaving was a falling-out with Alexander, or a falling-*in* with Miles.

I was still thinking of what a good time we'd had last night. Was it possible we were going to turn into something more?

Walt lifted his eyebrows. "Unless what?"

I grinned. "Unless I just get so tired of sticking thermometers up broodmares' butts that I can't go on another day."

He laughed. "That'll only last through next week, tops, unless someone spikes a temp. And remember," he added, his voice growing serious again, "if you're at a barn that doesn't work this hard to keep their horses healthy, you don't want to be at that barn."

Well, that was the truth. "Got it, Walt." I started to slide open the stall grill, with Chessiecat already nibbling at my fingers. "Hey, can I ask you a question?"

"Course you can."

"What's this all for? What comes next for me?"

He scratched at his stubbly beard. "Well, I reckon it's to be Alexander's assistant when I leave," he said. "Head rider, training barn foreman, whatever you wanna call it. All the same here. Anyway, that's what Alexander told me when you started. Maybe I shouldn't say so, though."

"It's to take *your* job?" I was shocked. "Are you leaving? You can't leave!"

Walt looked up and down the shed-row, holding out a hand to warn me to keep my voice down. "I bought a place up near Lake City," he said quietly. "A nice place to retire, close to my wife's family. She's been askin'. When Alexander's ready to part with me, well, I'm goin'. And he thought your showin' up when you did was real good timing."

"I told Alexander I could be his assistant," I admitted, "but...can I? Really? I'm so new at this."

"You know how to ride horses, Alex. And you know how to train them. All you're learnin' now is the technique for racehorses. It's not like you're startin' out for the first time. Pay attention and read some books, and in six months you could be down at Tampa applying for your assistant trainer license so you can run horses for Cotswold Farm."

I couldn't even respond to that.

Walt put a hand on my shoulder. "Don't look so surprised. Most people who drive up that lane for the first time have barely even seen a horse. You show up, practically a professional already? Well, Alexander knows a bird in hand when he's got one. You're not gonna have to look for another job, kiddo. Not for years. Cotswold Farm is your home now."

His words stuck with me through my four rides of the morning, even when Wing spooked at a squirrel on the way to the track and nearly bounced me right out of the saddle, getting a good laugh from everyone else in the set. I'd left home less than a month ago on what had definitely felt like a wild-goose chase, trying to catch a dream which everyone had warned me against chasing. And in record time I'd found myself a new home, with spectacular horses, a grueling training program, the hope of becoming an assistant trainer...and Alexander.

Although I couldn't really say if I counted Alexander amongst my blessings or my curses.

Alexander rode up beside me as we walked the horses back to the barn. Wing was huffing a little; it had been a sharp pace out there, with Jacinta and Juan's horses leading the gallop and both of them feeling their oats in the fresh, cool morning air which had filtered in overnight. With his return from a lay-off so recent, Wing wasn't as fit as the other horses in his set, and it was showing now. I'd already leaned down and loosened his girth, hoping to help him catch his breath.

"Is he feeling okay to you?" Alexander asked.

I glanced sidelong at him; he didn't sound particularly interested in his own question. I thought there was something else on his mind. "Just a little out of his league this morning. They were setting a pretty tough pace."

Alexander was looking straight ahead—not at me, not at Wing. I thought he was behaving oddly. "Are you ready to ride more? The yearlings are coming in."

"Yeah...Walt told us. It's fine. I can take on more work."

He chuckled. "Well, hopefully not too much more. Don't want you running away from Ocala. Not that you really see much of it, I suppose?"

"It's nice. I don't see much of civilization, but when I do get out, it's nice."

"That's right!" Alexander's voice lifted as if a thought had just occurred to him. "You went out last night, didn't you? How was that?"

I looked at him suspiciously, but he was still gazing forward, his face still smooth and expressionless. "It was nice. I had some pizza, some dessert. It was a nice evening out."

"Just nice?"

I drew in my breath sharply. Alexander finally glanced my way. Was it my imagination or did his face redden ever so slightly? Maybe it was just the morning sun, appearing over the training barn roof. When he spoke, his tone was apologetic. "I'm sorry, I wasn't trying to pry. Just making conversation."

The likelihood of Alexander making idle conversation about his employees' dates was absolutely nil. There was no way. He'd been prying, all right.

I turned forward, away from the searching expression in those blue eyes. I ran my hand up Wing's neck, feeling the heat of his skin, willing him to cool down quickly. We were almost back to the barn, thank God. This excruciating little interlude could end.

He couldn't keep doing this, these meaningful looks and personal questions, then turning away from me at the last possible moment. I knew there was something between us, something urgent and real, but as long as Alexander could suppress it, I could do it, too.

It was just an unpleasant little race to the bottom, I supposed.

Still, I reminded myself, I'd had fun with Miles. I could do it again. Again and again, until I put Alexander out of my head.

And maybe he could do the same, if Adriene came back again. Or if, as I was beginning to suspect, she'd never really left. She'd been in Ocala the day I'd arrived. She might well still be here, biding her time. Just waiting to pounce on the farm and make us all miserable, if Walt was to be believed.

Alexander was looking at Wing's breathing, his gaze critical. "He's going to need to pull it together. I'm not impressed with him, to be quite honest. He should be in much better condition."

I felt protective of the colt, immediately forgetting my own problems. "He's doing just fine!" I protested. "Every horse in this set has been in work longer than him. He just needs a little more time to grow and get fit."

Alexander shrugged. "Everyone wants more time," he said cryptically. "Sometimes there isn't any."

I was in the tack room, putting away my vest and saddle, when Alexander came in, an entirely new light in his eyes. "Alex, just the girl I wanted to see!"

I turned and leaned back against a saddle rack, trying to look nonchalant. He looked so pleased to see me, I let myself think, for just a moment, he might be ready to do something crazy—like maybe ask me to dinner.

"Hey, what's up?" I asked brightly. Behind my back, I squeezed my hands together in a tight fist.

"It's about Wing—"

I unclenched my hands and flexed the fingers carefully, one after another. *Of course it's about a horse, you idiot.*

"Walt and I were talking about him just now, and we agreed he could use some extra conditioning. Can you take that on? It would be an extra ride in the afternoons—alone."

I was surprised enough to almost forget my disappointment—almost. "Extra riding? Is that a normal thing?"

"Perfectly. You just don't get to do it when they're living at the track, that's why you don't hear about it very often. Home farm advantage. Walt will give you all the details, if you're interested."

"Of course I am. I'd be happy to."

"Good, good." Our gaze met, and I watched his eyes darken.

I took a step forward. "Alexander, can we talk?"

Suddenly, his gaze was flitting around the tack room, landing on me, then bouncing away to jump from saddles, to laundry bins, to the leather bridles hanging against one wall. He wasn't meeting my eyes anymore. Something in the room had changed, as if the moment he'd stated his business, the shiny businesslike atmosphere had vanished.

"Alexander, is everything okay?"

"It's fine, why?" His eyes landed on mine at last.

"I feel like there's something you want to say to me. And I'm tired of dancing around it."

We looked at each for a long, breathless moment. I thought, at first, he might give in. Then I saw his lips grow tight, and I knew it was a foolish hope. Whatever he wanted to say to me, whatever he *felt* about me, he wasn't going to come out with it.

He was impossible, and I was tired of this game.

"Fine," I said, turning my back on him before he could fumble with an answer I didn't want to hear. "I'll go get started on my stall now. Ricky'll be waiting on me."

I didn't look back to see if he tried to stop me.

What did it matter? If he wasn't going to acknowledge that he felt something for me, what was I supposed to do? Beat it out of him?

Or just move on with Miles?

Chapter Twenty

Thε next morning I didn't have a horse in the first set; Chessiecat's temperature was slightly elevated and although she had no other symptoms, the grooms moved her to an end stall with no one else around her, and called the vet to come check her later in the day. We were all told not to go near her stall. I felt bad for her, but she was eating hay and didn't have a care in the world, so I supposed she didn't mind the impromptu quarantine.

Killing time in the training barn, I sat on a folding chair by the tack room door as the sun slowly tried to pierce the morning fog and the first set went jigging out to the dark track, and that's where I was when Alexander came into the barn on his pony, Betsy.

I was surprised to see him back so soon; he would barely have had time to escort the riders down to the training track. I looked over Betsy, afraid she might have hurt herself, but nothing about her stood out as problematic. She was a nice-looking bay mare, pleasant to work with—the sort of horse who most enjoyed walking, standing still, and eating.

Alexander let the reins drape over Betsy's neck and dismounted. "Hold her, will you?" he asked me, barely glancing in my direction as he walked into his office.

I hustled to take the reins, even though Betsy was going nowhere fast. I heard Alexander shuffling some papers around, opening desk drawers which squealed with damp. Ricky peeked around the shed-row wall, a pitchfork in hand, to see if he was needed. He noted that I was holding Betsy and ducked back out of sight, probably making sure he didn't appear available for any extra work the boss came up with.

Alexander came out a few minutes later with a notebook and a stopwatch. He nearly walked right past me, but then he stopped, gazing at me as if he had a question on his mind. Finally he said: "Alex, come walk with me back to the track, will you?"

I felt a little flutter of excitement and fear: something of *he wants my company* combined with *well, this is the way you'd fire someone.* Then I remembered I was holding the reins of his pony. I gestured to the dozing Betsy rather helplessly.

"Oh, right." Alexander turned and bellowed over his shoulder for a groom. Ricky appeared immediately—so quickly I had to think he'd been hovering just on the other side of the wall, listening to see what was coming next. "Can you put Betsy away? Don't untack her, I'll need her for the next set."

"Yeah, boss," Ricky said, and the look he gave me as he took the reins was one of farewell.

Jesus, I thought. *Maybe he is going to fire me.*

Alexander walked out of the shed-row and turned down the path towards the training track. I followed a few paces behind. The fog was still thick over the paddocks surrounding the training barn and obscured the rails of the track, but it eased the travel of sound. I could hear hooves in the distance, thrumming over the sandy surface of the track. The horses were still jogging, warming up before they galloped.

Alexander glanced back at me. "You don't have to walk behind me, you know."

"Sorry." I skipped a little to catch up.

"I was hoping for some help clocking this morning, but I think the fog might thwart that," he sighed, waving an arm at the drifting mist. "I needed to send out some reports to owners. It was nice of Wallace to keep some horses here this fall, but I suddenly seem to be behind schedule. Things jumped up rather quickly. I should have hired another assistant for autumn, but..."

"Wouldn't Walt help you clock?" I asked timidly. I really needed to figure out who was doing what around this place.

"He would, but he's needed on the track. The riders need a head, someone to set the pace, keep the tempo, watch for changes in gait and that sort of thing. I ought to have someone on the ground as well." He shook his head. "Well, we can't have everything. I'll teach you how to clock, though. Maybe we'll have some overlap while Walt is still here."

So it was true. I was going to replace Walt. I bit my lip and looked at the ground, concentrating very hard on where I put my feet. Mist swirled around my boots as we trudged through a particularly thick patch of fog.

"Ocala gets crazy foggy," I said.

"Reminds me of home," Alexander replied. "Horses appearing out of the mist, then vanishing again."

"I'd love to see it."

"You'd love the family estate. I can't say the same for the family. One or two of them are all right but…I like our distance just fine. You know," he went on confidingly, "my entire family are in horses. But we've scattered a bit around the world."

I already knew this, from the magazines, but I wasn't about to tell him that I'd read half his life history before we'd met. "Really? That's nice."

"Yes…*nice.*" He sounded as if it was anything but. "My father trains in England—near Cheltenham. We're from the Cotswolds, that's where the farm name comes from…do you know anything of the U.K.?"

"I know about Ascot," I offered, feeling rather foolish. "And the Grand National. And…Redcar, I think?"

Alexander laughed. "For God's sake, how do you know about Redcar?"

"It gets mentioned in James Herriot books."

"Who, the vet?"

I nodded.

"Oh, that's too funny. Redcar. Heh. That's up in Yorkshire. In the north. Well, so my father trains in England; one of my brothers trains in Australia, and I train here. I have a cousin who used to ride jump races, National Hunt, it's called there, but she's bouncing around the U.S. galloping right now. Last time I saw her she was settling in New York and making Jimmy Wallace crazy. But of all of us, Alex, do you know who the most successful is?"

I knew for a fact that his brother ran one of the most successful breeding and training operations in the Southern Hemisphere, but I doubted this was something he wanted me to recite back to him. "Is it you?" I attempted, pitching my question in hopeful tones.

Alexander kicked a rock off the pathway. "It is not."

We walked in silence beneath the still palm trees. He seemed to have tired of the subject, even though he'd been the one to bring his family up in the first place. I tried to concentrate on seeing through the fog, but there wasn't a breath of wind in the whole gray morning, and the mist seemed to grow thicker still as we neared where the training track ought to be. I could hear hoofbeats thrumming, that rapid three-beat pattern.

"Here's the stand," Alexander said, veering off the path. The wooden observation stand appeared before us, a platform about five feet off the ground. "But I don't think we're going to accomplish much. Come on up."

We climbed the stairs and leaned, in one identical movement, against the front railing. I could see the dark sandy footing of the track, the white inner rail, and then the fog cut everything off. The drumming hooves drew nearer.

Everything felt very right, standing there. I glanced sideways at Alexander, and I knew this was all happening for a reason.

I made a decision. *Take charge now, Alex.*

"Whatever happens," I said, "I want to be your assistant. Walt told me that's what you want, and it's what I want too. I won't go off to some other farm. I'll stay here and do my best for you. Just tell me what to do. We can make this work, Alexander." My voice nearly cracked on the last syllable, and I swallowed hard. I could feel the blush spreading up my cheeks as he faced me, his expression impossible to read. Where had that speech come from? I must be going crazy.

The horses suddenly burst into view, their nodding heads gleaming in a sunny patch of track. Within a few strides they had galloped past us and vanished again into the swirling fog.

Alexander looked at his stopwatch with sudden chagrin. "My God, I forgot to time them! It wasn't much, but they worked a whole eighth right in front of us that I could have recorded."

I bit back a laugh. "How could you forget? We were standing right there!"

He shook his head, his jaw suddenly tightening, and then I knew: he'd been watching me, not the horses, as they'd galloped by.

"You really do need a proper assistant," I told him. "Good thing you've got me."

❧❧❧❧ ❧❧❧❧

He didn't forget his stopwatch when I took out Wing. The colt was moving smartly, as if he wanted to make up for yesterday's lackluster gallop, and Alexander nodded approvingly from his spot on the rail as we jogged onto the track. He was leaning against the railing above us, the same spot we'd been earlier, but now the fog was nearly gone. He'd see our entire ride.

"We're going to work the last quarter, kids," Walt had drawled as we rode out of the barn. "Alex, you stay right next to Jacinta, and tuck in on the rail. My colt is quiet enough for you to run up his tail, but don't get too close or someone will get hurt. Jacinta, you keep an eye on her. The first time working can be kinda...exciting."

My mind was full of racetrack accidents as we started to jog around the track. Clipped heels, stumbles, all of the classic ways for a horse and rider to go down. I started to sweat from sheer nerves, feeling steamy inside my vest. It felt like every week this job presented a new challenge that terrified me down to my core.

"You alright there, rookie?" Jacinta asked me, grinning. "I can't catch ya, now. Keep a leg on each side."

"I've galloped before," I said stiffly. "Every day, actually. With you."

"You haven't breezed."

"I've gone faster than our gallops before."

"That's right," she agreed. "You're one of those eventing girls, right?"

"Something like that." I nodded, thinking Jacinta wasn't ready for a discussion of all the ins and outs of English riding tribalism. "I've done some galloping."

"Been run away with, too, I'll bet."

"That too," I agreed.

"It's like that," she suggested. "But not."

"Perfect, thanks."

We jogged around the track, then turned and cantered along at our usual pace. As we passed the gap for the first time, Walt called over his shoulder, "At the quarter pole!"

"Follow my lead," Jacinta told me. "Everyone gets a little space now. Don't want to trip anyone up."

I found Jacinta moving out nearly to the center of the track, and backing off so we were a good five or six horse-lengths behind Walt's horse. I instantly missed my buffer zone.

Wing was an experienced horse, and he knew what was up as soon as we spaced out. He ducked his head, digging his jaw against the bit, and when Walt's horse suddenly stepped up the pace, he was ready to bolt after the colt. His entire body shifted. Suddenly, Wing accelerated to a pace far beyond anything I'd felt before. In my wildest dreams, I'd never imagined a horse could feel like *this*.

Oh my God, I thought frantically. *This is actual galloping.*

And we weren't even close to our fast quarter yet.

I dug my heels in and tilted my body forward to keep from being unseated, my hands desperately yanking back on the yoke strap. Wing seemed to think that meant he should dig in and go faster. We were overtaking the colt ahead at an alarming rate.

I squeezed on the reins, hoping to slow Wing's furious strides, but instead the colt bowed his neck and dug down even harder against the bit. I remembered that little line of cottage wisdom which gets thrown around at riding stables: *when you pull back on a racehorse it means go faster.* I'd always doubted things were that cut-and-dry, and it definitely wasn't true at slower paces, but there was no denying that right now I was pulling back on Wing and he was responding by going even faster. We were right up on the front colt's heels and Walt was looking over his shoulder, his frown giving me a stern warning.

"Back off, kid!" he shouted.

I stood up and dropped my weight into my heels, shoving against the stirrups with everything I had, and leaned back with the reins at elbow-height. This got some response from Wing, as if my lifted hands sent some sort of message in a language I didn't yet speak, and he slowed his strides at last, although he kept his head tucked close to his chest in a position I found nothing short of terrifying. Horses with their heads down were free to do a lot of things I didn't want them to do: buck, or bolt, or dart in a new direction. Luckily, he just kept galloping along the rail, his legs churning with furious speed.

My shoulders were aching and my legs were screaming and I just wanted this ride to end. I wanted to get off. I wanted my mom to come and pick me up.

We spun around the turn, and when we hit the quarter pole things moved into a new, more alarming level. Walt shouted and flung his elbows out, and his colt shot forward as if he'd been walking before. A dozen feet to my right, Jacinta was yelling, too. There was no choice. I grabbed mane, squared my shoulders over Wing's neck, and shouted.

"Get up!"

Wing launched beneath me, his entire body thrusting with the effort of his gallop, and as we swept through the turn and into the homestretch, I felt like he was just moments from taking flight. Not in a smooth and beautiful way, like a falcon, but in a powerful and industrial way, like a 747.

That didn't make the feeling any less magical. In that instant of pure speed, everything changed.

My fears disappeared; there was no room left in my mind for terror, there was no place for anything but sheer exhilaration. All I had to do was keep Wing from running up on Walt's colt, and everything else was up to him—the rail kept us direct and safe; a quick tug of the rein and a kick were enough to get him to switch leads as we hit the straightaway.

We flew, and we flew, and we flew, and I never wanted to land.

Then Walt's colt began to slow and I realized we'd traveled midway down the track, past the pole that marked our imaginary finish line. Our work was over.

And I was very tired. I had burning muscles in my legs I hadn't known about before; I had prickles in my little toes where they were pressing against the stirrup irons and cutting off my circulation. It was time to slow down, time to stop and rest. I knew Wing had to be exhausted.

I closed my fingers and leaned back gently on the reins, but I didn't get the response I wanted. Instead, Wing's strides *lengthened,* his grip on the bit deepening. We swept past Walt's colt and I think I might have emitted one single, terrified *peep* as I saw his astonished face, then we were racing back up the track all alone, his hooves rumbling like thunder.

Wing was running away. For ten terrible strides, I thought: *I'm on a runaway,* and my brain couldn't come up with a solution. Nothing worked! Then I stood straight up, jammed my feet forward, and braced back against him, hands in the air. It was everything I would never do to a horse, but desperate times...

Wing lifted his head and shook it furiously, but he slowed.

By the time we were down to a trot, we were already on the far turn again, and we had to jog all the way around, alone, to reach the others. They'd pulled up and gone back to the gap already. Alexander was sitting on Betsy, his hands crossed over the saddle's pommel and his expression bland. Walt was sitting next to him on his sweaty colt, looking like he'd be only too happy to fire me on the spot. The others were walking their horses back to the barn. Even Jacinta had left me, I thought desolately.

Walt opened his mouth as I approached, ready to launch into a tirade, but then Alexander spoke up.

"You'll get there," Alexander said gently, turning Betsy around. "First works are ugly. Wing's a good horse to practice on. You two know each other better now."

I looked at Walt, and he shrugged, shaking his head as he let his colt follow Betsy. I had no choice but to ride in behind them, my hands shaking, wondering if I could ever just have a normal day at work.

Chapter Twenty-one

I LET MILES TAKE me out to dinner on Saturday night, because Jacinta was sitting around the trailer with a cold and I couldn't bear to sit next to her on the couch, listening to her sniffle. She swore her colds only lasted twenty-four hours and she'd be perfect on Monday morning, ready for our first day of yearlings, but that didn't make our one and only day off any more bearable if we had to spend it in each other's company.

We went to a Mexican restaurant where everything came smothered in cheese, which was basically a best-case scenario for food in general, in my opinion. The servers put down the plates while wearing heavy oven mitts and saying, "Hot plate, do not touch!" over and over again, a special level of drama I had never experienced with food.

I touched my plate.

"Oh my God!" I stuck my finger in my mouth.

Miles looked at me like I was crazy. "Did you *not* hear them say it was a hot plate?"

"I was curious," I mewed, but I moved my finger surreptitiously to the side of my frosty iced-tea glass. "How did they get it so hot?"

"I think they stick them in the oven to melt all that cheese."

"Genius."

We talked about horses as we worked our way through the cheese and everything under it: tamales, enchiladas, burritos. Ocala really had the most magnificent Mexican cuisine. Nothing in Calusa could match it.

"So you used to be in show horses," Miles said. "Where did you compete?"

"Oh, nowhere special. I rode green horses almost exclusively. I rode a few in jumper classes in Fox Lea, but that was unusual." Fox Lea Farms was a showground in Southwest Florida which hosted fairly large and relatively prestigious horse shows. "And I evented a little bit, but events are rare down there and we changed disciplines because it just wasn't easy to get up here for the decent cross-country courses."

"I still think it's amazing you ended up in racing," Miles admitted. "You're just not a typical racetrack girl. You know what I mean, most of them are trainer's daughters and grow up in the sport."

"But that's true of any equestrian sport," I argued. "Look at you. How many guys get into horse showing organically? You grew up with horses, so it made sense to you."

"You're an outlier, is what you're saying." He grinned.

I shrugged. "I'm not saying anything. I'm saying if you have horses in you, you have horses in you."

"Racing's different," he persisted. "It's...I don't know, it's messier, for one thing. Racing has a terrible reputation even with horse-people."

"It's just what I want," I said. I offered him a shrug and a smile. That was the best I could do. "It's what I'm supposed to do."

"Are you a fatalist, Alex?" Miles asked, grinning.

I considered the question carefully. "I might be," I said eventually. "I believe some things are meant to be, anyway."

Miles looked at me from across the table, and I thought again how utterly gorgeous he was. Such a damn teen dream. I'd called it right the first night I'd met him. What was I doing on a date with this handsome young man, this professional rider, in a horsey town with endless possibilities for a passionate, dedicated equestrian? How on earth had I gotten here?

Maybe some things were meant to be?

I closed my eyes for a moment, and tried to pretend it was Miles I saw behind closed lids, instead of Alexander.

Nothing doing. I opened them again. If I was just going to imagine Alexander, well, then I wouldn't imagine *anything*. I'd experience life in real-time. "Tell me about your horses," I said.

Surely, I could appreciate any guy who could talk horses to me. Especially when the request made his face light up the way Miles's was right now.

⁂

"I'm glad you came out with me tonight," Miles said as we walked across the parking lot. We'd come in separate cars again; I still wasn't sure what to do about the whole situation with the Cotswold Farm gate. I felt like I was living inside palace walls; they were shut at night and there was no admitting strangers inside. At least it felt safe; my mother had been absolutely thrilled when I told her about the magical gate that closed at seven p.m. every night.

"I'm glad I came," I agreed. "It's chilly out tonight, isn't it? I'm going to need a jacket if this keeps up." I was wearing a sleeveless dress, which was basically a uniform in balmy Calusa, but Ocala's October nights could occasionally err on the cool side.

"We get an actual winter here, you know," Miles said absently. He put his hand on my car and I assumed the position, leaning against my car door. He was going to kiss me again, and I wanted him to do it, if only to drive the thoughts of Alexander from my head. If I spent enough time with Miles, I thought, surely I'd get over Alexander. Sooner or later. And as soon as I stopped thinking about Alexander while I was waiting for Miles to kiss me, things would definitely be looking up.

Tonight was not that night, unfortunately.

Miles looked down at me with a lazy smile, evidently blissfully unaware I wasn't daydreaming about my boss. "What are you doing next Wednesday?" he asked.

I pretended to consider the question. "Gosh, probably going to bed at eight o'clock to get a good night's rest."

"Why don't you come over to my place, meet my horses? I'll bet you'd love them. And I'll order us dinner. I don't want to brag, but I live within delivery distance of a real, live Chinese restaurant. It was the main reason I rented stalls at this farm."

"Amazing," I replied. "You should buy the place."

"Maybe I will." His lips were bare inches from mine now; my heart was hammering in my chest, and I was sure he could see pink on my cheeks. Even if he wasn't the one I wanted, I was still up for a little kissing in the moonlight. There hadn't been much of that in my life so far, and I was ready to take what I could get. "I have horse shows coming up the next few weekends, but I want to be sure to catch up with you as much as I can."

"Horse shows?" I asked, momentarily distracted from the promise of a kiss. "Where at? What classes will you be doing?" I suddenly wanted to hear all about it. Despite my shift to racing, there was still an allure to Miles's upper-level showing. I hadn't gotten far, what with all my horses selling before we were jumping more than three feet, but I'd once thought I had a serious jumping career ahead of me.

"There's a series at Jacksonville Equestrian Center. Some decent money classes, a Grand Prix."

"Oh, that's cool. I—"

Miles cut me off with a hard kiss, pushing me back against the car. I gasped against his lips, somehow equally aroused and unnerved. "Miles," I breathed, the moment I could get any words out. "What the hell?"

He stepped back, chagrined. "I'm sorry. I thought..." His voice trailed off.

I rubbed my hand across my lips, feeling a little bruised. "No, I get it," I said. "That's just...you surprised me."

"I'm *really* sorry." He looked like he meant it. "I should have taken my time. I just—you look so beautiful out here in the moonlight. I got carried away."

His words should have taken my breath away. I wished, for a hard, sad moment, that they had.

I should call this off, I thought. But what was waiting for me back at Cotswold? Just awkward pauses, abbreviated conversations, one pretty half hour when we'd held hands and watched the rain.

"Let's…" I sought out words I'd never had to speak before, and finally took refuge in the sitcoms I'd grown up watching. "Let's take it slow, okay? I have a lot on my plate right now."

"Yeah, definitely." Miles put his hands in his pockets, which I took as a sign we were done for the night. Probably for the best. "Well, listen…my offer still stands. Any time you want to come over and meet my horses, just call me, okay? I'd love to have you."

"I'd like that," I said.

We faced each other uncertainly, the few feet of asphalt between us yawning like a chasm.

"Goodnight," I said finally. "Thank you for dinner."

"You're welcome," he said, and he watched me as I got into my car and drove away.

The drive home felt long; the Ocala night felt even darker than usual, even with the moon glinting on mailboxes and metal barn roofs. At the start of the night, I'd felt so brave and untouchable. I was the woman with the good job and the nice guy who liked her and the big future. Now, I just felt naïve and vulnerable. The nice guy wanted more than I was ready to give him; the wrong guy barely gave me the time of day—but he was the only person I could think about.

I'd thought that finding work and learning to ride would be the toughest things about coming to Ocala. Now, I was learning, those were the easy parts.

Chapter Twenty-two

Yearlings today," Jacinta said, right after she'd polished off a taco in three bites. "You ready to take them out in the paddocks?"

"I'm going to say no," I answered. "I've been thinking about riding yearlings, and I have to tell ya, it doesn't sound great."

There couldn't be a good reason for getting on horses before they were two years old. I imagined a squirrelly little pony version of a Thoroughbred, afraid of everything and spooking at its own shadow. The rest of the civilized world waited until horses were three or four. Why should we be different?

"Nah. It's nice and easy,' Jacinta said, swatting away my opinion. "We go out for some nice, long pasture rides. Everyone relaxes. It's like trail riding for money. Right, Walt?"

"Check," Walt agreed, talking around a mouthful. "Nice, easy walk and trot work. Just like you've been doing with Wing every day."

I did have to admit I'd been loving my afternoon rides on Wing. We went out in a big back pasture adjacent to the field where the retired geldings lived. Wing was still young and hot enough to like throwing a few spooks from time to time, but he mainly just trotted along with his head held high and his ears swiveling, taking in the natural world around him. I had to admit, more of that kind of ride sounded fine, even if I wished the horses were a little older and knew a little more.

They were so awfully young, though. All of the yearlings would turn two on January first, which was only two months away, but of course that was just their official birthday, for records and racing purposes. Most of them had been born between February and April. Some were closer to eighteen months than two years old. That was young in horses, despite the expert conditioning they'd received leading up to the sales, which had them tall and muscled beyond their years.

"You still look nervous," Jacinta observed. "What's wrong?"

"I've just never ridden horses so young. I'm worried about what they're going to do out there. I mean, a young horse is generally trouble out on the trail."

"Oh, that's the best part." Jacinta laughed. "You got it all backwards. They're so young, they don't think to argue with you! It's not like riding a big, confident three-year-old, now. These are babies. They still want to please mama, and *you're* mama to them."

I was helping the groom with my first yearling, a chestnut filly called Carson Princess, when there was a shout. Manny, the groom, went to the door and yelled back in Spanish. "I gotta go help Ricky real quick," he told me. "Can you finish her up?"

I looked at Carson Princess, who was gazing back at me with wide eyes from her spot against the back wall. She was a spooky little thing, and I was already nervous about taking her out. But

I could saddle her up alone. "I got her," I assured Manny. "Don't worry."

He nodded and hustled out, whistling to the other grooms as he went.

I had her tacked up before Manny came back, and I went to the door to make sure I wasn't missing the other riders. No one else was in the shed-row yet. I turned around and Carson Princess was looking at me, blinking with her wide, white-ringed eye. "Baby girl, don't kill me out there," I told her gently. "I have got enough on my mind without trying not to die, too."

Manny came back to help me mount. He looked grim.

"What happened?" I asked.

He waved his hand. "Juan's filly acting up. We had to use a couple guys to get her tacked up."

Huh, I thought. Didn't sound like they all wanted to please mama that much, after all.

Manny gave me a leg-up, and after a few quick parades around the shed-row, we headed out of the barn. I had to admit, I could have used more time in the barn. I'd lengthened my stirrup leathers on Walt's advice, who insisted that long stirrups were a must on slippery little yearlings, and I was grabbing at the irons a little as my legs complained about the new length. Not to mention that I was on a small, albeit long-legged, horse I didn't know.

Carson Princess seemed to have her doubts about the whole situation as well. As we rode out of the shed-row and into the sunlight, she blew loudly through her nostrils, and looked back and forth at the surrounding paddocks, swinging her whole head from side-to-side so that I felt like I was on a carnival ride.

"Ride her up real close to me," Walt called over his shoulder from the front of the line. "And I'll keep an eye on you out there."

Ashamed to be called out as the new girl but still grateful for the support, I took Carson Princess out of our place in line and pushed her to pass the horses in front of us. Jacinta, Juan, and Billy all slowed their horses to let us pass, making some room for me to slide in behind Walt's mount. Wedged in there between the two senior riders of the farm, I sat miserably in the exercise saddle, my heels nudging the filly forward, feeling conspicuous.

We rode out around the big back pasture in the hot midmorning sun, the golden light picking out each dewy blade of grass. The yearlings started out with swiveling ears and bouncy gaits, but their high spirits quickly began to flag in the humid air. Carson Princess grew sweaty beneath the straps of her bridle and along her neck where the thick racing reins rubbed, and she began to shake her head, more worried about buzzing flies than anything she might need to spook at.

"We'll trot them along the back fence," Walt called over his shoulder, and everyone said *uh-huh* or *yup,* except for me. I just sat tight in the saddle, my heels down and my heart racing, and hoped for the best.

The big shady patches along the fence-line made everyone feel better—even me. We trotted in a decorous straight line, all of the babies nose-to-tail, hugging one another for comfort. Jacinta was right; they didn't want to argue with us at all.

This isn't so bad, I had time to think, just before Carson Princess jerked her head down and started to buck.

"*Whoa,*" I blurted, my hands full of her wispy mane and the thin nylon of the training yoke. The first few hops weren't too bad, but then she got into the swing of things and really let it rip, leaping and snorting and throwing her hind legs up in the air. I had my heels jammed down and my legs so far forward they were banging into her bony little elbows.

She'd made it out of line and was tugging me past Walt's filly, who just looked startled, and was starting to throw her head from side to side, getting her shoulders into the action so that she could really rip me out of the saddle, when my grip hit the knot in my reins and she finally realized she couldn't tear them out of my hands. It felt like she might just throw herself down on the ground to get away from me when suddenly she stopped, shook herself all over, and looked back at the group.

They were all circling by the fence, the riders turning their little impressionable minds away from the trouble Carson Princess was causing, lest anyone get any big ideas. Walt came jogging over first, his heels thumping against the sides of his lazy bay filly. Carson Princess shied away from his filly and then immediately seemed to change her mind, picking up her pace as she tried to tug me back to the group.

I was utterly confused by this little witch of a filly, but something in the back of my mind told me no one was more confused than the filly herself.

"What the hell was that?" I asked Walt breathlessly.

He pushed his filly alongside mine. We were so close our stirrups clanked together. The fillies touched noses and blew comfortingly at one another. "I guess she just took it into her head to buck," he said. "They do that sometimes."

"For no reason?" I knew I sounded shrill, but I wasn't really happy with his dismissal. That had been a *big* blow-up. And where

I came from, when horses took a bucking fit, you figured out why. "Every horse has a reason," Diana used to tell me, as I struggled with some bratty beast in the arena. "Figure it out so you can fix it for them."

Walt shrugged. "There's a lot of new stuff going on for her today. Maybe a bee stung her, or a branch brushed against her leg, and it just pushed her over the edge. Babies are like that. Can't say for certain why they take some things into their heads."

Well then maybe we should ride grown-up horses instead, I thought fiercely, but I could feel Carson Princess wringing her tail again and I concentrated instead on keeping her from having another conniption.

We made it back to the barn in one piece and a few people, Jacinta included, congratulated me on riding my first temper tantrum, as they called it. I was feeling a little sick and shaky, which I decided to pass off as a touch of heat stroke. I went into the tack room and took a bottle of water from the fridge, standing next to the air conditioner as I drank it down.

I was still standing there when Alexander came in.

His presence put me on edge immediately, the flutter in my stomach somehow easily distinguishable from the queasiness my bucking bronco had given me, and I suddenly felt tired of it—tired of the wondering, tired of the longing, tired of the confusion. We'd barely spoken in the past few days, our conversations limited to quick backs-and-forths about how a horse was going, or how I was riding, and I just wanted something more—or nothing at all. *Anything* was better than this middle state, the way he simultaneously made me feel that he knew there was a rich and vivid connection between us, and that he didn't have any desire to explore it.

If there was something stopping him, well, that wasn't my fault, and there was no rule that said I had to be sympathetic to it for the rest of my life. Maybe we just needed to have a fight, or kiss. Pick one and stick to it.

A gust of wind came up the aisle and the door blew closed behind him with a bang.

We were alone.

I held out the water bottle. "Drink?" I couldn't imagine him sharing a water bottle with anyone.

To my surprise, he stepped closer and took the bottle. "Thank you," he said. "It's hot out there." He tipped the bottle back and drank.

"Alexander," I began, "there's something I want to talk to you about."

He took the bottle from his lips and looked at me gravely. "Right now?"

"I think it has to be said. I feel like if I don't just say it, we never will, and I'm tired of dancing around you like it isn't real."

His lips parted. He knew what I was talking about. I took a step closer, tilting up my chin. He was taller than I was, but there was only one way to say this.

It was happening.

And then it wasn't.

Alexander put his hands, strong and hot, on my bare shoulders. "Adriene is coming this afternoon," he said. "And I don't want to tell you this has to wait, because that's not fair to you. You're right that we need to talk. But—well—this has to wait."

Miles called while I was walking slowly down the driveway, looking from side to side at the horses grazing in the paddocks. I let the phone ring almost to voicemail, trying to decide if I should answer. At the last second, I flipped it to my ear.

"Hey Alex," he said happily, "How have you been? I feel like I've been on the road forever, but I'm back now...wanna get some dinner with me?"

I bit back a sigh. Where was my resolve to get over Alexander when I needed it? I should go out with Miles. After I'd just been so gently dissuaded from pushing things with Alexander, this could hardly be more obvious. He was going to be with Adriene this afternoon. *Legs up to there.* I didn't stand a chance.

A woman who kept coming back, time and time again, was not going to back off because of some college drop-out working in the training barn.

"Yes, let's get dinner...but not tonight," I said finally. "I'm a mess."

"I bet you're a cute mess."

I laughed, swinging my free arm a little. Fact: I could have fun and talk to a guy, and it wouldn't be anything like the stress of talking in pointless circles with Alexander. "*So* cute. I have hay in my hair, dirt on my cheek, and we can't even discuss what's happening under my fingernails."

"Well, I think that sounds charming. I should come right over and see."

Motion up at the stallion barn caught my eye, and I paused, looking up the hillside. Was that Alexander up there? He'd left the tack room in a hurry after he'd dropped his little bombshell about Adriene. I hadn't even gotten a chance to ask him what he meant—was she coming to work? To have a meeting? To win him back? I assumed all three. My teeth caught at my lower lip.

"Alex? I was joking, I'm not going to come right over. You can stop panicking about your fingernails."

"What's that? Oh, no, I know. I just saw something...sorry." I forced a laugh, angry with myself that my mind was already back on Alexander. "Let's get dinner...did you say when?"

"Tomorrow?"

"Yes, please." I answered him before I could stop myself. I had to stop getting in my own way.

"Perfect." Miles sounded satisfied with himself. "And I'd like to pick you up this time, if I may. Not very gentlemanly to leave you to drive yourself all over town."

"Oh! That would be great. But it will have to be out front...I'm really not supposed to give out the gate code. I can park up there and wait for you. Seven?"

"I will rescue you from your tower at seven," Miles vowed. "Until then, my lady."

I slipped the phone back into my pocket and looked back up at the stallion barn. Clouds had shifted across the western sky and the sunshine had been stamped out; now a breeze was touching the boughs of the oak trees standing around the barn. The little barn was a dark silhouette against the sky. A man walked out of the barn aisle, and stood looking over the farm.

I almost ducked through the fence running along the driveway; I almost crossed the grassy pasture and climbed the long slope running up to the barn. I almost went to see him. I could make him talk to me. I could make him understand. I stood there in the driveway, the cool wind blowing my hair into my eyes, and I made up my mind.

He'd told me to wait for the last damn time.

I went home to pick at my lunch.

Chapter Twenty-three

Envision and Nelly came back to the training barn that
afternoon. I was busy doing up legs, moving from stall to
stall with a bucket of poultice and another bucket full of standing
wraps. One by one, I went into the stalls of horses who had breezed
that morning, tied them to the wall with a hay-net for company,
and slathered the cold, menthol-scented clay all over the forelegs.
By the time I was halfway through, I could feel the prickling iciness
of the poultice everywhere I'd accidentally smeared it: on my arms,
on my neck, on my forehead, even a dab on my ears. It was kind
of refreshing, especially when the fitful breeze flitted down the
shed-row.

I'd just come out of Wing's stall, trying to wipe poultice out of
my pony-tail without much success, when I heard the growl of a
diesel engine and the creak of a trailer coming up the driveway.
Ricky shouted for some grooms to come meet him at the loading
dock. My name wasn't included in the summons, but I wandered
down anyway.

The loading dock was a big earthen ramp at one end of the
training barn, with a section of fencing on either side to keep a

horse from falling off. A semi-trailer was pulling up alongside it. A half-door was open in the center, and I could see four horses inside, looking around with pricked ears. One whinnied anxiously, and they all joined in.

The grooms made quick work of pulling open the bottom half of the door, and slamming a ramp down on the loading dock. To my surprise, there was a man already inside the trailer—he'd been riding in the back with the horses, apparently—and he was unfastening chains from the halter of the nearest horse. I leaned against the barn wall and watched, absently pushing back my hair with clay-covered fingers. I'd never seen horses moved by semi before, rather than the more domestic-sized truck and trailer, and I felt like I was learning about a new, more efficient world.

While Ricky was taking Envision's lead from the groom in the trailer, the driver got down and walked into the shed-row with a clipboard in hand. He spotted me and headed in my direction.

Whoops, I thought. *He thinks I'm in charge?*

I held up my poulticed hands as he came nearer. "I'm not the manager," I said.

"Well, who is?" The trucker had a sharp Southern accent and a handlebar mustache.

I considered Ricky the boss when Walt wasn't around, and I didn't know where Walt could be. "That guy there," I said, pointing.

The driver considered Ricky, who was wearing an oversized Garth Brooks t-shirt over cut-offs and a pair of manure-stained sneakers. "That guy?" He sounded doubtful. "You sure about that?"

"I'll sign for him."

That familiar voice came from behind me, clear and powerful and crisp. I whirled around, my clay-coated pony-tail swinging to brush my cheek.

A tall woman, dressed simply but expensively in beige linen pants and a white buttoned shirt, was approaching us quickly with a long, sure stride. She had dark hair cut in a bob, curling around her sharp jawline with a simple elegance, and dark brown eyes accented by perfectly curving eyebrows. At first I couldn't quite place why she seemed so larger-than-life and put-together; then I realized it was just money. Everything about her was expensive.

She smiled as she saw our surprised expressions, and I recognized the confidence in her own charm that she'd radiated from the winner's circle at the Breeders' Cup.

Beside me, the trucker sighed with relief. Obviously, this expensive intruder looked like his idea of a Person in Charge. I glanced sidelong at him and saw his lips slide into a welcoming smile. *He knows her?*

"Ms. Hartwell," the trucker said. "I have Envision Light and Appleton Nelly here for ya."

⁂

Adriene Hartwell stood by the stall door and watched Ricky strip the shipping bandages off Envision's legs. The colt was sweaty from his ride up from South Florida, and he'd lost weight during his few weeks at the track. I hung out in the corner of the stall, ostensibly learning by watching as I was the barn apprentice, but really just desperate to hear every word which came out of Adriene's mouth.

Unfortunately, she didn't seem to talk to the help much.

"*You're* not doing much," she said to me eventually, cocking a silken question mark of an eyebrow.

I blushed. She was the kind of person who could make an adult feel like a child with one acidic glance. "I'm an apprentice," I told her. "I'm meant to be observing anytime Ricky's doing something new. Bringing a new horse into the barn counts as something new."

"Hmm." She gave me a closed-lip smile which clearly said: *you're full of shit.*

Ricky didn't say anything to support or deny my claim. He stood up slowly, tossing the last bandage aside, and went to Envision's halter. The horse was already tugging at a hay-net and didn't seem to be too bothered about having been returned in disgrace to his training barn stall. Adriene looked over the horse with a trace of a sneer.

"He's no good," she announced. "He ran like an absolute donkey at Gulfstream. He should have been in better condition."

I didn't say anything. She didn't want my input, anyway. Weirdly, something about Adriene reminded me of Diana. They couldn't have been more unlike one another in looks or background, but in a few minutes she'd made her personality very clear, and I could see the resemblance. Both of them were so cocksure, so certain *they* were the one with the answer, *they* were the one being wronged when things didn't go their way. It was a confidence which had tied me to Diana for eight years; I could see how Alexander might have fallen into the same trap.

"I thought I could trust Alexander," she went on, stepping back so Ricky could lead the horse out of his stall and walk him down the shed-row to get a bath. "He said he'd handle things just fine.

But it's clear he's lost his touch. There was no reason for this horse to run so badly. It's an embarrassment to the farm."

I thought I spotted an opening. "I don't know much about owner-trainer relationships," I said carefully. "Can you tell me a little about the decision to run him? Who makes that call?"

She shrugged, somehow making it an elegant gesture. "In an ideal world, the trainer makes the call. In real life, it varies. And in our case, it's a shared decision because...well, because I am his business partner, and we have a long history of running horses together. Although it might be time to move on."

"Meaning, you'd move your horses?"

She eyed me sharply. "*If* I thought it was best."

Obviously, as his employee I couldn't get her to tell me what she was planning to do with her horses. But I did think I could get a better handle on what was in their past. "What was your partnership like, before? When you were running horses together? I'm just trying to learn, so I can be a trainer someday."

"It was stormy," Adriene replied, with a little laugh. "But...no. It was good. We were old friends before, you know. In the U.K. And when he decided to come to the States and train, I came along. For the ride, and to help him get started. His father wanted him to stay. But Alexander...he's independent." Her gaze wandered up the shed-row, suddenly distant. "He didn't want to be tied to his family's name. Impossible to escape them in England or Australia. You know that much, don't you?"

"Of course," I assured her. "And so you two just worked together?"

Adriene looked back at me and I saw a little smile tugging at her lips. "Yes," she said in an amused tone. "We *just worked together.*

And not very well, recently. We had a few good years, but then…I wanted to take things in one direction, he wanted to go in another, and here we are. I stepped out of the training game and let him go it alone, but, well, I'm sorry to say it, your boss is in a slump. It won't end. Every time I come back to offer my help, I end up swearing I won't do it again. I don't think he *wants* to win anymore."

Everyone knew Alexander was in a slump. That wasn't really her news to break. I nodded carefully, as if I was considering everything she had to say with great attention. The only revelation I really cared about was that there was nothing romantic between them. Hah! The grooms had been wrong. Adriene Hartwell wasn't his fancy piece from back home. She was his business partner…and she was coming off as pretty nasty, actually. There was something in her tone which made me think she was almost *delighted* he wasn't doing well.

"It's too bad things didn't work out," I said. "I'm sure you guys had a good run."

"We did," Adriene replied, her gaze suddenly focusing at something behind me. "But I'm willing to give it one more shot."

I turned around, filled with sudden dread, and saw what she was looking at.

It was Alexander, standing in the shed-row, his expression unreadable.

⁕ ⁕ ⁕

I waited as Alexander came down the aisle, hoping for a significant glance, a nod, a wink, *anything*. After all, he hadn't said no to me this morning. He had just said our conversation had to wait. If there was some chance he was coming over to my way of thinking...but no. I didn't get it. Whether he kept his gaze studiously on Adriene in order to deflect attention from me, or because he was absolutely riveted by her, was more than I could say. I stepped to one side as he smiled, took her hands, kissed her on the cheek in his English manner. And then I watched as he led her up the shed-row, away from me, without a word of goodbye.

They went together in the office and closed the door. I had no choice but to go back to my poulticing. The legs of tired racehorses waited for no man, I told myself. And certainly not for me.

Ricky came down to check on me after he'd hosed off Envision and put the colt in a little paddock to stretch his legs. The hot afternoon was fading at last, and a cool breeze was playing up the shed-row. "That your last horse?"

"Yes," I said, carefully winding a bandage over the plush pillow wrap. There was an art to pulling the bandage securely over the pillow wrap without sending it sliding around the horse's leg, especially when there was also a layer of wet brown paper and clay to add extra slipperiness to the entire situation, and I was concentrating hard on my task.

"You talked to Adriene?"

"A little."

"She say anything about the horse?"

"She was disappointed in his run." The Velcro at the end of the bandage appeared at the right moment, just below the knee. Triumph!

"She say anything about Alexander?"

I pulled the Velcro snugly around the front of the horse's leg. "She did, actually." I rocked back on my heels and looked up at him. "She said something about one more shot."

Ricky's face clouded. "Damn. She's bad news. I wish she'd just go."

"Something tells me she was planning on it until she saw him." I paused, hating to say it out loud. "She's in love with him, right?"

He nodded grimly. "Not in a nice, happy couple way, though. She makes him miserable."

Something in his voice made me suspicious. "She said they'd never been together."

Ricky shook his head. "Oh, they were together. Whenever she wanted, which wasn't usually very long. I've seen her in and out of this place for years, and every time she shows up, she gets what she wants until he loses it, they have a big fight, and she's gone again. It never changes."

I was at a loss for words. I just crouched there, ankle-deep in shavings, as the horse next to me happily ate his hay. *You have a dinner with Miles to look forward to,* I told myself, but the truth was, I just didn't care.

I would have to try harder.

Ricky leaned over the stall webbing and reached out a hand for me. "We've got nothing left this afternoon. I'll stick around and feed...you take off."

I brushed shavings off my jeans, trying to keep my expression neutral, but inside I was deeply annoyed. Naturally, *today* was the day I could knock off early...and I could really use the break. But if I left, how was I going to keep an eye on Alexander and Adriene?

Ricky was eyeing me suspiciously. "Usually if Walt or I tells you that, you'd be halfway down the shed right now."

"I'm just curious about what's going on with those two."

He nodded as if he got it. "Well, Maureen isn't around today. I was going to take Victor up to feed the studs tonight, but...you want to do it?"

"You want me to feed dinner in the stallion barn?" That was kind of an honor, since I hadn't been trusted to work up there alone yet. "But no offense...how does that help me?"

"They'll head up there next," Ricky said. "They always do."

He didn't have to tell me twice.

❧❧❧ ❦❦❦

The stallion barn didn't need much work in the afternoon; since the stallions spent the morning and early afternoon outside in their paddocks, their stalls were still pretty clean, the aisle was swept, and the evening feed was already set up in little buckets. All the evening groom had to do was top off waters, give fresh hay, and dole out grain. Maureen usually fed them around four-thirty, giving me a little bit of time to kick back and relax, enjoying the views from the hilltop barn...or do a little more poking around in the notebooks in the tack room while I waited for Alexander and Adriene to bring their party to me.

But I couldn't really focus on the breeding pairings and cryptic notes in the books. Now that I was sure it was all for Adriene, I was less interested in deciphering the codes. I looked at the last note in the book again and again. She was signing on for another year. *She's back for good.*

The thought was devastating. Somehow, I knew Adriene was the one thing which really stood between us. With her back, I didn't stand a chance. Who could fight a personality like that? Not some overgrown schoolgirl like me, that was for sure.

A half-hour passed…then forty-five minutes. It was almost time to feed the horses, and still Alexander's truck and Adriene's sedan hadn't moved from the training barn. What could they be doing down there?

When they came at last, I was in the best possible place to eavesdrop: up in the little hay-loft. It was unusual for a Florida barn to even have a hay-loft, so it was pretty lucky I was up there, filling hay-nets for the stallions, when they came in separate cars and walked into the barn aisle.

I heard their footsteps as they scuffed around each other on the soft aisle pavers. At last, Alexander spoke, and his voice was tight with anger. It sounded as if they'd been arguing for hours. For as long as she'd been here.

"You aren't getting any of this, Adriene."

Adriene's voice was amused. "These are my horses. This farm is all my doing. And we're not together. So, tell me why I should let you keep it?"

"It's half-mine," he growled. "And you've sabotaged it again and again, trying to keep me down. You want me to quit and walk out. It's not happening."

"Is that what you think? I'm not the problem. *You're* not on your game, Alexander. You're burned out. You've lost your passion. And I think I know why. But you don't want the solution so…why not just sell it to me? I can handle this without you. And you can start over anywhere you want…Canada, France, hell, you can go to

Barbados and train a few in between snoozes on the beach. Or you can never look at a horse again. Whatever you want."

I took a deep breath and sank deeper into the hay. She was trying to buy him out.

Alexander was quiet; I wondered, with rising terror, if he was considering her offer. If he left, everything was over. I'd lose him—I'd have to leave the farm—find somewhere else, some farm where his ghost couldn't haunt me. Start all over.

Try to forget him.

The silence deepened over the stallion barn. Even the horses were quiet, waiting.

Finally, I heard Adriene again. "You don't want this to go away, do you? And you don't want me to go away. Admit it—you're a better trainer, and a better man, with me around."

He said something too low for me to hear, and she laughed at him.

"You're just saying that because you got used to having me gone."

I heard her smart shoes click on the concrete aisle as she began to walk away. "Dinner tonight, Alexander. We'll talk more then."

Her car started, and she was gone.

I knew Alexander was still just below me. I peered over the hay bales I'd been hiding behind and saw him standing in the aisle, looking winded. My heart wrung; I wanted to go down to him, wrap my arms around him, show him there was more than one woman in his life. But nerves kept me back, and my suspicion that while I was ready to go all-in, Alexander hadn't quite gotten there yet. Otherwise, wouldn't he have let me speak earlier? Wouldn't he have heard me out, before he heard what she had to say?

I rocked back on my heels, ready to wait for him to leave so I could finish chores unseen.

And then my phone rang.

Chapter Twenty-four

His head whipped around; his gaze shot around the barn. It only took a moment for Alexander to look up, and then he spotted me.

A strange expression came over his face: regret? Shame? Anger? I couldn't say—maybe it was all three together. I certainly felt all of them.

"Come down from there," he said, his voice oddly neutral.

"I'm getting together hay," I replied, stalling. "Let me just finish—"

"*Please* come down."

I couldn't say no to that. I scrambled down the stairs.

"You were listening?"

"I *overheard*—"

"You were up there listening to us." Alexander shook his head. "Alex, you should have said something. You should have told us. That was *private*."

"You started before I could stop you," I lied. "I was in the back filling hay-nets and I didn't realize you were here until you started talking."

He crossed his arms, looking skeptical. "What you heard—that's just her usual nonsense. She doesn't want to buy the farm, or the horses. She just wants me to be afraid of her. She likes holding the purse-strings."

"And you like letting her think that."

He raised his eyebrows. He hadn't expected me to talk back. "I do what I have to do to keep this place running."

"She told me you're in a slump because she's not around to help."

"I'm in a *slump* because I've been trying to get her to go away. But she keeps coming back."

"You're afraid to kick her to the curb," I told him.

"What do you know about it?" He was getting angry now, building up the head of steam I'd heard in his voice when he'd told Adriene she couldn't have the farm.

"I know you're trying to prove you're someone without your family," I said. "And you can't do that with Adriene running you into the ground, but you can't do that without this farm, either."

His jaw dropped, but it wasn't because of my amazing perception. "That's incredibly presumptuous," he blustered finally. "You're really getting ahead of yourself, Alex. I think you should go."

I stood my ground. "I have to feed these horses. I can't leave."

He shrugged. "Well, I can."

The missed call was from Miles.

Of course it was.

I found out the truth after I'd sat in the hay for a while and cried until I felt completely washed out. It was easier to survey the world with practical eyes once you've sobbed out all the emotion—I'd learned *that* working for Diana. Lifelong lessons from that one, I thought soberly, pulling out my phone to see who had caused the argument.

Miles. I considered the caller. He was simpler than the mess I'd gotten into here. If I told Miles I'd moved to Ocala, fallen for my boss in a case of love at first sight, almost managed to get a kiss out of him, and then got torpedoed by his crazy ex-girlfriend-slash-business-partner, he'd probably laugh and buy me a drink.

"Ocala," he'd say. "Typical Ocala."

Typical horse-girl crazy, he'd think.

And he'd be right.

I considered my sinking ships, trying to decide which one to try and salvage.

⁘⁙⁘ ⁙⁘⁙

Barn chore time is the best thinking time, and I found plenty to do despite the clean perfection of the stallion barn. Once the horses had eaten, I took out their buckets and scrubbed them, setting them against the front wall to drip dry. I swept the aisle again, removing every single blade of loose hay from the pavers. I wiped the dust from each stall door's brass nameplate. I wanted to pick the few piles of manure from their stalls, but knew I wasn't supposed to be in their stalls and decided I'd better not risk it.

All of this work, but I couldn't get over one repetitive thought, hammering over and over again in my brain. *This isn't going to work.*

I wasn't about to go through another collapse. I'd wasted years of my professional life on Diana's barn, watching everyone else leave and find success elsewhere while I held on to the memory of a friendship we'd once shared.

I was in love with Alexander, but I could get over him. Indeed, it looked like I would have to.

I called Miles back.

"Hey!" he said warmly. "I know we're going out tomorrow but...come and see me right now."

"Why?" I asked blankly. I didn't have any emotion left for Miles.

"Because I *miss* you," he said. "Because I like seeing you. Come and talk to me."

I looked around the quiet barn. I was always alone. I worked on a farm with a dozen other people, at least, and lived in a trailer with another human, and yet I was always alone.

"Okay," I said.

❧❧❧❧ ❦❦❦❦

The arena lights were lit overhead, and the white-sand footing was gleaming. Miles was cantering a big gray horse around a colorful course of jumps when I arrived, parking my car by his impressive barn.

I leaned on the fence to watch. He raised a hand to wave hello, then took the horse around the course. I was overwhelmed by the size of the place, by the magnitude of this setting. Everything was huge: the fences, the horse, the barn behind me, the pastures I'd driven between on the way here. I knew Miles was just renting stalls here, and everything was shared, but even so, it couldn't be cheap. This equestrian center was A-Circuit quality.

I supposed that meant Miles was, too.

His light gray horse went flawlessly around the jumps, flicking his dark tail after every fence. I suspected this was Otis, the best horse in Miles's string of jumpers and one he was hoping to show Grand Prix in the coming Winter Equestrian Festival. The way things were looking right now, he wasn't going to have any trouble with the big courses or the international company he'd face during Florida's lucrative season.

"Hey," Miles called to me, trotting the horse over after the last fence had been cleared with panache. "It's so good to see you. I can't believe I convinced you to come on such short notice."

"I was done early," I said, trying to play it cool. In reality, I was salivating over his horse. "You caught me at just the right time. Is this Otis?"

"It is! And you have to get on him. Did you wear your boots?"

I'd run back to the trailer for the quickest of showers, then pulled on clean jeans and paddock boots. I planted one foot on the arena fence, displaying my footwear. "Why, yes I am, as a matter of fact!"

"Perfect!" Miles dismounted in one smooth moment and led Otis to the gate. "Come on, there's a mounting block over here in the corner."

"You're just going to hand me your big horse?"

"He's not that big…"

"He's like, seventeen-two, so that's big, and anyway I meant big like your top horse, your best horse. It must be a racehorse thing."

"You're picking up all of their lingo," Miles laughed.

I closed the gate behind me. "Don't say it like that."

"Like what?"

"*They,* and *their*. That's my world now. That's who I am. It's not a phase or something."

"Then why are you looking at Otis like you could marry him? He's not even close to a racehorse."

It was true. Otis was some kind of European warmblood, and *not* one of the ones who was basically three-quarters Thoroughbred. He was big-boned, broad-chested, wide in the ribs and heavy in the head.

For all of that bulk, Otis rode like a dream. We cantered around the arena, and I savored the feeling of a horse who arched his neck and curved his spine, rather than sticking his head straight up every time my fingers touched the reins. I'd forgotten how nice it was to ride an adult, trained horse. Six weeks on youngsters really amplified the experience of an actual, good ride.

"You look like you're in ecstasy," Miles called.

"I love him! This is amazing!"

"Take him around the jumps."

I picked out a few easy lines and sent Otis cantering up to them. The big horse found every stride, asking me only to stay in the middle of his motion and out of his way.

"What a dream." I patted Otis under the curve of his dark mane. "You're so lucky. I've never had a horse like this." I'd ridden horses with the *potential* to be this nice, but they were always sold long before they reached these heights.

Miles was laughing at me. "How long has it been since you jumped?"

"Just a few months," I said. "But wow, it feels good."

"You know…if you ever change your mind about racing, you could work here. I could really use the help, and there's room. You could have a stall, bring on a young horse of your own."

I felt myself freeze. Otis, feeling my taut fingers and rigid seat, came to a sudden halt.

I looked back at Miles. He was smiling as if he'd just won a prize.

"I'm working in racing," I said stubbornly, but a voice in my head whispered: *for how much longer?*

❧❧❧ ❧❧❧

In the tack room, Miles poured me a Dixie cup of white wine, and waited until I'd taken a sip before he brought it up again. "So listen, about what I said out there…I know you're here for racing. I just wonder if it's time for a change."

"I just changed my life like two months ago," I said with a half-hearted chuckle. "Can I change it again so soon? Isn't there a waiting period?"

Miles ran his thumb along the stem of his wine glass. "You know…I've been thinking about this for a few days. It's crazy, sure, but we move fast in this business." He leaned forward, fastening his eyes on mine. "My show season is about to ramp up. You know how to ride jumpers. You can groom. So, why *not* come work with me? We'll go to Wellington, we'll go to Jacksonville, Tampa—anywhere there's a jumper course with a check at the end, I'm going for it. Come with me."

I opened my mouth, but found I had nothing to say. I'd come to Ocala to learn racing, not continue working in horse shows.

But...why not? I was good at riding jumpers, just like he'd said. Maybe, with his help, I could go from scrappy and able to pick-up rides on anything green with four legs, to educated and elegant, ready to ride more advanced horses. Maybe I had an amazing career in the show jumping arena waiting for me.

Seriously, why not? There was certainly nothing standing between me and show-ring brilliance besides good-enough horses and someone to set fences and give me good solid advice on when to rate and when to push.

I'd come here to go racing, but if I was about to leave the best farm in Ocala—and let's face it, I probably was—what on earth came next?

Maybe, I thought, my heart beginning to beat wildly, *I actually came to Ocala for the wrong reasons, but I could still end up in the right place.*

"I don't know," I said, trying to be careful, trying not to jump into something without taking the time to think it through—a favorite trick of mine. "I don't know if I want to go back to horse showing so soon. I just started riding Thoroughbreds...what if I realize in a few years that I should have seen it through?"

Miles reached out and took my hand. "I know you wanted to try it, but you have now. What else do you need to prove?"

"I really, really appreciate the offer, but I'd have to think about it."

"Do a pros and cons list," Miles advised. "And don't forget to put housing on there."

"Housing?" I echoed, surprised. Miles didn't have another apartment for staff.

"Obviously I'd have to provide you with a place to live," he said, and his smile practically twinkled at me.

Oh.

"I'll put it on the list," I promised, making an effort not to give away my feelings on the matter. We'd been on *two* dates. Unless you counted tonight. But three wasn't much better.

Why did the guys you want never make a move, and the guys you didn't jump ahead five spaces?

But I was trying to want Miles, trying so hard.

"Which side will it go on? Pros or cons?" Miles asked with a wink.

"I'll never tell," I replied, and I gave him a smile which definitely made him think it was a pro.

"Let me take you out for dinner," Miles suggested, corking the wine and slipping it back into the tack room fridge. "We were supposed to go tomorrow, but there's no time like the present."

❧❧❧ ❦❦❦

"This is the best barbecue in Florida," Miles announced, parking in front of a low-slung building just outside the commercial sprawl of Ocala. "And the sweet tea! It's like ambrosia of the gods."

"Music to my ears," I said, although I was just glad it wasn't the barbecue joint where I'd met Alexander. I never would have been able to concentrate on him there, and that wasn't fair. Miles was a great guy! I needed to give him a chance to outshine Alexander. Miles was the one driving me to the best barbecue in Florida, after all. What else could a girl ask for?

Oh, and he was thoughtful, too. He had followed me to Cotswold Farm and waited while I parked my car just inside the gate, so that he could drive me home from dinner later.

So we sat at an old-fashioned booth with high wooden backs, kicked our legs like little kids, and drank our sweet teas while the chefs in the smoky kitchen chopped meat and sang along to the country station on the radio. We talked horses, and I told him about breezing Wing.

"When they get up to that speed, it doesn't even feel like a gallop anymore. He stops feeling like a horse. He was like this machine I was balancing over top of. And they're all kind of like that, but Wing, it's a whole other dimension. He's something special."

His eyebrows went up. "But is that...fun? Machine horse? It doesn't sound like it."

"It's *incredible,*" I insisted. "Honestly, it's all I can think about sometimes."

He didn't make any comments about balancing on top of large, thrusting bodies and I was very thankful for that. *Miles is a nice guy,* I thought again. *A Nice Guy.*

"I'm going to look at a new horse tomorrow," he said. "At Hearthstone Thoroughbreds. Do you want to come along? I'm not going until two, three o'clock."

"I'd love to, but I have to work. I'm still apprenticing as a groom in the afternoons, remember? But hey, I'm surprised you're looking at a Thoroughbred. I thought you preferred warmbloods for big jumper classes."

"Just kicking tires, I guess. It's a nice farm, so when they have something for sale I like to look at it. I looked at a horse there last month. An older gelding ready to retire. So yeah, *sometimes* I slum it with Thoroughbreds," he added with a smile, just to tease me. "But I try not to make a habit of it. His feet were too flat, anyway. I could have taken him, but I didn't think he'd hold up forever. So I told them to find him a home with someone who didn't jump as high as I do."

"That was good of you." I turned back around and smiled at him. Miles was careful with his horses. He was the opposite of Diana—at least, late-stage-alcoholic Diana. Probably Adriene, too. "I like that about you—you always put the horses first."

Miles stretched his arms out wide. "I would rather put you first. Why don't you come sit on this side of the table, little lady?" He put on a mock Southern accent, and I hoped none of the wait staff heard him. Their accents were real and I didn't think they'd appreciate his joke.

"I don't want to be one of those couples," I told him. "Everyone will think we're gross."

"Everyone will think we're *lucky.*"

I couldn't do it. I wasn't ready to move that fast. Maybe I wasn't even ready to move at all. "I'll stay put for now. It's only our third date. You have time to convince me I should be gooey with you."

His grin was almost a leer. "I'm going to wear you down, Miss Stand-offish. You're a total mare, by the way. I mean that in the best possible way."

"I'm not offended. Mares are tough and mean and get what they want."

"And they're beautiful," Miles said, looking me in the eye. "Athletic, intelligent, graceful—"

"Please stop." I was blushing.

"You should get used to compliments."

"I can't. I never will."

"Not enough in your life?"

"It's not that. I'm not some poor unappreciated thing. I just don't like them. I don't think about myself very often. I think about horses. I think about my riding. I think about getting better, doing a better job. But that's it."

"So if I want to compliment you…"

"It has to be about my riding," I confirmed.

"You'd better keep coming out to ride with me, then," Miles said. "Because I'm never going to make it out to your place early enough to see you gallop. Anyway, I want to win you away from them."

I smothered a smile. Luckily, a pigtailed waitress brought us our food just then: a big metal platter covered with brown paper, and laden with ribs, cuts of brisket and pork, and sausages.

"Oooooh," I sighed. "Now *that* is beautiful."

Miles just shook his head at me, his eyes filled with laughter.

***

He kissed me again by the farm gate.

I was ready for it by then; we'd had a nice evening, the stars were glittering overhead, the breeze was cool and pleasant, feeling almost like real fall in a real place where the leaves changed and people drank hot chocolate and said things like "sweater weather!" to one another.

I was ready, and I didn't mind it when he closed the car door behind me and then pulled me close, tilting my chin up with his calloused fingers and leaning down to meet my lips. I let him kiss me, let myself feel worthwhile for just a few moments, a girl someone wanted instead of a girl fighting for someone who didn't let her speak.

I left him after a few minutes, parting with lingering fingertips and the feeling of his eyes on my back as I slipped through the opening gate, hitting the button to close it again before it had even opened halfway, heading for where I'd parked my car in the shadows behind the front hedge. Because as good as he made my feel, I was still feeling guilty beneath it all, that I was doing all of the taking and giving back nothing.

He was being everything kind and good, but even as I enjoyed dinner with him, enjoyed driving with him, my thoughts were back here at the farm.

I leaned on my car for a moment, soaking in the Ocala night. The croaking frogs in the ditches, the perky song of the whip-poor-will, the constellations wheeling overhead: this place was so dark, so natural, so different from the suburbs where I'd always lived. I didn't love all the turmoil which being here had brought into my life...but I sure wasn't sorry I'd come here, either.

Then I heard footsteps on gravel, and my entire body froze. Surely there couldn't be someone wandering around the property at ten o'clock at night. Visions of grisly deaths came into my head. Florida had more than its share of weirdos. I shouldn't be out here, alone, in this empty space. I clutched my car keys. How quickly could I get inside and lock the doors? Was I fast enough?

"Alex?"

My muscles loosened all at once; I nearly fell alongside the car, onto the gravel driveway. "Alexander," I gasped. "You scared me."

"Did you think I was an ax murderer?"

"Literally exactly what I thought, yes." I put my car keys back into my purse. "What are you doing wandering around out here? It's late."

"Oh, sometimes I take a little walk, make sure the property is still here." He laughed gently. "Did you have a nice night out?"

The conviction came to me with utter certainty: he had been waiting up for me. He'd been watching out his window, or maybe on the grainy gate camera, to see when I'd come home. Then he'd slipped on his shoes and—

No. That couldn't be true. He'd been going out of his way to avoid giving me the slightest encouragement. He'd been blatantly ignoring all the signals our bodies were throwing at us. He didn't want to see me like that. We'd literally parted after harsh words just a few hours earlier.

But maybe he couldn't help it, just like I couldn't help holding him up against Miles at every attempted embrace.

It didn't matter. I couldn't keep doing this. I meant it this time. Really.

"I'd better head home and get to bed," I said. "Early morning tomorrow, and all that."

He came closer. The moon had set already, but the starlight was enough to shine on his sun-kissed hair, his expressive eyes. He was looking down at me as if I was a prize he wanted to keep for himself. My heart quickened, exactly the way it *hadn't* when I'd been with Miles tonight.

For a moment I really thought it would happen. Then he seemed to straighten up, to square his shoulders, and I knew once again he'd fought back his impulse, his own instinct. A weary rage flooded through me. Why couldn't he just see what we had was good and real? Why did it have to be his British stiff upper lip, every single time?

I was done. Really, truly done. Adriene could have him and best of luck to her.

"Goodnight, Alexander," I said, not bothering to hide the coldness in my voice, and I fished out my keys again, opening the car door. I was halfway in when his hand reached out, caught at my hair. My bun had been loosening all night as my hair dried and now it came free, sweeping around my neck. I looked up at him, my lips falling open, daring him to come closer.

He took the dare.

Chapter Twenty-five

I WOKE UP LATE the next morning, Jacinta's voice at my door telling me to shut off my alarm. I pawed at my clock radio, turning off the beeping alarm and sliding the button over to FM. The calm voice of a BBC presenter arrived in my room, describing some sort of calamitous revolt in an African country I couldn't have placed on a map. I barely heard the words, though. The presenter's voice was what mesmerized me. His crisp accent immediately took me back to the night before.

We kissed.

We'd kissed in the starlight, kissed in the shadows, kissed against the cool siding of the office wall. We'd kissed next to the side door of his house, and we'd kissed on the stairs, and we'd kissed in the living room, our bodies pressing close in the darkness. We'd kissed the way we'd both been longing to for the past month, until my lips were sore and my chin felt raw, and we'd finally parted with nervous laughter and whispered apologies: *I'm so sorry, no really it's fine, never should have waited so long, things were confusing, it should have been different, it can be better, I'll do better, I mean it, I mean it, I mean it...*

All of that had happened just a few hours ago, and now I had to go down and work with him as if it were all a dream.

The other riders were gathered around the horse assignment board, arguing.

I sidled into the barn casually, hoping whatever had the riders up in arms would take their attention away from me. I was certain last night's events were written all over my face. My chin definitely had a pinkish hue to it. I hid it with my coffee cup.

Juan was rapping his finger against the board like a hammer. "When you do this I lose money," he snarled, looking at Walt. "These is two horses I lose! What are you going to do about it?"

Walt had his arms folded across his chest. "Seems like you think I do the hiring around here," he told Juan. "Take it up with the boss."

"I don't *see* the boss," Juan snapped. "I see you, and you're his boy, and this is what you do? You add a rider, we all lose money!"

"There are more horses coming," Walt said calmly. "We'll put Envision and Nelly back into work tomorrow. They needed another day off today. But next week, you'll be back to eight horses. Rest of this week, you have six. Call up some buddies if you need more rides."

"We all quit our buddies," Jacinta snapped. "Because we were told we'd have eight or nine every day here and we couldn't leave before noon. It's backwards, Walt, that's what we're saying. You done us wrong."

I was just starting to wonder where this new rider was when a small, dark-haired woman entered the fray. She'd come out of the tack room, already wearing her vest and her helmet, which had a green silk cover and a big fluffy pompom on top. I tried not to stare at it, but I'd never seen anything so silly in my life. Then my eyes drifted to the face beneath the helmet, and I realized she looked oddly like Alexander. The same piercing blue eyes, the same patrician nose and strong chin.

"I can give up a couple of rides, if it's going to cause so much fuss," she offered. She had the same accent as Alexander, too. "I'm not here to cause trouble."

Walt held his hands out in a placating gesture. "There's no fuss, Gigi. This is just the way our riders welcome new members of the team."

Juan scowled. "Hey, if she want to give up the horses, you let her."

"I'm not rearranging that board. It's done."

"So now it's about us losin' money over work *you* don't want to do?" Jacinta asked.

"Fine," Walt spat, exasperated at last. "Gigi, I'm taking you off the last two. That okay?"

Gigi shrugged her slight shoulders and smiled. "Whatever works. You're the boss, Walt."

There was a grudging consensus, and the riders began to move off into little discontented couplets, where they could continue bitching about the morning's rides. Gigi was left all alone. She didn't look too bothered by her exile, but I decided to be the outgoing one and walked over to meet her.

She looked up at me with bright eyes. I wasn't particularly tall but Gigi was tiny—maybe the first person here who actually fit the lay rider's mental image of a jockey. She had to tilt up her chin to make eye contact. "Well, you kept quiet in all that, didn't you!"

I liked the way her statements were questions and her questions were statements. Alexander had a similar manner of speaking. "I'm sorry. I'm new around here, and I try to keep out of any disagreements. It's safer that way. Also, I'm kinda shy."

"Couldn't tell that with the way you stepped right up to say hello! Unless you're looking for an ally, in which case, good choice. I'm an excellent confidante and I'll keep all your secrets. Where do you want to start? The juicier, the better. Any murders or bank robberies you want to confess to someone, let's get it out."

I was too surprised by her speech to do more than blink at her.

Gigi burst into laughter. "Oh, I'm only pulling your leg. Except that I'm not; I *am* very good at keeping secrets. If you ever want to tell any, I'm your woman. Anyway, I'm used to being the new girl; I like moving around. I'm the cousin from back home in the U.K., so I ride for Alexander and Adriene from time to time when I need a place to regroup."

My breath caught in my chest. "Alexander and Adriene?"

I hated hearing their names together, the alliteration, like they *belonged* together. And I'd suddenly remembered something: he'd had dinner with her last night.

That hadn't come up in all the kissing we'd been up to, and I'd forgotten until this instant that when Adriene had left the stallion barn yesterday, her parting words had been about talking things out over dinner.

She raised slanting dark eyebrows at me. "Yep, that's right. Is there something you've heard about the two of them? Because you're looking awfully pale. Makes me think there *are* stories to be told."

Just then, there was a crunching of wheels on gravel. I spun around, unable to keep the eagerness from my eyes as Alexander got out of his truck. Our gazes met and locked, and for a moment we were the only ones in the barn.

"Alexander!" Jacinta shouted. "You're cutting us out of horses, boss! Don't make this a habit."

He turned from me, and I felt the loss of his attention like a cold wind. Beside me, Gigi laughed, a delighted little bubble of sound. I looked down at her and she grinned back, her expression positively joyous.

"So it's like that, is it? Guess I better be keeping your secrets. None of this lot will."

❧❧❧❧ ❧❧❧❧

It can be hard to gossip in a training barn. You're kept busy for ninety percent of your workday, and the other ten percent is just brief breaks of five minutes or so between sets—enough time to grab a drink of water, or run to the bathroom.

The best break was when the Taco Lady arrived, in midmorning. We usually grabbed about fifteen or twenty minutes to sit around and eat, bullshit, and digest before we went to get on the next horse. And so naturally when the Taco Lady arrived, I was the one to sit down next to Gigi with my foil-wrapped taco, desperate to get some gossip on Alexander and Adriene.

"Now, *this* is a proper taco," Gigi announced, tearing into her breakfast. She pronounced it the British way, with a short *A*. "Right, what do you want me to tell you? I know why you're sitting next to me, and it's not because we're best friends, although we could be if you're in the market."

I was so embarrassed, I wished I could fall through the bucket I was perched on and vanished beneath it. "That's not what I want at all," I lied.

"Oh please! You want to know everything about Alexander and you figure *she's English, she's the cousin, she knows what's going on.* Well, you're right and you're right."

"So you'll tell me?"

Her laugh was enough to turn heads. "Sorry, sorry," she sighed. "I'm not much of an ally when I'm making everyone take a look-see, am I? I'm out of practice. I left New York two weeks ago and I've been riding up at this crazy lad's barn in North Carolina, I was the only one there for eight horses and finally I said, best of luck to ya, I'm going to Florida where it's fun! He was utterly furious, but what can you do, I was sick of him. He had ideas he shouldn't have, and there was a person who might have objected. It was like that, you know."

I didn't know. "Ah," I managed.

"So, I called up Alexander and said, look, your old cousin needs a place to crash, and here I am. But listen, to the point, you don't want to get involved with him. Alexander is not into relationships. He might get you all starry-eyed but it's going nowhere. Take it from someone who knows. And if Adriene is here, it's best not to get in her way. That's been dragging on for so long, I think she may just win in the end."

She had lowered her voice by now, but I felt like she was screaming in my face. "So they're really—are you sure?"

"I'm not. But I've known him forever. I've seen him break hearts. He doesn't even mean to, the big dope. He's one of *those.*" She paused for a bite, chewing thoughtfully while I waited anxiously for her to swallow. "And I saw Adriene do an absolute number on him, and every time she comes back, she sinks her claws into his back again. He can't be rid of her, no matter how hard he tries. You know she owns most of these horses, and some of the farm. That's hard to fight."

I nodded, not trusting myself to speak. My taco was sitting unnoticed in my lap.

Gigi saw my consternation and was about to speak again, but just then Walt stood and announced: "Everyone back in the pool!"

I hadn't even eaten, and break was already over. I looked uncertainly at the taco in my lap. My stomach was quivering, full of butterflies from talking about Alexander, from thinking about Alexander, from remembering, over and over again, the kisses we'd shared last night and the more recent realization that they'd probably come after he'd gone to dinner with *her*. I didn't even know why I'd bought the damn thing. I was too frazzled to eat.

Gigi glanced at my uneaten taco with amusement. "You need me to eat that for you, love?"

I handed over my breakfast without a word.

"Early love is the best diet," Gigi said cheerfully. "But you know, you put it on again with the heartache."

Chapter Twenty-six

ALEXANDER CAUGHT UP WITH me after the barn had cleared out for lunch. I'd decided to walk home for lunch, and I was halfway down the lane when I heard his truck rumble up behind me. As I slowed and turned, he smiled at me through his open window. "Well, hello, Alex. Can I give you a ride?"

My heart leapt up in my throat. He was grinning down at me with mischief in his eyes, looking boyish and ready to cause a little trouble. This felt like the moment in the rom-com where we went skinny-dipping in the lake and kissed in the cattails, but in Florida we were liable to get eaten by an alligator if we tried anything that cute.

"Why don't you walk with me instead?" I suggested. The late-October sun wasn't as hot as it had been in past weeks. We were fully into Florida-style fall, meaning the temperature was eighty-five degrees instead of ninety-five, and the slanting yellow sunlight made the day feel old before it was halfway done.

"It would look pretty odd if I left my truck in the middle of the barn lane," Alexander pointed out. "Much more normal if I'm just picking someone up and giving them a lift."

"Is that normal? You'd just give anyone a lift, would you?" I went on walking, forcing him to idle the truck alongside. "Random drifters, wandering the roads..."

"Fair-haired women, roaming my farm," Alexander finished for me. "Keeping me awake at night."

I stopped sharply, and so did he. The truck rocked back and forth gently on its tires.

I looked him in the eye, challenging him. "Mmm...you look pretty well-rested," I decided. He couldn't be entirely let out of the doghouse after leaving me alone all morning. He'd managed to either be on horseback or on his phone every time I'd seen him out of the office. "I don't think I believe you."

"If I look refreshed, it's only because I'm quite used to functioning on two hours of sleep," he countered. "And, I might add, because you wake me up, completely."

My heart fluttered. I didn't know what to say. What did you say to things like that? None of my brief boyfriends had prepped me for a man who was so at ease with short, impactful sentences.

The accent probably didn't hurt.

"Get in the truck with me, Alex."

I walked over to the truck, and as I began to pass the driver's side window, he reached out and took my shoulder. With the gentlest of tugs, he pulled me close and touched his lips to mine.

The kiss was short and sweet, infinitely tender, and my knees immediately began to wobble. Before it had even ended I was thinking: *Oh no.*

I was in so much trouble.

I thought he'd just take me back to the trailer; Jacinta had gone to lunch with the other riders and he wouldn't be seen there. I had no idea what would happen once we got there, and my mind was racing in a million directions at once as I climbed into the truck at last, my lips still half-open, living on the memory of that kiss.

Alexander reached across the wide seat and took my hand in his. "Let's go get some lunch," he suggested. "Have you been to Horse and Hound?"

Everyone went to Horse and Hound. I had heard the place brought up in a hundred conversations already. Miles had talked about business lunches at Horse and Hound, Jacinta had talked about celebratory dinners there. It was the place where horse-people went in Ocala when they wanted to feel a little sophisticated, when they wanted something to eat but they also wanted everyone to know they were equestrians of substance and style. Whether that was true or not.

If he took me there, he wasn't hiding me away. People would see us, recognize him, and wonder who I was.

The thought was equally exhilarating and terrifying. A public date with Alexander was proof we were really moving forward...but, I wasn't ready to be the subject of tack room gossip, either.

Or maybe I was blowing things completely out of proportion. Alexander was still letting the truck idle along, bumping gently towards the end of the lane—where I'd have to tell him to turn left or right.

"Alex?"

His voice was concerned, as if he was suddenly worried he'd read the situation wrong. His lack of confidence gave me a rushing boost of my own.

"Lunch would be wonderful," I told him. "I've heard Horse and Hound is great."

"You'll love it," he said, squeezing my hand and putting his foot down on the gas. "It's just your kind of place."

It turned out that secrets *could* be kept at Horse and Hound. In a dark and cozy corner, we ate lunch and chatted away, and I didn't notice a single curious glance in our direction. On the way out, Alexander waved hello to another man, in a button-down shirt and khakis like a vet would wear, but that was the extent of his man-about-town status.

I wondered how to feel about it, and decided to be okay with it. I hadn't felt hidden away, even if we had sat in the dimmest corner when there were other, brighter places to dine.

Plus, we'd both had a really nice time, which was what counted. Alexander was easy to talk to, and genuinely interested in my life. He gently prised all sorts of stories from me, things I'd half-forgotten about riding with Diana over the years, emotions I'd mostly buried after years of having no one to share them with.

"I can see what drew you here," Alexander said, tipping back the last of an iced tea as we finished our sandwiches. "At first I just assumed it was ambition, but you're not like all of the win-at-any-cost personalities I'm used to. You're genuinely here out of passion for the horses."

"That's exactly it," I replied, thrilled to be understood for once. "This isn't about money or fame and it didn't even feel like a choice. Once I knew I *could* do it, I think I *had* to come. It was like…" I hesitated, but decided Alexander wouldn't laugh at me. "It was like a calling."

He nodded. "I understand that completely."

But I thought his voice sounded a little thin, and he didn't meet my eyes for a few minutes after that. A silence fell over the table, and it wasn't until several minutes later, when we were suddenly discussing the differences between my flat home-region of Florida and the leafy hills of Ocala that he looked back at me with that steady, insightful gaze. I ate his last French fry and tried not to wonder what that lull in conversation had been.

"I can't believe you ate my last French fry."

"You weren't going to eat it." I leaned back in my chair. "You just let it sit there."

"It's the *principle,*" he told me. "We haven't even discussed eating off one another's plates."

"Share some cake with me," I suggested. "We can see how it goes."

He grinned. "I like the way you think."

"Good," I said. "So listen…can I ask you a question? A personal one, I mean."

Alexander lifted his eyebrows, but at least he looked interested. "Fire away."

"What happened with Adriene last night?" I asked him. I looked down, toyed with my napkin.

"Just more arguing. She told me what she wanted, and I told her she couldn't have it, and then she told me what she was planning to do anyway."

I wondered if she had said she'd wanted *him*. "So what is she planning to do?"

"Oh...the usual. She's going to interfere a lot, and stir up some trouble with the staff, and get mad at me for refusing to run horses in the races she chooses, and then, in a few months, she'll go away again. It's her usual pattern. She's like, I don't know, a migrating bird or something."

"But, why? I mean, I'm sorry, I just don't understand what's going on between you two." I suddenly felt emboldened enough to ask. If we were going to be together, I had a right to know.

"Why does she do this? The hell if I know, Alex—"

"Don't lie to me," I said softly. "I might be only twenty-one, but I'm not an idiot."

He nodded and sighed. "I apologize if I was holding out. I just hate talking about her. She wants to be The Famous Trainer." I could hear the capitals in his voice. "It has nothing to do with *me*. I'm just a means to an end. I'm the path she's found towards her goal. We aren't anything more than business associates."

"Always?"

"No, not always. But not in a very long time. The truth is, she was my best client, she was my biggest investor, and that wasn't enough for her. She has to be the muse, and the genius, and the goddess, all at the same time." Alexander looked into his glass. "She'd wear any man out within a few weeks of knowing her. And the problem is, everyone warned me. Everyone knew it. My father, my brother, *Gigi*—yes, Gigi even told me to steer clear of the wealthy, gorgeous Adriene, but all I saw was my ticket out of England, my own farm and my own career and my own name. I didn't know she saw herself the same way, with *me* as the vehicle to fame."

"But that's it?"

Alexander's smile seemed sad. "That's it. Isn't it enough?"

"I didn't mean it like that," I said. "This is hard. I'm not good at talking about...I don't know, about *people*. About feelings."

He reached across the table and put his hand on top of mine. Warm and solid, calloused and strong, his touch offered me a strange measure of comfort. "Maybe none of us horse-people are. But I understand what you're saying. I'm sorry. This is an awkward situation to put you in, having her around. But I don't really have any way out."

"There's a way out of this," I said. "I'll help you find it."

Chapter Twenty-seven

Alexander dropped me back at the training barn after lunch. "I have to go back to the farm office and do some work," he told me as he parked, not bothering to unbuckle his seat belt. "So this is a love you and leave you, I'm afraid."

"You mean you're going to annoy Emily all afternoon," I teased him. I lingered in the truck, leaning gently in his direction. I knew a kiss in front of the training barn was a terrible idea, but I wanted one anyway.

"Not here, Alex," he said with amusement, but his eyes lingered on my mouth.

With a sudden rush of decision, I did it for him. Why should Alexander call all the shots? I leaned across the truck seat and brushed a soft kiss across his lips.

His hands came to my face and for just a moment he gave in, pulling me closer. My soft, chaste kiss goodbye became something more, and then there was a hoot of laughter from outside the truck which broke us apart instantly.

Gigi was walking out of the barn, a duffel bag slung over her shoulder. She waved as she passed us, heading for her own car.

"Don't let me stop you!" she shouted, loud enough to be heard over the truck's idling and, naturally, inside the barn. "I just forgot my gear before. Carry on, lovebirds!"

I scooted back to my side of the truck, mentally counting my life's bad decisions. There seemed to be a lot of them, but kissing Alexander in front of the training barn felt like one of the larger ones.

"It's okay," Alexander said after a moment, reaching for my hand again. "Gigi won't go around telling everyone. But we should be more...discreet. We don't want to set the staff talking about us."

"You really think she'll keep this to herself? She *said* she would, but she also seems to think it was pretty funny."

"She's my cousin," Alexander said with a shrug. "I might have to remind her that if she starts any trouble at my farm, I can call her mother."

"You'd tell on her?" I burst in laughter. "To her *mom?*"

"You laugh, but you've never met my family. The men are formidable enough, but the women are absolutely terrifying. Trust me, a fear of Mother is valuable currency in my family."

❧❧❧❧❧ ❧❧❧❧❧

Jacinta was in the trailer when I got back that evening, making grilled cheese in a smoky pan. There was a haze in the living room and I noticed the smoke detector was already hanging off the wall, batteries dangling. At least she knew her cooking skills had their limits.

"Smells good," I offered, pulling off my boots at the door.

"You were late tonight," she called. "Want a sandwich? Everything okay up there?"

"Just helping a new groom learn the ropes." One of Ricky's friends, a hot walker named Victor, had just arrived in Ocala, and Ricky had convinced Alexander to take him on. He hadn't done much with horses in his old job at Gulfstream besides take halters on and off. "It's hard to believe I'm already training new people. And yes, I would really like a sandwich, thank you." I was drenched with sweat and filthy from head to toe, but in a household like ours, that didn't mean dinner had to be delayed.

Jacinta brought out sandwiches on paper plates, along with a bag of Ruffles. "These were buy-one get-one at the Winn-Dixie," she said with satisfaction. "I love me some Ruffles. Now, I hear you had a fancy Ocala lunch today! What was that all about?"

I'd just picked up my sandwich, stomach rumbling; now I put it back down and stared at Jacinta. Had she been making me grilled cheese just so she could pump me for information? Was this gossip grilled cheese? I'd hoped it was friendship grilled cheese. I forced a grin that I hoped was convincingly casual. "Oh yeah? Where'd you hear that?"

"Well, *I* heard it from Bunny Grafton at the leather shop, but she heard it from Willie Reese over at the farrier supply store next to Horse and Hound. I had to pick up my leggings with the busted zipper and Bunny was there dropping off a saddle needing new fenders. She's been ponying horses at Classic Mile all summer and that old Western saddle of hers looks like she found it in a back barn somewheres. *Anyway,* if Bunny Grafton's tellin' folks Alexander Whitehall's taking his riders to lunch at Horse and Hound, everyone in Ocala'll know by nightfall." Jacinta turned and elaborately lifted the blinds of the windows behind the sofa. "Which is now, actually."

I took a bite of sandwich and chewed slowly, thinking about the best way to approach this. "Well, we did have lunch today, but it was just to talk about some work stuff. I hope Bunny didn't tell you we were having some sort of romantic interlude."

Jacinta guffawed. "Romance didn't come into it. But if that's what you like to tell yourself..."

"Jacinta, I'm not having some sort of affair with Alexander."

"Well, he ain't married so I don't know I'd call it an *affair*, anyways."

"Nothing is going on," I insisted, doubling down on my lie. "I hope Bunny didn't go too crazy making things up."

"Well, she didn't," Jacinta said, looking decidedly down at the mouth. I had the impression she'd been hoping for something juicier than what she'd heard. "She just said you was sittin' together and laughin'. But you laugh pretty easy. I told her that." Suddenly Jacinta was my staunch defender. "I told her you were a real giggler and it didn't mean anything."

I was pretty sure I wasn't a giggler, but whatever. It worked in my favor. "This is a good sandwich," I told her. "Thanks for making it for me."

Jacinta shrugged and smiled. "I'm glad you like it," she said. "The secret's mayo."

And while I tried to figure out what she meant by that, Jacinta turned on the television, and I realized with some relief that the conversation was over.

The next awkward discussion didn't come up until morning.

"I thought it was cute," Gigi said, walking her colt close to Wing.

"It was embarrassing," I said. "Can we not talk about it?"

"But tell me if I'm right," Gigi persisted. "I knew you were messing with him. But Alex! The way you look at him! You really are in love with him, aren't you? Even though I told you not to be? You don't listen at all."

I'd been in love with Alexander since the moment I'd seen him, but that wasn't the sort of thing you said out loud to his cousin. Or at all. Who believed in love at first sight in these un-magical times? "Come on, Gigi."

She peered at me and then nodded, satisfied for the moment. "That's fine, if you don't want to say it out loud. I understand. But listen to me, please. Like I said before, he is not great at relationships. I'm not sure he's ever been in a proper couple. You'll want to play it cool with him. Who knows, you might pull it off! But you two shouldn't be bouncing around at Horse and Hound like a pair of pin-hookers getting in each other's pants between sales, and you *definitely* shouldn't be necking in front of the shed-row! You've met my good friend Ocala, haven't you? She doesn't keep secrets very well."

I turned Wing onto the track and Gigi kept her colt tucked in alongside him. "Why do we have to keep it a secret?" I asked, as if I didn't know already.

"For your own dignity," Gigi informed me. "Alex, they'll talk about you something awful! You're younger than he is, for starters. You're a rider. The optics are terrible. You *can't* just be seen as his latest plaything. You're better than that. You're made for better things than that."

I bit back a retort; I was certain I wasn't a plaything, but there was no telling Gigi that. For one thing, I didn't have any reasons. I just had *feelings*. And I knew Gigi wasn't the sort to trust an emotion—anymore than she'd trust a wall-eyed colt, like the one suddenly popping a buck beneath her. I picked up Wing's reins and sat back, just in case he got any ideas.

Gigi shouted and gave her colt a crack with her stick to straighten him out. Wing immediately swerved sideways to escape the scary monster-lady. He nearly took me straight into a palm tree, offering a dangerous but well-timed end to the conversation.

"Straighten it out, ladies!" Walt called from behind us. "Don't make me regret this!" There was a titter of laughter from the string of riders following; upsettingly, the highest and most amused one came from Jacinta.

I sighed. I really hadn't wanted to get laughed at this morning. Because today, for the first time ever, I was in charge.

Well, co-charge. Gigi and I were leading this set. Walt had told me it was time for me to start heading out in front. I'd be regulating speed, keeping the horses in a straight line, and showing everyone my riding chops.

I'd been tempted to argue I had no riding chops, but apparently this was not the case. Walt and Alexander insisted I just needed to finesse my understanding of technique and racetrack protocol.

Other than the palm-tree incident, things on this first set as head rider were going pretty well. The sun was rising and shone into my eyes as we trotted up the outside rail, heading clockwise around the training track. Wing put his head down and chewed at the bit, snorting into the early morning air. This was the nicest part of the day, and I hoped I didn't do anything to screw it up. I glanced over at Gigi, hoping to exchange a nice smile, but instead, she cast me a wicked grin.

"*What?*" I asked suspiciously.

"I'm still trying to get over the college girl who comes up to Ocala with a suitcase full of dreams, falls in love with one of the town's most eligible bachelors, and thinks she can pull it off without becoming the town's most amazing gossip item. You're cute. I mean it, Alex, I really like you. I think you're adorable."

I had absolutely no interest in being cute or adorable to Alexander's glib cousin. I cast a glance behind me, making sure Walt and the others were a decent distance behind. "Come on, Gigi, let it go. They're going to hear you."

She looked over her shoulder. "You're safe. Too far away. All this jingle-jangle of tack is insulating you. Listen, you need a plan which gets you from casual girlfriend to serious partner. I mean it. Because at some point, if you want to keep this going, you're going to have to own it. The Whitehall family doesn't keep things to ourselves. We go whole hog and then rub our success in everyone else's faces."

"I'm not a member of the Whitehall family," I argued. "I'm an O'Connor, and we don't do anything a certain way, because it's just our last name and doesn't mean a thing."

"Apples and oranges," Gigi said comfortably. "And I wouldn't be so sure about keeping that last name for long, anyway. I'll bet in no time at all, *you'll* be the new face of Cotswold Farm—don't shake your head at me! Head rider, then you'll be assistant trainer, and all the while you'll be wiggling your way right up to the ultimate top spot next to Alexander. You'll be everywhere, at sales and at the races and in meetings with bloodstock agents and owners. And honestly? I think you're right for the job. Just get on top of my clown of a cousin before someone takes him from you, and you can have the whole shebang."

I glanced at her uneasily. "None of that is even remotely possible."

Then, Wing decided to spook at an upcoming bush, and suddenly it took everything I had to keep him from swinging out and into Gigi's horse. Or maybe it just seemed like he needed that much attention. Either way, I made it obvious I couldn't keep up with the conversation *and* settle my horse, and we rode in silence for the rest of the set.

And yeah, other than that big spook, my first set as leader went pretty well. Maybe I *did* have chops.

All morning, I found myself keeping a weather eye on the other riders and grooms, listening in on their conversations whenever I could, hoping no one else had heard the rumors Jacinta had—or overheard Gigi while she cheerfully accused me of somehow wheeling for the farm. Did she really think I had some deep plan to sleep my way to the top and become Mrs. Alexander Whitehall? She was out of her mind. I had literally never seen myself as a future wife; when other little girls were holding play-weddings, I was building steeplechase jumps out of sticks and cantering myself over them.

Luckily—for whatever that term was worth—things quickly became far too crazy for little old me to register on the farm's gossip scale. Because while I was out on Wing, giving him a nice steady gallop and praising him for being a good boy, Adriene returned. And this time, she showed up in boots and jeans, ready to work.

We saw her the moment we turned the horses back to the gap. Gigi had been saying something about her colt, but whatever she'd observed vanished forever when she saw the female figure standing alongside Alexander. They were both up on the viewing stand; Betsy was tied to the railing, waiting patiently with one hind leg cocked.

"Shit," Gigi whispered. "Adriene's really here."

"It's early," I replied. "Guess she wanted to see her horses go?"

"You idiot," Gigi said, though without any real malice. "If Adriene's here at six a.m., it's not because she wants to watch the gallops. She's here to take over."

Chapter Twenty-eight

THE TACO LADY HAD driven away, and we were huddled over our breakfasts, eating quietly. There was no room for gossip or conversation; everyone knew Adriene was right next to us, closeted in the office with Alexander but capable of emerging at any moment. We were shoveling our food down, and I think there was definitely a shared belief that if we could just eat and get back on our horses, we could put off whatever was coming, maybe forever. But the quiet couldn't last. Everyone had something to say.

Billy was complaining into his tacos that Adriene had criticized the way he held his reins.

"And you know I'm sensitive to that kind of thing," he sighed, his voice an even deeper shade of blue than usual.

"You do just fine," Walt assured him. "Don't let a loud-mouth make you feel bad when Alexander knows you're a good rider."

"But she overrules Alexander in everything," Jacinta hissed. "And the problem is, she don't know a damn thing about trainin' horses."

"She knows *somethin'* about training," Walt said dourly. "Problem is, she don't know enough. You can't take half a class and ace the final."

I glanced at Gigi.

"You're wondering if she's *really* that bad," Gigi murmured, her voice audible only to me. "She is. Avoid her, Alex. Don't give her one chance to notice you. *Especially* you, got it?"

I had just rolled up the greasy foil from my tacos when the door opened. I heard sighs, quickly stifled behind hands and brightly-colored Mexican sodas, as Adriene emerged and looked us all over.

She was still dressed expensively, but instead of the tailored linens she'd been wearing the first day she'd been here, she was decked out in beautiful jodhpurs and a lovely checked riding shirt. Her look was very vintage, very chic, very high-maintenance. I knew my jeans and t-shirt were all that was required of me, but they made me feel inferior anyway.

"Hello, team," Adriene announced, fastening that gleaming twenty-four-karat smile on her face. "I know most of you, but some of you are new. If you're new, here's what to expect from here on out. Everyone, it's time we pick up the pace. Alexander has agreed to bring me back on as a trainer and we'll be consulting on all decisions. We have some of the best bloodlines in the country in this barn. It's time they started training like it."

Jacinta gave me a sidelong glance. *This old line,* she seemed to be saying. I had to admit it did sound like something out of a feel-good sports movie. Except that picking up the pace to build winners in a human sports movie ended with a trophy, whereas with horses in real life, it usually ended with lameness. If the horses were moving slowly, Alexander had to have a reason. Why did Adriene think she needed to rush the process?

Adriene was looking around as if she was hoping someone would have a reaction to her speech, but we were all just watching her warily. We must have looked like a lot of cornered rabbits, watching the cat, hoping it would lose interest in us and walk away.

"Breezes tomorrow," Adriene said finally. "Be ready. I want timed works on every horse of racing age."

She picked her way past us and went out to her car, a gleaming silver Mercedes. After a moment, the car went purring off down the lane.

There was an excited burst of chatter, grooms and riders alike spouting off in several languages and dialects. I pushed myself back against the wall, not ready to get involved. Anyway, Alexander was just inside the office, and the door was still open. He could hear every one of their complaints. He knew what they thought of her.

I slipped into the office and closed the door behind me.

Alexander was sitting behind his desk, his face resting in his palms. He looked up at the sound of the door closing, his face weary. "Alex, you shouldn't be in here alone with everyone just outside the door."

"I'm not allowed to have a private conversation with my boss?"

"We have enough trouble right now. That's all I'm saying."

I lingered at the corner of his desk, torn between wanting to slip behind it and wrap my arms around him, and wanting to sit on the other side, arms crossed over my chest, a person whose opinion should be taken seriously. Halfway wasn't good enough, but I popped my hip on the desk and owned it anyway. "You can't let this happen. No one will stay. Walt told me when the yearlings come in, people start moving around. If they think you're not in charge anymore, what's their reason to stay?"

What's my *reason to stay? There are other places to ride.* My sensible brain wanted answers, but I swatted it aside. Alexander was my reason. I had to help him dig out of this hole.

"They'll stay for good horses and good pay," Alexander said shortly.

"No one's going to stick around if the horses are getting pushed too hard. That's dangerous for riders and it's stressful for grooms. If they got another offer, they'd take it." I had stayed at Calusa Lakes long past that job's expiration date—I knew this now—because Diana had been so absent. If she'd been on top of me, every day, with her increasingly erratic demands, I wouldn't have stayed. Adriene's presence, though sober, felt the same. She was dangerous. I could feel it. "Good riders aren't going to work for a bad trainer."

He leaned back in his chair and looked at the ceiling. "So *this* is when you choose to tell me you'd rather just be friends?"

I stared at him for a moment, and then I saw the corner of his mouth twitch. I burst into startled laughter. "You jerk! Of all the times to make a joke like that..."

Alexander leapt up from his chair and came around the desk. Suddenly he was in my space, his mouth very close to mine. I looked him in the eye, daring him to do something about it. As he leaned forward, I scooped handfuls of his shirt into my hands, pulling him into me.

Oh no, I thought, somewhere in the clouds of my deep consciousness, *I think I might love fighting with this guy.*

Maybe I didn't actually accomplish anything by my attempted chat with Alexander, but at least I left the office with the happy buzz of a successful make-out session. We'd kissed until I'd fallen backwards across the desk, my shoulders tipping his training diary and pen onto the floor with a clatter. I'd pushed to get up, afraid someone would hear us, but he shook his head and muttered, "No one's coming in here now," before wrapping an arm beneath my shoulders, pulling me against him, and launching another attack.

It was the most exciting five minutes of my life, saddle-time excluded, or, if I was being really honest, maybe it was even more exciting than galloping Wing, but I couldn't be sure and I wasn't about to ruin a good thing by analyzing it.

Anything could have happened in there if we hadn't heard Walt shouting, "*Okay cowboys, time to mount up!*" and there was no doubt in our minds about the extra volume he'd used for today's call back to riding. I'd given Alexander a rueful smile and he'd grinned right back, his eyes crinkling merrily.

"I guess I better let my rider get back to her duties," he joked, tugging at my shirt as if it had gotten badly disheveled during our little encounter. Of course, it was a shirt which had been pinched under a tight, sweaty, high-impact foam vest for five gallops already, so there wasn't much more we could do to it just by rolling around on his desk.

"Yeah, stop distracting me," I replied, elaborately dusting at my jeans, permanent stains and all. "Some of us are trying to be professional."

"Meet me later?" Alexander asked in a different tone, picking up the books and pens on the floor. "Stallion barn, five o'clock?"

Maureen would be gone by then. "Sure," I agreed. "It's a date."

"It might be our best chance at one," he said, suddenly looking a little glum. "I seem to have lost control of my farm, and she has a tendency to show up in the evenings wanting to go over plans."

I could hear Walt stomping around outside, trying to get my attention without actually opening the door. I wondered if Gigi had told him about us—if only to stop him from coming inside. "Alexander, we have to get her out of here. There *has* to be a way."

"I've tried. I've been failing elaborately for years now, and she keeps coming back. I'm starting to think all I can do is cut my losses, like she wants me to. Sell her my share and go somewhere new. Otherwise, all I can do is keep a low profile and wait for her to leave again." Alexander sat down and looked at me with an empty expression. From behind the cluttered desk, he looked like a weary office drone, overwhelmed with paperwork and pointlessness.

The very life I had come here to avoid.

"We're getting rid of her," I told him.

Alexander gently spun his chair from side-to-side. "Never sell your soul for money, Alex, it's not worth it."

I laughed. "Don't worry about me and money, Alexander. I've literally never chosen money over my own freedom."

"I could learn something from you, then."

"Maybe you could." I liked the idea of teaching him something. This relationship looked pretty one-sided on paper, but maybe there was more to it than that. More to *me*.

There was a soft knock on the door. "Alex?" Walt asked. "Can you come now, so we can get this set on the track?"

Alexander bit his lip comically. "Well, Alex, can you?"

"Oh my God, Alexander." Louder, I called, "I'll be right there, Walt!"

"Sorry," Alexander sighed, but he was still grinning.

I wished I had something to throw at him. "Focus up, gross boy. Let's think about this for a second. Failing hasn't worked. She still thinks she can swoop in and fix things, and even when she can't, she just blames you again, right? So being useless isn't enough. It's like a challenge she can't resist. You have to do something *final*. An ultimatum."

He lifted his eyebrows. "A final challenge? Like a reality show?"

"Honestly, yeah. Something like that. Raise the stakes. She wins or she's out."

"What on earth would that look like?"

"I don't know," I said, shrugging. "You think about it, though. I'm going to go ride your horses."

Chapter Twenty-nine

ALEXANDER WAS WAITING FOR me in the stallion barn, a smile on his face and a wicker basket over one arm.

I hesitated when I saw him, feeling suddenly shy and uncertain. What exactly was happening right now? My brain was overwhelmed by the implications of this moment: of that handsome man, of that winning smile, of that perfect little hamper with its perfect crease of gingham table-cloth poking out of the top. Things between Miles and I had been so simple because he was close to my age, and we were on even ground. Things between Alexander and I would never, ever be simple.

But some things aren't choices.

Coming to Ocala hadn't felt like a choice, and neither had falling for Alexander.

I swallowed back my indecisiveness, because it was pointless to pretend any of this was optional, and let my feet resume their course. I was still in my work clothes, and my paddock boots were businesslike on the rubber pavers of the aisle.

"What have you got there?" I asked, adding a hint of tease into my voice. "I hope there's a tandem bicycle parked behind the barn, too."

"It's not a bad idea. We could put our feet up and go sailing down the hillside. Who knows how fast we'd get?"

"We'd hit peak velocity right before we crashed into a paddock fence." I reached him and turned my face up to his. Alexander put his free hand beneath my chin and gave me a lingering kiss.

"Well, hello, miss," he said afterwards, while my skin was still tingling. "So are you going to make fun of my picnic basket, or are you going to eat the nice things in it? Because you can't have both."

"I guess I'm going to make fun of it," I sighed, shaking my head mournfully. "And then steal it when you're not looking."

"I never look away. I'm all-seeing."

"That's part of being the boss, right?"

He laughed, a low chuckle which seemed to linger somewhere deep inside of me. "Alex," he replied, "you should know. Something told me you'd be boss here someday. The very day we met, I felt it."

I met his gaze, feeling the thrill of this moment, savoring his confession. For a moment, I let myself revel in his words, and then I said, "Fine. I won't make fun of your picnic basket."

His smile deepened. "Hay-loft? There aren't ants up there; I can't say the same for the grass."

❧ ⸱ ☙

The picnic baskets of my childhood were all straight out of the grocery-store deli: fried chicken and potato salad, pickles and potato chips. Alexander's picnic basket was mail-order from England, with crisp water crackers and tiny jars of jams and marmalades, hard wedges of cheese and thin slabs of dark chocolate. There were two small bottles of champagne, which he tipped, fizzing, into thin plastic flutes.

"No glass flutes in the barn," he said, passing me my bubbly. "You'll probably have to learn that lesson the hard way, though."

"I'd love to pop the cork after a big win." I took a sip and lifted my eyebrows, impressed. This was my first taste of the real thing, although I wasn't about to tell him that. "How big a race does it take to warrant champagne?"

"Oh, it's more about milestones. The first win for an apprentice, the first win for a horse everyone is high on, the first stakes win, that sort of thing."

"The first win after a slump?" I asked daringly.

He shrugged and gave me a lopsided smile. "That would be a good reason."

My heart went out to him. "I'm sorry. I don't want to bring up sore subjects. I'm just trying to figure out how I can help you, and so that's the biggest thing on my mind right now. When we can break out the bubbly for a good reason."

His gaze was steady. "I think *you're* a good reason."

I nearly dropped the glass, which was exactly why we were drinking out of plastic flutes. "I think you're a pretty good reason, too."

"But it's complicated, you know."

"What is?" I pretended I didn't know what he meant; it gave me time to sip my champagne, think of a defense.

"You and I."

There were bubbles in my nose and I held back a sneeze with difficulty. This wasn't the moment for big, funny sneezes. I swallowed and winced, looking down to hide my watering eyes. "Because of Adriene," I gulped finally, getting a hold of myself.

"Because of Adriene, because of the town, lots of reasons. Walt told me he wants to leave after the new year; you'll be taking his place. Don't look at me like you won't be ready! All you had to do was learn our procedures. You know how to run a barn and keep a horse sound. Conditioning you'll learn from me. There's nothing stopping you from taking over tomorrow, except Walt is still here. And Adriene is still here."

"And she wouldn't let me take over?"

"If she was here when Walt left, she'd insist on hiring someone herself. He'll have to stay until she goes."

I sighed and looked into the basket. I spotted a package of chocolate chip cookies and pulled them out. This was definitely a moment for cookies. "Maybe we should just run away together," I suggested moodily. "Fresh start, no Adriene."

"Maybe." Alexander's tone was thoughtful. "I've considered leaving before, but I never had such a compelling reason before."

I glanced up at him through my eyelashes. He was eyeing me with a pensive gaze, as if he was taking my pouty little idea seriously. "You can't be serious."

"I am serious. Legally, I'm only part-owner here. There's nothing I can do to avoid her. Why not just take her money and run? It's what she wants. Let her stay here and fail on her own terms. At least then she can't blame me. Maybe it will do her some good. And us? We'll be long gone." Alexander leaned forward. "What say you, Alex? If I cash out now, we can go anywhere you want. Except the U.K., that is. Going home in disgrace is off the table."

There were a thousand places I wanted to go, a million. I stared at Alexander. His face was just inches from mine, his eyes were boring into me. I opened my mouth, ready to answer as soon as the right place came to mind. We were going to do it! We were going to run away together! Life *was* a movie, I didn't care what anyone said. Everyone had been wrong: Professor Blake, my parents, Diana, even Lucille. They'd tried to tie me down to one kind of life and all the while, this moment had been waiting for me.

Alexander saw the gleam in my eye. "Go on," he whispered. "Say it. Take us away from here."

His voice seemed to catch on the last word.

That was the moment I knew.

"No," I said, my heart lifting in my chest. "This is where we're supposed to be."

When we clambered back downstairs, the sun was setting over the pastures, silhouetting the boxy angles of the house where Alexander lived and the distant, more pleasing lines of the broodmare barn. The paddocks and training barn below us were bathed in golden light. We stood in the driveway and looked over the farm, our hands clutching tightly together.

"This farm is worth figuring out," I told him.

"I know," Alexander agreed, but his voice was somber. "I think I'd try anything at this point. If I didn't feel like I already had."

We walked out a little further and I heard a whisper of wings behind me. I turned to see bats fluttering against the deep blue of the eastern sky, heading out on their nightly hunt.

"Alexander," I whispered. "I think I have an idea."

He looked down at me, eyebrows lifted. "Oh, really? Where do you want to talk this out? Shall we walk down to the house?"

I was on the edge of something, and I didn't want to give it time to fade away. "Do you have a condition book for Gulfstream up here?"

"There's probably one in the tack room. We can go look." His expression was quizzical. "Are you planning on racing us out of trouble?"

"Something like that," I muttered. "But shhh! Let me think."

Chapter Thirty

THE CONDITION BOOK SPREAD open between us, I leaned over the desk and flipped the pages, searching for inspiration. Every race for the upcoming race meeting was listed, along with their individual conditions: length, course, starting requirements, age of horse, things like that. Hence the name, condition book. It had taken me a while to figure it out, but it was basically a prize list for a horse show, expanded for an entire season.

Alexander offered a running commentary as I searched for the winning combination of factors. I needed something far enough in the future to prep, but not far enough that we'd all lose our minds from Adriene's overbearing presence. I was thinking specifically of Wing as I looked for a race. He'd been going so well with his extra workouts over the past month, and despite Adriene's cutting criticisms, I knew he was becoming really fit, his body hard and muscular.

I thought back to the way I'd conditioned ex-racehorses to prep them for hunter-jumper shows, which could be real marathons: full days spent in the Florida sun, standing at the in-gate between flat and jumping classes which went on for division after division.

I hadn't realized it before, but I *did* have experience conditioning horses...just for endurance, instead of speed. Racehorses needed both. Now, maybe, I could put it all together and build a winning racehorse.

A likely race jumped out at me, and the more I read the conditions, the more I liked it.

"Here," I told Alexander, putting my finger under a race's name. "Wing, in this race. Your way. Your win. Get her to agree that this is the last deciding factor, and we'll win it."

Alexander glanced over the page. "The Hibiscus Stakes," he read. "A mile and a sixteenth on...turf?" He glanced over at me. "You want us to put the farm up over a turf race? What makes you so sure of that?"

"Wing loves the grass. Don't forget, I ride him in the pasture every day. I can feel the difference between his stride on grass and dirt. He's a better horse on the grass. It suits his movement, too—his long pasterns, his springy gait. Maybe he didn't move this nicely before his growth spurt, and that's why you didn't try him on turf before."

"Is that so?" Alexander leaned back on the chair, his gaze drifting to the ceiling. "I suppose you might be right. My mind has really been elsewhere."

"I'm right," I said. This confidence felt new, but warranted. I knew what I was talking about. "He'll be ready. And that race is two months away. We can put him into an allowance a few weeks beforehand, sharpen him up and remind him of his job."

Alexander's eyes shifted to my face. "You're starting to talk like a racetracker, Alex."

"That's what I am," I informed him. "And this is what we're doing. We could go anywhere in the world. You said so. Well, I want to go to Gulfstream with my horse and win a race. And I want the prize to be this farm."

A smile crept across his face. "*This* farm? Have you looked around that awful house of mine? It was designed by drug lords from Miami. We got this place from a government auction. You might change your mind when you get a proper tour."

"I have my trailer," I reminded him airily. "I'm perfectly fine down there."

"Honestly, those trailers should be sold for scrap. I'm embarrassed to have a lovely little groom like you living down there." His arm slipped around my waist and tugged me closer. "I have half a mind to evict you."

I burst out laughing. "Then I'll live in this gorgeous tack room. Maureen won't mind as long as I clean up after myself."

"She'd *never* let you stay up here. She'd probably have a fit if she knew we were in here right now. Maureen only lets me use this desk because she knows sometimes I need the quiet to get all of these damn breedings done."

His words reminded me of the notebooks. I wriggled free of Alexander's grip, ignoring his protests, and pulled the notebook from its drawer. "Can you talk to me about this, please?" I asked, opening the notebook to the last page of matings.

"What, right now?"

"Yes," I insisted. "While I'm thinking about it." I put my finger under the line at the end of the hypothetical matings: *A wants top nicks by Oct—full bookings by Nov—commits to full year??*

"Ah," Alexander sighed. "I do owe her those top nicks. Her arrival distracted me."

"What does this mean? Is it going to be a problem?"

"Just another one of the places we differ. Adriene wants to massively increase the breeding operation by sending our mares to outside stallions. I want to support the ones here with good mares we already have. The nicks we talked about before...those are the scores each mating gets on paper. Then we have to hash out which stallions to book. And then that turns into *another* year of her mares here, on top of the farm's mares she also has a share in. It's a way for her to dig in deeper."

"But we can get her out of here before that happens," I said. "The stallions aren't booked yet."

"If your idea works out, yes, I suppose we will."

"It's going to work out."

Alexander closed the book and tapped the cover. "This is just one more reason it *needs* to work out. If it doesn't, we're leaving."

I looked at him evenly. He'd used the word *we* without pausing, without emphasis. It simply was. We simply were.

"That's fair," I agreed. "But we'll come to that when we have to."

I knew in racing, as in any life with horses, there were no guarantees. Still, when I let Alexander pull me tight against him again, it felt like there might be. Just this one.

Outside the barn, a car door slammed.

⁂

We both jumped up from the desk, our minds on hiding the evidence. My face flushed as I pushed away from Alexander, while he swept the condition book into the desk drawer. Looking for some innocent reason I might be in the room, I ran to the feed bins lining the wall beneath the window, dumped out the morning grain Maureen had carefully set up, and set the buckets on the floor beside me.

When Adriene came into the tack room, I was setting up feed and Alexander was sitting behind the desk, studying the breeding notes.

"Good evening," she said coolly. "Chores running a little late?"

This was directed at me. I glanced over my shoulder and gave her a short nod. "A little."

She waited a beat. I didn't feel the need to say anything else. I took down a jar of Farrier's Formula and sprinkled it over the buckets, just for something to do. I didn't know if the stallions usually got it in the morning, but a little extra wouldn't hurt them.

Adriene lost interest in me. "Alexander, I was wondering if I could interest you in dinner tonight."

"Don't think so," he said mildly.

I heard her sigh, sharp and exasperated. "I want to talk about the breedings."

"Working on that now, as it happens." A page flipped with elaborate slowness. "Making sure there are no mistakes. Only the best to the best, right?"

"That's right." Adriene's boots tapped around the tack room.

I was out of innocent vitamins to add to the buckets. I put the morning feed back into the grain bin, settling the buckets carefully one atop each other so nothing would tip over, and closed the lid. I dusted my hands on my jeans as I turned around. "I'll get going now. Alexander, will you turn the lights out?"

"I certainly will," he said absently. "Thank you for your hard work today."

It was all I could do to bury a smile as I hustled out of the room. The stallions watched me through the stall bars with interest, probably because I'd been rattling the lid of the grain bin, but no one made any noise as I went down the aisle and hung a hard left, scooping up the abandoned picnic basket as I went. I clutched it to my chest all the way down the driveway, breathless with fear in case she drove by, caught me in the headlights, and spotted me with my armful of pretty wicker hamper.

But Adriene didn't leave the barn until much later that evening. I knew because I sat at my bedroom window, slowly sipping one of Jacinta's cheap beers, and watching impatiently for the lights to go out.

Chapter Thirty-one

I WAS MOODY WHEN Alexander came into the barn the next morning, the result of not enough sleep and far too much thinking. I hadn't heard from him again last night, and I thought a quick text would have been the least he could have done for me. Something to say he'd gotten rid of Adriene for the night, so I wouldn't have had to stare into the darkness of my room until the wee hours, wondering if she'd gone home alone, or if she'd stuck around his house to enjoy her own little bottle of champagne.

I was new at this relationship game, and even so, I knew this wasn't an easy one. Sure, it was fun, and thrilling, to talk about running away together under the spell of a pretty sunset, some bubbles, and the idea that we were up to something secretive and special. All that rom-com stuff might not mean a thing in real life, though. If lovely, loaded Adriene had chosen to put the moves on Alexander, which everyone thought she was doing at every second of the day (when she wasn't in the barn, fighting with him, of course) then who was to say he wouldn't see the clear advantage of giving in to the woman who owned his life and didn't want to let it go?

So I tightened the girth on Chessiecat, who was still my first ride of the morning after all of these weeks, buckled my helmet strap, and accepted my leg-up from Ricky. Galloping was becoming old hat to me now. I'd gotten used to the little saddles, the light snaffles, the new kind of balance required of me. I had moved past the tenuous, scary, beginner's stage and I was actually starting to get good at galloping, maybe better than some of the other riders, if Ricky and Walt could be believed.

Ricky was standing in the doorway as I took Chessiecat on her first circles around the stall. "You gonna work a half this morning?" he asked, watching the mare with a critical eye.

"Probably." I was able to shrug it off. Working at speed was still new to me, but I wasn't afraid of the flat-out gallops anymore. I was looking forward to the thrill of it, actually. "I guess Adriene will make that call when we get out there."

Ricky scowled. "She ain't even here. Neither's Alexander. Might be Walt's call."

"If Walt's riding, how can he time everyone?" I asked, but that wasn't the question which mattered. They *both* weren't here? That couldn't be good.

It didn't mean anything.

It might.

Ricky stood aside and I let Chessiecat trip out of the stall—literally, this time, as she nearly fell over the sill of the door and I had to catch the weight of her head with the reins. Jacinta, a few stalls back on her filly, laughed at our ungainly entrance into the morning.

"Leave my filly alone, Jacinta," I called over my shoulder. "She hasn't had her coffee yet."

"She better wake up and give her daddy a fast quarter or she's gonna get sent up to the broodmare barn," Jacinta crowed.

"That's not true," I told Chessiecat, patting her neck. "Don't listen to mean ol' Jacinta."

"It's true, all right," Jacinta insisted. "Jimmy Wallace comes down every winter and he's not gonna hang on to anything that isn't running by January. And Adriene will tell him she's no good. Trust me on *that* one, newbie."

"How do you know Jimmy Wallace?"

"How does anyone know anyone? It's racing, you get to know folks."

"I know Jimmy Wallace," Gigi announced, joining us on her dark bay filly. "Nice guy."

We turned the corner and went up the front side of the shed-row. I glanced over the line of pick-ups and cars pulled up near the center aisle. Neither Alex nor Adriene's vehicles were there. Pre-dawn's pearly gray was creeping over the sky, but beyond the dark shadows of the paddock fences, no cars were making their way up the lane.

"Are they just not coming?" I asked no one in particular.

"Hold back!" Walt's voice came from the center aisle, and I reined back to allow him to ride his filly through and cut in front of us. She was a tall chestnut by one of the farm's stallions, and she looked sensational, her coat gleaming and her muscles sliding cleanly, her svelte lines making a pretty picture even under the unflattering fluorescent lights hanging over the shed-row. "Thank you, ma'am," Walt said as he reined her into the shed-row ahead of Chessiecat and me. "Looks like we're running this show by ourselves this morning. You got a watch?"

I glanced at my wrist, at my little gold watch I wore every day, despite the tan-line. "Not the kind you want."

"Damn. Maybe someone can spare up another one in the tack room."

"No need," Jacinta announced. "Here they come."

❧ ❧

They came in separate cars, but their synchronized arrival still gave me a sick feeling in my stomach. I supposed there was a slight chance Adriene had pulled into the driveway just as Alexander was backing out of the garage, but it seemed far more likely they'd left the house at the same time. *The same house.*

He wouldn't have, would he?

He wouldn't kiss me and offer to take me anywhere in the world, and then just as quickly spend the night with another woman, would he?

They'll eat you alive, Lucille had said.

I felt her meaning now. I felt gnawed on, torn at, ripped to shreds. But I'd never let anyone see it. That much, I owed to Lucille Cornett—and just maybe to Diana. The old Diana, who had built a farm and a career from nothing, and had never let anyone break her spirit. Diana had broken herself, but, she'd probably say, at least a man hadn't done it.

I deepened my seat, sat up straighter, and pressed my feet into the stirrups.

I smiled and patted Chessiecat beneath the ripple of her short mane.

He looked at me as he went into the barn, one quick glance, and then he looked straight ahead again.

Let him go, I told myself. *You didn't come here to fall in love.*

That part had been an accident. Whatever else happened, I couldn't let it slow me down.

Walt turned his tall filly out of the shed-row and down the horse-path to the track. He glanced at me over his shoulder, his grin bright in the half-light. "You ready to go fast?"

❧❧❧❧❧ ❦❦❦❦❧

We were galloping together, our horses neck and neck, striving to hit the finish pole first, when Walt's filly bobbled. The change in her motion shocked me as much as it did Walt; we were so close together, it was as if I was riding two horses instead of one, both of their heads bobbing away just in front of my eyes. So when her head came up too high, and then just as quickly dipped too low, I instinctively reined back on Chessiecat, trying to slow her strides. We were at racing speed now, the height of our work, and she turned her head against my hand, her mouth gaping against the bit.

Walt's filly was slowing in a hurry, falling back behind me. I heard shouts as the other riders began to catch up, our careful distancing falling apart in a matter of seconds. I wanted to turn Chessiecat around and send her back to Walt, but with the other horses fanning out across the track, there was nowhere for us to go but forward. She cantered raggedly, still shaking her head at my tight hold on the bit, before slowing to a jog on the turn. I looked over my shoulder to see what I'd left behind.

The pale morning light was just beginning to turn from gray to gold. It picked out Walt, standing by the inside rail, his filly's reins in his hands. Another horse and rider were near him—Billy, I thought. Juan and Jacinta were cantering their horses the wrong way up the track, heading back to meet them. I watched Walt bend down to pick up the chestnut's foreleg, and started to turn Chessiecat back, to see how I could help them. Then Jacinta looked over her shoulder and saw me. "Get to the barn!" she shouted. "Let them know!"

I waved a hand in acknowledgment and kicked Chessiecat back into a slow gallop, heading around the turn towards the gap. I figured Alexander and Adriene would be on foot at the viewing stand by now; they'd have timed our works, or what we'd managed to get of them. If we hadn't done works this morning, Alexander would have been on Betsy; he could have gone back to the barn for help already—although I didn't know what *help* entailed in this case. Walt and his filly were as far away from the training barn as they could be. There was no ambulance to come cart her back if she couldn't make it under her own steam, and it was a long walk home.

Alexander met me at the gap, his phone in hand. There was no time for anything but the business at hand; I managed to avoid casting any dark looks in the direction of Adriene, still standing on the viewing stand behind him. "I called Ricky and the boys are bringing out some emergency supplies."

"What can they do?"

"Emergency triage, to see where we're standing. Did she look bad?"

I noticed Chessiecat was blowing, her skin suddenly turning dark with sweat as the humid morning and her gallop caught up with her. Funny how standing still was what made you hot. I nudged her away from Alexander and walked her in a big circle. "She just ducked her head a little and then it came up a little higher than usual. There wasn't any sound." I had an idea that a broken bone would make a cracking noise. I hoped I was right.

❧❧❧ ❧❧❧

I was right...at least, I was right that it hadn't been a fracture. A bad step, sure, but these things happened. She needed time off and snug wraps, but the chestnut filly still had a future on the track—to say nothing of her life.

After gallops Ricky sent me to the tack room to fetch standing wraps. We had a long list of workers to do up in poultice. I grabbed a basket and filled it with pillow bandages, green standing wraps to go over them, and the squares of brown paper bags I'd cut up on slower afternoons. The paper soaked in buckets of water, then I used it to mold around the wet clay. I balanced my chin atop the heap of supplies and stepped into the center aisle—only to stop short as I heard sharp words inside the office.

Did they think they were alone, the riders gone and the grooms in the stalls, working?

"It's ridiculous that these horses can't even stand up to a regular breeze," Adriene snapped. "Alexander, I have to tell you, if I could fire you, I would."

"I tell you what," Alexander replied, his voice dangerously low. "I'll give you the chance. You don't think I can manage this stable, and I don't think I can with you around. You get the hell out of here and let me run horses my way. I can't keep having you back here, undermining me constantly. *You're* the one making a hash of this place."

"So why don't you win a race when I'm gone?" Adriene's voice was skeptical. "I'd tell you to prove me wrong, but you've already shown me you can't."

"You've done no better."

"I can't clean up the utter *mess* you make every time I'm gone for a few months!"

He slapped his hands on the table and I flinched, nearly dropping the entire basket. A single wrap fell from the stack and went wheeling across the floor, unspooling green cloth as it went. I held my breath, certain it would give me away...but the wrap stopped just short of the office door.

"I'll prove you wrong. January. The Hibiscus Stakes. Wings and Prayers. He'll win it, and you'll never bother me again."

There was a moment of silence. Then she laughed, a delighted cackle. "Wings and *Prayers?* Surely not. You've really lost your edge."

"He'll win it," Alexander insisted. "And when he does, you can take every one of your mares, all of your racing stock, and that will be the end of it. But you'll relinquish the farm and the stallions."

I held my breath. This was my play. He'd taken me seriously last night. Whatever had happened or hadn't last night, he'd taken *my* side.

Adriene laughed again. My heart fell to the floor, another bruise I'd have to learn to live with. She thought it was a joke. My idea was laughable.

"You'll have nothing left," Adriene told him.

"I'll have enough."

There was a pause.

"Done," Adriene said.

My head came up.

"Done?" Alexander sounded surprised.

"Oh, why *not?* We've been fighting this out for years now. If you can't give me another Breeders' Cup win—and you won't go to Europe—what the hell are we doing here? I spent all night trying to persuade you, and you won't have it, you won't just listen to sense. So fine, Alexander. We can end it. A wager like this is the elegant way to end a partnership, anyway. I like it. Was it your idea? Or was it hers?"

"Hers?"

"The little groom, Alexander. The one you've got on the easy horses in the morning. You've been treating her like a pet, so I know there's something going on there. Don't think I didn't notice! But if you think *she's* going to get the win out of Wing, I think you're fooling yourself." There was the sound of a chair scraping back, the jingle of a purse being picked up. "But that suits me just fine."

Chapter Thirty-two

I DON'T KNOW WHAT I'm doing for Thanksgiving, Mom. Probably working." I had the phone wedged under my riding helmet's harness as I walked a yearling out to his paddock for the afternoon. The colt was eager to meet up with his friends who were already out, and it wasn't the best time to take a phone call. But we were so busy these days, so desperate to get everything right, that there was no time to waste, and definitely no time to stand off to one side and listen to my mother chastise me for not coming home to visit.

My mom sighed, her annoyance audible from two hundred miles away. "It's *Thanksgiving*, Alex. You can't come home and celebrate with us?"

"Not now," I said, biting back my impatience. "Not without some notice, anyway. Things are crazy here."

Crazy, and getting crazier.

"Everyone takes off Thanksgiving, Alex!"

"It's our busiest season, Mom. We have yearlings about to turn two who are prepping for the two-year-old sales in March. We have two-year-olds about to turn three who are prepping for the racing season down at Gulfstream. And the broodmares are like six weeks away from starting to pop. November's crazy in Ocala." And, I thought, we had Wing, training for a race in the new year which could change everything. I doubted I'd be willing to leave long enough to see them for Christmas.

I wasn't going to bring that up quite yet.

The yearling at the end of my right arm started to prance as we neared the paddock gate. Worried I might have a kite situation on my hands, I wriggled the phone free with my left hand. "Gotta go, Mom. I'm sorry! Talk soon!"

I wedged it back into my pocket and clamped my other hand on the leather lead-shank just as the yearling snorted and dug his forelegs into the ground, pushing off hard as he tried to bolt away from me.

"Uh-*uh!*" I snapped, hauling back with everything I had. "You stay *with me!*"

The yearling came back to the ground and eyeballed me. He shook his head and snorted, blowing black horse-boogers all over my jeans. Then he reached down and snagged a bite of grass, as if that was all he wanted.

"Jerk," I told him. "Blue-blooded brat." The colt just went on eating. That was the thing about racehorses of all ages, I reflected. One second they were out for blood; the next they were just back to eating. Staying calm and riding out the wild moments made racing a deceptively dangerous game. Miss one little sign of pending shenanigans, and you could end up with a hoof to the skull.

"Weather's got them riled up," Walt proclaimed as I came back into the barn, still rubbing at my fingers where the lead-shank had dug in hard. "Gonna storm tonight."

"It looks nice now," I said, glancing up at the blue sky overhead. "But I guess that's how Florida works."

"Always tryin' to fool us. Especially this time of year. We get some big cold fronts up here, now. It's not like down in south Florida where you just get a lotta rain. We get some rough weather."

"We get plenty of rough weather," I sighed. *Really, Walt? Another Florida versus Florida argument?* "I guess I better be ready to get in my bathtub tonight, huh?"

"If it gets too bad, you and Jacinta just come up to this barn and get in the tack room." Walt put his palm on the concrete wall. "Sturdy enough to see ya through, not like those trailers under all those oak trees."

"I'll do that." I started to pass him. One more colt to go out, and I was going to take a Diet Coke break. The sun was hot, I'd ridden eight horses before lunch, and Walt had found plenty to keep me busy all afternoon.

His voice was a grumble as I passed. "I mean it, now. Don't go riding out any tornado warnings in that trailer."

"I won't," I promised. "Really. My mom would kill me if she found out I did, anyway."

Walt grinned. "Moms can be good that way."

"Breathing down my neck from two hundred miles away?"

"That's it," Walt agreed. "She's doin' a good job."

I figured she wasn't doing a terrible job. She'd let me come here against her better judgment. Although...did that make her a good mom or a bad one? I popped open a soda from the tack room fridge and considered the contradictions of parenting. I'd better not have a kid, I figured. It seemed far too complicated to handle along with everything else life could throw at you.

Things like Alexander, I thought, as he came into the tack room, his face lighting up gratifyingly when he saw me. He was holding his training diary. "Alex! What are you up to right now?"

I considered the clock. "I just finished turning out yearlings and now I'm going to fold laundry. And then I'm going to take Wing out for his afternoon jog, and then I'm going to help feed dinner." Just another twelve-hour day on the farm. "Oh, and hope Walt doesn't say to bring the yearlings back inside for the night, but he probably will."

"That's a lot of answer for *right now.*"

"I didn't want you to get the idea that I have any spare time or anything."

"Fair enough." Alexander flipped open the book. "I just wanted to go over Wing's works for the past couple of weeks and make some notes."

I drained half the soda in one tired gulp. "The past couple of weeks? You want a play-by-play?"

"Whatever you've got."

I sighed. "What if we do this. I write down notes, you fold the laundry for me. It's just saddle towels and polo wraps, anyway."

He shrugged and handed me the book. "Deal."

I was jotting down everything I could think of when I heard Gigi's delighted squeal. "What is *this?* Alexander, you're doing actual work? I'm so proud of you!"

"Don't get used to it."

I looked up, folding the page over so I wouldn't lose my place. "Gigi, what are you doing here at this time of day?"

"Oh, looking for this man here." She gave Alexander a poke in the side. "Listen up, old fella. I'm fielding employment offers from a certain Adriene Hartwell and I wonder if you might give me a reference?"

She burst into laughter at our shocked faces.

I recovered first. "Gigi, what are you talking about?"

"Adriene is already recruiting for life post-Alexander and Alex. She's asked me if I'll take over head rider after you're all gone. Which is presumably any day now? Should I get ready for my big promotion?"

"Hardly," Alexander said scornfully. "I hope you don't get ahead of yourself and buy the big car now, because there won't be a pay-off later."

Gigi clapped him on the back. "So frowny, old man. Listen, I've just come by to give you that little tidbit, because it was too good to keep to myself, and to offer my services for *anything* the two of you should need, gratis. You don't have to play this little game on your own, you know. I've known that old bitch as long as you have, my dear cousin. Back when she was still sniffing around the house after—"

"That's enough!" Alexander exclaimed. "No need to drag up the whole story now."

I raised my eyebrows. "Is there not? Some of us haven't heard it."

Gigi swatted Alexander again. "You haven't told your girl? Alexander, really."

He pursed his lips together, looking so grumpy I almost felt bad. *Almost*, not quite. "Tell me, Gigi."

"It's not that interesting, but it's still a detail. Adriene was engaged to Alexander's brother back in the day, and that's how those two got to know each other. She was always determined to snag one of the Whitehall brothers."

I couldn't believe it. "Your *brother*?"

Alexander folded over a saddle towel with prissy precision. "He went to Australia to get away from her."

"And you went to America." On her dime, of course.

"And it wasn't far enough!" Gigi snorted. "She just keeps coming back, that woman. A bad penny if I ever saw one. But this will be the end of it."

I didn't like it. I knew about determined women. I had run away from one, and I was turning into one myself. In my experience, we generally did whatever we wanted to do. "How do we know it's the end? What if she keeps coming back?"

"Oh, it's different this time," Gigi assured me. "Alexander, tell her the difference."

They looked at each for a moment, a long, knowing look which would have made me jealous if they hadn't been cousins. And then Alexander's gaze swung to me. "It's you," he said simply. "I didn't have an Alex before."

⁂

Jacinta was drinking when I got back to the trailer.

I'd only seen her go past the point of tipsy once or twice, but tonight was different. As soon as I walked into the trailer, I saw the bottles lined up on the coffee table: five in all. A sixth was clenched in her ropy hand.

She tipped the bottle back all the way; her muscles worked as she finished off the beer. Then she leveled her gaze on me, standing in the doorway, and she asked in a husky voice, "What do you think you're doing out there, girl?"

I hadn't even taken off my boots. "I'm sorry?"

"Adriene talked to me. She's talkin' to everyone. Look, Alex, no one thinks she's any good but what the hell are you doin' with Alexander *Whitehall?*" She said his full name as if he was a stranger to us, a Hollywood star or a distinguished politician, not a person we spoke to and laughed with every day. "You shouldn't have come up here if you were just gonna skip the line by sleepin' with the boss. This town remembers everything. You'll never live it down."

Jacinta plunked the bottle next to its siblings.

I leaned down and unzipped my paddock boots one by one. "I think she gave you the wrong idea," I said slowly. "I'm not sleeping with anyone, for starters. And I'm not skipping any lines. Alexander and Walt were the ones who made that decision, months ago."

"It's not a promotion," Jacinta snorted. "It's a ruse. It's not a hop up the ladder to stardom, either. It's just head rider at a training center. It's not gonna take you anywhere. Do you think any one of us gets up in the morning thinking we're going to be some big-shot at the races? This is a sport for rich folks and tiny men. If you're not one of those two, you're just makin' rent and chasing your tail hopin' for anything more."

"I'm just doing what Walt says." I set my boots side-by-side next to the door, lining them up with pointless precision. "I'm just doing what I'm told."

"Walt's just like the rest of 'em." Jacinta closed her eyes, as if the conversation was exhausting. "I shot my shot with Walt, too. It didn't go nowhere. I'm still just sittin' on this sofa, goin' nowhere."

I felt a surge of guilt. I'd never known Jacinta wanted to go anywhere. Walt had said none of the riders had any aspirations, and I'd believed him...but I could have asked her. All of these months we'd lived together and I'd never asked her what else she wanted to do with her life. I'd just assumed she was done. "When we get this whole thing sorted out—" I began, but Jacinta sat up, startling me, and held up her hand.

"You hear a car?"

I cocked my head, listening. There was definitely a car outside. "Are you expecting anyone?"

"Nope," she said. "This must be for you." She leaned back again.

"I don't know who it could be," I hissed, feeling my heart starting to pump. "I don't know anyone who isn't here already."

Jacinta began to look mildly concerned. Footsteps ascended the creaky staircase outside, and then there was a soft knock at the door.

Too soft to be a serial killer? I wasn't sure how they announced themselves.

"Who is it?" Jacinta called with admirable stability in her voice.

The voice was muffled, but recognizable. "It's Miles."

She looked at me scathingly. "Really, Alex? How many men you got on a string?"

"I didn't tell him to come over!"

She snorted. "Make it quick. I'm going to my bedroom until he's gone."

I hadn't talked to Miles since our last date; he'd texted but I'd always been too busy to call him back. I'd usually just tapped in a quick reply: *sorry so busy* or something similar. As things intensified with Alexander, I grew less certain how to handle Miles.

I had a vague idea that you couldn't break up with someone over texts, and I definitely didn't want to do it over the phone. As usual, procrastination made everything worse.

I opened the door with a feeling of dread.

Miles gave me a hopeful smile. Under the porch light, his face looked bright and boyish. I remembered the night we'd met—his Teen Beat good looks had been adorable. Now, I found his boy-next-door charm slightly off-putting.

"Hey, Alex."

"Hey, Miles." I tried to think of something else to say. I ended up spitting out the first thing that popped into my head. "How did you get onto the farm?"

"I buzzed the office and someone let me in."

I chewed the inside of my cheek. That couldn't be good. Who was in the office at this time of evening? Emily was only here until four. No one could be in the office past seven but Alexander.

"Did they say who they were?"

"No, no one said anything at all. The thing beeped, I said I was here to see you, and the gate opened."

"Oh, God." I turned away and went back to the couch, leaving the door open. Miles trailed inside, his eyes darting around. When he saw we were alone, he shut the door behind him.

"What are you doing?" I asked. "You can't stay. You have to leave. We're not supposed to have visitors." That wasn't true, obviously, but it made for a handy excuse. If he'd listen to it.

"I came to find out why you never called me back. I guess I was worried about you. You just kind of disappeared. I didn't know what that meant. Was it about the job offer?"

The job offer was the easiest thing to turn down. How nice of him to start there. "I can't come work for you. I came here to learn about racing. I can't turn down this opportunity." I heard the floor creak in the vicinity of Jacinta's room—was she at the door listening? I fought back an internal cringe. "I know what we talked about, and it was generous, but I have to see this through. I'm really sorry if this puts you in a bind."

"Puts me in a bind? Alex? Did you think this was just about getting a groom?"

I'd kind of hoped it was. I'd kind of hoped he'd just nod and say it was for the best and walk out. Of course that wasn't going to happen...but a girl could hope for the moon, couldn't she? Or at least for a guy to not like her?

"No, of course not," I said. "But...I don't think we should date anymore."

Miles's face was working now, his jaw clenching and unclenching, and I had the unhappy realization that I'd genuinely hurt him.

I'd never hurt anyone before, never had the experience, didn't know how to cope with it. So when he left, slamming the metal door so hard the wall swayed and the blinds rattled in the window, I felt more wrecked than I'd felt in a long, long time.

Jacinta came out with a bang of her own. "That was pretty weak!" she crowed.

I shrugged. Then I noticed she'd changed clothes—she was wearing clean jeans with a Western blouse, and her feet were clad in brown loafers instead of boots. "Are you going somewhere?"

Jacinta slung a backpack over her shoulder. It looked pretty stuffed. "I'm takin' off for a few days. Didn't anyone tell you?"

"No?"

"Oh, right. That's because I just decided."

"Don't go." I glanced at the six beer bottles on the table. "It's supposed to storm tonight."

"Baby afraid of storms? Go up to the big house. Alexander will take care of you. I'm done with this place tonight. All the schemin', all the lyin'. I need a break from all you brats with your games." Jacinta pushed past me and opened the front door. A breeze rushed in and ruffled her faded curls. "See ya in a few."

I held the door as she trundled down the stairs. "What do I tell Walt?"

"Tell him I'm lookin' for greener pastures again." Jacinta got into her pickup and slammed the door. In the distance, lightning lit up the night sky, long tendrils of electricity rippling across hundreds of miles in milliseconds. I watched her tail-lights fade, finally disappearing behind the hillsides, and then I stood there a little longer, watching the bright, silent lightning. I felt a tremor in the air, distant thunder which couldn't yet be heard, and I had a feeling this long, long day was about to become a very long evening.

Chapter Thirty-three

I HAD FALLEN ASLEEP in front of the television.

That was what woke me. That awful, high-pitched tone local TV stations used whenever there was a weather warning. This wasn't just a crawl at the bottom of late-night sitcom repeats, though. This was a full-fledged breaking news bulletin. The meteorologist had tossed his jacket over a chair and rolled up the sleeves of his shirt. I'd been here just long enough to know this guy's jacket was a cult symbol in Central Florida: a sign that things were about to get rough for someone in the viewing area.

I rubbed at my face and looked at the radar map he was jabbing at with frantic fingers.

"Shit," I said.

That someone was me.

When I pushed out the front door, shoving it against the howling wind, I went into a changed night. Gone was the still waiting, the flickers of distant lightning. Now everything was in my face, reminding me that Florida was many things, but she was not subtle. The wind was lashing heavy raindrops against my face as I tripped down the metal staircase, and by the time I pulled at my car's door-handle, the gusts were so strong I could barely pull the door open. Lightning flashed nonstop, like a celestial strobe light. The rumble of thunder went on like a ship's engine churning just out of sight: an undulating roar which never stopped.

The wind slammed the car's door shut just as I pulled my legs inside to safety, and I sat inside for a moment, not moving, listening to the raindrops pounding on the windshield and roof. Then a tree branch landed on the windshield—not big enough to do any damage, but big enough to scare the absolute piss out of me—and with a shriek I turned the key and threw the car into reverse.

That was when I should have panicked, when the tires caught in the wet sand and for a moment spun instead of gaining purchase. But I was too keyed up to give it any thought, so I just pressed down on the gas pedal until the car finally flew backwards.

When I emerged from beneath the trees and came into the open fields, the wind really hit. In the distance there were power flashes, big electric-white bursts as transformers were torn down from poles and flung to the ground. I realized the flashes were growing closer, and *that* was when I panicked. So just a few moments late, really.

The car wobbled and weaved as the wind shoved at us. Branches were flinging themselves across the driveway, leaves and twigs and even pine needles, even though I was fairly certain there weren't any pine trees on the farm. A palm frond went winging by, smacking against the fence to my left. I clung to the steering wheel and bit back a squeal and kept on driving as fast as I trusted myself on the barn lane. I saw a blue-white flash ahead, near the main road, and the overnight lights in the broodmare and training barns winked out in an instant.

If there's a tornado on the ground, it's right there, I thought, and I started to reach a place beyond terror, something that was just grim and determined. I knew I shouldn't be in a car, but I was too far away from shelter to run, and dying in a car was surely better than dying in an old trailer.

Then I pulled into the driveway of Alexander's house and I was splashing through the puddles and up the stairs to the rarely-used front door. Alexander used the side door, but it faced west, where the last flash had been. If there was a tornado spinning up the driveway, I didn't want to give it a chance to pin the door shut with me on the wrong side.

Alexander opened the door as I came pounding up the last step and ushered me in, slamming it shut against the wind. The house was a lot of glass and concrete set against a steep slope, and we were already standing on the second floor, in a foyer with soaring ceilings. Alexander took my hand and started tugging me through the vast living room, then down a flight of stairs to the ground floor.

"I was calling you," he said urgently. "Your phone just rang and rang."

"I was asleep." I didn't tell him I'd turned off the ringer, in case Miles called me.

We went into a back room and pushed past what felt like a dresser and a bed, and then I realized we were in a closet and Alexander had pulled the door closed. It was utterly dark. He was standing against me, his chest heaving. I stepped forward and pressed my chin into his shoulder.

His arms came around me and he held on tight.

There was no great roar, it didn't sound like a train went by. We stood together in the dark and breathed, and finally it seemed like there was no sound at all, nothing but Alexander's heartbeats, my own breaths coming high and tight. My cheek turned to the side against the soft twill of his shirt, I opened my eyes and soaked in the darkness. I thought we must have been on the ground floor, we must have been tucked in tightly against that hill, or maybe whatever it was which had sparked the tornado warning, and blown me all over the driveway, and knocked out power in the barns, had simply evaporated back into the clouds.

Finally, the tension left his shoulders, and he stood a bit more upright, his hands sliding down my back.

"There's a light switch against the wall," he said after a moment. "I just thought it might be too awful if we had it on and it went out suddenly. But things seem to be passing over."

I reached past him and felt hanging clothes, a cool plastered wall, and then the smooth plastic of a light switch. I flicked it, closing my eyes as I did so, and white light spilled through my eyelids.

I felt Alexander flinch at the light. When I opened my eyes again, I saw we were in the tiniest of walk-in closets; there was barely room for the two of us. He stood with his back to the door and his chin tucked down, looking at me.

"Well," I said, "seems like we made it."

"So we did." He ran his hands down my back one more time, then released me. "Let's go make sure everything else did."

The house was untouched, its gray carpets and white walls unconcerned with the weather outside, its cool frosted sconces still lit. I padded up the stairs after Alexander and we came back onto the main floor, where the living room opened up to my right and a kitchen and dining area to my left. Alexander turned left, ignoring the television still showcasing the weather radar in the living room, and went into the kitchen. I followed after, noticing the white cabinets, the steel appliances. I hadn't spent much time up here, and the moments we'd stolen had been too hurried and impassioned for much reconnaissance. Now I realized it was a very modern place—not at all what I would have expected of him.

Alexander put a steel kettle onto the stovetop and flipped the burner on. "This night requires tea," he said. "With a dollop of something stronger."

I sat down at the breakfast table. It was tucked close to a big window; rain streamed down it, still pelting the glass with what felt like excessive force.

The silence between us was oddly comfortable. He sat down across from me and looked at the rain spilling down the window.

"A very modern house," I ventured at last.

Alexander's face split into a grin. "Yes," he agreed. "Isn't it awful? I told you. It came this way."

I was thankful he hadn't done the interior decorating himself...or the exterior, for that matter. "It's like a hospital," I said. "A high-end hospital. Or maybe an extremely minimalist hotel."

"That's it. We'll call it minimalist. It's the opposite of how I grew up, so maybe that's why I've never bothered to change it. I wouldn't say I like it, now. But having a little less around me for a while has been...sort of...relaxing."

"How did you grow up?"

"Oh, in a great big stone house filled with everything my great-grandparents and their great-grandparents had ever amassed.

Plus everything else. A painting on every square inch of wall space. A priceless vase or a centuries-old candlestick or a porcelain bowl on every table. I barely touched anything outside of my own bedroom for the first ten years of my life." He snorted. "Probably why I spent so much time in the stable yard."

"That's not why," I said instinctively. "You're a horseman. That's just who you are."

"That's a fine compliment. Thank you."

"So is that why you came to the U.S.? To get away from your family?"

The tea kettle began to whistle. *Personal!* It seemed to be shrieking. *Way too personal!*

Alexander got up and fiddled with the kettle, tipping steaming water into a teapot. I watched, fascinated, as he spooned actual tea into the kettle. I had a dozen questions, all of them related to making tea without tea-bags, but I liked how personal I'd gotten the conversation and I wasn't willing to give it up. The tea questions could wait for another time.

Hopefully this wasn't the last pot of tea we'd share.

Finally, Alexander brought the teapot to the table, and I refrained from commenting on the knitted sweater the pot was wearing, although it was the cutest thing I'd ever seen, and definitely had no place in this modern monstrosity of a house. His eyes were thoughtful, and he plunked a mug down in front of me rather absently as he considered his answer.

"I suppose to a certain extent, yes. I needed to prove myself, to me, to them, to everyone. I was training well enough there, but you're right, my father was there, my uncle, my brothers...all training or riding, all of us with the same name. Then, one of my brothers went to Australia and he's built himself an empire there. I thought, well, why not me? I didn't quite understand all of his reasons at the time, as I'm sure you've guessed."

"And why did you come to Florida?"

He shrugged. "It's warm. I like breeding and the incentive program is good here. And farms were cheaper here than in Kentucky. Still not cheap enough for me, but we made it work."

"Did you plan it this way? Was she supposed to come and invest with you?"

He shook his head. "No. I was going to work for other trainers, build myself up. She was the one who told me I didn't have to wait. She told me I could either slave away for someone else for the next ten years and hope for a break, or I could let her be the break." He smiled grimly to himself. "When a person puts it like that..." He glanced at the table. "Oh, milk." He went back to the fridge and got a carton of milk out.

"No, I get it," I said. I watched him pour milk into his mug; I shook my head when he offered it to me. "Just sugar for me, thanks."

He lifted his eyebrows slightly, as if I'd answered wrong. "Well, let's hope the old place is still out there in the morning. That training barn was *my* investment, and you know I paid a steep price for all of my improvements."

I couldn't help but shiver a little. Alexander tipped tea into our mugs. The steam rose up, fragrant and rich.

The silence stretched between us again. Eventually, I realized Alexander was watching me. "What?" I asked, suddenly feeling a little self-conscious. "Did I get something on my face?"

"No, silly," he said gently, and then he leaned over and kissed me, a lingering, gentle kiss which took my breath away.

❧❧❧ ❧❧❧

It wasn't until later when I sat up in the darkness and looked around. Alexander stirred beside me. "What is it?"

"I'm just worried, is all."

"I thought we'd put all that to bed."

"Not about *that*. But the storm…I just have a weird feeling, that's all."

He sighed. "You know what my mother used to say about intuition? Still does, in fact, every chance she's given."

"No…what?"

"She'd say it's usually worth trusting."

❧❧❧ ❧❧❧

We got into the farm truck, a big hulking Ford with the farm name stenciled on the doors. By now the rain had dwindled to a soft drizzle, but there were deep pools in the barn drive and a lot of tree debris scattered across the pavement and the grassy embankments: twigs, leaves, small branches that crunched under the tires. I noticed palm fronds plastered across the fences on the southern side of the drive; the north wind had torn them from the palm trees around the barns and slammed them against the fences a full quarter-mile or more away. It had been really, really serious out here.

"The barn lights are still out," I pointed out. "Wonder how long that will last?"

"Could be days," Alexander said with a sigh. "When the power goes out in Ocala, it tends to stay out."

"Looks like they're out down at the houses, too."

"Let's drive down there and take a look."

I felt my fingernails clenching the edge of my seat. I'd been up at Alexander's house for hours already. What if Jacinta had come back? Would she be glad to know I hadn't been killed by a tornado, or would she just start in on me again?

But we couldn't get to the houses. An oak tree had fallen across the drive just before the trailer court. Alexander put the truck in park. "Damn," he sighed. "Want to get out and take a look?"

I gazed at the tree. There were bright white scars where huge branches had been snapped off. This tree hadn't just been uprooted, torn out of wet soil by high winds. It had been battered and broken until it gave up. And there were a lot of oak trees shading those trailers.

"We'd better check," I said.

I managed to scramble up through the fork in the downed tree, but it was too dark to see past the tangle of leaves and branches. I heard some rummaging in the truck behind me, and then Alexander was grunting, pulling himself up alongside me. He held up a flashlight.

"Emergency torch," he said, and flicked it on.

We took in the sight, laid bare in the spotlight of the powerful beam.

"Oh, Alexander," I breathed. My fists clenched together, fingernails pressing into my palms.

There was no telling how many of the gorgeous old oak trees had come down, or what they had crushed beneath their trunks and branches. I could see one tree leaning across the empty trailer that had been Pablo's, and I could see a heap of broken branches where the front of my trailer ought to be. I thought about my car, sitting right there less than an hour before...and of myself, sitting on the couch. If the power had gone out before the tornado warning woke me up, what might have happened?

"Damn," Alexander murmured. He reached out and touched my shoulder. It felt as if he was making sure I was really there, beside him, and not in the trailer.

I sighed and slipped back to the wet ground, landing on a patch of sodden leaves. I didn't want to look anymore. That trailer court had been so pretty, despite the sagging, rusting trailers. The trees had been enough to elevate the most dilapidated of homes. Now they were scattered across the ground. A little bit of beauty gone from the world.

To say nothing of my home.

"I didn't have much," I sighed, as he slithered down from the tree. "Now I'll have nothing."

"Well, maybe nothing happened to your things. We can't really see in there. And we can't look in case there are power lines down. But it could be fine."

I knew it wasn't fine. "It's mostly just clothes, anyway," I sighed, trying to shrug it all off. "I didn't bring much up here. And my riding gear is in the training barn. But..."

If I said it, was I going to look like I was asking for it? Well, I had no choice.

"But?" Alexander was turning the flashlight's beam across the pastures, looking for broken fence. I saw another downed tree a few hundred feet away.

"But that was where I lived." Surely he saw the problem.

"Oh, that's not a problem," Alexander said, still gazing out at the broken tree. "You'll come and live with me."

Chapter Thirty-four

I T WAS ALL SO easy, once the decision was made, once it was said out loud.

We went back to the house, where the coffeemaker had been busy, and we ate thick slices of toasted white bread spread with soft butter, and then Alexander set out a travel mug for me which I filled with more rich, black, life-saving coffee and we got into his truck and drove down to the training barn.

It was all so easy.

It was all so easy, so simple and so natural. Riding into work with him felt like my rightful place. I forgot it wouldn't be for anyone else. I was really lulled into security for a few minutes that morning, feeling somehow that if Alexander and I could coexist in such quiet harmony, the rest of the world would certainly be onboard, as well.

Of course they weren't.

Walt had already arrived and set up a generator, which was growling away to itself behind the barn. It lit up about a quarter of the lights, giving the barn a dim, dreamy quality.

Jacinta hadn't shown up, but Gigi, Billy, and Juan were standing around in the center aisle as usual. The guys were clutching convenience store coffee cups instead of their own mugs, a telltale sign of late night and maybe a power failure, but no one looked really bothered. Of course, an early morning was an early morning, whether you got three hours of sleep or six.

Juan was the first one to see me sitting beside the boss as the truck pulled up. I saw his eyes go wide; I saw him pat Billy on the shoulder and nod in my direction. I saw Billy stop talking and gesture, I saw Gigi turn around, a smile slowly spreading across her face. I saw Walt emerge from the tack room, and then watched his hand go to his chin, and rest there thoughtfully.

"I can't do this," I said, gripping the truck's door handle.

Even Alexander looked uncertain. "We may have miscalculated," he admitted.

I felt myself pressing down into the truck seat. "I'm embarrassed. Maybe that's not the right way to feel, but it's what I've got."

Alexander gave me a quick, questioning glance, but he didn't say anything. I felt the uncertainty rise between us and that was even worse.

"We have to talk about this," I said. "What we're going to say. We should have planned."

"We're not going to say anything. We are going to get on with the day and they are, too."

"Look at their faces! They're going to think the worst of me."

"Alex, they don't know about the trailers yet. You need to think sensibly. Let's remember that your house is behind a fallen oak tree. Where else would you have been after that, but in the house with me?"

That was true. They wouldn't have seen the trailers. They were staring now, but they didn't know my house was gone. Walt couldn't have expected me to stay in the tack room all night.

"I'll do the talking," Alexander promised.

"I can work with that," I agreed.

Alexander opened his truck door and whistled. Like an obedient collie, Walt came trotting over. He leaned on the open door and gave me a pointed glance before saying: "Good mornin', boss."

"Good morning Walt," Alexander said genteelly. "Did your family fare okay with the storm last night?"

"We did fine," Walt said. "Some of the other boys lost power. No one had any damage."

"That's good news. We did have some serious damage here."

"I saw a lot of limbs down, and there's some trees out on the highway verge."

"The back fence-line, where the oaks are, was hit pretty hard. And the housing court, I'm afraid."

"Oh," Walt said. Then he looked at me again. "Oh, not the trailers?"

"They're either crushed or just damaged, it's impossible to tell before we have some daylight. They're inaccessible, as well. I'll have a crew out as soon as I can to clear the driveway and see what's going on back there."

Walt straightened. "Well, I know Jacinta spent last night in town. She sent me a text to say she wouldn't be here today." Walt looked past Alexander to meet my gaze. "I hope you weren't hurt. Were you in the house?"

"Yeah, I went straight up there, as soon as they issued a tornado warning."

"It's a damn good thing." Walt glanced over his shoulder at the shattered trees. "I'll have to text Jacinta once we've seen what's down there. She'll want to know how much of the house is damaged before she sees it with her own eyes."

"I'd appreciate that," Alexander said. "It would be a big shock to drive up the lane and see those trees down without any warning. As for Alex and myself, we had a very late night and I think we will just leave you to manage the horses today. You can call me if there are any issues, of course. But we wouldn't be much use to you around the barn."

He'd done it so smoothly. I had to admire him for that. Walt was nodding, understanding written on his face, and then he slapped the truck door and stepped back. Alexander pulled the truck door shut and turned the key in the ignition once more.

"So we *aren't* riding?" I asked.

"I just realized Adriene will probably show up shortly to assess any damage. And I would rather do anything than see Adriene this morning," Alexander said. "Now, let's go find some breakfast," he announced, and he looked positively cheerful when he said it.

❦

There wasn't much late-night dining in Ocala, but early breakfasts were easy to come by. Alexander turned up 441 and drove north a few miles, finally stopping at a roadside diner. Gingham curtains in the windows: check. Semi-trailer parking around back: check. Wrinkled men in trucker caps sipping coffee from brown mugs: check and check.

We sat at a booth with a view of the wakeful highway, and ordered eggs and toast and sausage. A leather-faced waitress grimly poured our coffee from a steel carafe. I pulled out the little plastic tray of sugars and creamer, certain this coffee was going to need some doctoring; Alexander simply tipped his back, black as midnight, and made no complaints about its non-Italian origins.

For a few minutes, there was no sound but a gentle tinkling of lite FM and the sounds of silverware clinking on heavy plates. I sipped my coffee—it was terrible—and avoided Alexander's eyes. There was a talk coming, and I wasn't going to start it.

"So," Alexander said eventually. "How do you want to do this?"

I leaned back in the booth. "Do what, exactly?"

"Move up to my house."

I bit my lip and looked back down at the creamy white coffee in my mug. I wished I could start over again. The sugar was going to make me sick. I could already feel the discomfort tugging at the edges of my stomach.

Okay, maybe that wasn't the sugar.

"Unless you don't want to." His gaze shifted away, roved over the dining room.

He was...*disappointed?*

"Actually, I do," I blurted, not willing to hurt his feelings. "I'm just—nervous. I didn't expect this."

"Expect a tornado? We seldom do."

"Come on. I just...we've been together like, ten minutes, Alexander."

"It's a big house," he said mildly. "You can have your own bedroom. There are five, you know."

"I'm not joking," I persisted. "We aren't going to act out *The Odd Couple* in your giant house. It's not that simple."

Alexander shrugged and sipped his coffee. He seemed to think it was, in fact, that simple.

"I'm serious. I don't think this is a good idea." Even as I said it, the quiet pleasure of our early morning together came back to me. Hadn't sitting across from the kitchen table, quietly buttering my toast, felt like home to me?

"Alex," Alexander said, tapping the table. "Out with it. What is the problem?"

I tipped back a sip of coffee, buying time, and looked at him over the rim of the mug. He looked tired, drawn, and inexpressibly handsome. He looked, as he always did, like a person I had known for my entire life. I shook my head slightly, because I knew I was making a mistake, and I said, "The problem, Alexander, is that I'm in love with you."

He nodded slowly, considering this. "I see. And that's a problem, is it?"

I shrugged. "Seems that way to me."

"I'm not sure it has to be."

I sighed. "Are we going to just play games now? Because I'm really tired and I don't think I am up to it."

"No," Alexander decided. "It's just hard to get the words right."

We sat in silence for a moment. There was a wash of wet tires on 441 as truck traffic went by.

"I don't know how to be in love with someone," he said eventually. "The way to behave. I don't want to do something wrong." He paused, dipped his head to escape my gaze. "I don't want to break your heart."

I looked at him thoughtfully. "Maybe the mere fact that you'd worry about breaking someone's heart means something."

"Not *someone's*. Yours." Alexander sighed. "Why are you different from every other girl?"

"I'm not sure I am."

"No, this is all different. With you—I knew you the moment I saw you. Don't ask me how. I couldn't possibly begin to explain...but it was there. Instant recognition. I was literally working on autopilot when I told you to come to the farm. It was like...you know those dreams where you already know the plot, and you have to work your way through it, scene by scene?"

I stared at him. "I thought I was the only one who had those dreams."

Alexander smiled and shook his head. "You're not."

The waitress dropped a bottle of syrup on our table with extraordinary ennui, and kept walking without breaking stride.

I remembered something then. "When I was sixteen, a guy asked me to a school dance. I said no. He was nice, he was fine, but there was a horse show that weekend. It would have been impossible to do both. My grandmother came over for dinner that night. I told my family what had happened and she said, 'Alexis, thank goodness you don't have a heart.'" I paused, thinking of the way her words had confused and upset me.

"She called you Alexis." Alexander smiled.

"Oh, always. She was stubborn that way. Anyway, I asked her how she could say that about me. She said, 'I can tell you've made up your mind to never love anything but horses. I think you'll be lonely, but I'm not sure you'll be able to tell. You just don't have that kind of heart.' And I never told her how much that shook me, how much that hurt me. Because I'm lonely all of the time." My voice shook a little. "Do people not see that? Do people not understand you can be more than one thing? Or that some things don't come easily to everyone?"

I wasn't sure what I was mad about, but suddenly I was trembling with rage. I put down my coffee cup and pressed my hands into the table. My right thumb landed in something sticky. I registered this fact just as Alexander reached forward and pressed his hands over mine.

"I believe in your heart," he said. "I think it's just like mine."

⚜

When we got back to the farm, the sun was up, lighting the broken branches and uprooted trees with a cheerful yellow glow. The entire scene felt inappropriate. Alexander drove straight past the turn-off to the training barn, the truck tires crunching over battered palm fronds and sending up sprays of water as we passed through deep puddles. The destruction to the back tree-line was evident from a distance: white gashes on the trunks of distant trees, sprawled masses of uprooted trees pushing against their still-standing neighbors. I thought of the rides on the yearlings along that tree-line and how different and exposed those rides would be next year.

He stopped the truck where we'd parked the night before, right at the base of the massive tree blocking the entrance to the trailer court. I couldn't believe we'd climbed up it in the rain and the dark. The tree rested on the banks on either side of the drive, so that the top of its trunk was a good six feet in the air. If there weren't so many branches and leaves beneath it, we could have scrambled underneath.

Alexander got out of the truck. "Ready to climb back up?" he asked.

"I liked it better in the dark."

"You'll probably prefer the view in the dark too, I'm afraid."

He was right. Daylight gave away the true measure of damage. Three huge trees had come down on the trailers. Pablo's old trailer was utterly destroyed. Mine had a tree in front of it, and another leaning on the back half—where Jacinta's bedroom was.

"I guess I'm homeless," I said.

"You know you aren't." Alexander looked over at me and shook his head. "We'll get your things out of there and put them in the truck. I meant it, by the way—you can have your pick of the bedrooms if that's what you want. But that's entirely up to you."

I nodded towards the training barn. "What will *they* say?"

"They'll say nothing, or they'll be looking for new jobs," Alexander said grimly.

Chapter Thirty-five

Mom, it's not—"

"No, listen to me. We didn't—"

"Mom, I swear to God, would you just *let me explain*—"

We'd been on the phone a quarter of an hour, and I still couldn't get a word in over all of my mother's anger. She was up to threatening to drive up to Ocala, pack up my things, and drag me home. This came after scolding me roundly for getting involved with my boss and for letting things get so out of hand that I was now living in his house with him. "Like a kept woman," she kept saying. Again and again.

"I'm not some sort of *concubine,*" I finally exploded, my words overpowering hers at last. "How could you think that of me? When have I ever, even one time, chosen a man over myself?"

"Alex, I don't think you're understanding me. You simply cannot move into your boss's house. Especially when he's—how much older is he?"

"It's not that much. It's ten years?" It was a little more than ten years. It wasn't conventional. But it wasn't out of the question.

And it wasn't a choice I'd made based on age. Hell, it wasn't even really a choice. It simply *was*. "He's in his thirties. You're making it out like he's seventy years old and looking for some hot young third wife."

"Well, which wife *would* you be?"

I couldn't believe it. "He's never been married, Mom, and that's not exactly relevant to the situation. I moved into the house because a tree fell on mine. My job provides me housing, and this is housing. It's that simple."

It wasn't that simple, but I wanted the world to see it that way. My bags were in my own bedroom, my clothes were in my own closet. Maybe I wasn't sleeping in my own bed, but I certainly had that option.

My mother's sigh nearly took my ear off. "None of this is simple. You know it isn't. A young woman moves into a rich older man's house—"

"He's not rich—"

"Oh, of course, a middle-class racehorse owner's house. Hmm, funny, that doesn't sound at all plausible."

Now she was just getting sarcastic. There was no reasoning with sarcasm. "I have to go, Mom."

"Think about what you're doing."

"I love you, Mom. Bye." I tossed the phone across the breakfast table. Then I tipped forward and rested my forehead on the table, too exhausted to bother holding my own head up.

I was still sitting like that a few minutes later when Alexander came in. He'd been working in the office all afternoon while I'd been in the training barn. I'd noticed Emily's car was still outside.

"Did Emily chase you out?" I pushed myself upright.

"She did." He took down a highball glass from a cabinet and meandered into the living room. I heard the doors of the liquor cabinet open and close, and he came back with a bottle of whiskey. "She said I was being too loud and she needed to finish payroll, so I had to leave."

I grinned. I admired the way Emily pushed around Alexander. "She was probably right. Were you on the phone with one of your cronies up in New York? You seem to pick up on their energy."

"How would you know that?" He snorted, pouring himself a measure of whiskey. "And do you want a drink?"

"No, thank you." I'd never had whiskey straight. I wasn't sure what it would taste like and I didn't want to look silly in front of Alexander if I choked on it like someone in a sitcom. I made a mental note to try it when he was out of the house. I'd work my way through the entire liquor cabinet, taking experimental sips, so I'd have actual opinions if it came up in conversation. "I was just on the phone with my mother."

"Oh?"

"She is not happy about my new housing arrangement."

"Fancy." He sat down across from me and took a sip of his drink. His smile was knowing. "Fancy a mother who doesn't want her dearest daughter living in the house of a deranged racehorse trainer. You shouldn't have told her."

"I know that now."

"Mothers. They're very hard to handle. My own mother doesn't think I should live in Florida. She thinks I should be at her side, escorting her to flower shows and race meetings, bringing her drinks and whispering the winners into her ear."

I tried to think of how to answer that. "My mother thinks I should still be in college," I said finally.

"Oh, she's definitely right about that," Alexander agreed cheerfully. "But the heart wants what the heart wants."

I eyed him carefully. If he was talking about himself, I'd have to smack him, just to keep things honest. In whispers over tacos this morning, Gigi had told me that the key to managing Alexander was not to let him get so pompous all of the time. The minute he got precious with her, she said, she made up some new rule that had the ultimate effect of putting him back in his place. "Very important," Gigi told me, wagging a red-taloned finger. "He'll walk all over you. And the sad thing is, he doesn't even mean to! It's just how he was raised, I think."

He sipped his whiskey and grinned at me.

I shook my head at him. "Right now, just so you know, only *you* believe I should be here. The riders won't speak to me. Ricky looks at me like I signed my soul over to the devil. And my mother thinks you're—she thinks I made a mistake." I wasn't going to tell him my mother thought he was a dirty old man. That was just unkind.

Alexander swirled his whiskey and tried to look contrite. "The riders will come around. So will Ricky and the crew. In all likelihood, so will your mother. Any word on Jacinta, by the way?"

Jacinta wasn't answering her phone. No one had seen her; no one had heard from her. No one was particularly concerned, either. Apparently riders did this all the time. Racehorse people weren't the best at putting down roots and sticking around. I'd asked Emily what she was going to do with Jacinta's last paycheck. She said she'd just stick it in the safe and give it to her if she ever showed up for it. "I keep them six months," she'd said. "After that I tear it up. That's the system."

"You have a system for this?" I'd asked, shocked.

"Honey, these people come and they go," Emily had replied, shrugging.

"No one has heard a thing about her," I said now. "Walt said he was going to put out the sign this afternoon."

"Oh, that's what he was doing. I heard him stop in and talk to Emily while I was on the phone."

"So there's a sign out front now that says *Riders Wanted?*"

"Should be. A few will probably show up in the morning. Don't be surprised if you trial some newbies on your middle sets." Alexander picked up the *Thoroughbred Daily News* sitting on the table and began to skim the front page. "Her things will be in the maintenance shed, just in case she comes back."

❧❦❧ ❦❧❦

If people just disappeared in this business, I suppose I couldn't have asked for better timing for Jacinta to drop off the face of the earth. Things were difficult enough with Adriene still showing up in the morning, making caustic remarks, trying to pilfer all the riders for her own purposes. She had divided out the horses she owned in full from the handful of trainees and sales horses Alexander had in his own name, and was sending them out in separate sets, on a training schedule of her own devising. The result was chaos.

In all the confusion, Jacinta's absence felt like a double stroke of luck: no one was following me around hissing in my ear like a personal nemesis, and no one had felt the need to tell Adriene I was living in the house with Alexander. Billy and Juan were wary of Adriene, and of course Walt and Gigi were on our side. The riders she'd hired didn't know us, or our dramas. They just showed up, got on their horses, and tried not to learn our names—which made it easier for them to crowd us on the training track and rush the grooms between sets.

"Can't you find *any* way to make her leave?" I hissed to Alexander, as we rode in from a gallop and Adriene immediately sent out two riders of her own, causing consternation from the grooms who were suddenly being asked to do twice the work in half the time.

"Just wait her out," Alexander advised. "She'll send some of them to the track and this will get easier."

I took over some extra duties to ease things on the grooms, and spent my lunch break doing one-handed work like cold-hosing. I found I could eat a sandwich with one hand and hold the hose in the other. The real hard part was keeping the horse from taking my sandwich.

"One more hand," I told Ricky, who was jangling a colt's lead-shank to keep him still for the hose, "and I could hold the horse, too."

Ricky just snorted.

Working lunches weren't the only way my days got tougher. Walt was starting to get short-timer's syndrome, thinking more of his approaching last day than anything else, and he reacted to his own minor slip-ups by getting even harder on my work.

"Wrap it again," Walt demanded, leaning over Wing's stall webbing. I looked helplessly at the leg I'd just done up in a sweat:

a bottom layer of canary-yellow nitrofurazone mixed with clear DMSO, covered over with plastic wrap, then cushioned with a padded quilt and wound tight with a green standing wrap. I thought the leg looked gorgeous at first glance, although I could admit there was a tiny pucker visible in the leg quilt, just peeking out from under the standing wrap. He pointed at the offending gap. "No wrinkles. That's the rule."

I sighed and pulled out the safety pin anchoring the standing wrap in place, then started unspooling the wrap. Wing shifted restlessly, ready for me to be finished and out of his stall. I had to wiggle backwards to avoid getting stepped on, adjusting my position while still in a squat. Everything in the training barn was a balancing act: try not to topple over while wrapping legs; try not to topple over while schooling a baby bouncing on two legs; try not to topple over while the workdays grew longer and the people grew colder.

Still, I wrapped the leg again without complaint, because Walt told me to—and in a few weeks Walt would be gone and I would be head rider and everyone would be looking to me for guidance.

That's what he kept telling me, anyway. In fact, everything hinged on Wing, and whether Adriene would really leave when he won his race.

Gigi swung through the barn, looking for her half-chaps, which she'd left behind yet again. She spotted me kneeling in the stall and popped her head over the webbing. "Sweats, huh? I didn't realize Walt had you doing those today."

"Everyone who worked is getting them. That's seven horses. This guy is number four."

"Oof." Gigi glanced at her watch. "You might be done by nightfall."

"Only if I get a lot faster, really quickly."

"I think that's how *practice makes perfect* works, actually. You struggle and struggle, then all of a sudden, you're an expert. Say, speaking of struggle-buses, how is my dear cousin? He doesn't speak much these days."

"Can you blame him?" With Adriene a constant presence on the shed-row and the track every morning, Alexander had grown rather quiet and morose—both in and out of the barn. "I'm worried about him, honestly."

"What's it like living with him?" Gigi leaned against the concrete wall and folded her arms, ready for a comfortable chat. "I mean, seriously. You've been living with him for what, two weeks? That's got to be some kind of record for Alexander. He never lets women stay more than a few nights."

I frowned.

"Oh, sorry, but you know, you're hardly the first girl he's ever been with. But you're definitely the first girl he's ever been in a relationship with. It's fascinating to watch, if you don't mind me saying so."

I had to laugh at that. "He's fine to live with," I said. "He's no trouble at all."

"So you guys just...work." Gigi sounded impressed. "Wow. Who would have guessed?"

"It's like we've always lived together," I admitted. "We're quiet. We're not on top of each other all the time. We talk. We drink coffee. It's very domestic." I pulled the standing wrap snug. "I hope that doesn't sound boring."

"No, not at all. It sounds really nice. I'm getting married soon, and I rather hope it's like that, although he's not nearly the gentleman Alexander is."

I nearly fell over into the shavings. *"Married?* What? I didn't even know you were *dating."*

Gigi laughed with delight. "Oh, sorry, but it's old news. I've just been running around Florida getting my jollies out before I give in and marry the sod. Remember I told you it was a bit complicated with my last gig? He's why. Anyway, he'll be down here soon enough. We're getting married in Miami next month, while Gulfstream is still on. Fits his schedule, you know."

I thought Gigi looked quite content with her lot, despite her deprecating way of putting things. But I was still choking on the news. "Who on earth are you marrying?"

"Jimmy Wallace."

I goggled at her.

"What? You don't see me with a sharpshooter from New York City?" Gigi laughed. "He's really great, honestly. And loaded. My mum always said I'd need a rich husband, and she was right. But I like him, too. He's not controlling—obviously. When I said I needed a break from him for a few months, he was fine with it."

I felt absolutely dazed. "Wait...you've been down here galloping just to get away from your fiancé?"

Gigi grinned knowingly. "He was getting a bit wearing, you know, and I wanted to remind him of how much he'd miss me if I was gone. That's the problem with these privileged guys, Alex. You have to keep them wanting more. Otherwise, they forget they can't buy whatever they want. They get very complacent. Can't have that in a man."

I filed that nugget away, as no doubt Gigi expected me to, and got back to Wing's leg. I tapped the Velcro down on the standing wrap and secured it all with the safety pin. No folds. A perfect finish. My knees cracked as I straightened up, one hand on the colt's shoulder to keep my balance. Luckily, Wing stood still long enough for me to get back to my feet. "Thanks, good boy," I told him.

"He's so nice," Gigi said appreciatively. "Are you excited to take him to Gulfstream next week?"

I stared at her. "Excuse me?"

Gigi smiled unapologetically. "I figured he hadn't told you. He's not used to having a partner he can trust, remember. You'd better go talk to him before he makes all the plans without you."

❧❧❧❧❧   ❦❦❦❦❦

He already had, of course. "Alex, you *knew* we were going to Gulfstream."

Emily slipped out the door, saying something about checking the mailbox.

"But I didn't know when. Were you going to tell me about this? We're supposed to be training Wing together."

"It's not just Wing. That's why we're heading down next week. We're taking Jimmy's horses, too. He's heading down and he wants to see them running." Alexander handed me a legal pad, scrawled all over with his sure, even handwriting. "Here's the list. Can you give it to Walt when you go back to the barn to feed? I want to be sure everyone's prepared."

Alexander had an incredible way of missing the point. "Were you going to make sure *I* was prepared?"

He blinked at me. "Well, of course. I only just called down to the track to check on stalls. Gigi happened to be sitting across from me at the time. It's not as if I've been plotting this behind your back for weeks."

I sat down in one of the office chairs, feeling like I was arguing with an owl. Every time I asked a question, he just spun his head around and said: *who?*

"I'm just saying I would have liked to know in the planning stages," I said wearily.

"That's fine," he replied airily. "Next time, I'll include you. Oh, and ask Walt to give you a rundown on racetrack etiquette, please. Distance from other riders, where to gallop in the track, that kind of thing."

I felt a little dizzy. He could *not* be serious. "Why?" I croaked, although I could easily guess.

"Well, you're my rider, aren't you? You'll get a license first thing and then you'll take the horses out in the mornings. No better way to learn."

I wasn't feeling particularly domestic that evening. Gigi hadn't been kidding when she said Alexander wouldn't know how to behave in a relationship; he barely knew how to behave as a boss. His little intel on taking horses—our horses, the ones *we* were training—to Gulfstream and then his reveal that *I* was supposed to be riding them every morning left me feeling like some alone time was definitely in order.

(I mean, riding them on an actual racetrack! With other riders out there! This would not be like the morning gallops with four or five other horses. I was in full panic attack mode.)

I decided to take one of the training books Alexander had set aside for me and drive into Ocala for a little pretend normalcy. Ocala was on the small side, but it was still a city—of sorts—and there were a couple of cafes which could lend a certain urban studiousness to a coffee break. So I ducked out of evening feeding with Walt's blessing, took a quick shower, and bounced out of the house before Alexander had even come up from the office. I just needed a *little* break.

In a cozy cafe hidden in an unassuming strip mall, I gathered a foamy latte and settled into a quiet corner to try and read.

The book I'd selected was incredibly technical, really scholarly stuff. I was deep into a paragraph of seemingly unrelated words, trying to keep my eyes from crossing, when I heard my name being called.

I looked up to a man standing near my table, clutching a coffee cup in one hand.

"Miles!" I gasped. I hadn't seen him since the night of the tornado—the night I'd broken up with him. A wave of guilt rushed over me. I hadn't treated him well at all. "I'm really sorry for everything, Miles, I—"

Miles held up his free hand, and then, with a gesture I found pretty bold, he pulled out the spare chair at my table and sat down. He pushed back his hair, which was just as smooth and pretty as ever, and gave me a rueful smile.

"I heard about you and the boss," he said. "I know why you didn't leave."

"You heard wrong—" I stopped myself. There was no point in denying it. I bowed my head, ashamed of myself for trying to pretend. "I'm sorry," I said again.

"You should have told me yourself," he said. "You didn't have to ignore my calls and then lie to me. You could have been honest. That's all I'm saying. That's all I wanted to tell you." He paused. I looked at the lights reflecting in his eyes. "I hope it works out for you."

"I hope so, too," I said. "I mean—thank you."

He looked at me closely. "Is everything—are you okay?"

"I'm fine. It's just...there's a lot of moving parts. I'm not trying to excuse myself, but, it's not as simple as it looks."

Miles nodded. "In this business, it never is. Good luck, Alex."

Pushing back, Miles took his coffee and left the cafe without looking back.

I watched the door after he'd gone, wondering if in the end, he would have been the simpler, saner choice.

As if I had a choice in the matter.

Chapter Thirty-six

I HAD HARBORED A secret hope to ride in the back of the horse van, the way I'd seen the groom do when Envision and Nelly came home, but it turned out the shipping companies supplied their own staff. So, instead, I rode down to Gulfstream with Alexander in his gleaming BMW, a car he assured me was all for show, and felt fancy as I lounged on the tan leather seats.

It was a long trip through the center of the peninsula. Florida seems to mostly consist of four ecosystems: pine forests, swamps, suburbs, and cities. We got to enjoy the whole cursed quadrant on the way to Gulfstream. At least in the forests and swamps, there was the occasional bird to look at. As the turnpike drew even with the coast and turned south, the Floridian jungle turned concrete and stayed that way. By the time we exited off I-95 in Hallandale Beach, I felt absolutely smothered by the traffic and low, ugly buildings surrounding the interstate.

Gulfstream Park in those days was a little bit more rickety than the glitzy shopping mall that has overtaken the grandstands today. You had to look for the glamour in those days, the remnants of celebrity in its sunburned dirt and grass ovals, which ran right up to the high-rise towers overlooking the Atlantic. Gulfstream in those days felt like a remnant of mid-century South Florida: beehive hairdos, cats-eye sunglasses, and shark-fin cars. Funny how everything in the fifties got its name from the animal kingdom, isn't it?

The cramped backstretch complex had found just enough room to squeeze in our four horses. Alexander had hired a groom from a friend's stable to prep the stalls before their arrival, and our horses were all snug in their boxes by the time we got there, eating their hay and looking generally pleased with themselves. The hired groom was seated on a folding chair nearby, a dark-eyed Cuban-American who went by Sunny. He was drinking a Coke and flipping through the day's program.

"Hey, Sunny, studying on my dime?" Alexander greeted him, and Sunny laughed, closing his book.

"Man, it's not like you pay me by the hour. I got them off the truck and they're happy, what else you want?" He stood up and gave Alexander an enthusiastic handshake. "It's good to see you, man."

"You too, Sunny. Thanks for stepping up to help. Everyone good here?"

"They're all good. A little on the chubby side, especially that bay filly." Sunny gestured towards Chessiecat, who was, indeed, looking a little flabby next to the sleek racehorses in neighboring stalls. "Man, what are you feeding her?"

"Well, they're all just here for the experience," Alexander said. "I like to run them fit, you know. They train well at home but I find the long runs on the big track are what really get some horses in condition."

"It works, man. My guy Cyrus has been running the tough ones fit for years. Some horses just don't get it in the morning works. You drop them into some back-to-back sprints and *pow,* man, you got a nice fast horse. You got a win." Sunny was grinning at Chessiecat, who was eating with exuberance. "I won't bet her the first time, but I guess the second time maybe she run to show." He glanced my way. "Hey man, I'm Sunny. I didn't see you back there, hidin' behind Alexander."

"Hey, I'm Alex," I said, ignoring the indiscriminate use of *man.* Sunny clearly had a word addiction.

"What you doin' down here?"

That was a good question. "I'm a rider," I decided. "A farm rider."

A rider who is not willing to ride on that track out there. I felt like I'd hit my limit for death-defying acts in a single season. Learning to gallop at Cotswold had been scary, but fine. I still needed more mileage before I went out on a track with a hundred other horses, though.

If only Alexander understood that!

"She'll be riding them in the mornings," Alexander was telling Sunny. "No point in hiring some busy rider to gallop just before the track closes when I've got perfectly good riders at the farm."

"Nice!" Sunny enthused. "Better go grab your license, though. They don't play around with no unlicensed riders, man."

"We're going to the frontside right now," Alexander assured him. "Just wanted to check in on the horses. You're good to watch them a little longer?"

"I'm good, man. Gonna go up front in a few to make a little money, but you'll be back by then."

We were out of the barn and heading back to the car before I told Alexander, *again,* that I didn't want to ride on the track.

He shook his head. "You'll be absolutely fine."

"Alexander! I'm not ready for this. Why won't you listen to me?"

He opened my car door. "I've told you time and time again to trust me on this. You're perfectly fine riding out there. I have a plan. We'll go out first thing. The track opens at five-thirty and it won't get too crowded until seven. You'll stay on the rail and mind your business. It's just like a warm-up ring at a horse show."

"But with more galloping," I sighed. "It's *nothing* like a warm-up ring."

"You might be surprised," Alexander said mildly. "I've seen those mad-houses. Now come on, we have to hurry up and get your license in order before the secretary closes up shop."

The afternoon passed in a blur, and by sundown I had a track license with my face on it—not smiling, despite instructions from the staff member who'd taken the shot—and was standing in a dim elevator, slowly heading upwards to Alexander's condo. The doors rattled gently as we passed the sixth floor landing.

"They always rattle there," Alexander said. "If they don't rattle, get out at the next floor and take the stairs the rest of the way."

"This place is a little, um, worse for wear," I suggested. The carpets in the lobby were ragged at the edges, paint was peeling next to the abandoned front desk, and the elevator floor had almost enough sand on it to start a second beach. Not exactly what I would have expected after the relative luxury of the Ocala house, for sure.

The elevator emitted a lazy *ding* as the doors opened at our floor. Alexander hoisted our bags and led the way. "I started out training down here," he explained. "This was my first place after I left home. So don't expect much. I've never updated it or anything."

The corridor was stark white and open-air at each end; the air was salty and humid. He led the way to a white door, unlocked it, and escorted me inside.

I looked around the little condo with raised eyebrows.

Alexander's condo was like a time capsule of old South Florida, with pastel pink accents and sagging white furniture everywhere. The front door opened straight into the living room, and I could look across the eggshell-colored carpet, past the shiny white dinette set, to old-fashioned louvre windows on a set of double doors. When I wrenched the louvres up, I could peer through the pebbled-glass slats to see the dark ocean crashing on the pale beach below.

"Was this place a drug dealer auction find, too?"

Alexander laughed. "Amazingly, no. It was some granny's place that a friend of mine sold me. Why? You don't like the decor?"

He grinned and flicked the white plastic frame surrounding a pale, abstract print of an egret standing in a pool of water. "This is classic Miami, right here. Pink, green, and white."

"And faded to perfection, with a soft scent of mold?" I teased.

"You got it."

"It's charming," I said, and I wasn't lying.

"Well, Adriene hated this place, for what it's worth."

There was silence for a moment. Bringing her up seemed to conjure her into the room. I went into the little kitchen and began opening cabinets. There were dishes and glasses, but almost no food.

"Do you want me to order dinner?" Alexander started to pick up our bags again. "Or shall we go out? We don't have to stay here."

"Let's stay in." I liked the sound of the waves crashing outside. "We can eat on the patio."

"That's a good idea. We can turn in early, too. Early morning tomorrow." Alexander went into the bedroom with the bags.

Early morning tomorrow.

I'd had a brief vision of myself enjoying this little trip to South Florida, almost like a vacation. Instead, I was going to be out on that track tomorrow, in the melee of morning works, surrounded by dozens and dozens of much more seasoned horses and riders. *Competitive* riders, men and women who rode to win.

I felt faint just thinking about it.

I put my hand in my back pocket, touching the hard plastic of my rider's license. The woman in the secretary's office had been brusque and efficient—she'd taken the brief application from me, noted Alexander's signature as my sponsoring trainer, and told me to stand against the wall with my feet on the X taped to the carpet. Within five minutes I had a racetrack ID with my own frightened face looking out of it. Just like that, I was transformed from farm girl to racetrack rider. It seemed like there should be more to the process.

"I've put your bag on the bed," Alexander said, coming out of the bedroom. "You can have a dresser drawer or the closet, there's plenty of room."

I went past him without meeting his gaze. I felt his eyes following me, then he went into the kitchen and started opening the same cabinets I had, probably hoping for a forgotten box of tea.

The bedroom was just as aged as the living room: faded pink duvet, old white furniture. I opened the mirrored closet doors and started to hang up my shirts. My safety vest was at the bottom of my bag, resting flat. I paused, brushing my fingers over the sleek nylon surface. The hard foam padding would be all that was between me and hooves if I came off on the racetrack.

I had grown used to the risks on the training track. I accepted the vest, the hard hat, the occasional brushes with danger. I had thought I was a gallop girl, really and truly a racing girl at last, but now I knew the truth. I was fooling myself if I thought I was tough enough, brave enough, bold enough to ride on the racetrack. I could gallop around a half-mile oval on the farm with a handful of coworkers I knew and joked with every morning. I couldn't possibly go out into the chaos of the real thing, surrounded by professional riders and jockeys, and expect to come out unscathed.

I'd seen pictures of morning gallops, the sheer number of horses and riders sharing that space. No matter what Alexander thought, mornings on the track weren't anything like a warm-up ring at a horse show.

Why didn't he listen to me?

He could have brought Gigi, I thought angrily, my fingers closing around the heavy padding of the vest. Her *fiancé* was here, for God's sake. He could have brought Walt. He could have *listened* to me when I said I didn't want to do this, that I wasn't yet ready to make this leap.

"Alex?" He was in the doorway. "Delivery's too slow. I'm just going to pop out and get us some supper. Do you want to come along?"

"No," I said. "I don't feel like going out again."

"No problem. You take a shower, have a drink. You'll feel better by the time I'm back with the food."

I walked across the pale carpet and gave him a cool kiss. "Thank you," I said. "See you later."

⁂

I didn't really expect to leave. I had put my shirts back in my bag, and my bag over my shoulder, and stepped out of the elevator and onto the street before I even realized what had happened. Even then, looking down at my feet on the sidewalk, I wasn't sure I was actually going to take off. As I started walking down the busy pavements, the concrete towers rising around me, traffic snarled with expensive cars and pedestrians in bathing suits, I didn't really think I was going to run away.

I wasn't really thinking at all.

My feet led me to the water. When I reached the beach, I took off my shoes and tucked them into my backpack, shoving them against the unforgiving bulk of my safety vest. The sand was cool against my skin, powdery between my toes. I had lived in Florida all of my life, mostly within twenty miles of the Gulf of Mexico, but I hadn't been to a beach in at least two years. I'd thought beaches were for people with spare time, spending money, friends to hang out with. I still had none of those things, but now I could see I'd been wrong. The beach was for loners, people without a hope in the world, people with empty pockets. I'd always belonged on the beach, hadn't I?

I found a spot near a dune where I thought I could sit without being noticed and tucked myself up in the sand. I tugged a granola bar and my water bottle out of my bag—I might have sleepwalked my way out of the condo, but I'd been conscious enough to fill up my bottle on the way out. "Look at you, taking care of yourself," I said quietly.

The sky over the sea was a velvety black. The condos at my back scattered yellow light across the beach, but the ocean remained dark beyond the breakers. On the horizon, more lights glittered—cruise ships, I figured, maybe freighters. The Gulf Stream ran very close to land here, with deep water for shipping lanes just offshore. I gazed at the ships, finding them impossible to reconcile with the countryside I'd woken up in that morning.

It was amazing the way Florida could be one thing—farms and fields and fast horses—and then another so different—ships and surf and soulless towers shadowing the beach.

My phone buzzed a few times from my pocket. That would be Alexander coming back with dinner, finding me gone. I wondered if I'd left a note. What would I have written? Why couldn't I remember?

My father had told me I shouldn't run away, and I'd told him I wasn't, but here I was, months later, sitting alone on a dark beach with just what I could fit into a backpack. As if Ocala, and Alexander, and plans for a brilliant future, had never happened at all.

I should go back, I thought, but back felt too far away to process. My instincts had said, more clearly than ever, to run away. *Trust your instincts.*

I tipped my head back on my bag, on the unyielding bulk of my safety vest, and fell asleep.

I woke up to a moonrise.

The ships on the horizon were gone and the enormous moon, almost full, cast a silver track across the water. It glittered on the ripples far out to sea before sparkling into a million points of light on the short breakers, like a pathway rolling nearly to my feet, a road I could follow if I just swam out beyond the surf.

It was beautiful, and lonesome, and I took a few deep breaths of the briny air, soaking it all in.

Beside me, half-covered with sand, my phone buzzed.

I picked it up. There were twenty missed calls. *Twenty!* All of them from Alexander.

Suddenly, I seemed to wake up properly. I realized what I'd done with shock. It felt as if a stranger had been in charge of my body.

"Oh my God," I whispered.

The phone said it was nearly midnight. Six hours ago, I'd walked out of the condo and down streets I didn't know until I'd crossed over to the beach. I didn't know where I was, or where the condo was, or why I'd done any of this.

Had I just had a mini-nervous breakdown?

My phone buzzed, and I answered it.

Chapter Thirty-seven

H E WASN'T ANGRY.

I was ready for him to be mad. I was willing for him to be mad. I would approve of him being mad. It turned out that I *hadn't* left a note, and he'd been out of his mind with worry. Apparently Alex taking off from the condo wasn't like Jacinta disappearing from the farm.

"Did you know you can't call the police for a person until they've been gone a full day? You could have been murdered already, for God's sake. This is *Florida*, Alex."

His voice carried across the empty pavement. When he'd called, I had crossed back over to the sidewalk and looked at the nearest street sign. He'd been there to pick me up in less than five minutes. I hadn't walked very far.

I got into the car without saying a word.

"What the hell happened, Alex?"

"I panicked."

I felt his eyes on me. The car purred gently, still in park, still pulled off into a metered parking space. The spots had all been packed at sunset. They were empty now. No one wanted to go to the beach at night, even a beautiful moonrise night like this one. This was *Florida,* he'd said. Bad things happened here on beautiful nights. I shouldn't have gone out alone.

"I just panicked," I repeated.

"You panicked."

"About riding in the morning."

He tipped his head back against the car's headrest.

"About living with you," I said, following some inner train of thought now. "About everything happening so quickly. I didn't expect any of this. I didn't know how to deal with it."

Alexander put the car into gear. "This isn't how to do it."

I didn't know how to respond to the sudden harshness in his voice, so I looked straight ahead and waited.

He backed onto the empty street, and sighed.

"I'm sorry, Alex."

"I'm sorry, too."

"You can't just run away, you know. That isn't fair to me."

"I wouldn't have, if I'd been thinking straight."

"Is this something you do? Is this something I should know about?"

I thought about the question for a moment. I owed him a real answer. "Yes and no," I decided. "Usually I stay. I stay until things are so bad, I don't know how to get out. This was different, though. This...it was a panic attack, I guess."

The car was stopped at a red light. Alexander looked at me. "You know I'd never put you in harm's way."

"I know."

"Things aren't going to get bad with us," he said. "Trust me on that. I won't ever let things get bad."

❧ ❧

I fell into a deep sleep in the wee hours. I awoke to an empty bed and the sound of Alexander making coffee in the kitchen. He came in with a mug and set it on the bedside table, a white wicker number with a glass top which rocked gently when anyone walked through the room. "Do you want some toast?" he asked. "I bought bread last night. Or, I think there are some breakfast burritos in the freezer."

I sat up slowly and the butterflies in my stomach awoke. "Oh, I think toast," I said. "Dry." The idea of a breakfast burrito made me positively queasy.

"Coming right up." He went back to the kitchen, and I slowly got up and dressed in clean jeans, my Cotswold Farm polo, and a pair of boot socks. Then I sat back down on the side of the bed, feeling nauseous. Was I really about to go to Gulfstream Park and ride on the racetrack?

There was no way I was ready for this, no matter what Alexander said.

I'd never put you in harm's way. Was I ready to trust him? Last night, it had felt like the better choice—running away felt like a mistake. For the first time, things had gone too far. I'd come a long way since my days of climbing out my bedroom window.

"Alex? Toast is warm."

My stomach growled despite my mental state, and I remembered that I hadn't had dinner the night before—just the granola bar scrounged from my backpack. I dragged myself out of the bedroom.

Alexander put a plate and coffee mug on the glass-topped table next to the kitchen. He sat down, pulling back the vertical blinds in front of the patio doors, but there was nothing to see besides our own reflections. The sunrise was still hours away. I yawned, and he smiled sympathetically—more sympathetically than I deserved, I thought.

"You shouldn't worry so much. We'll get you out there right when the track opens," he assured me, sipping his coffee. "You'll beat the traffic."

With my first couple horses, maybe, I thought. *But not with the last three.* Riding four horses would take close to two hours. With the track only open from five-thirty to ten, there would be a hundred other horses out there by the time I'd finished my second gallop.

"Alex," he said gently, "I wouldn't send you out to do something you can't handle."

I nibbled at my toast. "I know," I sighed finally. "Why is this hitting me so hard? I can't explain it."

"It must feel more real then you're ready for. That's all I can think of."

"That's it," I agreed. "When did everything get so real?" *Everything:* from being the next head rider to moving in with Alexander to this morning, prepping to gallop my racehorses on the track at Gulfstream. All of it too real to even believe, happening at the speed of light.

"Things move fast in racing," Alexander said. "You get used to it."

The stabling area was shadowy and quiet at five o'clock in the morning, with most of the horses still asleep and the barns' overhead lights still switched off. The tack and feed room lights were on, though, and as we walked up the smooth clay shed-row where our horses were housed, Sunny popped his head out of an open door with the unwelcome grin of a morning person.

"Hey man, you ready to start this party? I'm just going to throw everyone a little scoop of breakfast and then we can get busy. Alex, man, we'll have you up in the saddle in thirty, I *promise.*"

"Great," I said weakly, feeling queasy all over again.

Alexander looked me over. "There's a sofa in the office," he said finally. "Go and sit down until we're ready for you. Sunny and I will get Wing tacked."

I settled into the sofa, because following instructions seemed easier than anything else right now. The office was dark, and I thought I might drift off again if I could just get my heart rate down to normal. I stretched out, my feet towards the door, and looked across the shed-row. A bay horse with a big white star was watching Sunny intently, waiting for his breakfast. He was one of Jimmy Wallace's horses, from the string who had been racing this autumn. Eventually, I guessed, he'd be one of Gigi's horses.

The horse turned his head away from Sunny and looked down the shed-row in the opposite direction.

Someone was coming.

I sat up a little on the sofa, readying myself in case the owner of the office came in.

But the new arrival in the barn didn't even look my way. She went straight to the horse across from the office, opening her arms as if she was going to give him a big hug. I had just enough time to recognize her before she turned her back to me.

"Lucille?" I gasped.

She turned around, her fingers still coiled in the horse's mane.

I knew I was gaping. Lucille, on the other hand, seemed untroubled by my appearance. After a moment's thought, I realized she probably had no idea who I was. She would be thinking of a younger, softer girl than the hard-muscled, tough woman I was turning into.

"I'm sorry," I said, scrambling up from the sofa. "It's Alex O'Connor—Diana's old girl. I called you a few months ago..." My voice trailed off, my vocal cords stilled with the enormity of everything that had happened since the day I'd convinced the track secretary to give Lucille my message.

Now her eyebrows went up. She looked me up and down, taking in my boots and leather leggings, my safety vest and jockey skull-cap. "Well, I'll be damned," she drawled in her husky, smoke-roughened voice. "You went and did it."

"I did," I agreed, a grin breaking free. "I really did."

She laughed. "And did you believe me? When I said this was no place for a girl, did you think *that old woman has no idea,* or did you say to yourself, *it doesn't matter, I have to go,* and come find out for yourself?"

"I think a little of both," I confessed. "And I did what you said. I went to a training farm. I've been in Ocala all this time. This is the first morning for me at the track."

Lucille glanced up the shed-row. "Is that Alexander Whitehall I see throwing feed?"

I nodded. "That's my boss." *Among other things.*

"That's good. I don't think you could do better."

"Neither do I."

Lucille dusted her hands on her jeans and took her leave of the bay horse. "Well, I just was coming to visit this one. Jimmy and Tyson claimed him from me last week and I know he's going to do great things in this barn. But I still hate this sport." She cocked her head at me. "You know what I mean?"

"I think I do." I joined her in the shed-row. I could see Sunny and Alexander clipping feed buckets into place inside each stall. My eyes drifted back to Lucille, taking in her overall air of exhaustion, and her half-amused, half-irritated expression—the same one she'd worn when dropping off horses at Diana's. Horses she'd probably spent thousands on in upkeep, horses for which she was just hoping to find a good home and maybe get back a few grand to put into the next ones. This wasn't a sport for the soft-hearted, this was a sport which rewarded the hard, but it was essential for the horses that we keep some gentle part of us intact. Half-amused, half-irritated: that was probably the best-case scenario in this game.

"He's a good one," Lucille said. "Stick by him. Listen to him. He'll never steer you wrong."

"I will," I promised, and not just because I'd already come to that conclusion early this morning. (Or perhaps, late last night.) The truth was, I believed Lucille, who had been honest with me about racing from the start, more than anyone else. "Thank you."

She nodded. "See you around."

I watched Lucille stride up the shed, heading for the opposite doorway from the one we'd come in. She must have other horses here somewhere, horses who hadn't yet been claimed or retired, horses who gave her a chance at a win and enough money to keep clawing forward in this aching, back-breaking, heart-wrenching business.

But it's the only place for us, I thought.

I went into the tack room to find my saddle, ready to take my next step.

Chapter Thirty-eight

AT FIVE-THIRTY, THE TRACK was nearly desolate, just as Alexander had promised.

A few other horse and rider duos were walking along the paths from the barns to the on-gap, which let us onto the track somewhere in the middle of the backstretch. Wing saw the other horses and stretched out, striding as quickly as he could until we were half-jogging. He turned his hindquarters to one side as he tugged at the bit, twisting beneath me. I wished Alexander had brought a pony; Wing and I both could have used the support from quiet little Betsy.

We weren't meant to do much out there, either, which meant I had to hold back all of this energy for a full mile.

"Just jog him once around this morning," Alexander had instructed as I'd knotted my reins. "Let him look around, get to know the place."

I wasn't sure how much either of us would get to see. The track lights were on, but we weren't talking brilliant illumination here. There were plenty of shadows and spook-worthy pools of darkness to jog through. The grandstand loomed above the homestretch like a massive haunted house. I doubled my grip on the reins and the neck-strap, anchoring myself to the colt as best I could, and then let him stretch into a trot along the outside rail, posting as slowly as he'd let me. He snorted with every stride, peering into the darkness beyond the rail.

"Take it easy, Wing," I muttered, remembering how tough he'd been when I'd first started riding him. Not that long ago, the key to Wing had been softness, but how was I supposed to keep him to a trot when he was digging against the bit, begging to be let loose? If I softened up, we'd be galloping the wrong way around this huge racetrack, twice the size of our training track at home...and twice as occupied, with strange horses and riders who were beginning to pass us on the inside. There were already other early birds to contend with.

"Easy, easy, easy," I sighed, as he jerked hard on the reins, trying to chase after a horse who went flying past us at a gallop. The rider was standing in the stirrups; the horse's head was straight up in the air. We weren't supposed to gallop the wrong way, only jog, but something told me that horse was doing whatever it wanted, rules be damned. "Slow, slow, slow," I murmured. "Just a jog, just a jog, just a jog."

Wing had always liked chanting; his ears flicked back as I thought of short phrases to coo to him. Fortunately, I didn't have to be nice. It was all about tone. A whispered, *"Dumb, dumb, dummy,"* got him to ignore a horse who went by with an extended trot like an Olympic dressage horse, and a hissed, *"Ho boy, ho boy, ho boy,"* relaxed him as we passed the chute, with the starting gate looming in the shadows.

A striped pole came and went along the inside rail, and I flexed my shoulders, sighing at the cracks my joints made. We'd managed to jog a quarter-mile. Just another three-quarters or so to go.

"Good boy, good boy, good boy."

We approached the grandstand from the clubhouse turn, somehow finding ourselves alongside a horse who had passed us earlier at a swift trot but who was now cantering sideways, occasionally throwing in a buck. I was starting to think all of the bad horses got sent out first. Or maybe all of the horses here were just bad? I remembered Walt telling me to ignore the temptation to ride at other farms, that Cotswold's horses were all quality and that quality mattered when you were out on the track. Chances were good not every horse on this track was quality, I thought grimly. And now I was about to run right into one.

The troublesome horse was starting to bounce into our pathway, and my sudden sweat wasn't just from the morning humidity. *"Settle-settle-settle,"* I droned, as Wing fixed his ears with extreme curiosity on the crow-hopping bronco in front of us. They bounced into the middle of the track, giving me a moment of relief, and then I saw the rider swing his whip in the air. My hands tensed on the reins.

Crack! The whip came down on the horse's hindquarters and he darted forward, straightening out and giving up on his shenanigans in favor of a Standardbred-worthy trot along the rail. I would have been impressed with how quickly his attitude turned around if it wasn't for the twisting, buckling feeling between my own knees. The crack of the whip sent Wing into a state of panic, either because he was afraid the next one would be for him or simply because loud noises were scary. He flung his head in the air, spit flying from the bit, and threatened to rear.

"Hustle up, hustle up, hustle up," I called, my tone urgent, my voice louder. "Wing, buddy, whoa, whoa, whoa!" I actually said *whoa* instead of the usual *ho*, putting the two syllables together like a magic incantation. *"Whoa settle whoa down whoa cool it."*

A few riders jogged their horses past us as I struggled to get Wing moving forward again. I heard a crack about lady drivers, I heard a snicker in reply. I bit my lip, not prepared to be the new joke on the backside. Wing seemed to hover over the track, his legs dancing in place.

Then, without warning, he jumped forward.

I went with him, bending over his neck and letting his strides flow in an easy canter despite our instructions to jog, and despite the clear rules about galloping the wrong way. Flouting the rules my first time out was probably not a good idea, but I was hardly the only one letting their horse gallop along the outside rail and anyway, if this was how Wing felt secure his first time out on the track, this was what I was giving him. His neck rounded, his mouth softened, and for the first time since we'd left the shed-row, he felt comfortable and happy.

Trust your instincts, I thought.

"I saw you galloping him," Alexander harrumphed. He had met us at the off-gap, clipping a lead-shank to Wing's bit and parading us back to the shed-row as if the most dangerous part of our morning was yet to come.

"It had to be done," I said with a shrug. It felt so good on my tired shoulders I did it again. "He wouldn't settle in the jog. And I saw plenty of other riders galloping the wrong way."

"Don't make a habit out of it," he blustered, but I could tell he was going to let it go. "He'll be better tomorrow," he added in a softer tone. "The first day is always toughest."

I thought of the three fillies waiting for me. "Boy, *that's* the truth," I muttered, hopping down.

Sunny was waiting for me in Chessiecat's stall, her coat already gleaming beneath a single bare lightbulb. "We just throw the tack on, man, and boom, out the door!" He took the saddle from my arms and tossed a saddle towel over her back in one smooth movement. She was tacked in what seemed like seconds.

"Whoa," I said, impressed. "You're good."

Sunny laughed and held out his hand to give me a leg-up. "I'm *the best.*"

He led Chessiecat as far as the end of the shed-row, then told me to take a turn around the barn and head to the track when I was ready. "Alexander's hosing Wing, man. We all pitching in to get this done fast."

"What's the rush?" I asked. "You're not hurrying on my account, are you?"

"Nah," Sunny said, grinning at me as he turned to leave. "We're just trying to beat Jimmy, man."

Of course! We were borrowing Sunny from Jimmy's operation…without telling Jimmy about it. *Crafy, Alexander,* I thought appreciatively. Without Adriene's checkbook, times were lean—but they wouldn't be forever, and in the meantime, borrowing from clients was a tricky way to get through the race meeting without looking too shabby.

It probably didn't hurt that Jimmy would soon be marrying Alexander's cousin. If we were caught, it would be much easier to ask for forgiveness with a wedding on the way...and Gigi would find the whole thing hilarious.

Chessiecat remembered Gulfstream, and she was a perfect lady about her jog around the track. My arms needed a break after Wing's little fit, so I was grateful to just let her trot along the rail, snorting occasionally as we passed suspicious shadows in the gaps between the track lights. The sky was beginning to shift from deep black to gray as we jogged up the homestretch, and we had plenty of company. A rumble like thunder caught both of us by surprise, and we watched as two horses came galloping up the inner rail at racing speed, soaring past us and continuing down the track towards the clubhouse turn, their riders shouting to one another.

"Holy cow," I told Chessiecat, who was so interested she'd actually turned her head to watch the galloping horses disappear around the turn. "Everything seems faster here, doesn't it?"

"Well, lookee-lookee! Who do we have here?"

I turned in the saddle so violently that Chessiecat bounced sideways, sending my left leg into the rail. I had my hands full for a minute, straightening her out, and that was all the time Jacinta needed to draw her horse alongside us.

I bit my lip as I glanced over at her. We hadn't parted on good terms, after all. Shadowed by her helmet, her expression was impossible to read. "Hi, Jacinta," I said uncertainly.

"Miss Alex," she replied, turning her head. I could see her teeth glinting in a feral grin. "You've graduated to the big track!"

"Yeah, lucky me. How long have you been here?"

"Since I left Ocala," Jacinta said nonchalantly, as if she hadn't just abandoned her clothes and scant possessions, to say nothing of her job, without a word. "Decided to move in with a friend. Wanted to spend some time by the beach, get some good use outta Florida."

"We boxed up your things. If you want them, Emily would probably ship them to you."

She glanced my way. "What, did they need my room so bad? You end up with a new roommate?"

"Did you never check your phone? Your messages?"

"Nah." She reined back her horse, who was stronger and faster than Chessiecat. "I lost that thing."

I wondered if I should tell her. She'd left a few hours before everything had changed: the tornado, the crushed trailer, my move up to Alexander's house. If that part even mattered to her. I was starting to see that none of it had ever really mattered to Jacinta. She was a drifter. Things came and things went, but she'd always just keep turning up in new places, finding horses to ride, a couch to crash on. All of the bitterness of our last night together fell away. I was just glad she was okay. "It's good to see you," I told her. "I was worried."

Jacinta shrugged and snapped her gum. "You're an okay kid, Alex," she said. "Don't get too attached to anyone, though. We're not like you horse show girls. We don't like to get stuck in one place."

With that, she opened up her reins and let her horse trot away from us. I watched her go, my hands high and tight as Chessiecat pulled, begging to follow. What strange reunions I was having this morning. And yet, there was something promising about both of them. I was new to Gulfstream, but I had already run into two people I knew.

Maybe I wasn't really such a rank beginner, after all.

Chapter Thirty-nine

GULFSTREAM LIFE BECAME A routine so quickly, by the end of the first week it felt like I'd always lived here. The day moved in rapid chapters: training hard every morning, a quick nap after lunch, then a visit to the beach or back to the track for the races in the afternoon, depending on how much energy I had left. Alexander went to the races every day, networking and pressing palms as if his life depended on it, but I found that much human interaction on top of the strain of morning gallops was too exhausting to handle everyday. It was exciting, though, seeing live racing for the first time in my life. At last, I was watching horses gallop past in front of me, instead of on television, and it was pretty cool that they did it on a track I was beginning to know as well as Diana's riding arena.

Alexander's motive each afternoon was clear: he was making the rounds, making sure everyone knew he was back in the game, and he had his new assistant with him. No one asked where Adriene was when I was at his side. If they wondered, they were at least thoughtful enough to save their questions until I was out of earshot. "This is Alex O'Connor," he introduced me again and again. "She's going to be my new assistant."

The title wasn't real yet. My license said exercise rider, and there was no calling me trainer on paper. Even so, the horsemen gradually began to recognize my position alongside Alexander. Jimmy's Gulfstream trainer, Tyson Romero, ceded us a corner of the shed-row office, and after gallops, Alexander would sit down and I would perch on the corner of the sofa, and we would go over the training book and the condition book together, checking our progress against the races we wanted to put our horses into. When trainers and agents came by, looking for conversation or gossip, that was where they saw me—not in the stalls as I had been at Cotswold, but in the office, working at the business of racing.

Tyson was kind and subdued, a man who enjoyed summer in Saratoga more than winter in South Florida, and his presence in the room was less a distraction and more of a comfort. Occasionally he would hum a little tune while he made notes and flipped pages. Other than that, and visits from other horsemen on the track, the office was pleasantly quiet.

The frontside of the track was another story. Up there it was all backslaps and handshakes and big-chested attempts at showing up one another. The atmosphere in the clubhouse, the paddock, and the apron in front of the finish was almost entirely male. Alexander had no issues holding his own in this world, but I could feel the weight of all those male gazes on me as I walked through the afternoon crowds. Most of my riding jeans were interchangeable as my everyday jeans, and they were skinny-cut because that's what worked under tight leather leggings. Under the constant scrutiny of the leering racetrack boys, though, I wished I had some baggy mom jeans to cover me up. On the beach, I wore a t-shirt over a one-piece. The atmosphere in South Florida felt predatory.

We entered Wing into his first start two weeks after we'd arrived. The December day started humid and warm, and I was sweating through my morning gallops as if it was midsummer's day, but by the time we started prepping Wing for his four p.m. post time, a damp wind was whipping through the backside and the clouds over the grandstand were thick and pale gray. If we could have seen west, if buildings hadn't been blocking our view, I knew the distant horizon would be deep, forbiddingly black as a storm front slowly pushed across the peninsula.

"If it storms right before the race, will they take it off the turf?" I asked. I was pulling a comb gently through Wing's tail, loosening each strand with care so I wouldn't break a single hair. He wasn't blessed with a thick tail.

"They might," Alexander said noncommittally. "Depends on how hard it rains."

"And then he'd have to run on a muddy track instead."

"That's right."

Not only that, I thought gloomily, but we wouldn't really know how he performed on the grass. The Hibiscus was in three weeks, and we were gambling on my own conviction that Wing was a turf horse.

"Alexander," I said, "what's going to happen to us if we don't win the Hibiscus?"

"We'll have to start over, I suppose. I'll have some money coming in—she'll have to buy me out, so even if I don't *want* to lose the place, at least we'll have some seed money to start with. We'll rent a place and we'll start over, smaller. Our way. And hey, it could be good. Remember, I said we could go anywhere you wanted?"

He sounded brave, and I had to admit his plan sounded like a fine way to start again. I knew it was all a front, though. Alexander loved every stone and every blade of grass at Cotswold, and giving it up would be like leaving his family home all over again.

"You built too much to lose it," I said. "So, we're not going to let that happen."

"Not if you have any say in it?" he asked, grinning.

"That's right," I said stoutly, coming over to the webbing and leaning over. I took his chin in my hand, meeting his eyes. "Because *I've* worked too hard on your horses for you to lose them. Wing is just one of them, you know. I've poured my heart and soul into every horse in that training barn. Twelve-hour days, and extra riding, and—"

Alexander surprised me with a long, deep kiss.

"I love you, you know," he said. "I always wanted to meet a girl like you. I was starting to think you didn't exist."

We smiled at each other, and I was just congratulating myself on the perfect romantic moment when thunder cracked through the heavens.

***

"The footing's heavy," Alexander reported, slipping his phone into his pocket. "But we're not moving off the turf."

"Oh, thank goodness." I had been slowly rubbing Wing's racing bridle up and down for the past ten minutes as rain drummed down on the barn roof, polishing the leather for lack of anything else to do with my hands. Once Wing was groomed and wearing a light sheet to keep him clean, I'd been forbidden from messing with him before the walkover to the track. Alexander said horses shouldn't be fussed with before a race; it could put them off, make them nervous. I thought about how much time we'd always spent on our horses at horse shows and wondered if they'd go around the ring better if we just knocked the dust off and let them doze until showtime.

"They're going to call us over any minute." Alexander picked up a bucket and handed it to me. Inside there was a body brush, a hoof pick, a sponge, and a few leather odds and ends. "That's your bucket for the paddock. I'll lead him over this time, so you can watch. In a couple races, this'll be your job."

I followed him out of the tack room and into the office, nearly bumping into him when he came right back out waving a teal-colored piece of fabric. "Oh, is that the pinny?"

"Teal, for number six." He tugged on the smock. "When you lead the horse, you'll wear it."

Wing was watching us, his chest pressing against the webbing. Alexander slipped the chain gently over his nose and dropped the webbing, letting Wing hustle out of the stall alongside him. He looked over his shoulder at me. "Don't forget the bucket!"

We were going racing.

❧❧❧❧❧ ❧❧❧❧❧

The paddock was a whirl of confusion, horses everywhere, bright colors flying, tails swishing, hooves clattering over pavements and thudding on grass. There were spectators, bettors, entire families of owners spilling over the center of the paddock, smiling daughters and embarrassed sons in their Sunday best, blue-blazered businessmen shaking the hands of their trainers and trying to look as if they understood what was going on around them. I watched it all and hoped I didn't look as cheerfully clueless as they did.

Wing looked pleased to be back in the swing of things, even if he was being a big baby about puddles and refusing to get his pretty toes wet. Alexander pointed me to the number six saddling stall and told me to stay out of trouble until it was time to bring Wing in for tacking-up, then he gave the colt a few turns around the paddock. I leaned against the wall, my bucket at my feet.

I nearly jumped out of my skin when Adriene appeared next to me, seemingly out of thin air.

She smiled at my reaction. "First race has you a bit nervous, I see."

I shrugged, not willing to agree with her, even though the truth was obvious. I was scared to death. "You startled me," I protested. "You can't just sneak up on a person like that."

"Well, you'll get used to the paddock soon enough," she went on, ignoring my words. "I suspect you have a long career in front of you."

"What?" This time, my voice betrayed my surprise. "Why do you say that?"

Adriene laughed, leaning against the wall beside me as if we were old friends. "I know girls like you, Alex. I *was* a girl like you once. A horse show girl, who couldn't take any more velvet hunt caps and show bows. Oh, we have it all in the U.K.! We *came up* with all of that nonsense. My heart was here," Adriene went on, looking around the paddock with satisfaction. "And with him," she added, and her voice momentarily flattened. "But we're oil and water. At least, that's what we are to him."

I was too astonished to answer. Alexander was on the far side of the paddock, his back to us. No rescue was forthcoming from that quarter...except that Adriene was being *nice?* Did I need rescuing? Things were progressing too quickly for me to keep up, as usual.

"What happened with you two?" I heard myself asking.

"Nothing to worry you," Adriene said. "I've always known him. Did Gigi tell you I was engaged to his brother?"

"Yup."

"We had a fight and he went to Australia without me. He wanted someone more subservient than I could ever be. He didn't want a full partner."

I didn't know a thing about Alexander's brother, but I had to suspect the truth was somewhat more complicated than that. Adriene didn't want a full partner, either. She wanted to be in charge. So I simply nodded. "That's too bad."

"Alexander isn't the same man as his brother, but he isn't entirely different, either."

I heard the warning note in her voice. I turned my head. She was studying me with those long-lashed eyes. So carefully made-up, a woman dressed for the paddock as owner or trainer, but not a common groom, as I was. I should have dressed better. I should have pulled on nicer slacks. Too late now. I had to stand up with what I had.

"What are you trying to tell me?" I asked her, adding a note of challenge to my voice. I was tired of Adriene calling the shots when we were together. "Just say it already."

Her lips parted in a slight smile. "To always be like *that,*" she replied, amused. "To push back. He'll walk all over you, Alex. That's who he is. That's how he was raised. He knows more than you now, but he won't always. Someday you'll be just as clever with a racehorse as he is, and you'll have to force him to see it." Her eyelashes fluttered, as if she was remembering something she'd tried to put behind her. "Don't let him get in your way."

We both looked towards the walking ring. There was a cluster of people between us and Alexander, but any moment now, he'd come clear of them and see us. I stiffened, not wanting to be seen fraternizing with the enemy. But Adriene was already slipping out of the saddling stall, a cherry-red handbag over her shoulder. She cast me a frosty smile as she went, and then she was gone, striding across the paddock and towards the gate with her long, sure step. The bag was like a bright flag, waving bravely behind her. She was leaving at last, but she wasn't retreating. Adriene would always be sure she'd left on her own terms.

My gaze flicked back to the walking ring. Alexander and Wing appeared, both of them looking our way. Wing's pricked ears and high step gave him a positively joyous look, and Alexander looked sure and right at his side. My heart lifted, bursting free of whatever fears Adriene had momentarily cast on it, and I waited for them to arrive, for the next step, for whatever was coming.

❧❧❧ ❧❧❧

Gabriel Ramos rode Wing with a cocky, comfortable seat. I watched Alexander hand off the pair to the outrider, studied the way he coiled the lead-shank in his hand and stepped to one side as

Wing shoved against the track pony. I made a mental note of every move Alexander made, because it would be me out there soon. Alex the assistant trainer. From horse show girl, to gallop girl, to assistant. This life was dizzying.

I sidled up alongside the rail, trying to avoid the cigarette and beer fumes from the men who had spent the afternoon alternating between the apron, the clubhouse bar, and the betting windows. Alexander would come and meet me here, but until he arrived I felt keenly alone, unsheltered and obvious to all of these coarse men, most of whom would be perfectly polite and well-behaved in different surroundings. The racetrack seemed to bring out the worst in so many people. It must have been all the money flying around, an invitation to a kind of raw machismo these guys wouldn't display anywhere else.

At least, I didn't think they would.

Alexander slipped alongside me. "Alex, do you know Jimmy?" He gestured to a man at his side, good-looking in a slick kind of way.

"Alex, good to meet ya." Jimmy Wallace shoved his hand at me. His grip was too tight, but I didn't complain. "I've heard so much about ya from Gigi."

I tried and failed to imagine petite, pixie-like Gigi with this sleek, dark-haired man. He was wearing a guayabera in deference to the steamy heat we'd had earlier in the day, but something told me he had plenty of shiny suits in his closet. As I took my hand back, a cool wind whipped through the grandstand and I saw him shiver just slightly. I grinned, pleased to spot a chink in his glitzy armor. "Cold? I thought you were from New York."

"When I'm in Florida, I dress for Florida!" He grinned back, showing off a mouthful of expensively white teeth. "Gigi said you were one to watch around here. Hands and seat that just float. You gonna stick around Gulfstream? I could use a rider like that."

I found myself glancing at Alexander to save me. Then I remembered Adriene's warning. If I didn't take care of myself, Alexander would be glad to—but was that really what I wanted? And how would we ever make it together if I had to rely on him for everything? I turned back to Jimmy before Alexander could say anything. "I'm not planning on sticking around here too long, but thank you. Gigi's too kind."

"She knows what she's talking about." Jimmy shrugged. "All right. But you know where to find me. I've always got some light-mouthed fillies who would rather have a woman on their back, and if Alexander's riding you, I know I can."

I blushed, and Jimmy laughed. It took me a moment of flustered embarrassment to realize what he meant by *riding me.* It was just a racetrack phrase for using me as a rider.

The track announcer broke in to save me with a cheerful: "The horses are at the starting gate, they've reached the post."

I'd been so distracted by Jimmy, I hadn't even seen Wing warming up. I turned towards the big screen, hoping he'd go into the gate like a good boy. I hadn't broken him from the gate here; Gabriel had taken care of that during his getting-to-know-you rides, handling Wing's timed works as well.

Suddenly I wanted to know what it was like in that starting gate. I'd been afraid of it before, not really ready to find myself inside a steel cage on top of a ragingly ready racehorse. But now I knew it was just part of the game, and I found myself newly eager to get a taste of everything this sport had to offer.

Everything it demanded.

Rain started falling again as the horses loaded into the gate. I pulled my hat more firmly over my forehead, blinking against the sudden downpour. As shouting bettors started to run for the safety of the clubhouse, I leaned forward against the fence, not willing to miss a single moment of Wing's race.

"And away they go!"

Chapter Forty

WE WAITED FOR THE rain to stop, but it didn't.

After his race was run, we met Wing on the muddy dirt track, Alexander murmuring directions in my ear. Catching a horse after a race was the groom's job, so I had Wing's halter over my shoulder and the bucket slung over my other arm as I squelched across the soggy ground. There were numbers along the track rail, a place for each horse to pull up, and I got to the six just as Gabriel jogged our muddy horse up.

I wanted to wrap my arms around his filthy neck and hug him with everything I had, but Wing was wild-eyed and blowing through red-rimmed nostrils, refusing to stand still. The rain hammered down as Gabriel hopped down from the saddle and started to undo the saddle girth. I watched him, my hands frozen on Wing's reins, until Alexander hissed for me to slip on the colt's halter and start sponging the mud from his face.

I jumped to attention, but the rain was doing my job for me, dirty water streaming from Wing's forelock and dripping from his muzzle. I dabbed at the mud around his eyes while he blinked and tugged away from me.

"He sure got dirty for second place," Gabriel said, swiping at the dirt on his own face. "So did I."

"Next time you'll go straight to the front," Alexander replied, studying the horse. "And you'll win. Nice and clean to get your picture taken."

"You got it." Gabriel gave Wing a farewell clap on the neck and left us there on the track.

I turned to Alexander. "Now what?"

He wiped water from his face. "We walk back, we cool out our horse, and we have a whiskey," he told me. "No champagne for second place."

I grinned at his dour expression. "Next time, right?"

Alexander didn't reply, but I knew what he was thinking. *It better be.*

❧❧❧ ❧❧❧

The rain fell all night, soaking the patio furniture, hammering on the empty beach. It fell on my helmet the next morning as I galloped the fillies, their hooves squelching in the sucking mud. It fell on Alexander as he walked Wing in the morning and the afternoon, stretching the colt's legs out after his race-day. It fell on our hunched shoulders as we walked back to the car in the evening, thoroughly chilled and ready for the dry, sunny Florida winter to come back.

Surely it will clear up tomorrow, we told one another. *Rain like this never lasts in winter.*

And then, for the next two weeks, the rain just kept coming.

I poured myself another cup of coffee from Tyson's coffeemaker, which was perched rather dangerously on a rusting filing cabinet in a corner of the office. For three mornings now, the track had been closed, and we'd arrived even earlier than usual to jog the horses around the shed-row before the other trainers started their horses. I'd finished our horses before the rush, but it was on now—a constant thudding of hooves and swirling of dust as horse after horse was trotted down the shed-row. It was impossible to get any work done with the barn aisles transformed into impromptu training tracks, and fairly dangerous to do anything as innocent as try to walk from the office to the tack room, so we hunkered down and drank too much coffee, waiting for the hordes to retreat so that we could finish our morning's chores. The side door was open, letting in pearly gray light as water pooled on the pavement outside.

This rain was beginning to feel Biblical.

Everyday we woke up and hoped for sunshine to return. I would have welcomed heat, humidity, a mild case of sunstroke. But everyday, the clouds thickened over the ocean and by noon, even a dry morning had turned into a rainy afternoon. Sometimes there was thunder, but more often it was just a steady, hammering, tropical rainfall.

"South Florida has a sense of humor," Tyson had said on the fifth day of rain. "This happens sometimes." On the tenth day, he said, "Okay, this is getting ridiculous." On the fourteenth day, yesterday, he said, "I'm about to just pick up and move back to New York year-round. At least at Aqueduct I can train all winter even if it snows."

"You've never felt wind like that in your life," Alexander told him. "Aqueduct is the coldest racetrack in America. The wind comes right off the ocean there."

"Anything has to be better than this," Tyson had sighed.

Hooves thundered past the door, the constant rumble of trotting horses burrowing into my skull. I'd never realized the sound could be unpleasant. Enough of anything could wear on a person after a while.

I closed my eyes and leaned my head back against the couch cushions, imagining a sunny morning, the flowers outside the office door nodding in a gentle sea breeze.

"Alex! Look!" Alexander's voice was alarmed.

I opened my eyes, nearly spilling my coffee as I sat upright. "What?"

He pointed at the office door, and my eyes widened.

Water was lapping at the door-sill.

"When did that happen? There were just puddles before!"

"I don't know," Alexander said, jumping up. He looked out the door. "The whole pavement between the barns is like this. I don't know where it's coming from."

Water spilled over the sill and pooled around his boots. We looked at the new puddle in shock.

I was the first one to move. I hopped up and pulled our books and files off Tyson's desk. "We need a plan. This stuff goes in the car right now—you go and drive it off property to a road that isn't flooding. And call the office and find out what's going to happen with the horses. They must have an evacuation plan, right?"

Alexander looked over his shoulder at me. "Did you have an evacuation plan at your old stables?"

I paused in the doorway, my arms piled with paperwork. Our horses' health records, our training diaries, any number of forms and agreements—all of it needed to be protected. But nothing was as important as the horses themselves. The problem was, I didn't know how to save them. I needed someone else to have made that decision already. We were in the middle of a city, for God's sake. "We would have just loaded them up in every available trailer and driven away," I told him. "But there aren't enough trailers here to get all of these horses out. So there must be something else. Maybe there's higher ground on the property?"

A train of three horses trotted past, reminding me that training hours were still taking place in the shed-row. I watched their hindquarters muscle down the aisle, past my own horses, all pulling at their hay-nets. There were other trainers in this barn who were still so wrapped up in conditioning, they didn't know the waters were rising around us. Even Tyson was in the saddle right now. "Alexander, call the office. We might be the first ones to realize what's happening."

Water spilled across the office floor. Suddenly, it was everywhere, little streams tickling at my boots. I looked both ways, made sure the shed-row was clear, and then made a run for it, our files clutched to my chest.

❧❧❧ ❦❦❦

By the time the loudspeakers in the stabling area crackled to life, water was pouring down the ruts in the shed-row, trainers were dragging spooking horses from stalls, and trucks were pulling up in the ankle-deep water outside the barns, drivers hurriedly checking hitches and dropping ramps, hoping to get their horses loaded and out of the stabling area before the water was too deep for their engines. Like most trainers on the backside, we didn't have our own trailer, relying instead on transportation companies to handle any hauling. We had haltered all of our horses, tugged on our Wellington boots, and borrowed some hotwalkers from other trainers. We were ready to leave—but we had no idea where to go.

Through it all, the rain kept falling.

I stood by Wing's stall, watching him eat, still tugging meticulously at his hay-net for the best bits of alfalfa, though every time another horse went splashing past or a horse trailer set up a wake zone outside the barn, his ears pricked and he stopped chewing. He snorted occasionally at the water streaming along the shed-row, but all in all, Wing was unconcerned. I found that cheering.

I myself had entered some strange state of calm which had pushed my initial panic aside. I was centered. I was ready for whatever came next. I wasn't afraid—though I knew, deep down, I should be.

The rain kept falling.

A man's cough sounded out, amplified over the loudspeaker. Wing jumped and snorted. I think I did the same. Beside me,

Alexander shook his head. He had been muttering about gross incompetence for the past twenty minutes, ever since he'd called the office and found they were totally unaware of the floodwaters rising in the stable area. Then the instructions came, garbled at first, then repeated at a slower pace, as if the speaker couldn't quite believe he was saying them the first time around.

We were to lead our horses out of the shed-rows, up the driveway that led to the frontside, and to the main parking lot, where trailers would be organized to evacuate everyone to a training center outside of town.

"Okay," I announced, shaking my hands out as if I was getting ready for a fight. "It's go time." I reached for the lead-shank hanging outside Wing's stall.

Alexander put his hand on my arm. "Are you good with him? I can lead him, if you want. Or get one of the boys to do it." He nodded to the hotwalkers he'd rounded up, who were coiling lead shanks in their hands, ready to start as soon as we gave the word.

I could have taken one of the fillies—Chessiecat would have been the easiest. But I wanted Wing. He was the horse who had brought us to Gulfstream; he was the horse we had been prepping to go to post in a week and fight for the future of Cotswold Farm. Wings and Prayers: he carried everything on his back, and even now, with the rain tumbling down and the water spilling into the shed-row, I trusted that he could carry the weight of all those hopes. I wanted his lead-shank in my hands. "I'll take him," I said.

Alexander squeezed my arm. "Then it's time for the strangest walkover of our lives."

Chapter Forty-one

T HE HORSES WERE STRANGELY calm on the walk over to the frontside. Maybe the swirling waters, rising to our knees by the time we got everyone to higher ground on the driveway, was enough to keep them honest. They knew what was happening—at least, they knew what we were fleeing. And while some tugged at their leads and a few pawed at the water, splashing everyone—we were already soaked from rain, so it couldn't possibly matter—we made an oddly solemn procession for the most part, marching through brown water under the featureless gray sky.

Waiting for our turn to load onto a trailer was a little more wild; horses whinnied and snorted, reared and tried to bolt. Still, the rain beating on their heads and backs seemed to quell high spirits; no one had too much extra energy with all of that chilly water hammering on them constantly as minutes turned into hours. When I finally walked Wing up the ramp of a trailer, he lowered his head and sighed, utterly relieved to be out of the weather, and I couldn't say I disagreed.

At least I got my wish to ride in the back with the horses—we all stayed with our horses, standing at their heads and swaying dramatically as the horse van rumbled through the traffic of Hallandale Beach. Salvation was an hour away, at a training center near the Everglades, and when we finally had the horses in bare, dry stalls, I sank onto a straw bale, my legs trembling, and put my face against my knees.

Alexander sat next to me, his knees cracking. "Oof," he grunted, wrapping a wet arm around me. "Today has to be the strangest day of my life. Are you all right?"

I didn't pick up my head. "I'm just exhausted," I mumbled. "I feel shaky all of a sudden. I was fine all this time and now...I'm wrecked."

He tugged me closer, until I finally brought my head up and rested it on his chest. "You're soaked," I said.

"So are you."

"What else do we have to do?" I wondered how we'd get home. The car was somewhere back in Hallandale Beach, wherever Alexander had parked it. The city itself hadn't been flooding—just the big bowl of the stabling area.

"Bed down the stalls, find hay and grain, find buckets..." Alexander's voice trailed off. "Well, look at this."

I picked up my head. "What?"

"Helloooo!" a chipper voice trilled. "I heard you might be in need of some assistance!"

"Gigi?" I blinked at the woman approaching. She was pushing a wheelbarrow heaped with bags of grain, buckets, and coolers. "Where—how—when—"

"I was already in town," she said, setting down the wheelbarrow in front of us. "I'd just come in. Alexander, you should know Jimmy's called me in. I'm quitting Ocala forever."

"That's a very dramatic way of putting it."

She crossed her eyes at him and laughed. "I'm a very dramatic person, you know that! Anyway, I'd just come into town, and when I heard about the track, I stole Jimmy's good truck and went to the feed store and just loaded up. A groom is right behind me with hay. We'll get these babies all bedded down for the night and then I'm taking *you* drowned rats home for soup and sympathy."

"Gigi, you're like a guardian angel," I said gratefully. "I'm pretty sure I've never said that to anyone before, too."

"I'm pretty sure no one's ever called me an angel," Gigi chortled.

"Jimmy certainly won't, when he realizes his good truck is missing." Alexander got up from the straw bale. "Any chance you brought coffee, too? I'm freezing."

"In the truck. It's at the end of the barn," she said. "Go and fetch it while Alex and I get coolers on these horses. They're just as half-drowned as you are, I'm guessing."

An hour later, as darkness spread across the wilderness just outside the training center, we pulled the wet coolers off the horses, smoothed our hands over their dry coats beneath, and finally headed for Gigi's borrowed truck. Everyone was bedded down in straw and enjoying a full hay-net. Gigi had really come through for us. I'd have hugged her if I wasn't still so wet.

We sat together on the bench seat of the truck, crowding together without complaint. She turned the heat on low and pulled the truck onto the two-lane county highway, heading back towards the city lights. For a few minutes, we were silent, soaking up the warmth and the joy of simply being off our feet at last. I rubbed at my thighs. My muscles were sore from wading through the deep water on the backside.

Gigi was the first to speak. "They say the backside won't open for at least a week. Assuming the rain stops."

I glanced at Alexander. "Will racing be cancelled?"

He didn't answer.

"The track won't be able to open until they can sort out the footing," Gigi offered. "The good news is, it's supposed to stop raining in a few days. But it won't be in time for your race."

I watched the lights of the coast grow nearer. We passed under the turnpike, and I-95. The sprawl reached out and clutched the truck, drawing us into the congestion of the beachside cities. Gigi hummed along with music on the radio.

Upstairs, she threw her purse on the sofa and swung her arms, spinning around the tiny living room.

"Alexander, let me have this condo. I like being so close to the beach."

"Jimmy's condo is ten times nicer than this one," Alexander said dismissively. "Go and live with your fiancé."

"I will live with him if I have to, but I'd rather have this place all to myself." Gigi laughed at herself. "Listen to me, I sound as if I don't love him madly."

"Well, do you?" I asked, feeling the question was intrusive, but also incredibly curious. Anyway, I was too tired to be courteous. I threw myself down at the kitchen table and started tugging at my soaked socks.

"I do, actually." Gigi waltzed into the kitchen and plucked a bottle of white wine from the refrigerator. "He's funny, and he spoils me, and he loves horses. He can't help that he's from Queens and has that ridiculous accent, and no notion at all of how to dress." She started pulling down wine glasses with a practiced air, and I realized she must have stayed in this condo before.

"Are you going to fix him?" Alexander asked, standing on one leg by the door. He had one sock off and it dangled from his hand like a drowned rat. "Going to buy him some tweeds and a pair of Hunter boots?"

"I might buy them for him, but I'm not going to force them on him." Gigi handed out glasses brimming with chilled wine. "He's his own man. Everyone has that right, I think. Take people or leave them, but don't try to change them."

"It would be nice if more women shared that view." Alexander's voice was skeptical.

"You've had bad luck," Gigi told him sympathetically. "Alex, are you trying to change my cousin here? Because he's a stick-in-the-mud. You'll never succeed."

I bit my lip. Gigi's frivolity was infectious, and heaven knew I could use a laugh after the day we'd had, but I was still trying to work out what came next. I sipped the wine, hoping it would loosen my brain. We needed a new plan. Everything had hinged on the Hibiscus—we had arranged it that way ourselves. And while Adriene's constant threat had felt diminished during our Gulfstream days—I hadn't seen her again after the day in the paddock—she still held half of Cotswold Farm tightly in her grip. A flood wasn't going to change that.

"We're going to have to find another way," I said aloud.

Alexander tossed his wet socks into the closet where a small washer/dryer huddled. "You don't think it's time to concede?

Maybe this Act of God is telling us something, Alex. Maybe Cotswold goes, and that's the way it's supposed to be. Maybe this is a sign that we're meant to move to the desert."

"God moves in mysterious ways," Gigi suggested, flinging back half her wine in one swallow.

"No," I insisted. "I know when it's time to run away, and when it's time to stay and fight. Trust me on this one. It's the one instinct I've got."

"So what will you do?" Gigi asked. "Find another race?"

"No," I decided. "We will go home and fight on our own turf."

Gigi laughed. "You know, for that, I think I'll go back to Ocala. Just to watch you beat her."

Chapter Forty-two

I FELT NOTHING BUT relief when we turned in the gates of Cotswold Farm.

We drove past the house and up to the training barn, where the van was parked by the ramp. By the time we arrived, the horses were already unloaded, back in their stalls. I glanced in at each one—they were circling their stalls, sniffing the fresh bedding, making themselves at home.

Ricky leaned against the wall next to Wing's stall, watching the colt paw at his shavings. He nodded at us. "Good to have you back."

"It's good to be back," I told him. "Now I don't have to do all the work."

"Watch it, or I'll have Walt get you in there pulling off their bandages." Ricky glanced over my tidy clothes. "Even if you're dressed all neat and pretty."

I pretended to scurry after Alexander, but I tossed Ricky a grin over my shoulder, just to let him know.

I'd really missed him.

I'd really missed *the farm*.

Going to the racetrack had been my dream from the beginning, but I felt more like myself here. That might change someday, but for now, I knew where I wanted to be.

Right here at Cotswold Farm.

Home.

Walt was chatting with the driver by the truck cab, their voices raised over the growl of its idling engine. He turned as we approached, eyebrows lifted. "Well, you're back! Welcome home, you two."

Alexander shook his hand, and then the driver's hand for good measure. "Everything signed off on?" he asked, and the driver nodded. "Good man. Thank you."

Walt gave the driver a nod and he headed back to his truck. "So, flooded out. That has to be a first."

"It certainly is for me," Alexander sighed. "And the timing couldn't have been worse. Has she been here?"

"Almost every day. She'll disappear for a few, leave instructions for her riders, then come back. I kind of thought she was headin' down to bother *you.*"

"I haven't seen her." Alexander shook his head.

I swallowed. Now was the time to admit it, I supposed. "I saw her the day Wing raced," I said. "In the paddock. She came up to me while you were walking him."

Now Alexander's eyebrows went up. "And you kept it quiet? Why on earth for? What did she say?"

Nothing that you need to know. How could I tell Alexander that Adriene had warned me not to let him take charge all the time, that I'd have to push against him if I wanted to be my own person, to become a trainer in my own right? No, that was private.

"Not much," I said instead. "She just wanted me to know she was watching, I guess."

The men exchanged glances.

"What time does she come in the morning?" Alexander asked eventually. "I want to talk to our riders before she's here, if I can."

"Not until after six," Walt assured him. "You can do it."

"I'll see you at five-thirty tomorrow, then." Alexander glanced my way. "Alex? Shall we go back to the house and unpack our bags?"

Walt's eyes rested on me, gently curious, and I was forced to accept that he must know now that I hadn't just been staying in the house out of convenience's sake. Walt had been with Alexander a long time; chances were good he knew all about the condo in Hallandale—specifically, that it was a one-bedroom. I smiled weakly at him and shrugged—*what can I say?* "Sure," I said. "Let's go home."

❧❦❧ ❧❦❧

The morning meeting was like a call to arms, and everyone loved it.

There were a few new faces: with Jacinta, Gigi, and myself all gone, Walt had to hire three new riders. Billy and Juan were still there, though, and the new riders, two guys and a lone woman, all seemed to be on their team. None of them were impressed with Adriene.

"She's a pain in the ass," complained the woman, Eleanor, when Alexander was done introducing himself. "She shows up late, gets in our way, and criticizes everything. I wouldn't have stayed after day one if Walt hadn't promised she'd be out of here soon."

Alexander glanced at Walt, who shrugged. I felt a bloom of warmth in my chest. Walt had believed in my plan. He'd believed in *me*.

The fresh boost of confidence made me speak up, raising my voice to gain everyone's attention. "You know, bullies don't stand up for themselves when they're outnumbered. That's a proven fact. If we let her walk all over us, she'll never leave." I paused, thinking about my years with Diana. "I'm done getting walked on. Let's be clear about how we feel, all of us. I'll bet every single one of us put up with someone when we shouldn't have, maybe for a long, long time."

There were a few solemn nods from the riders, Eleanor included. Behind them, Alexander watched me. I met his eyes, and he nodded once, sharply.

Emboldened, I went on. "I can't promise anything. But I bet if we show Adriene she isn't wanted here, she'll take her toys and go home."

"What do you suggest?" Billy asked. His habitually sad eyes were suddenly interested. "She has her own riders. She doesn't care what we think of her."

Just then, a car door slammed behind me. I spun around, afraid it was Adriene herself, but a woman carrying a helmet and safety vest entered the training barn. "Are you one of Adriene's riders?" I asked.

The woman nodded warily.

"Work for us," I told her, "and we'll make it worth your while."

Adriene's riders weren't hard to steal. It turned out they weren't getting paid as much per horse as Alexander's riders were, and the incentive of more cash alone was enough to make them turn their coats. When Walt gently pointed out that we didn't have enough horses for two more riders, I suggested putting them on a weekly salary instead. "We'll have more horses in a few weeks," I told him.

Even Alexander was watching with a slightly stupefied look at this point. "We will?"

"Easily. All we have to do is empty Adriene's stalls, and we can fill them up with better owners." I spoke with confidence. I'd just watched Alexander spend weeks on end shaking hands and slapping backs with every owner and trainer in South Florida. A few phone calls and some outlandish promises, and we'd be bursting with horses. He knew how to make connections, but I strongly suspected he didn't know how to make good on them. Well, I'd cold-called Lucille Cornett, I'd accosted Alexander Whitehall in a parking lot, and with those two mad moves, I'd turned my life around. Now, I was ready to turn Cotswold Farm around. "Trust me," I added. "I have it all worked out."

"Alex," Walt drawled. "It's after six o'clock. You want to send out a set this morning or what?"

I didn't even register that Walt was asking *me* for instructions until much later. For the moment, I just went with it. "Yes. Give me just a minute while I rearrange the sets." And without even thinking about what I was doing, I walked up to the whiteboard, added Adriene's riders to our list, and moved horses around.

I realized what I'd done about halfway through the task, and glanced at Walt, but he just nodded. After I'd finished, he looked over my work and made a few suggestions. "You ready to send them out?" he asked at last.

"Almost," I said. "Can you just gather everyone down here for me, please?"

Walt nodded and set about collecting the grooms and hotwalkers who were scattered around the training barn. When the entire staff was assembled in the center aisle, I looked them over appraisingly. I felt Alexander at my back, and I knew if I couldn't think of the words to lead these people, he'd speak up for me. But it was time for me to stand up and take charge.

"Team," I said, "it's time for her to go. You're the people who make this place work. You have a voice. I know it doesn't sound like much protection, but there are forty horses in this barn who need taken care of, and based on that alone, she can't fire all of us. And if we're all in this together, she can't just fire one or two of us. It has to be all or nothing."

Ricky looked impressed. "So you're calling a strike?"

"No. We have to get through training. I'm telling you to pretend she isn't here. Ignore her. If she pushes you, remind her you answer to Alexander."

"And to you," Alexander interjected. "Walt, you ready?"

Walt nodded. "Team," he began, echoing my use of the word, "A lot of y'all know I'm movin' to Lake City. I want you to welcome Alex as the head rider and Alexander's assistant. She's a good horsewoman and she'll always put the horses and you first. I think she's provin' that to you right now."

My heart thrummed in my chest like a taut bowstring. I reached my hands behind my back, and Alexander clutched them tightly. This was happening. This had *happened*. I waited for their response, breathless with anticipation and frayed nerves.

Ricky was the first to speak. "Congrats, boss," he told me. "You worked hard for this. Everyone? What did I say about this girl, one week after she get here? I say, no one cares as much as she does. I say, I've never seen anyone work as hard as she does. And look here, I was right!"

One by one, the other riders and grooms spoke up, agreeing with Ricky. "Congrats, Alex," they said. "Nice work, Alex. You deserve it, Alex."

"Thank you, guys," I managed to choke, holding back tears with an effort. "Thanks so much. We can do this."

With nods and waves, the grooms went back to the shed-rows, and the riders went into the tack room to gather their saddles and bridles. I looked over my shoulder at Alexander.

"We can do this," he echoed.

"We can," I told him stoutly. "Today, we win this."

Whatever Adriene threatened, she was only one person. I had the entire farm behind me, and the courage of my convictions.

I was keeping Cotswold, and there was nothing she could do to stop me.

Chapter Forty-three

B Y THE TIME ADRIENE had arrived, I had sent out the first set, put Alexander on Betsy to lead the way, and was seated behind the desk, going over the past week's training notes. If there weren't enough horses to go around, I decided, I wasn't going to take another rider's horse. I could sit right here and catch up on what had happened while I'd been away.

I glanced up when I noticed her. She stood in the doorway dramatically, fixing me with her most overbearing expression. "Oh, hello. You're very late," I said.

"Alex, what on earth are you doing here?"

"Working," I replied simply. I dropped my eyes back to the training diary. My nerves were quivering beneath my skin; I felt nauseous at the thought of the fight ahead—but the same sense of calm which had strengthened me as the backside flooded was beginning to flow through my veins now.

Adriene didn't start a war right away. Instead, she settled with elaborately displayed comfort into one of the ancient office chairs and gazed at me thoughtfully. Her entire person oozed cool, casual friendliness. I didn't believe it for one second. She had shown me support at Gulfstream, but now I brought the battle to home turf. She wanted this farm. I was going to have to prove I was strong enough to take it from her. So I simply lifted my brows at her, and waited.

"I see you're taking my advice," she said finally. "You're taking some control of the training from Alexander."

You have no idea, I thought. Aloud, I replied, "The timing is right. Especially with Gulfstream closed for the next week. Tampa opens in a couple of weeks and we'll run some horses there."

This was an executive decision. Alexander and I hadn't discussed Tampa at all yet, but I knew from listening to backside chatter that horses seemed to love Tampa's track, and it was close enough to haul in for just a few days before and after a race. That sounded better than moving lock, stock, and barrel to the track right after we'd come home. *Mental note,* I thought, *tell Alexander we're going to Tampa.*

"Tampa's nice," Adriene allowed. "A little pedestrian, perhaps. California would be a more challenging choice, for better horses, but of course your string isn't there yet."

A smile twitched my lips. That was a poorly-aimed shot, and she had to know it. Plenty of big-time East Coast trainers based in Tampa for the winter. She was way off the mark. She was floundering. "California? Is that where you're sending your horses? When *are* they running, by the way?"

She worked her tongue around her teeth. "I haven't found the right spot for them yet. They were very behind. Totally out of condition. We're playing catch-up now."

I smiled. "We?"

"My riders," Adriene said. Then she looked at her watch. "Speaking of which—where are they?"

Outside the door, Ricky shouted, "*Horses in!*"

"They're right outside, I guess," I told her. "But they're my riders, now."

❦❦❦

Adriene leapt up, a growl in her throat, and I slowly followed, flexing my fingers at my side. For some reason, my hands and feet had gone numb. Her fake friendship and her sweet gentility were about to vanish, and I didn't know what kind of enemy was waiting within. I came out of the office just as the riders filed into the barn on horseback, and she skidded to an astonished halt in front of them, narrowly avoiding getting trampled by Walt's big colt.

"Jaycee! Ricardo! What the hell are you doing?" She didn't scream it, but she might as well have. The outrage in her voice quivered through the shed-row, and a few horses actually snorted. They weren't used to anger. This was a calm barn—or it was when Adriene wasn't around.

Jaycee was on the second horse, right behind Walt, and her glance raked over Adriene with insulting swiftness. She couldn't have been more dismissive if she'd tried. Jaycee turned her horse up the shed-row and calmly walked the colt into his stall. The other riders, Ricardo included, followed suit. No one acknowledged Adriene. Every single one of them looked my way and nodded. I felt a surge of pride, and suddenly the feeling came tingling back to my extremities. These were my people. I had done this.

The farm was going to rally behind me.

Adriene watched them go, her hands clenched at her sides. I watched her from behind, noticing the questioning tilt of her head as the horses split in front of her, turning left and right as if she were standing at a fork in the road. Then Alexander appeared, pulling up Betsy just outside the shed-row. The mare dipped her head to tug at the grass, and he dismounted, leaving the reins slung over the saddle horn.

He nodded at Adriene. "Good morning."

"What did you do?" she snapped. "You can't just ride Jaycee and Ricardo on your own horses. They're *mine.*"

Alexander leaned against the wall and picked up his coffee mug, which he'd left balanced on the shed-row's outer rail. "They quit, and Alex hired them."

"*Alex?*" She cast a quick look at me over her shoulder. "Since when does Alex run this barn?"

Alexander rubbed his jaw, feigning confusion. Then he smirked. "Oh, of course! You must have gotten here late. Since this morning. She was promoted about forty-five minutes ago."

I pressed my lips together to hide a triumphant smile.

❧❧❧❧❧ ❧❧❧❧❧

The rest of the morning turned into a standoff between Adriene and the entire staff of Cotswold Farm (including Jaycee and Ricardo), and frankly, I couldn't think of a better way to spend my day than watching her get iced out by an entire crew of grooms, riders, and hotwalkers.

Finally, our horses were finished. Every horse in the stable, from yearling to four-year-old, had gone to the track—every horse except the six Adriene held in her name alone. They banged at their stall doors and kicked at their walls, impatient to get out and gallop.

"What do you want done with those horses?" Walt asked me, his voice low. Adriene was leaning against a railing, staring moodily at the training track in the distance. "They've got to get out. We can't take this out on them."

"No, of course not." I didn't want Adriene's horses to suffer, but I wasn't going to offer her back any riders, either. Nor did I want her concession to be to put them back into Alexander's training program. I wanted them at another farm, under another trainer, being treated well but totally out of our hair. In the meantime, though, I had open paddock space. "Adriene?" I called.

She turned, and the dejection in her face gave me a moment's pause. Chances were, I realized, no one had ever stood up to Adriene before, let alone an entire stable of workers who refused to even glance up when she called out to them. She had been rendered a ghost in the barn she had controlled effortlessly for years, and she simply didn't know how to cope with it.

"Yes, Alex?" she asked wearily.

"I wanted to know if we can turn out your horses for you," I said. "They could probably do with a few days of sunshine on their backs, and you could spend that time finding open stalls for them somewhere else."

Her jaw stiffened, and for just a moment I thought she'd fight back. Then she nodded. "That would be fine, thank you."

Declawed, Adriene turned back to her survey of the sunny morning, and I gestured for Walt to come and help me turn out her anxious horses.

Chapter Forty-four

TAMPA BAY DOWNS WAS like a county fair: striped awnings, the smell of fried chicken, families spilling out of picnic tables and onto the pavement, their kids drawing ponies on the apron with giant pieces of chalk. There wasn't a fascinator or a pair of stilettos in sight, and I felt a million miles away from the shiny-suited excess of South Florida.

Of course, all of that was on the frontside. On this sunny February afternoon, we were still in the shed-row of the low-slung green barn where Wing had been living for the past few days, getting used to the track and prepping for his first start of the year. Alexander, Gigi, and me: the dream team reunited to get Wing the race we'd promised him at Gulfstream weeks ago. Instead of the Hibiscus Stakes, the Apalachee Bay. Instead of the towers of Hallandale Beach, the slash pines of Tampa's exurbs. Instead of the constant fear that we'd get a bad run and Adriene would never leave, the knowledge that Cotswold Farm was free and clear at last. Everything about today was better than December at Gulfstream, and I had a feeling I'd always love Tampa Bay Downs based on the memory of how happy I felt on this warm, sunny winter's day.

We had been playing the waiting game all afternoon, and the heat was making us drowsy. Gigi was stretched out on the straw bales stacked at the end of the shed-row, fast asleep. Alexander kept checking his watch. Finally, he stood up. "We can give him a few turns around the barn," he said. "They'll be calling us shortly. Do you want to do it, or shall I?"

"I'll do it." I hopped up, grabbing Wing's lead-shank from the peg by his door. Wing whinnied, ready to go. We'd taken away his hay-net hours ago and he'd been alternating between chewing on the door-frame and making faces at us for most of the afternoon. Now he jumped to attention, and nearly plowed me over as I dropped his stall guard. "Slow down, cowboy," I told him, tugging back on the lead-shank.

Alexander stood back and watched, his eyes gleaming. "Amazing, to think he turned out to be our star horse. You really saw something in him, Alex. You saw something in the whole damn place, though. I'd already given up. And look at us now."

We'd already gone past him, but now I reined Wing back and looked over my shoulder at Alexander. The colt nipped at my hand, anxious to be going. "Alexander, answer me something truthfully, will you?"

He cocked his head. "Certainly."

"Did you *want* to lose the farm? Like, really, truly, did you want Adriene to just take it away from you?"

Wing pawed at the clay and squealed, anxious to walk on.

"I did," Alexander said.

Wing swung around me in an anxious circle. I stayed in the center, a bobbing stick in a Thoroughbred whirlpool. "But, why?"

"I thought it would be easier. You weren't here yet. You don't know what it was like, the pressure, the bills. Her constant threats." Alexander tipped his head back against the wall, and a horse from another trainer's string leaned over its stall webbing curiously, straining and stretching to try and nibble at his shirt. "So much had been set in motion by the time you'd come, I didn't know how to turn any of it around. I just wanted to be *done.*"

I was speechless.

Then hooves clattered outside and I had to pull myself together, tugging Wing back to his rightful place at my side, before someone from another stable saw us behaving like children in the shed-row. I started walking again, giving in to the racehorse's urgent tugs on the lead. If there was one thing I'd learned in this life, it was that Thoroughbreds must always be in motion.

Until *they* decided otherwise.

I put a hand on Wing's taut neck, a quick and thankful pat, my heart suddenly fluttering anxiously against my ribs. This race was just any other race now, and still, I wanted to pull the horse up, put him into an empty stall, and go running back to Alexander. I wanted to wrap my arms around him, and I wanted to shake him silly for all his foolish thoughts, and I wanted to tell him I loved him.

But every stall was filled with someone else's dozing horses, and as we rounded the corner at the top of the barn, the loudspeaker outside crackled to life.

"Horses for race eight to the paddock please. Race eight, you're up."

Work came first.

I sensed rather than saw my parents standing along the paddock rail, and I felt a little guilty I hadn't arranged for them to have passes for this, their very first racetrack experience. On the other hand, who would babysit them? Gigi had her hands full helping me get Wing tacked; Alexander was playing gentleman trainer in the paddock's little circle of green where the jockeys and owners congregated. Civilians loved the paddock, but allowing them into this little space, filled with fit, anxious racehorses, seemed like an accident waiting to happen.

I glanced their way and raised a hand in greeting. My father happily waved back; he looked over the moon to be here, watching his daughter girth up a racehorse. You'd never have known how hard he'd fought me on all of this. My mother's smile was more furtive; she wasn't ready to give herself away quite yet. But I thought in about fifteen minutes' time she might allow herself to be proud of me.

Wing suddenly spooked at a bird swooping through the rafters, trying to dart forward. I jiggled the chain over his nose, trying to keep his attention, while Gigi cast me exasperated glances from the saddling stall, where she had one hand on the saddle. The valet jumped out of the way with a curse.

"Stand up, Wing, stand up, stand up!" I told my colt in the singsong chant he loved. "Be a good boy!"

The valet narrowed his eyes at us and walked away, muttering about lady trainers.

Gigi gave me a look that was somewhere between resignation and laughter. "Love our jobs, right Alex?"

"Love our jobs," I confirmed grimly. "Okay. You're on the right. I'm on the left. Let's walk this horse."

We took Wing to our little corner of the walking ring, trying to keep our booted feet clear of his hooves as they dug and danced on the mulched pathway. He knew how to walk in the paddock, but there wasn't usually a festival crowd leaning on the rails, crowding the grandstand's concrete apron, pressing flesh in the paddock, clapping along with a band playing on the front lawn. His blood was up, and it took everything Gigi and I had to keep his hooves on the ground.

"You look very professional, sweetie," my dad called as we paraded past him, and I looked around Wing's profile to share a grin with Gigi.

"That's us," she murmured. "The professionals."

"Racetrackers," I said, savoring the word.

Wing broke well and settled in along the rail, running past us for the first time with his chestnut head in front of the pack.

We leaned on the chain-link fence, its uppermost wires cutting into our bare arms, and yelled his name like broke horseplayers with nothing left to lose. The horses flew around the clubhouse turn, scattering a flock of white ibis, with the ambulance hustling after them at a discreet distance. The *just in case* reassurances of the world's most dangerous sport.

I could see Gabriel in his green and white silks, hovering over Wing's long back. Gabriel was too tall to be a top jockey by American standards, but his height had always suited Wing, still so tall and lanky, and I was glad he was the one on top today. If anyone could help my big colt run home first, it was Gabriel.

There was a rustle of papers behind me and then I felt Alexander there, standing just an inch or two from my back. I took one hand from the fence and reached back, finding his. I gripped his fingers as tightly as Gabriel must be gripping those reins, and I felt Alexander's fingers squeeze right back. It was a message I didn't need, but I still appreciated: we were in this together, today and always. Whether it all went up in flames or we ascended to glory, Alexander and I would face the future together.

I fixed my attention back on the race, currently playing out on the infield screen, and I lifted my voice in another howl to the heavens, to the racing gods above. *"Come on, Wing! Come on Wings and Prayers!"*

⚘⚘⚘ ⚘⚘⚘

We were a short distance up from the wire, so we couldn't see the head-bob for what it was: the closest of close calls. No one knew, though—maybe one or two people stationed right near the wire, maybe a photographer, clicking their remote shutter at the moment of truth. We held hands in silence and waited as the jockeys galloped past, standing in the stirrups; as Gigi picked up her bucket and ran down to the track gate to meet Gabriel and Wing at their spot on the rail; as the horses came trotting back with their eyes wide and their nostrils flaring red; as the crowd roared and the blinking *Photo* sign shut off and the word *Official* went up next to Wing's number.

Win.

We bolted for the track.

After

THE DINNER PARTY AT Simon's Bayside Restaurant was long and loud. The Tampa horsemen had tipped me off that that Alexander had always celebrated wins here, and the entire track stopped in at some point or another—at least, that's how it seemed. *Simon's: The Place for Celebration,* the banner ads in the racing programs proclaimed, and the win photos on the paneled walls bore this out.

My parents, bewildered, stayed near me for the first hour or two; then, as Simon himself came out and insisted our party take over the entire back patio, they seemed to get into the spirit of things and ventured off on their own.

It was nearly ten o'clock and I was nursing a glass of water, hoping to rinse away some of the champagne I'd overindulged in earlier, as I watched my dad wave his hands in some earnest discussion with an owner from another stable. Alexander came up beside me, his face drawn but his eyes glittering with excitement and champers. "What d'ya think they're talking about?" he asked, his eyes following my gaze.

"Airplanes," I said. "Watch his hands for a minute." They rose and they fell in smooth lines. Pinkie fingers imitated ailerons, index fingers were landing gear. I had seen it all before.

Alexander nodded, impressed with my translation. "Quite," he said, and then, with a slow sigh, "This is a good day."

I tipped my head against his arm, feeling the roughness of his tweed coat against my sunburned cheek. The February air drawing across the bay was cold and damp, and I slipped my hands into his pockets as well, feeling the satin linings caress my calloused fingers. "We won," I said softly. "Everything. Can you believe it?"

The drama of the past few months slipped away—from Diana to Adriene, from the classroom to the flooded racetrack. I had run away from my old life and fallen into another one so rich and bright and colorful that sometimes I thought I could barely open my eyes all the way. Could scarcely take in everything that it was throwing at me.

A finger tipped my chin up; Alexander looked down at me with a suddenly feral gaze. I felt a stirring deep inside; I thought of our hotel room a few hundred feet away. *Simon's, the place for seduction,* the jockeys laughed, but they weren't wrong. Putting hotel rooms next to a celebratory restaurant was simply genius. My lips parted invitingly, then I checked myself. My father was *right* there, after all.

"Alexander," I began, but he cut me off with a quick shake of the head.

"Listen for a minute," he said, voice urgent. "Alex, let's do this right. Let's put things together and keep them that way, starting with us. Alex O'Connor, will you marry me?"

I heard a hissing intake of breath; a squeak; a yelp—one of those was mine, but I didn't know which. The room was turning, one by one, but the others existed only on the periphery of my consciousness. What really mattered, what really had me captivated, was him.

My fingers slipped from his coat pockets and slid up his rough cheeks. A man who hadn't shaved since four o'clock this morning. A man who had given me everything when he'd thought for certain he had nothing. A man I thought I'd known for the entirety of this life, and perhaps for all the ones before.

"Of course I'll marry you," I told him, half-laughing, half choking back tears. "You're such an idiot."

A ripple of laughter, cheers, Simon shouting *More champagne!* and the band striking up the Wedding March, my mother telling my father *I told you so,* Gigi's sniffled *I love you guys so much:* it would all turn into a watercolor in my mind, the colors seeping together and blending into one perfect, unforgettable, unbelievable moment. The night Wing won, Cotswold Farm overcame, and the entire racing colony of Tampa Bay Downs toasted Alex and Alexander...yeah, that was *some* night.

The End

The Story Continues

Ready to continue reading Alex's story? Jump into the next full-length book, *Other People's Horses*, or enjoy the short novella, *The Head and Not The Heart*, which started the series back in 2011. These books are filled with the allure and passion of the races, and they're the perfect treat for anyone who loves racehorses, the equestrian life, or simply escaping the everyday world.

The Alex & Alexander Series is available in paperback or ebook from your favorite retailer.

Thank you for reading!

Acknowledgments

Runaway Alex always seemed like an easy novel to write. I figured I knew the characters, I knew the story, I'd bang this sucker right out in a few months.

I couldn't have been more wrong.

Putting together a prequel story for Alex and Alexander was an absolute monster of a job!

Still, I'm thrilled I was able to do it, and I'm very thankful for my readers and Patrons who cheered me on, made incredible suggestions, and supported me through this entire process. Writing anything in 2020 has been a big ask—writing an origin story for a character who was originally written when I was just trying to figure out what on earth I was doing with my life at thirty? Freaking huge.

So thanks to everyone who made it possible!

My amazing husband, who handles the nuts and bolts of life so I can write, and write, and write.

My ARC team, who read the "finished" product and then got back to me with all the mistakes I'd made. Massive thanks to Christine for the teapot scene! I needed that lesson, Christine.

My Patrons, who support me every single day and make all of this possible—some of you have been with me for more than two years now! Much love and thanks to Heather Voltz, Cindy Sperry, Rhonda Lane, Princess Jenny, Emily Nolan, Lindsay Moore, Brinn Dimmler, Tricia Jordan, Megan Devine, Sarah Seavey, Cheryl Bavister, Zoe Bills, Liz Greene, Diana Aitch, Orpu, Kathy, Mary, Liza Sibley, Kathi Hines, Kaylee Amons, Heather Walker, Ann H. Brown, Dana Probert, Claus Giloi, Jennifer, Di Hannel, Risa Ryland, Silvana Ricapito, Emma Gooden, Karen Carrubba, Thoma Jolette Parker, Christine Komis, Peggy Dvorsky, Katy McFarland, Amelia Heath, Andrea Parker, Kathlynn Angie-Buss, Alyssa, Harry Burgh, Mel Policicchio, Nicola Beisel, and Leslie Yazurlo.

You have all made so much possible over the past two years and I'm incredibly grateful to you. Your suggestions throughout the process of *Runaway Alex* were so valuable. Stay amazing!

Thanks to every single one of you who has sent me an email, a message, or otherwise found some way to send me a cute picture, words of encouragement, or a suggestion. Your connections mean the world to me.

On to the next book!

About the Author

Like many of my characters, I live in Florida, where I write fiction and freelance for a variety of publications. In the past I've worked professionally in many aspects of the equestrian world, including grooming for top event riders, training off-track Thoroughbreds, galloping racehorses, patrolling Central Park on horseback, working on breeding farms, and more! I use all of this experience to inform the equestrian scenes in my novels. They say that truth is stranger than fiction, and those of us in the horse business will certainly agree!

Visit my website at nataliekreinert.com to keep up with the latest news and read occasional blog posts and book reviews. For previews, installments of upcoming fiction, and exclusive stories, visit my Patreon page at patreon.com/nataliekreinert and learn how you can become one of my team members.

For more, find me on social media:

- Facebook: facebook.com/nataliekellerreinert

- Group: facebook.com/groups/societyofweirdhorsegirls

- Bookbub: bookbub.com/profile/natalie-keller-reinert

- Twitter: twitter.com/nataliegallops

- Instagram: instagram.com/nataliekreinert

- Email: natalie@nataliekreinert.com